THE SEVENTH CIRCLE

Visit Paul Henke on his website
for current titles and future novels at:

www.henke.co.uk

or email Paul at

henke@sol.co.uk

THE SEVENTH CIRCLE

Paul Henke

To Moira,
enjoy!

Paul Henke

GOOD READ PUBLISHING

First published in 2009 by Good Read Publishing
A Good Read Publishing paperback

10 9 8 7 6 5 4 3 2 1

A CIP catalogue record for this title is available
from the British Library

ISBN 9781 902483 12 2

Typeset by Palimpsest Book Production Limited,
Grangemouth, Stirlingshire
Printed and bound in Poland by Polska Books
www.polskabook.pl

Good Read Publishing Ltd
Balfron
G63 0RL

Acknowledgements

Thanks to Isabella Jarvie for her meticulous attention to detail. Thanks also to Bruce Macauley and his team at Macauley Creative for their design and creativity. To all the book shop managers around the country who give me such a warm welcome at book signings. To Craig and Ruth Morrison and the staff at Palimpsest Book Production – as helpful as always. And finally to my wife Dorothy, for her love and support and for sharing this emotional rollercoaster.

From Dante's Inferno

Dante envisioned his Inferno as an inverted spiral, which narrows as the traveller passes through nine circles of purgatory. The souls of the lost descend through the circles according to their guilt, the greater sinners falling to the lowest, meanest spaces . . . closest to Satan.

The path to the Seventh Circle begins in a wild chasm of shattered rocks, which give way beneath Dante's feet. At the bottom of the precipice he sees a river of blood, which flows around the entire Seventh Circle and forms the first of its three divisions. Those who perpetrated the most terrible violence on earth are tormented in the river; some are immersed to their eyebrows, others to their throat. Troops of centaurs run along the river's bank, keeping each sinner at his proper depth. As Dante continues his journey downwards, the names of the suffering tyrants, murderers and assassins ring in his ears.

Prologue

ACCORDING TO THE statistics, Hurricane Janet was growing. The satellite weather tracking system showed the eye of the storm with depressing and frightening clarity. Winds were sustaining a speed of over 270kph with gusts in excess of that figure. She spanned an astonishing 1,100kms and had already sunk dozens of light craft as far apart as Cuba and the Cayman Islands. When still a baby storm, the embryonic hurricane had passed between St. Lucia and Martinique. Then only heavy rainfall and a few windy squalls spoiled the holidaymakers' fun. As she moved lazily across the open ocean Janet began to suck in power like a voracious monster. Passing over the sea she hoovered up water and energy, steadily growing in strength, quickening, moving majestically onwards, a live fury becoming so monstrous that when she unleashed her pent up energy she would destroy all that stood in her way.

Her change of direction seemed arbitrary. But Hurricane Janet was moving along preordained tracks as surely as if on a railway line. The laws of meteorology and physics had already dictated her route. Slowly she turned in a clockwise movement until, past Cuba, she was headed in a northerly direction. She would hit the southern states of the USA with her epicentre around Galveston. The order to move inland and evacuate the low-lying areas had been given. A state of emergency had been called and the National Guard deployed. Their instructions were specific. All looters were to be arrested.

Across the Gulf the oil rigs and platforms had their hatches battened down and doors tightly shut. Except the tug Goliath and her charge. They were headed straight for the oncoming maelstrom.

1

THE TWO MEN were bristling with anger.

'Ismael, you must.' The older brother spoke harshly.

'Jalal, I cannot. I will not return with you to Gaza. For four years I have trained as an engineer. When I have finished my degree I shall stay here in Cairo and work. I have been offered a good position with a company that is building the new dam. I will be able to send money home. Use it to help our people.'

'Palestine needs your skills, Ismael, to help us build our own roads and houses. We don't need the pittance you'll be able to send every month. We need your knowledge. Have you forgotten the promises we made, when our parents died at the hands of the Jews?' Like all Palestinians, Jalal Chalabi referred to the West Bank and the Gaza Strip as Palestine. Over half of the West bank was under Israeli jurisdiction and had been contested for decades.

Ismael sighed. Life for him had moved on. His older brother by ten years remained trapped in the warped hatred he felt for the Israelis – a hatred which blinded him to everything else. He had felt like that once but his education had helped him to build another life. The hatred was still there but he no longer felt the passion to do anything about it.

Ismael knew that what he was about to say would fan the flames of his brother's ire but he had no choice. 'Jalal, I have met someone. A girl. An Egyptian. Here at the university.' The words rushed out in a torrent. Jalal's anger at the news was written clearly on his face. 'She has a degree in computer science. We wish to marry. I am going home to meet her family in one week's time.'

His brother spoke in hissing fury. 'You will return to Gaza with me. You are to marry Kalal.'

Miserably Ismael shook his head. 'That is what you want, Jalal, not I.' This was the first time he had ever defied his brother.

Moments passed. Much to Ismael's surprise his brother suddenly took a deep breath and smiled. 'Why are we arguing, brother? I only want your happiness.' Ismael was astounded at the change of heart. Four years ago Jalal would never have backed down. Perhaps he too had changed in the time they had been apart.

Ismael swallowed. 'You're not angry?'

'Angry? Why should I be angry? I am anxious for you, Ismael. I worry so much for your safety. The Israelis still have you on their wanted list.'

'Jalal that was years ago. Six years in fact. I was only a boy.'

'You killed a dozen Israelis. You know they never forget.'

'Well they seem to have forgotten me. There have been many other bombs since then. Other slayings. Jalal, try to understand. I want none of it.'

'As you wish. Let us talk of more pleasant things. What is the name of your woman?'

'Roban.'

'Is she as pretty as her name?'

'Oh, yes. Well,' he qualified, 'I think so.'

It was Tuesday. The two brothers made plans to meet at the weekend. Ismael and Roban had been planning to attend a student rally on Saturday before going to the cinema and then on for supper to a small restaurant. Jalal agreed to go with them.

They parted amicably. Ismael was relieved his brother had agreed to his plans.

Back in his small hotel room Jalal paced the floor. Finally he made his decision. Ismael must not be allowed to follow his heart and abandon the struggle. He was needed for the fight against Israel. Reluctantly, Jalal Chalabi made a phone call to Doha in Qatar.

Saturday night found the Chalabis and Roban leaving the cinema after watching an Egyptian film whose interminable plot Jalal had not bothered to follow. Meeting Roban that afternoon he had been relieved to find that the girl was plump, simpering and, in his opinion, not very bright. The fact that his brother seemed besotted with her was beyond his comprehension.

The restaurant they had chosen stood at the intersection of a busy thoroughfare and was only half full. They sat at a corner table next to the window. In the background the raucous noise of rush hour traffic moving nowhere fast, competed with Egyptian muzak. When Ismael announced he was going to the restroom, his brother rose to accompany him.

With the door closed and a wall between them and the restaurant, Jalal entered a cubicle, sat down and took out a small radio control device. Without so much as a second thought he armed the device and pressed the button.

The plastic explosive was in a metal box wrapped with copper wire that acted as an antennae. Although the amount of PE couldn't have filled an egg cup, the explosion was devastating.

The blast shook the walls of the restroom, dust and flaking paint showering down like a blizzard. Ismael ran out, stopping in horror at the carnage he saw. Roban had been killed instantly, blown in half. Those at the next table had been seriously injured while some further away were crawling or trying to stand up. Jalal grabbed his brother's arm and dragged him away, uttering meaningless words. Outside there were more injured, many of them cut to pieces by the flying glass from the window or blown off their feet by the blast. Ismael stopped, in a daze, unable to move.

Jalal put one hand around the back of his brother's

neck, while with the other he grabbed his belt and he literally propelled him along the sidewalk. Ismael moved his feet to prevent himself from falling flat on his face. Jalal kept up a pace half walking, half jogging all the way to the tiny apartment near the university that Ismael used.

Ismael was incoherent, sitting on the bed, shaking. Jalal phoned for a doctor who came and administered Ismael with an injection that put him to sleep for twenty-four hours. Already, as a result of Jalal's phone call to Doha, Al Jazeera, the English language current affairs and news organisation, was broadcasting the information about the Israeli perpetrated atrocity in Cairo. Part of the story contained the information that Ismael and Jalal Chalabi, high on the Israeli's wanted list, had died in the blast.

Israel denied all knowledge or involvement in the incident. The more they denied it the more her enemies disbelieved them while her friends were, at best, ambivalent. The deaths of the Chalabi brothers was what gave Israel's allies cause to be dubious. As usual, nothing was said against Israel in public, though much was said behind the scene.

When Ismael learned that the Israelis had killed Roban in an effort to destroy himself and his brother, he made an oath. He swore to become the Palestinians' leading freedom fighter, determined to dedicate his life to killing Jews and their allies.

2

RICHARD GRIFFITHS CLOSED the front door and dropped his briefcase in the hall.

'I'm home!' His greeting was met by loud whoops as his children, Lucy and Phillip, came running to meet him. Tugging at his legs, talking simultaneously, the twins vied, as always, for his attention. Bending down, he lifted them up, tucked one under each arm, planted kisses on their cheeks and said, 'One at a time. And remember, Phillip, it's ladies first.'

Lucy, an impish grin on her face, poked her tongue out at her older brother – older by half an hour – and said, 'I'm a lady, so there.'

Richard, anxious to head off a bout of sibling rivalry, decided on a diversionary tactic. 'Tell me about school.' As the twins, veterans of a single term at junior school, prattled on about their day, he gazed lovingly from one to the other. His beautiful Lucy, with her shock of blonde hair and blue eyes dancing in her mischievous face, stole the limelight as usual, whilst Phillip regarded her dubiously with his mother's clear hazel gaze. Richard felt the rush of contentment he experienced every evening when he arrived home to his family.

'Where's your mother?'

As if she had anticipated the question, his wife Ellen called from the kitchen.

'Hello, darling.' She smiled her pleasure at his usual kiss, her eyes crinkling at the corners. 'Dinner's late. I forgot to defrost the curry.'

'In that case, I'll help myself to a whisky and soda.'

Recognising the beginning of a nightly ritual – mum and dad's ten-minute chat to catch up on the day's events – the twins ran out of the kitchen. At six they were still at an age when everything was done in a rush, life waiting to be embraced eagerly, time too precious to squander walking anywhere.

While he poured the drinks, he asked, 'How was your day?'

'Not bad. I've got a drug case to defend.' Ellen juggled the children with her career as a junior partner in a small, but busy, solicitors' practice in Portsmouth.

'Think he's guilty?' Richard asked cynically, handing her a glass of her favourite pale yellow sherry.

Ellen smiled and said, 'Thanks. It's a she. And yes, she's guilty.'

'It never fails to amaze me that you can defend them, knowing that.' Richard couldn't keep the frustration from his voice.

Ellen smiled, put a hand on the back of his neck, curling her index finger through his hair and said, 'Easy. She deserves it. Innocent until proven guilty. You're such a Goth.'

'A Goth?' He grinned but spoke with mock horror. He had once looked the term up in a dictionary. It described a Goth as a barbarian; a rude or uncivilised person.

'Belt them on the head and have done with them. Chuck them in prison and throw away the key. I married a Philistine. Thankfully, however, I love you, despite the fact you have no redeeming features.'

'None?'

'Give me time, Ghenghis Khan and I'll think of something.' Smiling, she kissed him briefly.

'So tell me about this girl you think deserves defending.'

Ellen shrugged. 'What's to tell? Comes from a broken home, an abusive father.'

'Not dissimilar to that case you defended last month.'

'So you do listen to my daily rantings,' Ellen teased him.

'Only for fear of cross-examination.'

Richard let Ellen do the talking, content to listen, enjoying the sound of her voice, watching her as she pottered about the kitchen. Ellen was a wonderful cook, an indifferent housekeeper and a great mother. He loved her with all his being.

Their relationship, begun in a night-club in Edinburgh when he was on shore leave, had rapidly progressed from a strong mutual attraction to love. Ellen had just finished university and they decided to wait before settling down. It was three years before they finally married. Since then, not a single day passed without him being aware of how lucky he was, especially when he saw so many other marriages failing. When Ellen became pregnant with twins, she had reacted with equal measures of horror and joy. Richard had been forced to tell her that it had almost been inevitable; there had been several twin births in his family history. She had been saddened to hear that of the first twins recorded in the Griffiths family, the girl had died in a mining disaster in 1890. Her school had been wiped out when a slagheap had engulfed it. Her brother, Sion, had survived. He was Richard's great – or was that great-great-uncle? Family history had never been one of Richard's strong points.

Thinking of the twins brought Richard back to the present. A pile of legal briefs lying on the dining room table told him at a glance that Ellen had brought work home.

'I'll bath the kids, shall I?' Ellen smiled her thanks. Putting down his empty glass, he called, 'Coming upstairs, kids?'

They came running back in with yells of, 'Carry me!' Richard swung Phillip onto his back and Lucy into his arms. He galloped off with them both shrieking in delight.

Upstairs, they redistributed the dirt, as Richard described it and climbed out to be wrapped in big, fluffy towels. Phillip was already insisting that he could dry himself, while Lucy still enjoyed the attention. When they were in their pyjamas, he left them in the living room watching a cartoon on the television while he crept up on Ellen, pulling her into his arms for a resounding kiss.

'Enough of that!' She pushed him away and stood up. 'I'm a respectable solicitor.'

'You know what solicitors do for a living?' he teased. 'They solicit. And the only other profession that does that . . .'

'Richard, I warn you,' she interrupted him with a laugh. 'Give the pot a stir will you, while I shower and change out of this suit?' She was wearing her standard business outfit, a very becoming grey skirt and jacket she referred to as her warrior's clothes. 'I'll only be a few minutes.'

After token protests, the children went to bed and snuggled down for the night. Richard read to them, a chapter of a Secret Seven adventure for Lucy and a ghost story for Phillip. He loved being scared, or pretending to be and often teased his sister. The truth was, they both enjoyed each other's stories and listened avidly. Finishing the second story, Richard closed the book and kissed them both goodnight before going back down the stairs.

Stepping into the hall the phone rang and he frowned at the interruption. He thought about letting the answering machine take it but changed his mind and lifted the receiver. 'Griffiths.'

'Richard, it's Brian.' Richard recognised the voice of Brian Williams, the Managing Director of Griffiths & Buchanan Offshore, the company Richard worked for as Operations Director. A blunt Welshman, Williams did not mince his words. 'You're needed.'

Richard stifled a groan.

'Bad news I'm afraid. Bill Peters has had a heart attack.'

'Bill? But . . . But he only had his medical last week. I saw the report. Fit and ready to resume command of the Goliath.'

'Well, it seems we can have a medical, walk out of the surgery and collapse minutes after being given the all clear. Richard, I know it means wrecking your family holiday, but we need you in the Gulf.'

The Goliath was in the Gulf of Mexico, towing a huge

new drilling rig out into the cluttered waters of the American southern states. It was often said, with some truth, that if any more rigs were planted there, it would be possible to step from Key West at the tip of Florida to Brownsville at the southern end of Texas without getting your feet wet. The Americans, with their insatiable thirst for fossil fuels, were finally doing something about the problematic and inefficient old rigs they still operated. Some were being mothballed, whilst others, cynically, were being sold to third world countries. Fewer of the new rigs were needed and so there was less likelihood of accidents leading to deaths or environmental disasters.

'I need you to cover for a few days, until I reshuffle the rosters and get a replacement out there. Jake Saunders could have come back from the Gulf of Oman, but with Christmas coming up, we're operating a skeleton staff as it is. Just a few days, Richard. A week at the most. I'll make it up to you.'

'I've heard that one before.' Richard frowned. There was something he wasn't being told. 'You still haven't said what the real problem is.'

There was a pause and then Williams gave a sigh. 'Unfortunately, nature doesn't know it's Christmas. There's a hurricane headed for the coast.'

'What category?'

'Have you ever heard of Hurricane X?'

'Sure. Everybody who has studied meteorology has heard of it. It's the killer storm that will make the monsters of Camille and Andrew seem like a wet day on the Fens.'

'Well, it appears to be brewing. Hurricane Janet has been given a category 4 status. That's only one step down from the most damaging and dangerous designation on the charts. It's forecasted that as she nears the coast and the water gets shallower, the build up will continue and she'll become the monster that has been predicted and threatened for the past thirty years.'

'I take it she's headed for the Gulf.'

'You got it. Right now, she's moving slowly and isn't expected ashore for about three days. The Americans have issued a warning of potential evacuation and are expected to implement the warning in twenty-four hours. If they do, then the states around the Gulf will be closed and you won't be able to get in.'

'I see. Who's the first mate on the Goliath?'

'Giles Woodstock. He's a good man, but he's too inexperienced to deal with this. He needs his hand held.'

'You're right. When do you want me to leave?'

'Now. There's a flight in three hours.' He gave Richard the details of the flight.

Replacing the receiver Richard went into the kitchen, frowning.

'Who was that?' Ellen looked curiously at him.

'Brian.' Briefly, he related the conversation.

Characteristically, her first thought was for others. 'Poor Bill. I hope he'll be all right.'

'The holiday's spoilt.'

'Don't be silly. You go and we'll fly to Colorado without you. Just try and be there for Christmas day. Shall I organise a taxi?'

He put his arms around her. Typical Ellen. Where other wives had histrionics, she made practical suggestions. He kissed her gently.

Leaving her would not be easy. It never was. 'Okay, we'll have a great time Christmas and welcoming in the new year together. Are the kids okay about Santa Claus?'

'Yes. I explained that their presents would be left by Santa for them. They took some convincing, I can tell you. Such cynicism in children so young! I wonder where they get it from?'

Richard smiled. 'I wonder.'

'Are you sure you've used enough explosive?'

'You worry like an old woman, Lamen. Trust me – half this amount would be enough.'

The man moulded the plastic explosives in his hand, softening it. Next, he took the now empty toothpaste tube and began pushing the PE inside. It was tedious work but there was no rush. Once he had the plastic in the top, he used a cotton bud to push it in further. Bit by bit, the tube began to fatten and fill. Finally, he replaced a small amount of toothpaste in the top. He weighed it in his hand. He squeezed it. He opened the top and smelt it. It was just like toothpaste. Nodding his satisfaction, he said, 'I meet Herr Fabier in two hours. He will supply the detonator. Then give the holdall to Nazrallah.'

'I'm still not sure we can trust him.'

'If Nazrallah fails, *Allah* will curse him.' The man looked at his companion and drew his finger across his neck. 'Him and his family. Now, let us go over the sequence of events once more.'

The two men parted an hour later.

In the main street in Valletta, Lamen Al-Ghoul purchased various items of clothing careful to make sure they were all the correct size. Paying cash, he turned his collar up against the rain and returned to the safe house. Once there, he set about cutting off the price tags. It didn't take long. Time hung heavily and, already nervous, he began to worry in case anything had gone wrong. He paced the room, looked out of the window. Saw nothing. Finally, he heard a key in the lock. His companion had returned from meeting the bomb expert, Fabier.

'What took you so long?'

'Lamen, calm yourself. I keep telling you, nothing can go wrong. No one will ever suspect us. *Bis-millah*, the sweet taste of revenge will soon be ours to savour. How the impotent West will rant and threaten. It will be a wonderful victory for our sacred Islam.'

The death of so many people would be a wonderful victory? Lamen knew better than to voice his doubts. He shook his head, running his hand through his thinning, curly hair. He lit yet another cigarette, his shaking fingers stained with nicotine. Anxiously, he pushed his tinted glasses back up his nose.

'Will the device work?'

'It is why I was so long. Fabier demonstrated it to me.' There was wonder in his voice. 'It is truly ingenious.'

Several hours later, Lamen Al-Ghoul rose from his prayer mat. He had made his obeisance to *Allah* and now he had work to do. From a cupboard he removed a holdall and filled it with the new clothes. The tube of toothpaste he placed in a toilet bag, along with his shaving kit. The can of shaving cream, he knew, was forbidden. The pen given by Herr Fabier he placed in an inside jacket pocket, along with his passport. There was a hint of rain in the air, but the poor weather did not detract from the island's festive atmosphere as the devout Maltese prepared for their Christmas celebrations. It was a festival despised by him and all true believers.

The taxi driver tried to engage him in conversation but gave up after receiving not so much as a grunt. Ignorant bastard, thought the driver.

Al-Ghoul found Nazrallah in the coffee shop. They exchanged greetings and Al-Ghoul handed over the bag. Next, he took the pen from his pocket, pressed the plunger on the top and pushed out the point. He ran it across the palm of his hand, showing it still acted as a pen. He explained how it worked. It was childishly simple.

'*Salaam Alikam.*'

'And may God be with you. I will see you back at home.' The two men shook hands and Nazrallah walked towards the departures gate.

Al-Ghoul stood near a pillar and watched him walk away. It was obvious to Al-Ghoul that his colleague was very nervous. He hoped that if a member of staff noticed they would put it down to fear of flying. Nazrallah passed through the gate.

Allah's work be done. Al-Ghoul smiled. It had gone

exactly as he had planned. The $50,000 would be sufficient for his mother and sister to live in comfort for most, if not all, of their lives.

The tug Goliath was currently towing the super rig for the giant oil company Esso, 150 nautical miles south of Louisiana. Richard was certain if they could get on station and bed down the anchors in accordance with the contract all would be well. If they failed, it would cost the company a fortune in penalties. He knew he was the natural choice for the job. No one knew the Goliath as well as he did. He smiled. Running the Harbour Acceptance Trials and Sea Acceptance Trials for the tug had been a high point in his career.

When he arrived in the hot, humid atmosphere of Houston he was as fresh as he could reasonably expect to be. His naval training – to grab sleep whenever possible – still stood him in good stead. God alone knew, but he doubted there was much chance of any sleep in the near future.

Already, clouds were beginning to appear as streaks high across the sky. They formed a circular pattern that would tighten as the storm approached. The wind was beginning to pick up and he could see the leaves in the trees rustling gently. So far, there seemed nothing unusual about the weather, apart from the cloud formation. To those with sufficient knowledge, it was enough of a warning.

At the airstrip, he climbed out of the air-conditioned cab, paid the fare and hefted his bag in his hand. He could hear the sound of helicopters in the distance but, more acutely, he was aware there was a lack of natural sounds. No chirruping from the crickets, no sign of any birds, no sign of Mother Nature. As always, she knew when things were going to get bad.

Taking a crumpled fax from his pocket, Richard checked the details of the helicopter hire company. His booking had been confirmed and the hire of a helicopter to take him out to the Goliath had been guaranteed. Walking into the company's reception area he encountered his first problem.

His initial impression of the woman behind the counter was less than positive. A size 18 body squeezed into a size 14 dress, visible roots and brassy blonde hair. Looking at the fatuous expression on her plump, painted face, Richard had difficulty keeping his temper in check. 'What do you mean,' he managed, 'you have no helicopter available? The booking was confirmed and paid for.'

'I'm sorry, Mr. Griffiths,' the receptionist replied, dripping insincerity, 'but every one of our helicopters is in use. We're evacuating as many rigs as we can. Because of the hurricane, you know.' She smiled, enjoying herself.

Richard considered arguing with her but he knew he'd only be wasting his time. Biting back his anger he insisted on speaking to the manager, only to be informed that he was helping with the flights. She could offer him a helicopter sometime the following afternoon. Thanking her for nothing, he stalked away.

Using his mobile he telephoned Williams and vented his fury.

'Damn! What do you plan to do?' His boss asked.

'I'll think of something. How's Bill doing?'

'We medevac'd him. The hospital says he's stable and hopefully he's on the road to recovery.'

'What's the latest on the rig?'

'Woodstock is going by the book. They're moving at the recommended speed of 6 knots and will be on station in five days or more. That's too long. You know what the contract says. Hell, you were responsible for some of its clauses. Esso will hold us to every one. If that damned hurricane stops us anchoring on station, on time, we'll lose a fortune. As first mate, young Woodstock will wait for the hurricane to move away and for the seas to die down. And no one will blame him for it. That's why we need you out there. Steal a helo if you have to!'

Nazrallah had the holdall in one hand and his boarding card in the other as he reached security. He was unable to speak, his mouth was so dry. Increased security at airports around the world meant that even Malta had to take the issue of terrorism seriously. He placed the holdall into a plastic basket and emptied his pockets. Keys, the pen and his wallet he dumped on top.

When he went through the archway the security sensor bleeped. He was beckoned across and stood in front of a security officer where he was told to lift his arms out straight. The man ran a hand held sensor over him and it bleeped at his waist. He removed his belt and walked through the arch a second time. There was no sound and he was given a nod of approval.

He walked over to the counter to retrieve his possessions.

'Is this yours, sir?' The guard enquired, boredom in his voice.

Nazrallah nodded.

'Are there any liquids inside?'

Nazrallah shrugged and said, 'Only shaving cream, but that is not a liquid.'

'Please show me, sir.' The courtesy was in the words, not the tone, nor the body language.

Nazrallah opened the bag and showed him. It was confiscated and Nazrallah accepted the fact with typical bad grace. He showed the man that there was nothing else to concern him and he was waved away. Nazrallah hid the smile that threatened to break out. He had done it! Although in truth, only so far. There was still a long way to go.

3

CHUCK POLANSKI RECKONED he could smell a customer at fifty paces. He watched Richard through the shop front window of his tiny brokerage. The guy appeared tall, fit-looking. He seemed to know what he wanted. Didn't spend more than a minute looking at the specs of small planes and choppers hanging in the window before entering.

'Need any help?' The accent was strong Southern States. He had a straggly, ginger moustache that matched the few wisps of hair still growing on his head. He appeared friendly enough.

'You've got planes and helicopters for sale in the window. I want to discuss buying a helo.'

Polanski looked at his potential customer, unsure if this was a wind-up or for real. Judging from his complexion he hadn't been sure if the guy was from up north where the sun rarely shone or from Europe. His accent clearly indicated the latter. He looked like he had money – neat brown chinos, white shirt. His jacket sleeves were rolled up. Judging by the muscles on his forearms, he was probably as tough as he looked.

'What do you need a chopper for?' The man's voice was rough and nasal, more adenoidal than standard Texan.

'Mind if I sit down?' Richard had been expecting the question.

'Help yourself.' Polanski indicated a battered chair and Richard eased himself into it.

'I want to get to my tug that's towing a drilling rig out into the Gulf. Unfortunately, all the helicopters in the area are being used to ferry people ashore. Despite confirming my booking, the evacuation of the oil rigs means I've lucked out.'

'Yeah. It's a madhouse around here.' Chuck touched his scalp as though hoping that his hair had miraculously grown back. Disappointed, he began to tug at his ear. 'Where do I fit in?'

'It occurred to me that I could buy a helicopter, hire a pilot and be. flown out there.'

'If that's your plan, you must be in an all-tearing hurry to get killed. You got a death wish, son? That hurricane is shaping up to be the biggest storm in a hundred years.'

'I have to get out there. Are you going to help me?'

The man shook his head. 'The truth is, I'm a broker. Some of the pictures you see there are just that. Pictures. Ain't no chopper to be sold. But I figure I have to make the place look as though it does good business. There's one or two I can get a hold of, but it generally means having to pull them in from other fields. That's the way we all work. I ain't got nothing that's suitable, my friend.' He paused. 'I'm sorry.' He made it sound as though he really meant it.

'Damn! How far is it to Galveston?'

'About 50 miles. But they don't have no choppers there.'

'I know. But I can probably hire or buy a boat. It'll take a lot longer but what the hell. I've come this far and I'm not turning back now. Thanks for your help.' He stood up to leave.

'Hold your horses, mister. Maybe there's a way I can help you. You must be desperate to get out to that rig right enough.' Chuck's brain was in overdrive. He could smell greenbacks. After the First Gulf War, he had drifted in and out of dead-end jobs for years, finally ending up at the brokerage. If he didn't subsidise his income by smuggling a little weed the place would have gone under years ago. Weed was harmless; the other stuff – skunk – did folks damage. Maybe here was a chance to make some money legally.

Chuck went through the hair checking process again,

sighed and said, 'Now listen. I got me a suggestion. I can't legally fly you out to no oilrig. I ain't got the licence for it.' He paused, frowned, thought some more. 'If I did, I'd lose my pilot's licence. You savvy?'

'Is this leading somewhere?'

'I've got a helicopter. She could do the trip. But if we went and I landed out there and got reported I'd be done. I ain't authorised to hire out to no one.'

With an intrigued look on his face, Richard sat back down.

'What I suggest is that you buy the chopper from me. We go for a test flight. Then I can go anywhere I damn well choose. And if I'm stupid enough to fly towards a hurricane with a fool Limey on board, then what the hell. I'll take you to where you want to go. Drop you and come back. Whadda ya say?'

'Sounds good to me. What do I do with the helicopter after I've bought it?'

'Why, son, sell it back to me. For a lot less, of course.'

'Of course. What sort of price did you have in mind?'

'Well, say I sold it to you for twenty-five thousand dollars. I buy it back for fifteen. We're both happy. You get to where you're going and I get a small profit.'

'Small? That's theft.' Richard looked around. The office was clearly the worse for wear. Clean and tidy enough, but there were tell tale signs that the brokerage wasn't doing well. 'I don't have ten thousand dollars.'

'That's all right. I can take a credit card.'

'You have a point there. I have a different proposition. I buy the helo for twenty-five thousand dollars and you buy it back for twenty-three. So I pay you two thousand.'

After haggling back and forth, they settled on a difference of $4,800. Richard knew that he was being robbed but had little or no choice if he wanted to get to the Goliath.

'Name's Chuck Polanski. At your service.'

'Richard Griffiths.' They shook hands. 'Right. Can we get on with it?'

'Paperwork first.' While Polanski drew up the necessary

papers, Richard signed five, one thousand-dollar travellers' cheques. He read and signed the purchase and sales papers where indicated, handed over the cheques and pocketed his copies of the agreements.

Polanski handed back two, grubby, one hundred-dollar bills. The deal would help him keep up his flying hours. During three tours in the Gulf he had been decorated for bravery several times and received the Purple Heart after he was wounded when ex-filtrating survivors from an ambushed platoon. But you can't eat a Purple Heart. Flying a helo was an expensive business. And flying was the only activity Polanski took seriously.

'Right, all done. Let's get the hell out of here and you can tell me where we're going.' With a jaunty step he reached behind a door and lifted out a baseball cap and a pair of green earphones wired to a jack plug while Richard told him where to take him. 'I might have guessed.' Then he shrugged, 'What the hell, you've paid enough. Come on, the old lady is across the way.'

Polanski led them out through a back door. Immediately, they were assaulted by the heat, the humidity and the noise of helicopters landing and taking-off. Men hustled back and forth. Walking at a brisk pace, they arrived at a hangar. Despite the doors being wide open, the air inside was as hot as hell. Polanski pointed into the nearest corner where an old and tired helicopter sat forlornly.

'Don't be put off none by the look of her,' Polanski tapped the side of the veteran helicopter. 'She's a Bell 212. Been working the oilfields for years. I got her about two years ago. Did her up myself. Been used a lot but nothing's worn out in the old gal.'

Climbing up where indicated Richard sat in the right-hand seat. The seat leather was practically rubbed away, polished by hundreds of bottoms which had sat there before him. The seatbelts were frayed but still service-able and, in one corner of the windscreen, he could see a few hairline fractures.

Richard looked out the side window and watched as two men in overalls came over to help Polanski push the helicopter through the door.

Polanski did his external checks and climbed aboard. From a side pocket he lifted out his checklist and began to work his way methodically through it. After a few minutes he turned to Richard. 'Important to get the check-list done right. Skimp on that and you're asking for trouble. Okay, you've told me where we're headed and given me the call sign and radio frequency for the tug. Once I start the engines I can't hear you no more. So is there anything you want to tell me before we leave?'

Richard thought for a moment before shaking his head. 'No. You've got everything you need to get us there. What about a weather forecast?'

Polanski looked at his passenger with pity. 'We already know the weather forecast, son. There's a hurricane coming. Now fasten up and let's get going.'

The plane arrived in Frankfurt. Nazrallah walked off, more confident as each hour passed. His connecting flight was two hours away. He sat in the departure lounge and drank coffee. He cursed the stupid European laws that prevented him from smoking. A few minutes before his flight he sent a short text to Al-Ghoul. There was no acknowledgement. But then, none was expected.

For the first time Richard wondered whether or not he should have asked to see an airworthiness certificate. He also questioned his own sanity. He was rushing towards danger from which any sensible man would run away from. There was one satisfying point and that was that Polanski was handling the helo like the veteran pilot he claimed to be.

Inside the cabin, the noise was horrendous and Richard wished he had some way of blocking it out. Once airborne the helo turned south and headed towards the deep blue expanse of the Gulf, now visible ahead of them.

In spite of the noise, Richard began to enjoy himself. The engine sounded sweet and strong, the buffeting from the wind was not unpleasant and the air was clear. They could see for dozens of miles all around them, the horizon far away. On the waters of the Gulf, supply vessels were trundling back and forth to the drilling and production rigs, tiny black spots on the ocean. Oil was a huge business, worth many billions of dollars every year to America. The hurricane could cause vast amounts of damage if she hit before the hatches were well and truly battened down. Hurricane damage in the past had been awesome as more Americans centred their lives on the coast, their ever-increasing wealth in jeopardy from global warming and rising sea levels.

The further they flew the more the curve in the clouds tightened. The wind was beginning to pick up and the blue sea was turning white with small, angry waves. The helicopter began to buck. The motion was still not uncomfortable nor did it feel dangerous. Polanski checked their flying time and went a few thousand feet lower. He pointed ahead and down. Richard could make out the largest platform they had seen so far and the tug towing it. The Goliath.

Taking one finger away from his ear, he pointed down and raised his thumb. Polanski acknowledged the message and his lips began to move as he made contact with the tug on the frequency that his passenger had given him.

The helicopter swooped straight down to the huge expanse of open deck. It was the size of half a football pitch and the uncluttered space made for an easy landing. As soon as they touched down they could feel the deck moving beneath them. Richard grabbed his bag and jumped. His feet had barely touched the steel deck when the helicopter lifted up and Chuck Polanski raced back towards the shore. Shaking his head to try and clear the buzzing, Richard made his way along the deck towards the rear entrance to the living quarters.

The tug was pitching gently. She was so heavy, she

just cut through the sea. The ease with which she moved through the water would lessen drastically when the Gulf became really rough, but for now she barely felt a thing. Glancing around him, Richard could see that everything was in good order. Not that he would have expected anything less from a master as experienced and professional as Bill Peters. Richard peered towards the stern. The tug's huge, self-tensioning drums were moving first clockwise, then anti-clockwise. They carried 8-inch extra-flexible-steel wire rope with a titanium core for added strength. Below decks he knew that other cleverly connected drums carried the same wire rope and could deploy a mile of wire and still have at least two cables – two tenths of a nautical mile – in hand should they be needed. Ships and other craft were never pulled with a taut line but always by the weight of the wire or rope connecting the vessels. He glanced at the sag in the wire. It was about what he would have expected.

There were two men standing at the stern watching the huge rig move through the water behind them like a giant stalker waiting to pounce. Looking up to the starboard rear control room Richard saw someone wave to him and returned the greeting. He couldn't see who it was but at least half of the crew on board would have sailed with him at some time.

Reaching a door, he stepped inside the tug. Outside, there had been the noise of the engines, the throb of the diesels beneath his feet and the wind whistling across the deck. Inside, soundproofing deadened the noise and ensured almost complete quiet.

Richard strode along the corridor to the lift and pressed the call button. He waited only seconds before the doors to the six-man lift opened. He pressed the top button. The lift shot skywards, up five floors, before it stopped and the doors opened with a hydraulic hiss. He stepped onto the bridge.

It was state-of-the-art. The control panel looked as if

it would be at home on a modern jumbo jet rather than on a sea going tug. A joystick had replaced the traditional wheel. If altering course sharply, bow-thrusters automatically cut in which enabled the tug to turn on her axis. The Goliath had two variable pitch propellers mounted on constantly revolving shafts, which controlled her speed. The greater the angle of pitch, the faster she went. She could move at speeds from a fraction of a knot to 22 knots at full speed. Glancing at the speed indicator Richard saw that they were making 6 knots through the water. At that speed they had no chance of getting to their destination on time. The speed was the recommended one for towing such a large and ungainly object as the huge rig astern.

Waiting nervously at the front of the bridge was the first mate, Giles Woodstock. He came forward with his hand outstretched. Broad shouldered, with a firm handshake, at five feet nine inches, he was forced to look up to Richard. Woodstock was in his twenties and Richard knew he had passed his master's ticket the year before. After four or five years on board the Goliath, learning from experienced masters such as Bill Peters, the young man could hope to be given command himself. Master of the Goliath for all of twenty-four hours, the strain was beginning to tell around his eyes. He had obviously had little sleep since Bill's heart attack.

'Am I glad to see you,' he said sincerely, his southern counties English accent clearly discernible.

'Tell me what's been going on since Bill was medevac'd,' Richard ordered.

'We've maintained course and speed, all systems are working perfectly and the tow is progressing smoothly.'

'Except for one little detail,' Richard remarked.

The other man shrugged and looked slightly sheepish. 'That would be the hurricane.'

Richard stepped into the navigation room at the back of the bridge and checked the automatic, computerised plot. The satellite tracking system was working perfectly and he pressed a button on the console. They had 430 miles to go to their station. At a speed of 6 knots that would take three days. By which time they would be in the middle of the hurricane with all hell breaking loose around them. It would be a miracle in itself if they managed to hold onto the tow. If they got blown away by the wind and heavy seas they would have to battle back into position, possibly losing days, which the company would have to pay for. Right now they were in a no-win situation. No wonder Woodstock had been relieved to see him arrive.

Stalking back to the forward control panel he checked the fuel. They had plenty. Next, he checked the strain on the tow and saw that it was well within limits.

'I have command,' he intoned.

'You have command,' replied Woodstock. The relief he felt was evident in the way he stood straighter and almost, though not quite, managed a smile.

Richard pressed the increase button designed to bring the tug's speed up at 0.1 knot increments while simultaneously taking down the handset for the radio. He called the rig astern. After identifying himself, he said, 'I intend increasing speed slowly until I am satisfied that we are making all possible speed. Over.'

'Understood. It's your call. But we're getting concerned about the weather. If it gets any worse, we're all for dropping anchor.'

I bet you are, thought Richard. To them it made no difference. The penalties for late delivery were so onerous they didn't bear thinking about. A year of the company's profits could be wiped out by a single job. That was the nature of the work – it was so competitive that one mistake – he shook his head. He knew it was why he had been sent.

'It's not if, but when and we'll cross that bridge when we get to it.' Richard watched as their speed crept up and the tension along the wire increased. The tension meter was calibrated all the way to breaking point and was the most important piece of information he had at his fingertips. He increased speed each time the needle on the tension meter stopped moving. At 7.4 knots he still had a way to go to the red zone. He checked the navigation plot. They had reduced their steaming time by 13 hours. It was a start. But nowhere near enough.

Lifting the phone to the stern control cabin he said, 'Who's that?'

'Hello, sir. This is Jock McVey.'

'Jock, it's good to hear you. How's it looking?'

'I've got the same dials back here as you have up there, sir. I reckon there's still a long way to go yet. She can take a lot more, believe me.'

As the tug's tow-master McVey was responsible for all aspects of the tow, but could be outranked by the tug's master. He was a complete professional and both men had worked together in difficult situations in the past. They each knew the other's capabilities and made a good team.

'I want you to pass out another two cables.'

'If you want my opinion,' McVey added, not waiting to hear whether it was wanted or not, 'I reckon we can go to 10 knots without any danger.'

Richard smiled in spite of the predicament they were in. 'We'll see how she bears up. I'll increase speed now while you pay out the tow.'

Down aft, the huge hydraulics kicked in and started paying out more of the wire rope. It passed from drum to drum, the wire threading over the stern now coated in thick, heavy grease from when it was originally put on board. The wire rumbled smoothly over the rollers and into the sea before snaking astern and up to the towing points on either side of the forward legs of the massive rig. Gradually the tug increased speed until she settled at 9.5 knots. Checking the navigation data Richard saw that he had reduced the towing time by a full day and he still had a bit of speed in hand. According to the tension meter they were still below the danger level. Now it all depended on the speed and direction of the hurricane.

During the night the wind began to increase along with the waves. The Goliath was now pitching more, but by no means dangerously or with too much discomfort to the men. The crew worked eight-hour shifts, twelve men around the tug at any one time, from the officer on watch on the bridge to the engineer below.

At 22.30 Richard was finishing a superbly cooked meal, washed down with water. He had been offered an excellent Californian red but drinking alcohol when faced with a hurricane was simply not appropriate.

He wondered if there was any more he could do. He had increased speed as much as he dared and still had a small safety margin in hand. All that was left was for him to get a good night's sleep before doing battle the next day.

Once on passage aboard a Royal Naval destroyer making for Singapore he had been caught in the path of a hurricane. The experience had not been pleasant, but neither had it been life threatening. Then he had been a sub-lieutenant on board the guided missile destroyer HMS Antrim. Perhaps he had been too junior to appreciate the danger. At the time, it had all seemed like one great adventure.

This was different. Now he was responsible for hundreds of millions of pounds worth of equipment and dozens of lives.

The other officers had departed, either to get some rest or to watch television. He descended to the master's cabin immediately below the bridge. If he was needed he could be on the bridge in about thirty seconds.

The cabin was luxurious. It stretched the full width of the tug and the view ahead and to either side was panoramic. His sleeping quarters, a day room and a study, were beautifully decorated. Throwing himself on the bed, he grinned to himself, remembering an occasion when Ellen had accompanied him. Her mother had taken the twins for a week and they had enjoyed a second honeymoon on a tow from Oman to Bahrain.

He was back on the bridge before daybreak, a steaming mug of coffee in his hand. The tug was really beginning to pound into the waves but he knew it would get a lot worse before it got any better.

Checking the tow, he fixed the tug's position and read the navigation data. They were no longer making the same speed over the ground as they had been. The wind and the sea were holding them back. He checked the tug's log, scanning below the entry which read, "Mr. Griffiths came aboard to take command. 11.03." Glancing through the hourly readings he saw that their speed had gradually dropped to 8.1 knots. He checked their speed and position again. They were still a frustrating 240 miles from the station. At their current speed it would take thirty hours. It wasn't enough. He phoned down to the towing station.

'That you, Jock?'

'Yes, sir,' came the cheery reply.

'Don't you ever sleep?'

'Plenty of time for sleeping when you're dead. Want to go faster?'

'Any more cable you can pass out without risking any slippage?'

'Sure, sir. About half a cable, maybe a bit more. I could then strop her if you like.'

Richard considered the suggestion to pass out as much of the tow as was possible and then fit preventer strops to hold the cables in place. The danger lay in the strops, which weren't as strong as the cable. If they broke, the cable might run away, hit the end securing shackle, rip it out and slide over the stern. He calculated the risk.

'Go ahead, do it. When you're finished get back to me. In the meantime I'll increase speed slowly.' As the speed moved back up to 9.5 knots the needle on the tension meter crept up to within a whisker of the red. There was practically nowhere else they could go with it.

All that morning they ploughed ever closer to the hurricane. Richard listened to radio reports about the pandemonium in the southern states as people tried to flee her path. On one interstate highway north there was a backup of cars stretching nearly 200 miles. All across Texas, Louisiana, Mississippi and Alabama, chaos reigned. He was absurdly cheered to hear that Janet would remain a category 4 hurricane and not grow into the mythical X that had been predicted. He had enough to think about without being distracted by what was happening on land. Shaking his head Richard turned off the radio.

As the Goliath raised her blunt bow she reared high in the water and came down with a mighty thump. From his commanding position the sea still didn't look threatening but Richard wasn't deceived. She was a cruel mistress – those who forgot her cruelty did so at their peril. She had taken millions to a watery grave and would continue to do so as long as time and man existed. A natural enemy, capricious as well as deadly, he loved pitching himself against her.

Sitting in the master's chair on the starboard side of the bridge, Richard grabbed a sandwich and chewed it slowly, monitoring everything that went on around him, his eyes never still for a moment. The glass continued to drop, the wind increased and the waves grew ever higher. It was now a gale force 8 with a sea state 6. He put the upper deck out of bounds. All hands were to remain between decks and to travel to and from their work places inside the hull. Their journeys were longer but safer.

Placing his drink in the holder on his right armrest he gazed forward and was appalled by the sight before him. Racing down towards the Goliath was a huge wave, the height of a tall building. It looked as though it would swamp them. As he grabbed the microphone to warn the crew, the mammoth wave struck.

4

NAZRALLAH'S FLIGHT WAS without incident. He followed
the other passengers towards passport control. There were
two queues, one for European passport holders the other
for non-Europeans. He joined the latter. The queue shuffled forward, twisting left and right. He knew it was for
the cameras situated in the ceiling, taking front, left and
right profile pictures. Computer scanning made for virtual
instant identification. It was why he had been chosen to
make the trip. In anti-terrorist parlance, he was a virgin.

Finally, he reached the control booth and handed over
his Libyan passport. It was carefully examined and placed
on a scanner. He was asked how long he intended staying,
replied only a few days, received a nod, had his passport
stamped and handed back to him. He walked towards
customs. Two hard eyed men watched him approach. His
nervousness increased. His lips felt parched, his mouth dry.
He desperately wanted to lick his lips, to look at the men.
To see if they made any reaction. If they suspected him.
He walked into the arrivals hall. He made it to the gents'
toilet just before he vomited.

He washed his mouth out, splashed water on his face
and left. Standing outside the terminal he allowed the
cacophony of Heathrow Airport to wash over him.
London! He'd made it!

The Goliath failed to lift up her bows. She struggled as
tonnes of water cascaded down on her, pushing her under
until Richard, horrified, saw that the top of the wave was

now towering above them. It beggared belief. He had
never seen or heard of a wave like it. A huge wave running
before the main body of the storm – it was preposterous.
Christ, it would push them to the bottom and take the rig
with them. He grabbed the joystick and pulled it back to
neutral, reducing the way on the tug. The sea washed
hungrily around them. The force of the water struck like
a massive blow and the tug shivered along her whole
length. She slowed down like a carthorse being pulled up
suddenly on her reins. Her nose continued to point down
as the water passed along and over her hull and then
started to move along her stern. Aft, the weight pushed
her stern down and her bow up and slowly she began to
rise again. Tens of thousands of tonnes of water began to
drain away from her as her bow broke through with a leap
into the air. She hung there for a second, half in, half out
of the water, threatening to fall backwards down the huge
cliff of water still behind her. She was in danger of flip-
ping over. If that happened, nothing could save them. It
would be a one-way ticket straight to the bottom.

By reducing speed, Richard had taken away a good
deal of the weight off the tow but there was no way of
telling whether that was enough. All he could do was sit
still and pray. She hung there for two seconds, an eternity, until slowly the water continued astern and her nose
came down. Reaching for the joystick he pushed it
forward, feeling the propeller biting, pushing her ahead.
Her speed increased and she moved through the water,
shaking the last of the huge deluge away from her.

But the danger was not over. The monster wave still
had the rig to pass.

Looking through the aft windows Richard saw that
half the tow was hidden by the wave. His heart was in
his mouth. If the rig capsized, it wouldn't be his fault.
Nobody could have foreseen a freak wave like this one.
But he'd still be blamed. It was the nature of the business.

Instinctively he acted. If the wave hit the rig with only the weight of the tow holding her she would probably topple backwards and be lost. Sunk in minutes. But if he could get enough tension on the tow ropes and they held, he might be able to prevent the rig from being pushed over, flipped backwards by a force greater than anything man could create. The joystick was at the forward stop and Goliath's speed was picking up. The tow was bar taut, the tension meter needle moving inexorably into the red. The strain would be showing down aft as the wire came clear of the water and stretched between the tug's stern and the towing points of the rig. With dread in his heart, Richard looked aft.

The rig was falling backwards, its huge flotation drums skidding out from underneath her. If she flipped over there was nothing he could do. He watched the red anti-fouling paint come clear of the water, lifting ever higher towards the sky. The rig hovered, stabilised for a second and then fell slowly forward, her flotation drums keeping her upright, the killer wave passing astern. Even as relief flooded through him Richard looked at the needle on the tension meter. It was all the way over into the red. According to the figures he held on file, the tow should have parted before now. He lurched forward, grabbed the joystick and pulled it back. The speed fell off quickly, as did the tension on the wires. Looking aft once more he saw the oilrig sitting serenely on top of the sea, the waves barely more than splashes around her base.

He grabbed the phone to the aft control room. 'Jock? You okay?'

'God's teeth, I think so. What the bloody hell was that?'

'Don't ask me, I've never heard of a huge wave like that running before a big wind.' He paused, almost afraid to ask. 'How does the tow look?'

'Hang on a second while I check the figures.' There was a slight pause. 'According to what I have here,'

McVey's normally gruff voice wobbled, 'we hit a reading that is double the breaking strain for our type of wire rope. How can that be?'

'I don't know and I don't care. I'll call the rig. See how they are. I'm going to increase speed. Knowing we have this much power and safety in hand we'll go for broke.' He hung up and radioed the rig. 'Are you all right back there?'

'Yes,' came a very shaky reply. 'That was close. I was sure we were going down. God help them ashore when that hits. It won't stop until it reaches Little Rock. I'll radio a warning to the coastguard.'

Richard knew any warning would be too late. The wave was travelling at the speed of an express train. 'Okay, it's might be worth it, but I doubt it.'

'What are your intentions?'

'I'm going to increase speed. That wave showed us that we have plenty of safety in the breaking strain and so we ought to be able to travel much faster than we have been. Does that give you any problems?'

'Negative. We'll go along with whatever you say. You still have overall charge until we part the tow.'

Richard increased the speed by small increments, but this time he forced himself not to look at the needle on the tension meter. He knew it would be moving steadily into the red.

The tow was settling down at the astonishing speed of 12 knots when the door to the bridge banged open and the first mate appeared.

'How are the men, Giles?'

'One of the seamen has a broken leg, sir, but the doc says he can fix it until we can fly him off. Some of the others have a few bruises and minor injuries but nothing serious.' Aghast, Woodstock pointed at the needle on the tension meter. 'Sir!'

Even after Richard's reassurances, the first mate didn't look any happier with the tug's rapid progress.

'I've checked the passage time against the track of the hurricane. At this speed we should get on station about six hours before the eye hits us. It'll be tough, but we ought to be able to manoeuvre the rig to get four anchors away and in place, one in each corner. Once we've done that they're on their own. They can use their anchors to steer into place. We'll have fulfilled our contract and can head for home.'

Woodstock nodded. Orders were orders, but privately he was thinking *easier said than done*.

The hurricane was still bearing down on them. All day the weather continued to deteriorate. The tow held even as the wind and waves increased. Richard moved the speed up a notch, trying to maintain their rate of progress so they could beat Hurricane Janet to the anchorage. All day he sat on the bridge, staring at the sea, restlessly running his gaze over the dials and indicators spread out before him. The radar showed their path was clear. They had a straight run to the oilfield.

At midnight he was still there, both hands gripped around a mug of tea. The seas outside were mountainous but in the dark he could see nothing. Goliath continued to rise up and plunge back like a thoroughbred, impervious to the water around her as though, having survived the worst the hurricane could throw at her, she was enjoying herself. The phone rang, disturbing his reverie.

'Griffiths.'

'Chief engineer. I've got a bearing running hot on the port shaft.'

'How bad is it?' If he was perturbed by the information, Richard's voice did not betray it.

'I need to stop the shaft, strip it and replace the bearing.'

'How long?'

'Well, by rights we should shut down the port engine and limp into a harbour somewhere. As it is, I can fix it in about eight hours.'

Damnation. Just as things were going so well.

'What will happen if we keep going?'

'It will eventually start to run rougher and hotter until it seizes.'

'The shaft will stop?'

'Yes. It'll probably buckle as well. I don't mean twist like a piece of spaghetti but even if it bends off its true by a few degrees it'll mean a new shaft and weeks in refit.'

If that were to happen, the company would not thank him for deciding to keep going. 'What's the best you can do?'

There was hesitation before any reply. 'If I repack the bearing grease and fix a hose to douse the housing with cold water we might delay the inevitable. But there's no telling.'

'We don't need to stop the shaft to pack it with grease?'

'No. There are two connection ports either side of the bearing housing. It'll all depend on how quickly the grease burns off. It literally evaporates. We've got enough for normal running but not to keep packing it in. If we train a water hose on it and keep the housing as cool as possible it'll reduce the rate of burn. But at some point we'll have to stop.'

'Okay, Chief, let's do it. Keep me informed. Is there anything you need from me?'

'Such as?'

'Written authorisation. Whatever you need to clear your yardarm.'

'Bugger off, Richard.' The phone went dead.

Richard grinned. He and Chief Engineer O'Driscoll had done the Goliath's Harbour and Sea Trials together. Friendship and mutual respect had grown quickly.

The time was now approaching 02.00 and he began to fill in the ship's log. Considering that everything was automatically recorded in different ways throughout the ship the log seemed to some an old fashioned concept.

For Richard, it served as proof that the men on watch were actually awake and at their stations.

Making the log entries took him a few minutes as he walked back and forth across the bridge, noting latitude and longitude, heading, speed, wind speed and force and sea-state. He included in the log his orders to the Chief Engineer. Responsibility rested solely with him.

As he was walking back to his chair the tug suddenly pitched up higher than normal and smashed back onto the sea. The next wave wasn't any better and he realised the sea was becoming rougher than ever. He guessed it was approaching state 10.

Hatches were battened down to the best of the crew's ability. All breakables had been stowed away and all hands, except those on watch, were safely tucked up in their beds, resting, if not actually able to sleep. There would be dangerous work to do once they got on station. Passing giant anchors attached to huge chains was a difficult job at the best of times. For a moment he wondered if he had made the right decision.

He dozed in the master's chair. He didn't have the luxury of going below to his cabin – even thirty seconds to get back to the bridge could prove to be too long if instant decisions were required. The night passed fitfully. Watches changed. Richard checked their position from time to time. He made sure their course and speed over the ground was what was needed. Breakfast was a bacon and mushroom sandwich washed down with mugs of strong coffee. Dawn broke. Richard couldn't decide whether or not seeing the maelstrom around them was an improvement or not. The waves were huge, the wind howling through the rigging a reminder of how puny man was in the face of a malevolent nature.

The morning passed slowly but without incident. With each passing hour Richard became more confident that they would be successful. Finally, in the middle of the afternoon, they arrived at their destination. The men were

weary with the constant motion, the need to hang onto
something when walking from one spot to another, the
necessity to be alert at all times. Although they had been
forced to slow down because of the over-heating bearing,
they had still managed to arrive on station on time. It
had all been to no avail. Richard knew that in such tumul-
tuous seas and heavy winds there was no point in even
trying to set anchor for the rig. It was just far too
dangerous. All they could do was stay there, maintain
their position and hope the hurricane passed quickly. In
twelve hours his company would be forced to pay for the
time on station. They had run out of contract delivery
hours.

Damn! There was nothing he could do about it. He
might take risks but he wasn't going to get anybody killed
over money. He agreed with the rig that they would hold
position until the storm abated. It was galling to have
come so close only to fail at the last minute.

5

NAZRALLAH HAD A room booked at the Travelodge at Heathrow. He knew it was pointless trying to take a taxi. Having queued for what was sometimes hours, no taxi-driver would take him such a short distance. He waited for the bus, sipping at a bottle of water he'd just bought, sucking greedily on a cigarette after each sip. His lips were no longer parched, his mouth no longer dry. The fear and trepidation he had felt had been replaced by elation.

At the hotel, he paid cash for one night. In his room he sent a text to an address logged into the mobile's memory. After sending it he wiped the memory clean. All he had to do now was wait. Wait for the martyr who would surely go to Paradise for what he did.

Standing in the chart room Richard double-checked their latitude and longitude by comparing a LORAN fix. Idly he looked at the picture and report of the hurricane, the centre of which was now only a few miles away. The winds outside were hellish, brutal. Their luck had been phenomenal. If the truth were told they had not deserved to get this far. Richard stared at the screen image of the hurricane's path. He realised that his prayer that the storm would veer away from them was going unanswered. It was evident that the eye had turned straight at them. They would pass right through the middle. Richard stopped, stunned by his sudden thought. Excitedly he reached for a manual on advanced meteorology. He looked up the

index on hurricanes and ran his finger down until he came
to the sub-heading – Eye of the Storm.

Quickly, he flicked through the pages and read their
contents. Grabbing the microphone to the ship's broadcast he said, 'Listen up. This is the master. All seamen
and riggers on and off watch muster on the bridge in
fifteen minutes. All seamen and riggers to the bridge in
fifteen minutes. That is all.'

The first mate appeared a few seconds later. 'Sir?'

'I think we've got a chance to pull it off.'

'I'm not with you.'

'The eye is coming right through here. I've been
checking the manuals. When it does the wind in the eye
will drop to nothing. Absolute calm. The sea will be
chaotic but not dangerously so. There'll be no wind whip-
ping across the water. If we pull our fingers out we'll
have about forty to fifty minutes to get the rig's anchors
down.'

Woodstock shook his head. 'Not enough. We need at
least thirty minutes for each anchor. You know that. Each
anchor has to be placed just so and that takes a lot of
manoeuvring. It's a good idea but. . .'

'Listen, Giles. That's in a perfect world. We don't
have time for that. I've read the contract at least half a
dozen times since I got here, looking for a way to cut
corners. It actually states that four of the eight anchors
have to be laid, giving the rig stability and a firm
anchorage. We spend time getting it just right more from
convention and . . . and sheer professionalism rather than
anything contractual. I need to fulfil the contract. You
can come back and finish the job afterwards. So we get
ready and we move fast. We need to pull the rig round
until one corner is facing directly into the wind. That'll
put the sea and wind on our port bow for a while. It'll
mean a lot of rolling and pitching, but that can't be
helped. We order the rig to drop its forward port anchor
and pay it out. We let go the port tow and recover the

cable. In the meantime we shorten the starboard tow to slipping length. That done, we order the rig to pay out on the anchor cable and to be ready to drop either the port or the starboard quarter anchor, depending where we fall back to. We let the sea push us into position. They drop one of the stern anchors and we drop the starboard tow. We take the starboard bow anchor and get that one in place. It will leave us with one more anchor to place.'

'Time will have run out by then,' Woodstock protested, not liking what he was hearing.

'At least we have a chance this way.'

The on-watch and off-watch seamen and riggers began to arrive. Richard briefed them quickly. He was met with sullen scowls and head shakes.

'Too dangerous,' muttered one of the men.

There were twenty-two men standing before him, all work-tough, hard men. They were there for the money.

'You'll each get a twenty percent bonus on your pay.'

'Now,' smiled the bosun, showing nicotine stained teeth, 'why didn't you say that in the first place, Mr. Griffiths?' He turned to the men. 'You know what to do. We've got forty minutes to do the bleeding impossible. Let's get ready.'

As they were leaving the bridge Richard radioed the rig.

'I hope you know what you're doing,' was the terse comment from the rig's master.

'So do I,' Richard replied laconically.

At the door to the departures lounge people were saying goodbye. As always, there was an air of excitement, as well as tears of happiness and sadness as families and friends parted. For some, their flight was to a holiday destination. For others, the separation would be for years.

Those passengers who were booked on the flight to Denver had already checked in and gone through to the

departures lounge. The air was festive. Christmas carols
were being piped over the tannoy system, a huge decorated tree stood in one corner and paper streamers hung
from the ceiling. There was even a Santa Claus grotto
for children to visit.

Lucy and Phillip were playing with the presents they
had just received from Santa. Unusually, they were
proving to be good value for money, thought Ellen. She
turned her attention back to a couple going on their honeymoon to New York. They had fallen into an easy conversation a few moments earlier. Ellen smiled inwardly. They
were terribly sweet, but far too young to be married. She
hoped they would find even some of the happiness she
shared with Richard.

It would be some time before their flight was called.
As was usual, boarding would be by seat row numbers
except for those passengers travelling with small children. The twins, however, were adamant that such a
description did not include them. They were big children
now. Ellen gave in to them.

Dressed in foul weather clothing, Richard opened the
doors on both sides of the bridge. Immediately, the wind
and the rain howled in but Richard knew he needed to
get a feel for the weather, for the way the tug would
respond. Once they had arrived on station Richard had
shut down the port shaft to give it time to cool. Now he
ordered the engine to be restarted. The picture of the
hurricane showed that the eye would be with them within
the next twenty minutes or so. There remained another
danger he hadn't shared with any of the others. The storm
could veer off in any direction without notice and the eye
could bypass them. Then they would be up the proverbial creek without a paddle. They would have no alter-
native but to sit out the worst of the weather and wait
until the wind and seas died down.

'Let go the port forward anchor,' he ordered the rig.

Richard stood on the port wing, peering aft, ignoring the rain and wind that howled across the skies and battered him and his tug.

The tug had shortened the starboard tow to two cables and was now dropping back with the rig as the rig paid out her anchor. They sailed in tandem for a full half-mile. He ordered the stern starboard anchor dropped. The tug then pulled the rig against the storm while the rig paid out on the stern anchor and took up the slack on the forward one as the rig crept forward. It was slow work; they had to fight the wind and the sea all the way. Even as the rig reached the midway point, the eye of the storm burst around them and the area was suddenly wind and rain free and bathed in a peculiar light from the afternoon sun high above them.

Grabbing the ship's broadcast he said, 'All right. This is it. Let's move it.'

He backed the tug to the rig. The starboard tow had been let go and the towing hawser was reeling in fast. They were under the starboard anchor of the rig within minutes and the anchor was lowered. It was taken on deck, shackled in place and ten minutes later the tug was moving away. Once in position the anchor dropped over the stern and the huge monstrous weight plunged out of sight. Three down. One to go.

Ramming the joystick forward, Richard quickly drove around the rig, the tug bouncing in all directions as the sea came from different quadrants. He checked his watch. Looking at the picture of the hurricane he saw that more than half the eye had passed over them already. They were running out of time – fast.

Ignoring what was happening, Richard continued with the manoeuvre. The tug passed around the rig and went astern under the port quarter of the huge edifice. The anchor was lowered and secured on deck just as the eye passed clear of them and suddenly the wind and the rain were battering them once again. This time the weather came from the opposite direction. The tug reared and plunged like a bucking bronco and the seamen scattered from down aft. Each was aware that one slip could mean their death if they were swept overboard. No bonus was worth dying for. All they could do now was hope for the best and wait for the weather to abate. It had been a gamble and they had lost.

At that moment, the door at the back of the bridge crashed open and Giles Woodstock appeared. He was soaked, wet and scared.

'Sorry. We did our best. We can't get on deck to slip the shackles.'

'Take the ship. Move her into position,' ordered Richard. 'You got her?' he demanded impatiently, waiting for the age-old words.

'I,' Woodstock paused, his eyes showing his fear, 'I have the ship.'

Richard leapt to the back of the bridge and into the lift, pressing the button for the main deck. He descended quickly. Fixed to a bulkhead at the door to the outside was a fire-fighting unit. A long hosepipe coiled up in the middle was attached to the fire-fighting ring-main. Pulling a seaman's knife from his pocket he hacked off the heavy bronze nozzle from the end of the hose. Tying the hose around his waist he slipped the knot to the middle of his back and unclipped the door, pushing it open. The deck was awash with water. The tug was plunging up and down, the weight of the anchor hardly damping down the movement at all. The wind was sweeping in across from starboard to port and Richard knew it was howling at speeds in excess of 120mph. Stepping over the combing, he clipped the door open and began to make his way along the deck. He was hidden from the wind for a few metres but then it hit him. Totally unexpectedly, he was thrown off his feet. He hit the deck with a bone jarring smash and got his hands to his head only just in time to stop it slamming into the steel. He lay there for a few seconds, winded. He didn't try to stand. It was far too dangerous. Instead, he snaked across the deck, using his elbows and his knees, ignoring the water swirling about him, protected from the wind by the three-foot high solid railing running both sides of the deck. He was soaked to the skin but ignored the discomfort. Halfway along the deck he looked aft to see the anchor looming in the murky light. He inched his way closer, until he was finally at the huge lump of metal. It weighed hundreds of tons and towered above him. The anchor was secured with two, specially designed, quick-release shackles, one either side of the deck. The stern had no guard rail, just a roller that stretched from port to starboard allowing the towing cable to run smoothly over the stern.

Timing was critical. The tug was plunging more than ever and he knew he needed to release the shackles as the bow went up, allowing the anchor to slip away. He stayed where he was for a few minutes, gauging the weather. Trying to establish a pattern was hopeless. There was no pattern. The sea was completely wild in its timing. Summoning his courage, he crabbed across the deck to the port shackle. In a holder next to it was a lump hammer. He pulled it loose, removed the shackle pin and swung the hammer. The shackle dropped clear. As the tug plunged down another huge wave, he scuttled across the deck to the starboard side. The anchor slipped a few inches towards him but was held in check by the other shackle.

Reaching the other side he removed the pin and paused. If he slipped the shackle at the wrong moment the anchor could slide down on top of him and crush him to death. The crewmen who had refused to slip the shackles watched him in horror. It was far too dangerous. Idiotic. What kind of a lunatic would take the risk?

Richard swung the hammer, releasing the shackle. It fell free and he staggered to his feet. As he did so the anchor lurched and slid straight at him. Avoiding being crushed by nanoseconds, he jumped on to the anchor.

The tug's plunge stopped and she reared up. The anchor slid over the stern taking Richard with it.

Much to Nazrallah's surprise it was a woman who came for the toothpaste tube and the pen. She was dressed appropriately all in black, a yashmak hiding her face. The double veil allowed only her eyes to show. She stood at the door and said nothing. Words were superfluous. He handed over the toothpaste tube and the pen. She bowed her head and left. For Nazrallah it was finally over. He could now return to Libya.

The woman waited only moments for the bus. She was quickly taken to the airport where she stood in line to check in. She ensured it was a female behind the desk. She handed over her Iraqi passport, unclipped her veil to show her face and replaced it after receiving a polite thank you. No, she had no luggage to check in, merely a small holdall which she held up for inspection.

Her boarding pass was handed over to her with a friendly, 'Have an enjoyable flight.'

'Thank you.' The voice of the nineteen year old was steady, her English tinged with a pleasant accent. If she was in any way nervous she didn't show it.

She went through to departures and passed smoothly through security. She sat demurely in the departure lounge reading her Koran. Finally, her flight was called. She sat in economy, in an aisle seat. Forty minutes into the flight she stood and opened the overhead locker. From her bag she took the toothpaste, her toothbrush and the pen. She had been told to wait two hours. However, her impatience to get it over with had gotten the better of her.

In the toilet, she sat on the seat and squeezed the contents of the toothpaste tube into her hand. Next, just as she had been taught, she moulded it into a pyramid and stuck it onto the outer wall of the cubicle. She unscrewed the pen and removed the specially shortened ink cartridge. She tipped out the glass detonator and pushed it into the PE. Next, she removed her high heel shoes and unscrewed the heels. From each, she took two AAA batteries. An elastic band held the short piece of wire across the negative terminals. As she worked, she fervently repeated over and over, *God is Great*. The mantra filled her with an inner peace. At last her pain would end. The death of her family at the hands of the Americans would be avenged.

As she touched the two wires from the detonator onto the positive terminals she repeated her mantra one last time.

Hitting the water, he let go the anchor, but was pulled down. His sleeve had become caught on something. He was being dragged to the seabed. The hosepipe reached the end of its length and he stopped with a backbreaking, air-expelling wumph. His sleeve tore free and he was left hanging in the water fifteen feet under the surface, drowning. He couldn't summon the strength to pull himself up. Jesus! He railed at the fates and his own stupidity. He was losing consciousness when he felt himself being jerked upwards. He had wits enough to keep his mouth shut and not breathe in, desperate though he was to do so. His head broke the surface, air mixed with the sea and he gasped. Groaning, he felt his back hit the stern of the tug and he was pulled smoothly onto the deck. For a few seconds he lay on his back, stunned, looking up. Towering over him was Jock McVey, his face a mask of anxiety.

Richard grunted and crawled unsteadily to his knees. 'Thanks, Jock' he gasped, holding his hand out to the Scotsman. 'Thank you. I owe you one.'

'Just the bonus, sir, that'll do.'

Free of the anchor, Woodstock had turned the tug so the wind was coming over the stern, pushing them away, the Goliath running before the sea. Richard was able to stagger along the deck. Falling over the combing into the corridor he stayed on his knees for a few seconds. Suddenly, he was plunged into a feeling of utter sadness. He shook it off. He should be rejoicing. He'd won! Life was great!

After a few hours sleep and freshly showered, Richard returned to the bridge. He was tired and bruised but the hot coffee he held in his hands was helping him to recover. His body ached. But he was exultant. He had fulfilled the contract. He would be in Colorado for Christmas. He was looking forward to telling Brian Williams. He picked up the phone, punching in the number from memory.

'Brian? It's Richard. We did it.'

There was no response. When his boss's voice finally came down the line it was leaden. 'Richard, I . . .' he cleared his throat. 'Richard, I have news. Bad news. Ellen and the children . . . their flight has crashed. There were no survivors. Richar . . . The man's normally brusque voice broke.

And Richard Griffiths' world shattered into tiny pieces.

6

THAT SINGLE MOMENT of revelation would remain with Richard forever. Slamming down the phone he had crashed to his knees. In the blink of an eye, his life was over. Throwing back his head he had howled, a dreadful, animal cry, raising the fear of God in those who heard it. In that moment he had been insane. The memory of that moment was accompanied by a debilitating anguish.

Shock, the body's natural protector, had moved in. For days he was numb. He ate, slept and lived in a daze. But then the yearning began, the hurting for Ellen and the children. The horror of their deaths played constantly in his mind. The numbers of the dead went round and round – passengers killed 206, crew 16. From having all that he wanted in the world he now had nothing. Without his wife and children he felt he was nobody, a non-person. His family had defined him. Made him what he was. The life's joy that had been such a strong part of his make-up was gone. Richard plunged into a deep, all-encompassing depression from which there seemed no escape. His anger consumed him. Yet, until the results of the inquest were announced, his anger had no direction, no focus. It ate at his soul. Sent him to the brink of madness.

He held himself together until the inquest, often spending days curled up in the bed he had shared with Ellen, weeping. The verdict, when it came, was shattering – death by a person or persons unknown. With no way of lancing the boil of his hatred, his depression engulfed him. He ceased to have control over his emotions. He was an automaton, going through the motions of being alive.

Reports of Libyan involvement in the disaster began to trickle into the media, first as an odd paragraph and then an onslaught, the full-blooded baying of wolves demanding revenge. Richard began to take notice. Pills enabled him to concentrate for a few hours. He began to follow the reports in earnest, reading everything he could lay his hands on. Soon, he was obsessively accumulating every article and tape, every news broadcast. He began compiling a dossier of the information he was gleaning. Friends cautioned him against it. But somehow he understood that he needed the dossier. Without it as a focal point, his feeling of powerlessness added to his hatred and fuelled his depression.

All his conversations revolved around the crash, their deaths, the Libyans. He was wound as tight as a spring, a powder keg ready to explode. People learnt to leave him alone. Diagnosing acute, reactive depression, his psychiatrist ordered him to leave work indefinitely.

His boss, Brian Williams, agreed with alacrity. Richard had money from an insurance policy on Ellen's life. Besides, his family was wealthy beyond avarice. They did, after all, own the company Richard worked for – one of many. His taciturn mood, his lack of pleasantness in everyday settings, was getting on everyone's nerves. He was avoided whenever possible.

Richard also began to shun people. He would sit for hours with his head in his hands, unmoving, unaware of his surroundings. His psychiatrist, Dr Reynolds, had patiently explained to him that depression was an illness like any other. He had nothing to be ashamed of. Millions suffered from it. He knew she meant well, but her words, delivered in a professional tone, offered him no comfort. The pills would help, she said. So he took the pills and felt worse as the chemicals were released into his bloodstream. Dr Reynolds suggested a brief stay in a sanatorium. The counselling sessions brought no relief from his pain. He sank lower and lower.

Members of his family rallied round. His younger cousin, Nick Hunter, spent time with him whenever he had leave from his busy duties as an officer working in the shadowy organisation known as The International Force Against Terrorism. He listened to Richard when he rambled on about Ellen and the kids, sharing his memories, his pain, trying his best to help. Others too, were sympathetic, whilst some told him to buck up.

His primary concern, his all enveloping focus, was to build the dossier about the tragedy. He began amassing information from the most unlikely sources. A pattern was emerging, though still too hazy to act upon.

Leaving the sanatorium, still on heavy medication, he went home. He still lived in the house that he had shared with Ellen and the twins. There, all his memories lived with him. He spent hours poring over photographs, watching videos recorded at birthdays, Christmases, holidays. Then, one morning, emotionally drained, Richard looked up from the screen and glanced at the clock. He started. He was late for his pills. Getting to his feet he shambled along to the bathroom. Taking down the correct box he shook a couple of pills into his hand. About to throw back his head and toss them down his throat, he caught sight of himself in the mirror.

For the first time in months he took a good look at himself and was shocked by what he saw. His sideburns were turning grey while the rest of his hair had stayed dark. His eyes were red rimmed, bloodshot and sunken. His face was lined and sallow and he looked what he was – a shadow of his former self.

It was now nearly four months since they had died and while others who had been similarly affected had moved on with their lives, he was squandering his, sunk in a morass of memories. Ellen wouldn't have wanted this. He hated himself.

He looked at the pills. They weren't the answer. Suddenly he was terrified of the future. What would happen to him for the rest of his life? God knows, he had considered it often enough, but suicide was no solution for him. He couldn't go on like this. His rage and hate were colouring every aspect of his life.

Filled with resolve, he shook off his apathy and returned to his bedroom. Quickly, before he changed his mind, he climbed into his running gear and let himself out through the front door. The house stood in an isolated setting, a mile from the nearest village of Fawley and overlooked Southampton Water. It was early evening in the middle of April and there was warmth in the air after a hard winter. He began to run, slowly at first, but picking up speed. He sprinted about 400 metres before collapsing, gasping for breath his body aching and the tears of self-pity welling up again. He ran back to the house and dropped onto the sofa in his living room. Exhausted, he fell asleep.

When he awoke, it was early in the afternoon. A black cloud was pressing down on him. He registered that he was still wearing his running clothes. The urge to take a pill was very strong. Summoning all his resolve, he decided to go for another run. Pulling on his trainers, he went outside. He began to jog. He returned home twenty minutes later, having run half a mile one way, half a mile the other. An hour later he went again. An hour after that he ran again. And he kept going. When he was running he became robotic, without emotion, the pain inside him was held at a distance. Physical pain became a challenge, defeating it was his reward. After a few days his natural fitness began to reassert itself. His desire to run, to feel the endorphins coursing through his veins became an addiction. Soon, he was jogging a mile in each direction. Then two miles. Then three. He had stopped taking the pills. In quiet moments he began to confront the past. He spoke less and less with Dr Reynolds. He drank less. His flab turned to muscle.

Even when it rained, he still went. Running gave him the only peace he knew. By the time summer passed he was running half-marathons in less than three hours. At last, he finally acknowledged to himself, the pain had become bearable. He felt ready – it was time to go back to work.

Eleven months after the tragedy he telephoned his old boss, Brian Williams. His hand was sweaty as he held the receiver in a tight grip. After a dozen rings he had just decided, thankfully, that Brian wasn't there, when a voice answered.

'Brian, it's Richard.'

'Richard! Great to hear from you. How are you? I haven't seen you in months.'

'I'm doing fine. Brian, the reason I called. I,' he paused, unsure of himself. 'I wondered if my job was still available.'

Brian Williams didn't answer.

'From your silence I take it the answer's no,' said Richard, anger beginning to rise in him.

'Not so hasty, Richard,' said Williams gruffly. 'Are you ready to come back? That's my worry.'

'Don't worry. I won't let you down.' Angry as he was, even as he said the words, he wondered if they were true. He felt okay, but there was no telling if the terrible blackness would descend on him again. He would have to be on his guard. 'Well?' The anger could not be disguised this time. 'Is my job available or not?'

'Not,' was the disappointing reply. 'That is to say, not straightaway. You have to appreciate, Richard, that we needed someone in the position of Operations Director. We gave the job to Bill Peters. Following his heart attack there was no way we could allow him to remain as a tug master. To be honest,' Williams' harsh tone softened, 'it was always intended as a stopgap. We had hoped you'd come back sooner rather than later. Bill understood it was a temporary position until you returned. But after six months I had no choice but to confirm him in the job.'

'I see.' Disappointment welled up within him. The mist was descending. He needed to get off the phone. 'Thanks, Brian.' He hung up before the other man had time to say anything more and quickly changed into his running gear. Outside it had turned cold, wintry, sleet was falling as he began to run. He did not hear the telephone ring as he stepped out of his garden and started along the lane. He envisioned his endorphins as white knights pitched against the forces of darkness. He concentrated on pounding one foot in front of the other. On building up speed and creating a sweat. He kept going. The day passed. When he turned around, he was 20 miles from home. His mind was clear. The white knights had won.

At the house he saw there were half a dozen messages on his answering machine. Five of them were from Brian Williams. One was from Bill Peters. Feeling in control of his emotions, he decided to tackle Bill Peters first. If Bill wanted to tell him to get lost, then so be it. Maybe he could have a job as a tug master somewhere. At least that would be a start.

There was genuine warmth in Bill Peters' voice. 'Richard! Brian phoned and told me you're after my job.' His next statement startled Richard completely. 'As far as I am concerned, the sooner you get back here the better. I can't think of anything I'd like more. I've only been keeping your chair warm for you.'

'Are you serious?'

'Never more so. When I had my heart attack I decided it was a warning and time to hang up my boots. We bought a cottage in Cornwall to be near our daughter and I still haven't managed to stay there for more than a few nights. Betty has really been chewing my ear off for the past six months, demanding that we leave Southampton and retire. But you know, company man and all that. So like I said, the sooner you get here the better.'

'Bill . . . I'm so . . . thanks.'

'Richard, there's nothing to thank me for. I told Brian that if you think you're up to it then you're ready to come back. I won't stand in your way. Quite the reverse. The first job you can have is to arrange my retirement do.'

Richard laughed – it was the first time in a long time. 'It's a deal.'

The following Monday he returned to work. The only change he made to his old office was the installation of a running machine. He threw himself into his work and drove himself harder than ever. The white knights continued to do battle while he ran the roads or used the machine.

The next step on his path to recovery was hard. He knew that if he was ever to leave the past behind, he needed to move. Physically move away. Leave the house with its memories, its history. The day he put the house on the market was a 30 miler. He sold it for less than it was worth because he wanted a quick sale. The day he closed the door for the last time he ran 50 miles. It was one year, three weeks and four days since Ellen and the children had died.

With the sale of the house he had nowhere to live. A house with a garden didn't appeal to him. Gardens were for families. For children to play in. A flat was a possibility, but somehow didn't appeal either. One thing did. It was what he and Ellen had talked about. Something to do when the kids were off their hands and they had more time to themselves.

As the new year started he bought an old, motorised fishing vessel with the intention of having her converted into something far more luxurious. She was fifty feet long and sixteen feet at the widest point of her beam. The wheelhouse was set a third of the way back from her bow and was big enough for four people to stand in. Inside lay decrepit old machinery and four cold, empty holds. Her only saving grace was her hull, two-inch rock pine on oak without an inch of rot anywhere. He had her taken ashore at an old boatyard up Fareham Creek and had a caravan placed on the site. He had chosen the place because of its owners, two brothers, Vic and Matt, both in their late sixties and craftsmen in boat building. With the advent of various plastic mouldings for boats' hulls and prefabricated items for internal fittings, the need for their talents had dwindled. Hanging on to the business by their teeth, they were delighted when Richard came along and made them a proposition.

As soon as the boat was ashore and on blocks they got started. Richard, meanwhile, threw himself into his work, all the while compiling his dossier, using his unique contacts in the world of Arab oil. Whenever he was home he was at the boatyard helping, although Vic and Matt grumbled good naturedly that he was more a hindrance than a help.

The inside of the boat was completely but carefully stripped, leaving the bare carcass of the hull. By April she had undergone a complete transformation. When she was finished she was immaculate. The engine room was fitted with a new Volvo Penta 350hp diesel, along with an independent, silent running generator and a water maker. Forward of the engine room lay the master bedroom, en-suite, with a double bed and loads of stowage space. Then came the combined living room and galley. Forward of that was a second toilet and shower to port, while to starboard a workshop held a complete set of diving gear and a small electric air compressor. Right forward there was another cabin with two bunks, one either side. In the forepeak was a locker that contained fenders, ropes, boat hooks and a myriad of other useful things necessary for the well-being of any boat.

The wheelhouse had also been removed. It was replaced with an area spanning nearly half the length of the boat but two feet short on either side, allowing complete access around the deck. The new wheelhouse was made from synthetic, lightweight materials, not to upset the boat's stability. The wheel was on old-fashioned one with spokes, but fitted with an automatic pilot. It had the latest Geo-Positioning Satellite system, superb radar and a radio capable of transmitting around the world. To port was a chart room and aft, through a door, a seating area that comfortably accommodated six people. A collapsible table stood in the middle. Throughout, the wood was dark oak, superbly finished. Only real craftsmen could have achieved these results. Richard thought it had been worth every penny and every moment he had spent on her. The therapeutic value alone was incalculable.

He named her *The Ellen*.

7

DREAMS KNOW NO limits. Nor do nightmares. Richard lived in dread of his – a constantly repeated nightmare, in which his wife and children tumbled through the night skies, screaming for him to help them, their eyes wide open, staring at eternity.

Once *The Ellen* was finished and afloat, he had hoped his enjoyment in her would help him to get over his pain. On a superficial level he took pleasure in handling her and living aboard, but there was a hard core in the centre of his being that was stripped of any gentleness or love. Instead, it was filled with a longing for revenge.

He was working harder than ever, filling his days and weeks, but it wasn't enough. It would never be enough until he found out who had been responsible and they were brought to justice.

He had one advantage which he used at every opportunity. His work placed him in unique situations that allowed him to make discreet enquiries. Although G & B Offshore was a worldwide business, Richard focused the company's efforts in the Middle East, desperate for clues that might lead to the identities of the men responsible. It wasn't difficult to do. The only resource standing between the Arab world's abject poverty and its great wealth was oil. Yet even that commodity they were unable to exploit for themselves. So western technology, skills and hard work were needed. The oil rich countries paid top dollar for the expertise and the West exploited the situation for every cent.

Snippets of information began to come his way. A certain amount of evidence pointed at the Libyans being involved, but Richard was sure they had not been the main instigators. The press blamed and vilified Muammar Harwazi, the Libyan leader, demanding new sanctions be imposed on the country. Richard, however, disagreed and continued his private enquiries. Harwazi had become the elder statesman of Africa. Libya's rehabilitation had been a long time in coming, but the lifting of UN sanctions had been a turning point for the country and its people. As a result, Richard couldn't see all that being thrown away again. However, he kept an open mind.

Early summer found Richard in Cairo. He had finished a meeting, shaken hands on an agreement to tow a construction rig from the North Sea to the southern end of the Gulf of Suez via the Cape and returned to his hotel. Papers were being faxed back and forth, standard contracts were being amended until both parties could agree to their terms and conditions. When that was done, Richard would sign on behalf of G & B.

Back in his hotel room, waiting on the paperwork, he received a mysterious phone call inviting him to a rendezvous with the caller.

'Why? What's it all about?'

'I know you look for information. I have some I think you will want to see.'

'Why not just tell me over the phone and I will decide . . .'

'Listen, I have written proof of something. I can assure you, you will want to read it. And I will want payment.'

That came as no surprise, so Richard said, 'Why not meet here, in the hotel? In the bar or in my room?'

'No! It is too public. I do not want to be seen talking to you. I can promise you that it will be well worth your time to see me.' The caller was adamant.

Richard, about to tell the man to get lost and hang up the receiver, paused a few moments. His curiosity was piqued. He agreed to meet but was insistent that the venue was of his choosing. He described a bar a few hundred metres away from the hotel . The caller knew it and they agreed a time.

Richard got there early and checked the place out. There was one entrance through the front that opened directly into a large room with a small stage in the corner. There were thirty or so tables, half of them occupied, facing the stage. A bar ran along one wall behind which two men were serving. Only there was nobody buying. The bar's occupants were too busy watching an Egyptian belly dancer. The music was loud and bad and fitting for the display the woman was giving as she undulated her stomach and shook her fat hips, flailing her arms around her head. Richard crossed the room, checked out the toilets and found a locked back door. The lock didn't appear particularly strong and he figured that if he had to, he could burst it open. He hoped it wouldn't come to that. Back in the bar, a reluctant barman served Richard with a bottled beer. The label said it was German, brewed under licence in Libya. Richard declined the offer of a glass.

He took a corner table and sipped the warm beer. He didn't have long to wait. A man entered, looked around the room, saw him and approached his table. The man was clearly very highly strung. Or, Richard suddenly thought, very frightened.

'Mr. Griffiths?' The man was sweating, nervously twisting his hands together.

Richard nodded, warily looking behind the man, ensuring he was alone. A quick glance around the room showed that they were still being ignored. The man gave his name as Abdullah bin Abdullah. He was short, fat and had a long black moustache – a caricature of a greasy Egyptian with slicked back hair held in place by some sort of sweet smelling unguent.

Abdullah licked his lips, looked about him, then leant

closer to Richard, his voice low. 'You are looking for information about the air disaster? The British Airways flight?'

Fighting back a desire to move his head back because of the Egyptian's bad breath, Richard said, 'Yes. I am. You told me on the phone that you had something that might help.'

'You pay?' Rubbing his thumb back and forth across his two fingers, Abdullah looked hopefully at Richard.

'If what you tell me is true and can be substantiated.' The look of confusion on the Egyptian's face required Richard to try another approach. 'Substantiated. Means if you can prove it from another source.'

'Ah!' The man smiled. 'Yes, of course. It is why I am here. I have information in my pocket. With proof. You pay?' He rubbed the tips of his fingers with his thumb a worried look on his face.

'If what you tell me is what I am looking for. What do you have for me?'

'A report about a meeting between a Palestinian with name of Jalal Chalabi and Colonel Harwazi.'

A tingle of anticipation thrilled along Richard's spine. He had heard the name Chalabi only recently. Then it had been in the context of a possible suspect. Perhaps here was confirmation of the Palestinian's involvement. Something of his excitement must have shown because Abdullah said, 'Ah, I see name means something to you. I have dates, places and I know what they talk about.'

'How did you get the information?'

'I stole it,' came the astonishing reply. 'I am a humble worker in government department. I find information on file that I should not see.' He shrugged his round, fat shoulders. 'It was accident. I take copy.'

'Why? Why take a copy?' Richard frowned.

'It is worth lot of money, I think. I think I take it to America or England but now not possible.'

'Why not?'

'My wife. She needs operation very fast. I have no time to do what I think is right. I must get money. I hear you ask questions about the plane crash and so I come to you.'

'How did you find out about me?'

'My cousin works for big oil company. He tells me about a man who was at Hurghada asking questions about blowing up of plane. That his family die in blast. That he offer reward. He told me how to find you. It was simple.' Abdullah shrugged again.

The story made sense, as Richard had been at the town on the Red Sea to look at the destination port for the tow he had been negotiating. As always, he had been asking questions. He thought, discreetly. However, the fact of the matter was, there were some people who were beginning to take notice of him. He had yet to decide whether that was a good or a bad thing. All he did know was that he'd get nowhere unless he did ask the questions.

'Will you show me what you've got?'

Abdullah shook his head. 'Not here. Outside, in my car.' He saw Richard hesitate. 'Come. It is no trick. If I was doing a bad thing, why I come in here? I could wait outside and pull gun on you. Come.' Getting up, he walked away. Richard had no choice but to follow. He left the beer on the table.

Outside, it was a clear, warm and dry night. It was not yet nine o'clock and the pavement was teeming with people. He followed the fat man to a dilapidated, old Citroen and climbed into the passenger's seat.

Handing over sheets of paper, Abdullah sat nervously licking his lips. 'The top one is in Arabic and the bottom one is a translation.'

Richard nodded. Used to reading complex contracts he scanned the sheet of paper. It was just what he was looking for. It wasn't all there by any stretch of the imagination, but it did show Chalabi's and to a lesser extent, Harwazi's, involvement in the atrocity. It made interesting reading. Richard knew that his investigation had just taken a giant step forward. Trying not to show his excitement, he asked, 'How much?'

'Ten thousand American dollars.' Knowing how excessive the demand was, the Egyptian's voice became suddenly squeaky. Abdullah coughed to clear his throat.

Handing the papers back Richard turned to get out. 'Forget it. I don't have that sort of money. And I certainly don't carry that much around.'

'Wait!' Abdullah was becoming desperate. 'Make me an offer.'

'One thousand.'

Shaking his head Abdullah said, 'I risk my life to be here and you insult me with one thousand dollars? My cousin say you are man of honour.'

Feeling slightly ashamed of himself Richard said, 'All right. I have three thousand dollars on me. That's all. Take it or leave it.' Seeing the man hesitate, he added, 'Well?'

'I take it.'

With the contract in his briefcase, Richard left Egypt the following morning, before the newspapers hit the streets. The headlines proclaimed the same discovery – a headless body had been found in the back streets of Cairo. The sensationalised report went on to say that although the torso had been difficult to identify the authorities were now sure the body was that of Abdullah bin Abdullah, a low-level office clerk in a government department. There was no apparent motive for the killing although three thousand American dollars had been found in his wallet. His wife had shown surprise that he had been carrying so much money.

The information Richard had received from Abdullah became the cornerstone of his enquiries. Continuously, he cross-referenced information, chasing leads, adding to his total knowledge, discarding what was proven to be a lie. Eventually, he had a clear picture of what had happened.

Following the war in Iraq and the toppling of Saddam Hussein's regime, the Iranian Parliament had become fearful that they would be the next target of the Americans. Particularly as so much was being said in Washington about a possible Iranian nuclear weapons program. They had wanted to divert the Western World's attention away from themselves. To have the West's intelligence agencies running around the globe looking for militant Islamic terrorists. Not paying attention to Iran – until it was too late.

The Iranians had begun by hiring Walid bin Sydal to plan the operation. As a renegade Saudi Sheikh living in Afghanistan, bin Sydal's avowed purpose in life was to kill Americans whenever he could. It was his task to make the necessary arrangements whilst ensuring the Iranians would never be implicated. Using his Jihadist organisation, bin Sydal in turn contacted FATAH in the Gaza Strip. He promised them ten million dollars if they would carry out the operation.

FATAH was a reverse acronym of Harakat al-Tahir al-Filistiniya, literally meaning Palestinian National Liberation Movement. However, hataf meant sudden death, whereas Fatah was used to describe Islamic expansion in the first centuries of Islamic history and hence was important to Moslems. Which was why the acronym was reversed. FATAH had declined the offer. Should the Americans ever learn of their involvement then the loss of aid to the beleaguered Palestinians would be far, far greater. What was equally important, no government in the world considered FATAH a terrorist organisation. Unfortunately, at the last election, it lost power to HAMAS.

Harakat al-Muqawama al-Islamiya meant Islamic Resistance Movement and *was* considered a terrorist organisation. HAMAS meant zeal and they were desperately short of funds. Hence, Chalabi had accepted the offer. He also relished an excuse to attack the hated Americans, the main supporters of the Israelis. But Jalal Chalabi had also needed to put distance between HAMAS and the operation. He had no illusions what the Americans would do if they discovered HAMAS' involvement.

One major problem faced the Palestinians and their desire for a homeland. FATAH were prepared to accept a two state solution with the Israelis. They would accept the West Bank and Gaza with East Jerusalem as their capital, while HAMAS wanted Israel wiped off the face of the earth. As a result, the two organisations were at each others throats, killing each other more often than they killed Israelis.

Chalabi's contacts had led him to Abdel Nazrallah and Lamen Al-Ghoul. Two men who hated the West in general and the Americans in particular. Sheikh bin Sydal had been paid a great deal of money by the Iranians, some of which he had distributed to the involved parties as fees and for operating expenses. Those men connected to the operation had been kept to a minimum in order to maintain secrecy. Bin Sydal's cell had been five strong, the Palestinians had numbered four and on the Libyan side only Al-Ghoul had been named. The list on the Iranian side would have been decidedly longer. Collective responsibility was a way of life in Iran.

Thanks to the information supplied by Abdullah bin Abdullah, Richard had a clearer understanding where to look for what he wanted. During the months that followed Richard passed what he learnt to MI6, convinced it would help in the case against the perpetrators of the horrendous crime. Repeatedly he was assured that it did and so he kept the information flowing.

Whenever he asked, Richard was told there was insufficient evidence to take to court. There were no witnesses prepared to substantiate what they had learnt. And without witnesses what could they possibly do? Richard's dossier was circumstantial, but it did name names.

Finally, December that year there was some good news.

A trial of the men who had committed the atrocity was to take place "sometime soon". That was perhaps an optimistic assessment of the situation, but it was sufficient to satisfy Richard's desire to see the guilty men brought to justice. So he waited. And waited. He kept in touch with MI6 but the responses he received were subdued to say the least. Finally, his patience at an end, he demanded a meeting and, after a number of phone calls, was invited to MI6 headquarters. He was kept waiting for nearly forty minutes before being shown into the office of Edward Pennington-Prentice, the Deputy Director of Operations. The two men shook hands and Richard was invited to sit down.

Pennington-Prentice said nothing, waiting for Richard to begin.

'Thank you for seeing me,' Richard said. 'I want to discuss the information I've sent you.' He had no need to elaborate.

The man in the elegant grey suit opposite nodded his head. 'So I gathered.' He said nothing more.

'The news talks about a trial coming soon. What does that mean? When is soon? Next week, next month, next year?'

'That I cannot say. We are collating information from all over the world. Not just what you've sent us. We evaluate and assess what we receive before passing it on to the authorities dealing with the incident.'

'Incident? Is that what you call it? Surely it merits a stronger term, like atrocity? Or mass murder. Because that's what it was.'

'Of course, Mr. Griffiths.' The bureaucrat spoke gently, as if to a wayward child, which irritated the hell out of Richard. 'We appreciate what you've been telling us but it's time to stop. We have all the information we need and are working towards a satisfactory conclusion.'

'A satisfactory conclusion? What the hell is that? I want the bastards responsible dealt with. Send in special forces and deal with them.'

'I'm afraid it doesn't quite work like that, Mr. Griffiths. It hasn't for a long time. Not since the raj in India, I shouldn't think. Just leave it to us. We know what we're doing. However, I can assure you, arrests and a trial will take place in the not too distant future.'

'Whose?'

'That, I am afraid, is classified. I am not at liberty to tell you more. I am sorry.' The words were meaningless, the voice dripping with insincerity. 'I have a request from Her Majesty's Government.'

'What's the request?'

'We, that is, HMG, wishes you to desist from any further action. Do not make any more enquiries. We find that you are . . . em, shall we say, muddying the waters and making life difficult for our investigators.'

'But that's ridiculous. I've provided you with information you would never have had otherwise,' Richard protested.

Pennington-Prentice held up the palm of his right hand. 'Please believe me when I tell you it is for your own good. We do not wish you to do anything further. If you want an official request I can arrange it. I thought it better we keep this quiet. Between ourselves, so to speak.'

Richard was boiling with indignation. 'Between ourselves? I'll go public. I'll send the information I have to every newspaper in the world.'

'That is your prerogative, of course, but I wouldn't advise it. You will make many enemies and we will not be able to protect you.'

'Is that a threat?' Richard asked belligerently.

'No. Merely an observation. For your own good Mr. Griffiths, get on with your life and leave this to the professionals. Furthermore, if you did make the information public then an argument could be made that any trial will be prejudiced. You could be the man responsible for letting the culprits off because of a technicality.

Mr. Griffiths, I really do have another appointment. I must get on. Thank you for coming.'

Richard stood up. Neither man offered to shake hands as Richard stalked from the room.

It was the end of March before it was announced that arrests had been made in connection with the BA bombing. Even when he discovered that it was merely two unnamed Libyans who were being tried Richard kept silent. Perhaps the authorities had more up their sleeves. Perhaps, at the trial, more of the vital data he had amassed and handed over would be disclosed.

Camp Zeist had once been used to try the two men known as the Lockerbie bombers. It was a forty-hectare abandoned military establishment, 10kms south-east of Utrecht. More than 120 Scottish court officials and police had been moved there for the trial. Under Scottish law, fifteen jurors hear murder trials, with an eight person majority sufficient for a verdict. To please Libya's Muammar Harwazi the jury had been replaced by three Scottish judges, two of whom needed to agree for a conviction. As the trial had been long and complex, it was just as well. No jury could have followed all the arguments and reached the correct verdict. It was asking too much of the judicial system.

Although they had been found guilty and the case closed, the world had known that the real culprits had not been tried. But, it being in the nature of politics, the true facts were swept under the carpet. Two lowly operatives would spend the remainder of their lives in prison, their pleas and arguments going unheeded.

Now, the camp was being opened for a second time, also to try terrorists who had committed an act virtually identical to the one over Lockerbie. Richard hoped the outcome would not follow the same path. He wanted others to be named; those responsible.

The prosecution had presented their evidence. Now,

the defence was at work. It was during this time that Richard berthed *The Ellen* in Holland. He was not liking what he had heard so far about events at Camp Zeist.

Sir Edward Pennington-Prentice was satisfied. He had made contact and a figure had been agreed. If he received confirmation of the payment in the next forty-eight hours he would make the necessary arrangements. His retirement was less than a year away. The coveted top job was not to be his, in spite of his years of loyalty and hard work. A knighthood did not compensate for the disappointment. Well, he would get his own back. He had only one more task to perform.

The British Airways plane had come down on the edge of UK territorial waters. Hence the trial was Britain's responsibility. Due to the number of different nationalities who had died it had been agreed that the trial would be at Camp Zeist. Security would be easier and the fairness of the trial transparent enough for all to see. There was to be no jury. Just like the last time, three judges would sit, listen and decide. This time though, they would be English judges.

Pennington-Prentice stretched an elegant and manicured finger across the desk and pressed a button. 'Mary, will you come here, please? I need you to take a letter.' While waiting for her to appear, he drummed his fingers impatiently on his desk, thinking over his plans.

After she sat down, crossed her legs and held her pencil poised over her pad, he began. 'Eyes only. To the Head of Security, Camp Zeist. Sir, as soon as the verdict is announced and if the prisoners are found guilty, we will make arrangements to transport them to Wormwood Scrubs. This operation will be classified top secret and known only to a very few people. Please liaise directly with me. All arrangements will be undertaken and supervised by this office. I have etc. You got that, Mary? Good. Then read it back to me.'

She did so.

'Excellent.' He was highly satisfied with himself. He would get rid of one nuisance, for a considerable sum of course and be in a position to avail himself of an even greater amount of money in the future. All of which contributed handsomely to his retirement fund. It was a pity, but some things had to be kept from the general public. It was too dangerous, otherwise. 'Now, I think I will have a cup of that rather fine Earl Grey you bought yesterday. Oh and one of the Digestives, if you please.'

Richard sat aboard *The Ellen*, blowing ripples into a mug of tea, lost in contemplation, woken early by his thoughts, his dreams. Looking through the window in the wheelhouse, he watched as the stark outlines of the buildings and dockside hardened in the growing light. *The Ellen* was berthed in a small marina, near Spakenburg, about 10 miles to the east of Amsterdam but, more importantly, only 15 miles from Zeist near Utrecht.

He went below and swilled out his mug in the galley. He stowed it away and went aft to change into running gear. Dawn was breaking when he let himself off the boat and began limbering-up exercises. With the kinks out of his muscles he began his run.

The holiday had been his idea. He had made all the arrangements, the bookings. A surprise for Ellen and the twins, although they had been too young to understand what was really going on. Even now, the guilt wouldn't go away. The sequence of events that had conspired to let him live had been mind numbing. If Bill hadn't had a heart attack. If another qualified and experienced master had been available. If he hadn't answered the phone that evening and had let the answering-machine deal with it he might not have been reached in time. If there hadn't been a hurricane in the first place. If the first mate had been more experienced. So it had gone on, round and round without end, until the "what ifs" had begun to drive him mad. In order to save his sanity, he was forced to accept that his survival had been a part of life's lottery. On the tug he had almost died when the anchor dragged him over the side. Anything could have happened during the hurricane. The fact was, it hadn't been his time to die. His family was dead and he was not.

The previous two years intruded into his thoughts. He had been dealing with some of the most important and influential men in the most vital industry in the world – oil – the life-blood of the West pumped from the Middle East.

Stretching his pace, he also increased speed. His role till now was solely that of information gatherer. Everything was passed to a higher authority to let them deal with it. After all, he was no longer a serving officer in the Royal Navy. In fact, although he had specialised in diving and mine warfare, his skills were inadequate for bringing terrorists to justice. He had not taken the next step into special forces like his cousin Nick. Richard was aware that his temperament was better suited to the commercial world than to the claustrophobic one of the military, with its rigid hierarchical structure and the long haul it took to get anywhere near the top. What was more, with a shrinking navy and reducing budgets, the ultimate goal, command of a capital ship, was less and less likely. So he had resigned his commission as a lieutenant and joined the family business. It was a sprawling mix-match of companies, varying from property to banking and insurance. There was one truly oddball business – the one he worked in. It did not really belong, but in some odd way it fitted, complimenting the remainder.

He'd had a number of regrets when he'd resigned his commission, but not for long. Command of a tugboat was almost as satisfying as command of a Royal Naval vessel. He grinned to himself. Well, not quite. But he was already the equivalent of an Admiral. Even an Admiral of the Fleet. In fact, he had more hulls than the current Admiral of the Fleet. The RN could muster a mere forty ships while he had forty-four to order around. As Operations Director it was his job to keep the ships fully utilised and to do so he had a staff of seventy-six men and women.

He followed a path alongside a canal, side stepping or overtaking other early morning strollers and joggers. The sun breached the horizon and began to burn off the low-lying mist. It promised to be another lovely, early summer's day.

When he returned to *The Ellen* he stopped a short distance away and took a close look at her. Everything appeared to be in order. Richard reached into a pocket in his shorts and extracted a credit card size electronic device. He looked at the screen and pressed a button. A green dot flashed briefly.

During the course of compiling the dossier there had been an occasion when he had not been discreet enough. He had been warned off. He had apologised, explained that it was a mistake. He was only asking out of interest. The incident had shaken him. He was not invincible. If he was going to be asking questions of terrorists, possibly stirring up a hornets' nest, then he could expect to be stung. As a result, he had taken a few precautions. He had hired a security expert to advise him on what locks and other devices he could use to stop anyone gaining access to the boat. It came as no surprise to be told that it was impossible to stop a trained and determined man or woman from getting on board. Instead, he had been taught about unit security. Hiding items of value in such a way as to be undetectable. As most break-ins occurred during the owner's absence it was most important to know if anybody had been on board or if they were still there. Hence the electronic sensors fitted throughout the boat. The green light told him nobody had been on board. If somebody had broken in then the dot would have flashed red. If that were to happen, he needed to press a second button. If it flashed green, it would mean that the intruder had left while a red one would warn him that an un-invited guest was still on board. Other features would tell him where the person or persons were located. Altogether, he considered it a very handy gadget to have, though he sometimes felt a fool for taking such precautions. *Better foolish than dead.*

The remainder of the day he spent doing chores around the boat. They were never ending but helped him to relax.

By 10.00 the following morning, he was seated in the public gallery at Camp Zeist. With his arms crossed, Richard glowered at the two men sitting at their ease, protected by bullet-proof glass. They were following the arguments through headphones, listening to the translator as the defence took apart some of the evidence that had been heard from the prosecution. At lunchtime, Richard left the court and took a taxi back to his boat. He had work to do. He was currently negotiating a contract with the Royal Dutch Oil Company to tow a rig from Europe to Nigeria. It was a standard job which dove-tailed in with another contract to South Africa. Together, they would be highly lucrative in a market place that was feeling the pinch of high oil prices and hence lower consumer demand. His thoughts, however, were on the trial.

He was sure that Al-Ghoul was guilty but less sure about Nazrallah. The latter's name had only come up once when he had been looking for the evidence, while Al-Ghoul's had come up time and again. In spite of agitating for the information he had supplied to be passed to the prosecutors, MI6 had again warned him to stay out of the proceedings. He had been told that everything needed to reach a satisfactory conclusion had been done. Those words had an ominous ring to them.

Checking his security arrangements on arriving back at *The Ellen*, Richard let himself on board. He changed into a sober dark suit, white shirt and blue naval club tie with the gold crown motif and took a taxi into Amsterdam.

He spent the remainder of the day arguing the finer points of the contract, aided by two assistants. It was nearly 19.00 before both parties were satisfied and a heads of agreement document was signed. The lawyers would have to battle over the even smaller print. He accepted an invitation to drinks and dinner and they moved to a nearby restaurant.

The party consisted of six men, three from G & B Offshore and three from Royal Dutch. The food was solid Dutch cuisine, but the wines were of the finest vintages. Everyone drank too much and by the time they parted company, the various schnapps they'd enjoyed took Richard over the edge of sobriety. He was nonchalant and careless when a taxi finally dropped him off at the marina.

The Ellen was berthed alongside a narrow wooden jetty. He let himself through the security gate and stepped carefully along the metal ramp that let down to the water's edge. He paused for a few moments and looked up at a clear sky. In spite of the light pollution all around he could still see the stars quite clearly. He searched his memory for the names of some of them. He thought hard, but for a few moments his alcohol fuddled brain failed him. He easily identified the Plough and the North Star and then, like a curtain being pulled back, a few other names came to him. Riga, Capella and Arcturus but he could not remember which was which. He gave up and continued towards the boat. He reached into his pocket for the security device and looked at it blearily. What the hell, he thought and placed it in his pocket. There was nobody there and he was too drunk to care anyway. It had been a long time since he had been the worse for drink.

He reached *The Ellen* and scrambled on board. Taking out his keys he fumbled for the lock. They dropped through his fingers and he cursed as he bent down. The move saved his life.

He heard the rustling of clothes, the shuffling of feet and he looked behind him. His head was bent and he half turned. The figure in black had his arm held high and was swinging it down. Richard instinctively blocked the move but the power was too much and he was hit across the arm and the side of the head. He flew backwards against the railing, tottered for a second and then fell overboard. His naval training kicked in. Whilst in the air he still had enough of his wits about him to take a deep breath, put his hands behind his head and curl into a ball. Dazed and drunk, his instinct for survival took over. The water was cold and cleared his fogged mind. He had no idea if the person who attacked him was alone or armed. Swimming down into the black depths he went under the keel and made his way slowly to the surface. He was between the boat and the bank and underneath the jetty. Reaching the surface, he trod water. Looking up, he saw the wooden slats of the jetty about two feet above him. It was pitch dark but he could see the edge of the boat against the night sky. Suddenly, a torch appeared and shone on the water. Somebody spoke in a loud whisper and a second person replied. He heard footsteps coming along the jetty. They stopped directly above him. A man with a deep rasping voice asked something in a language he recognised as Arabic, although he couldn't understand what was being said.

The torch moved along the side of the boat, pointing down at the water. It passed around the bow and came towards him. He took a deep breath and sank beneath the surface, swimming along the jetty, distancing himself from his attackers. When he could hold his breath no longer, he surfaced and gulped in air. He was at least a hundred metres, maybe more, from the boat. He watched the torch flashing back and forth for some time. Eventually, it was extinguished. It sounded as if the men were leaving. He decided to stay where he was just to be on the safe side. He would wait fifteen minutes. He squinted at his watch. It was 01.35. The cold was beginning to get to him but he thought it was better to be cold than dead. At 01.50 he decided to give it another ten minutes, just in case. His teeth were beginning to chatter like castanets but he was determined to wait longer. In spite of a headache and a feeling of nausea he was sobering up. Anger welled up in him. Not at his enemy, but at himself. How on earth could he have been so stupid as to drink so much and to become so careless? It was easy enough to say no, even to the most insistent host. Then not to check his security was beyond belief. At 02.00 he figured enough was enough. Swimming to the end of the jetty he silently climbed out of the water. He lay where he was for a few seconds.

All along his left side, boats were moored. *The Ellen* was fifteen or eighteen boats away. Keeping low he moved slowly back the way he had come. Looking all around he could see and hear nothing except the soothing noise of rigging flapping in the gentle breeze. When he was about twenty metres short of the boat he took out his security device and pressed one of the buttons. He was near enough to receive the signal and to read its message. Somebody had been on board and searched her from end to end. The device showed that whoever it was had taken his time. It showed where he went on board and how long he had stayed in each place. He had been longer in the engine room than anywhere else on the vessel.

According to the signal, the person or persons had left. Richard looked around but the marina was still and silent. Bent over, he had taken only a few paces forward when *The Ellen* exploded.

8

DEBRIS FLEW INTO the air in a fiery ball. *Whoever set the explosives used a large quantity,* Richard registered grimly. *Or maybe they disconnected the gas alarm and opened the Calor gas in the galley.* The vessels on either side of *The Ellen* had also caught fire. People were stumbling out from their boats, screaming and yelling for help. In the confusion, no one paid him any attention. He was bedraggled, filthy and dripping wet but the men, women and children streaming past him to get to the fire hardly registered him. Their attention was fixed on the conflagration.

If his attackers knew who they were looking for they would find him quickly, despite the dozens of people now trying to put out the fires either side of *The Ellen's* berth. Already, her hull was leaning out, away from the jetty, as water poured in through gaping holes all along her port side. As she settled, the fire died down. Holding onto the railing on the side of the jetty next to the bank, he walked backwards, away from the scene. Only when he was certain he was masked by darkness did Richard turn around and hurry along the jetty. No one noticed him leave. The marina was filled with frenetic activity.

At the end of the jetty he slipped once more into the muddy, brown water. Using a powerful breaststroke he swam steadily. Once outside the marina's perimeter he waded ashore and began to jog away from the orange glow which was beginning to die down.

Fear is a kind of warning device. He had travelled less

than a few hundred metres when he noticed two cars parked in a lay-by ahead. Cautiously, he stepped off the road and into the undergrowth. Creeping forward he could smell tobacco smoke and hear the low murmuring of voices. Surely the occupants of the car must have heard the explosion. So why were they sitting so calmly in the cars? He stopped. If he went any closer they would hear him. But in his present position he was too far away to hear or see anything. In the background he caught the sound of alarm bells and two-tone sirens. Blue flashing lights appeared in the distance, rapidly approaching the marina. Taking advantage of the cacophony, he moved quickly through the undergrowth until he was at the lay-by. Kneeling down he watched as two fire engines and a police car swept passed.

In the lights of the passing vehicles he could clearly see the occupants of the cars. The Mercedes nearest him had two occupants. A single figure was sitting in the second car, parked parallel to the Mercedes' driver's window. When the emergency vehicles had passed, the drivers of the two cars resumed their conversation. Richard could see the lower half of the face in the second car. The square jaw had a neat pencil-line moustache above the upper lip.

'You are sure he's dead?' The accent was unmistakably English.

The reply was harsh and guttural. 'If he didn't drown when he went into the water then he was blown sky high.'

'I will let your masters know. What plans have you?'

'We return to Beyrouth.'

An engine started and the lights on the second car came on. In the glow from the dashboard Richard strained to make out the driver's features. He couldn't recognise him. The car pulled away from the Mercedes and as the moving vehicle turned a bend, away from the lay-by, Richard smothered a shocked expletive. The car was carrying British diplomatic plates.

What the hell was going on? The Mercedes moved

away with a squeal of tyres. It turned and followed the other car, allowing Richard a brief glimpse into the interior. Both men had swarthy and, Richard thought, Middle Eastern complexions.

Leaving the marina it had been Richard's intention to go straight to the British Embassy and ask for help. Now, despite his contacts, the embassy was the last place he wanted to be.

Jogging at a steady pace he continued towards Amsterdam. Although it was early morning there were plenty of taxis about, taking late night revellers home or back to hotels. The ones he saw were all occupied. Finally, a car was coming towards him with it's light on. He hailed it and the driver stopped. Quickly, Richard slid into the back seat and closed the door. He knew he was a dishevelled mess as well as being soaked to the skin.

The driver turned his head to protest and said something in Dutch. Richard didn't need an interpreter to tell him that he was being told to get out again.

Reaching into his pocket he extracted his wallet and offered the man a 100 Euro note. 'I'll give you the same again if you take me to the railway station.'

The man looked at the money, licked his lips and nodded. He made comment about the fact that the money was soaking wet.

'And please turn the heating up full.'

For 200 euros to travel only a few kilometres the driver was happy to oblige. At the station Richard paid over the other 100 euros and hurried onto the concourse. There were very few people about. He found the toilets and went inside. It came as no surprise to find them empty. Richard, shivering and with his teeth chattering, stripped naked. He hung his clothes over the blow dryers and started pressing the buttons. His head hurt like hell, he had a streak of mud along one cheek and his hair was plastered to his head. He filled a sink with hot water and washed his hair and face and rubbed warm water over his body. While he did so he kept pressing the buttons to keep the blowers going. Not only did this help his clothes to dry but it added warmth to the place. Gradually, he began to shiver less, while his teeth stopped acting like castanets. He used toilet tissue to dry himself, at the same time bending awkwardly under the dryers for additional warmth.

Luckily no one entered. His underpants felt dry enough to wear and he put them on. His shirt followed. Checking his watch he saw it was nearly 05.00. The early workers who helped to kick-start a city into life would be arriving soon. Even as the thought entered his head a man came in. He gave Richard a curious look. Richard smiled back, said nothing, grabbed the remainder of his clothes and went into a cubicle. He sat exhausted on the toilet. Activity and adrenaline had kept him going. His trousers and socks were reasonably dry and he put them on. His jacket was still damp. He forced himself to leave the cubicle although he felt weary beyond belief. The room was again empty and he hung his shoes and jacket over the dryers and started them operating. Other people came in but he ignored them. He was respectable enough not to cause any comment even if he did receive some odd looks.

He thought about telling the police what had happened but dismissed the idea. The last thing he wanted right then was to be caught up the bureaucratic nightmare that was Dutch law enforcement. Furthermore, the car with the diplomatic plates really had him worried. He had intended to sail *The Ellen* back to Brighton. A day's journey was all it would take and he had been looking forward to the trip. Now, he needed to get back to England as soon as possible and report what had happened to MI6.

The thought gave him cause to pause. He assumed that the attempt on his life had been something to do with the enquiries he'd been making. Had he asked one too many questions and somebody had decided it was time to get rid of him? Had he made other enemies? Something to do with business? No! He rejected the ridiculous thought even as it formed. He was known as a tough negotiator, but he had never cheated anyone. To the best of his knowledge, he had never done anything that came remotely close to justifying his murder. Christ, who wanted him dead? Weariness and the events of the night had left him punch drunk. His thinking was sluggish as well as scrambled. But it had to be the file. It was the only thing that made sense. The only people who knew what he had learnt were MI6! MI6? Why on earth would they want to kill him?

Was this paranoia? Maybe! Panic welled up in him. He half closed his eyes, looking through slits as another thought occurred. The polite brush-offs, the lack of progress. His obsession with the dossier had blinded him to the obvious. For whatever reason, he had become a thorn in the side of MI6.

What about the voices he had heard in the cars? One English, the others, he was sure, were Arabic. Beyrouth was the Lebanese way of saying Beirut. He needed to find out who was after him and fast. Where on earth was he going to start? He had barely registered the profile of the Arabs, so he couldn't begin to make a positive identification, even if he could find them.

The embassy looked like being his best bet. Maybe he could spot the owner of the moustache? How many people worked in a major European embassy? A hundred at least. And if he found him, he couldn't just confront the man. An idea began to take shape.

Knowing the car hire offices would be open early at the airport he took a taxi to Schipol. He paid the driver using crumpled but dry Euros. It was often said that nowadays airports had become shopping malls with runways attached. He soon bought a complete outfit of clothes. For the first time in his life he was wearing designer labels, something he had sworn he would never do. A suitcase and toiletries completed the task. In the toilets he shaved and looked critically at himself. Apart from the bags under his eyes he looked what he was, a successful businessman. A coffee and a couple of painkillers helped his transformation back to feeling almost human again.

A Fiat Uno was the most inconspicuous car he could hire from Avis. He presented his driving licence at the Avis desk and paid cash. The car hire people would have preferred a credit card. Richard wasn't prepared to use one, in case somebody was able to track his transaction. He wasn't ready for the world to know he was still alive.

By 07.30 he was parked a hundred metres from the main gate of the British Embassy. Pulling a baseball cap lower over his eyes, he walked slowly towards the main gate. A sign gave the embassy opening times: 8.30am until 5pm, five days a week, Saturdays 9am until 12pm. Closed Sundays. There was no guard and the place looked deserted, but Richard wasn't fooled. He knew that he was currently being filmed and if he acted in any way suspicious a squad of armed guards would be on him like a plague of locusts. Security at embassies all over the world had entered the 21st century at long last. He paused and glanced through the railings of the gate to the huge, solid building. He had visited the embassy on many occasions, both on business and to attend formal receptions. If he needed to, he knew he could get an audience with the Ambassador, but that would draw too much attention for now. He continued around the block. As he had suspected, there was only one entrance. He had been fairly sure the staff used the same gate as the visitors.

Richard settled back in the car and watched. From 08.00 onwards there was continual activity as people began to arrive for work. He hadn't bargained for the number of people arriving by car. Sometimes he caught a glimpse of the driver as he or she opened a window to show a pass and speak to the sentry who had now appeared at the gate but Richard couldn't always see clearly. He certainly didn't see a driver with a thin moustache.

All morning he sat there, becoming more restless. He tuned the radio to BBC Radio 5 Live and listened to the morning phone-in show. As always, it was highly entertaining, facts seldom interfering with opinions. He fought his tiredness. The long day wore on and he was becoming distinctly uncomfortable. He had stocked up with food and cold energy drinks and the latter were now beginning to press heavily on his bladder. He swallowed more headache pills. By 18.00 he had watched the last of the staff departing and finally gave up. If the man with the moustache was in there, he needed to find another way of spotting him. When he drove away he knew he was in no fit state to be doing so.

He got to the airport without mishap and booked into a room at the Sheraton Amsterdam Airport Hotel. He managed to undress before he climbed onto the bed and instantly fell asleep.

It was a few minutes before 09.00 when he awoke. Groggily he sat up and groaned. he completed his ablutions before he rang down for room service and ordered breakfast delivered to his room. He broke the connection and then he called Brian Williams. He used the hotel phone as his mobile phone had given up the ghost after its sustained immersion in the marina.

'Brian? It's Richard.'

'Richard! Bloody hell! You're alive! We got a message that your boat had blown up. Bloody hell!' he repeated.

Richard had already decided tactics. 'Hang on a minute, Brian, are you telling me *The Ellen* has been blown up? When?'

'In the early hours. I was woken up about four-thirty by the military attaché in Amsterdam. He was quite convinced you'd been killed in the explosion.'

'My boat! Damn! She was unique. How in hell will I replace her?'

'I take it you were insured?'

'Sure. I used our underwriters at Lloyds.'

'Consider yourself lucky to be alive, Richard. Good job you weren't aboard . . .'

'I . . . got lucky. Stayed ashore. You know how it is.'

There was a tinge of envy in the older man's voice. 'At my age, just vague recollections, unfortunately. Well, as long as you're all right. I'll contact the embassy and put them in the picture. The last I heard they were looking for your body. Or at least, bits of one.'

After telling Brian he'd see him in the office in forty-eight hours, Richard broke the connection and thoughtfully lay back on the bed. The military attaché had phoned? Contacted his boss? How very interesting. Why had Brian been informed so quickly? It was definitely time to see what this military attaché looked like.

The next morning, Richard took a taxi back to the embassy. There was one person he had met on numerous occasions who just might give him a few minutes of his time without being given prior notice.

His passport got him into the building and through the X-ray detection system. Instead of following the sign for the public offices he went across to a door marked "Secretaries", knocked and went in. There were two women sitting at desks, typing furiously. One looked up politely and asked, 'May I help you?'

'Yes. My name is Richard Griffiths. I wondered if the Chancellor would be able to see me briefly?'

'Is he expecting you?'

'No. But if you give him my name, I'm sure he'll fit me in.'

The secretary looked doubtful, but picked up the phone. Richard waited impatiently while his request was passed through the Chancellor's secretary. The Chancellor, Oliver Pettigrew, was the Chief Secretary at the embassy and a man Richard had met on at least a dozen occasions. To his certain knowledge he was one secretary who had never typed a letter in his life.

'He'll see you straightaway. I'm to take you up.'

A secretary escorted him to the booth at the foot of the stairs and arranged a pass. Richard pinned it to his lapel and she led the way upstairs. He was quickly shown into the Chancellor's office and offered a cup of coffee, which he accepted.

Oliver Pettigrew was a career diplomat who could expect an ambassadorship in a year or two, probably of an African country where, provided he didn't succumb to sclerosis of the liver, he could work his way up the ambassadorial ladder. Within ten years he could find himself a cushy number somewhere in Europe. Pettigrew was already becoming plump from too many receptions and dinner parties, an occupational hazard that took tremendous willpower to resist. He was as tall as Richard and hid a sharp mind behind a lazy manner; he was not a person to underestimate. His greeting was typically to the point.

'Richard! We thought you were dead.'

'That's why I'm here. I just heard the news from my office so I came over to set the record straight.' He repeated the spiel of a romantic liaison he had given his boss.

'Tremendous piece of luck. They think it was a gas leak. I'll let the police know that they can stop searching for a body.'

The two men exchanged a few pleasantries until Richard caught Pettigrew casting covert glances at his watch. He stood up.

'Oliver, thanks for your time.' They shook hands. 'By the way, who's the MA these days? I thought a friend of mine from my navy days had the job.'

'No. This chap's an army major. Name of Clive Simms.'

'Simms? Tall fellow? Red haired with a bushy moustache? Royal Engineers?'

Pettigrew shook his head. 'He's tall, all right. But he's got a pencil moustache. He's from the Black Watch. Only been here a few months. Gone back home on leave, I think. Went this morning.'

'Obviously not the man I was thinking of. Oliver, thanks for your time, I'd better leave you to get on.' They shook hands again and Richard left.

At an internet cafe he Googled "The Black Watch". The regiment was currently serving in Germany. At St. Barbara's Barracks, Fallingbostel, BFPO 38. A map showed that was between Hanover and Hamburg.

The Black Watch was one of Scotland's most famous regiments, headquartered in Perth. It was now an armoured infantry regiment. They had battle honours stretching over hundreds of years and dozens of wars and skirmishes. Why would a major in the Black Watch want him dead? He needed to get some answers. He drove to the airport, returned the car and took the next flight to London.

In the British Library, a copy of the Army List provided more detail. Major Clive Simms. No medals. Regiment, The Black Watch. Date of seniority, 1.4.98. That meant he was out of the zone for promotion to lieutenant colonel. Another few years and he would be forced to retire. The MA job was probably his last.

The internet proved as useful as ever. It took only minutes to track the major down. So much, thought Richard, for security. It appeared that Simms had an apartment in Edinburgh. Before setting off north, he took an important detour south. He had to break the news about *The Ellen* to Vic and Matt.

At their run-down cottage, he was warmly welcomed. The place was more dilapidated than ever. He could see that the two brothers were continuing to live hand to mouth and guessed that any work that had been coming in had long since dried up.

He sat at their spotless kitchen table and recounted the story.

'That's a bad business and no mistake,' said Vic. 'Matt, get out the whisky. Tea's no good at a time like this.'

Eagerly, his brother complied.

'So what brings you here, lad? It was good of you to come, of course. But as you see, there ain't nothing much happening.'

Richard nodded. It was just as he had expected. 'I have a proposition for you. I want you to scour the coast until you find a replacement. Then I want you to re-fit her to the standard of *The Ellen*.'

The transformation before his eyes was astonishing. His two old friends seemed to cast off ten years as the prospect of work, real work, loomed before them.

'Where do we go for the hull?' Matt asked.

'You know something? There's a beauty at Salcombe,' Vic said to his brother, who nodded eagerly.

The two brothers were off and Richard sat back, listening to them argue gently. At that moment, the idea that someone wanted him dead seemed utterly preposterous.

He interrupted their discussion. 'You fix it and I'll pay you cash every step of the way.'

He spent an uncomfortable night on their badly stuffed sofa and the next morning he took a train back to London having left the brothers in funds. The dossier he had kept on board the boat had been the only hard copy he had. But everything had been backed up on memory sticks, one in his office, the other at his bank. He wanted to add some notes about recent events to the memory stick in the bank. It was in his will that in the event of his death the contents of the box at the bank were to be given to his solicitor for forwarding to his cousin, Nick Hunter. He was the one man who Richard trusted to do the right thing.

After completing his task, he caught the train to Edinburgh. Arriving in the middle of a thunder storm, he waited at Waverley station for the rain to ease. The sun came out and basked the city in a warm evening glow.

Walking out of the station, he crossed the road and

went up Cockburn St. This was the oldest part of the city and lay steeped in history. It was one of Richard's favourite places and he had often enjoyed a pint or two in the local pubs. He went down the High Street, past the Wax Museum and into the Cowgate. He found the address he was looking for. The solid stone apartments were four high, impressively substantial. An entry phone controlled the door. He carried on walking past.

On the other side of the wide street were bars and two cafes. Edinburgh had developed a substantial café society over the last decade and on such a pleasant evening there were tables arrayed outside on the pavement. Taking a seat at one of them, he opened a copy of *The Daily Telegraph* while keeping a covert eye on the door opposite. His luck was in. He was half way through a large cappuccino when a taxi drew up outside the house. Simms emerged from it and looked across the road as he turned to pay the fare. In Richard's over-heated imagination the major appeared to be looking straight at him. He dismissed the thought but there was no doubt about one thing. Simms was the same man he had caught a glimpse of in the embassy car. A jolt of hatred and anger made Richard sit up. He forced himself to relax.

Watching the major go inside, he ordered another coffee. As he lowered his head to the cup a curtain at the third floor window twitched.

When a table at the window inside the restaurant became vacant, Richard continued his surveillance from there. He had a clear view across the road. The waitress approached and, barely glancing at the menu, Richard gave her a token order, the first of several.

It was dusk and the streetlights had just come on when Simms re-appeared. Hastily summoning the waitress, Richard gave her twenty pounds and hurried after his quarry. The man was at least a hundred metres away but not walking very fast. Richard closed the gap until he was about a dozen paces behind. The pavement was packed with tourists and there were plenty of people to hide behind. His difficulty was keeping close enough to see where Simms went, while at the same time staying far enough away not to attract attention. With no training in surveillance he had to hope for the best. Richard had been concentrating so hard on following Simms that he lost track of his surroundings. When he looked round, he realised that they had walked the whole length of St. Leonard's Street and were now on Dalkeith Road. There were still pedestrians about but fewer than before.

Simms turned into Holyrood Park Road, crossed the roundabout and walked quickly towards the park. Now they were the only two men walking the street. Richard suddenly felt vulnerable. Night had fallen but the way was lit by the orange glow of the streetlights. As far as he could tell, Simms had not looked back once in his direction. For the first time Richard had the thought that he might be walking into a trap.

Simms began to walk faster, turning anti-clockwise around the volcanic rock of Arthur's Seat. The road bent to the right until Simms was out of sight. Richard rounded the bend to be confronted with an empty stretch of road. He stopped for a second then rushed forward, desperate to catch up with his quarry. He heard nothing. Awareness came only with the strong arm that wrapped itself around his throat. When the second arm clamped across the back of his neck fear washed through him.

9

THE PRESSURE WAS horrendous. Richard flailed like a landed fish. As he clawed at the arm strangling him, a voice hissed in his ear.

'Hold still or I'll break your neck.' To prove the point there was a sudden jerk and Richard's head was pushed forward. He couldn't breathe and the pain was excruciating. He stopped fighting.

'That's better. Now, I'm going to ease my hands and you'd better talk. If you don't, you're dead. Do you understand?'

Richard's head jerked painfully forward. He gasped for air and tried nodding. His head moved imperceptibly.

'First of all, who are you?'

Was it conceivable that Simms didn't know him? Of course! Simms had left his post, believing him killed. His boat had been targeted and he had been identified with the boat. If he knew the truth, Simms would finish what he had started here and now.

'Davidson,' he croaked. 'Saul Davidson.'

'What do you want, Davidson and why are you following me?' The pressure was applied once more, harder this time. 'I saw you in the cafe, you amateur. You've also been following me for the last half hour. Now what do you want?'

One story after another flitted through Richard's head, but nothing that would hold water. Too late he realised that he should have had a plausible explanation at the ready. He wasn't even carrying any fake identity. Simms only had to reach into his pocket to find his passport.

Richard realised that Simms couldn't locate his passport without removing one of his arms from the headlock. The thought seemed to occur to the other man simultaneously. Suddenly, from having his head pushed forward with his throat jammed between Simms' arms, Richard was jerked back. Now he found himself pinned against Simms who still had an arm around his throat and Richard's head held back. Simms' other arm was now free and he reached inside Richard's jacket pocket.

The pressure on his throat had eased. He had one tiny opportunity. The first clamp that had been around his throat was a lock he was familiar with. Against it he stood no chance. With the assailant's hands clasped to his own arms the assailant could exert an upward and forward pressure that would break the victim's neck. With that lock removed, he now had a glimmer of hope. Simms was strong but Richard was no weakling. Putting his right leg out before him he swung it back as hard as he could, while leaning backwards with all his weight.

The heel of his shoe connected with a loud crack, Simms let out a yell and both men fell to the ground. Richard smashed his head back and had the satisfaction of hearing Simms' head hitting the concrete. Simms' nose erupted blood and his grip on Richard slackened. Climbing groggily to his feet, Richard saw that the major was unconscious. He stood, at a loss what to do, until the loom of headlights showed around the bend and he dived into the shadows for cover. As the car passed Simms stirred. Before Richard could react, Simms climbed to his feet, looked blearily around and staggered back the way he had come. Richard stayed where he was. He did not relish a hand to hand encounter with the Black Watch major.

Minutes later, his throat hurting like hell, he began walking in the opposite direction. He cursed himself for the fool he was. The major had been right. Richard was an amateur. He had only succeeded in putting Simms on his guard. He needed a plan.

Like many modern cities, Edinburgh had its fair share of down and outs and beggars. In the summer time, they tended to congregate where the tourists wandered. The Cowgate was one such place and Richard had noticed a number of them sitting in doorways, dogs and begging bowls at their feet. Was there another way? The more he thought about it, the less sure he became. His dithering, in turn, made him angry – at himself.

He spent a sleepless night in a small hotel near the Haymarket. He awoke groggy, his throat aching, swallowing was unpleasant, though not impossible. Not bothering to shave nor wait for breakfast, he swallowed some of the painkillers he'd bought at Schipol and took the bus into the city centre.

The first thing he did was buy a mobile phone. The next was to enter an internet cafe where he bought a large Americano with milk and found the address he wanted. He took a taxi to his destination down Leith Walk. In a charity shop, feeling foolish, he bought an ancient, long, black coat and a battered sun hat. He tried them on.

Seeing the woman behind the counter looking strangely at him, he said, 'It's for a fancy dress.'

She nodded her understanding and smiled when he gave her four times the asking price. 'For the charity.'

Outside, away from prying eyes, he ripped the sleeves and trampled on the coat. A few doors along was a shoe shop. He entered and bought a pair of cheap trainers. Walking back along Leith Walk he dragged his feet, scuffing the shoes. Outside a convenience store he found a collapsed and folded cardboard box put out for the bin collectors. He slipped it under his arm and carried on.

An hour later, Richard once more took up a position opposite the major's flat, only this time, with a piece of cardboard under him, instead of a stylish designer chair.

He sat with his head bowed, copying two other down-and-outs further along. One had a mongrel at his feet, the other a sign on which was scrawled "Ex – Serviceman, Please Help". Both of them had tin cups at their feet.

Richard berated himself for his sloppy field craft, his lousy analysis of what he needed to do. He didn't dare risk staying where he was. He knew the major to be a highly observant s-o-b. He left his spot and went in search of a cup, more cardboard and a marker pen. He was back about an hour later to find the place he had been at was occupied. He moved further along, still able to keep the major's front door in sight.

While he watched the flat's entrance he kept his head bowed. In the late afternoon he saw Simms emerge and walk briskly along the street. Climbing to his feet, Richard shuffled after him. In his cup was 76p. He tipped it in his pocket, wondering how the others survived if that was all they'd been given. He kept his eyes down, stepped out of people's way, acting as if he expected verbal abuse at any moment. He was willing himself into the character of a down and out.

The major was checking he wasn't being tailed. He stopped suddenly or gazed into shop windows. He altered direction, doubling back on himself. Once he even brushed past Richard without a second glance. It was as though Richard had become invisible. Richard found the feeling disconcerting, his sympathy for those who did live on the streets growing by the minute.

A quarter of an hour later, Simms entered a busy bar in the Grass Market. Richard he took up a position not far from the entrance and watched the bar. After nearly an hour, just as he was on the verge of going inside to take a look, a figure stepped through the door. The man was wearing traditional tourist garb of jeans and an open-necked shirt and for a second Richard didn't recognise him. In fact, he probably wouldn't have, if at that moment

Simms hadn't appeared, exchanged a few words with the man and walked away. The shock of recognition sent a chill of fear along Richard's spine. The man Simms had spoken to was Pennington-Prentice, the Deputy Director-General of MI6.

Taking no further notice of the men, Richard went in the opposite direction. Seeing a beggar sitting on the side of the road he handed over the coat and the shoes along with £20. The man nodded and gave a surly thanks.

One thing was clear – he needed help. He was way out of his depth. If Simms was connected to Pennington-Prentice then was he working under orders from MI6? But why? Where was the justice? Was it so wrong to supply MI6 with evidence about the disaster which had killed his wife and children? Everyone understood the concept of an eye for an eye. So, he had made some noise. Too embarrassing for the Establishment? Fury ripped through Richard. All that trite bullshit they had given. They had been keeping tabs on him all along.

He knew only one man who could help him and thankfully he wasn't very far away.

He used the mobile he had just purchased. 'Nick? It's Richard. Where are you?'

'Rosyth. What's up?'

'I need your help. Any chance of meeting me?'

'When?'

'ASAP.'

'I'm finished here. Say an hour at the hotel near the Barnton roundabout?'

'I know it. I'll grab a taxi.'

Breaking the connection, Richard stripped off and went under the shower, keen to wash away the dust and feel of the streets. He took a taxi to the Barnton Roundabout and had just arrived when his cousin, Nick Hunter, entered the bar. Richard watched him approach with a feeling of great fondness, as well as relief. Hunter was an inch taller than his cousin, with the same dark hair. In contrast to his own, Hunter had dark blue eyes. He always reminded Richard of a panther, with his sleek walk, his awareness, his energy and strength. Nick had been a proud god-father to the twins and a special favourite with Ellen. He would never forget the support Nick had given him in the months after their deaths.

Nick and he had been friends all their lives, although Richard was five years older. Hunter had joined the navy and followed his cousin into the world of diving and mine countermeasures. But whereas Richard had resigned his commission and joined the family business, Hunter had gone even deeper into the world of special forces and now worked for TIFAT – The International Force Against Terrorism. The organisation had been established to fight terrorism world wide. It was staffed by special forces operatives from around the globe; the best each country had to offer. Hunter was regarded as one of TIFAT's most able men. The two of them exchanged handshakes and wide smiles. They spent a few minutes on pleasantries and then got down to business.

'Okay,' said Hunter, 'what's the problem?'

Richard quickly brought his cousin up to speed.

'You, Richard, have opened one stinking can of fish,' was Hunter's verdict.

'I need help, Nick. Can you use your contacts? Find out what's going on?'

There was no hesitation. 'Not a problem, but I don't think I'll have to look far. This is political, Richard. Once this trial is over, a global, diplomatic line will be drawn under the whole incident. Libya finally came in from the cold and is desperately trying to stay there. They are still hurting badly economically from the last lot of sanctions. The Palestinians are in deep trouble too, now the Israelis have a hard-line, right-wing Prime Minister. And there's nothing the West can do about Walid bin Sydal or the Iranians. The former is unreachable in Afghanistan or Pakistan, we aren't sure where and the Iranian parliament is simply way out of bounds. The West wants to keep a lid on the whole situation. The simple fact is, the world needs oil. What we don't need is some sort of holy jihad spreading its ugly wings across here. Believe me, Richard, we've got enough to contend with as it is. The word from on high is that the whole sorry mess is to be swept under the carpet and forgotten about.'

'How do you know all this?'

'TIFAT is in a unique position. You know only too well when not actually taking part in some operation, clandestine or otherwise, we play war games. We call them "What if" games. We've played every combination, every permutation you can think of in regard to the disaster. It may give you a little satisfaction to know that we came to the same conclusions as yourself. Our information was passed to our political masters and the word has come back. We're to stay out of it. No action to be taken.'

'What happens when the trial ends?'

'If the men are found guilty they'll go to prison. If they are found innocent, they'll be sent home.'

'Even if they are found guilty, Nick, you know as well as I do that they're just pawns. Foot soldiers acting under orders. What about the men who planned it? The leaders?'

His cousin shrugged and slowly shook his head. 'Don't hold your breath. I'm sorry, Richard, but soon you'll start to hear all sorts of excuses and platitudes. Resources could be better spent, the equivalent of ten jumbos of people die on our roads every year. More in America. Or what about the starving? What about the dispossessed caught up in civil wars? What about the disaster in Burma that killed tens of thousands? There will be as many excuses explaining why we have to move on as there were dead bodies.' He paused, seeing the hurt flash across his cousin's eyes. 'Forgive me, that was brutal. I didn't mean it to be. But it is what will happen. Believe me.'

Nodding his head, Richard looked at Hunter. 'I'm

surprised the Americans are going along with this. They usually aren't so accommodating when it comes to dealing with terrorists.'

'Their tacit agreement not to act is just for public consumption. The Americans have some of the brightest and most realistic politicians in the world. So don't let their rhetoric fool you. When they need to use the iron fist they will, but they know that the volatile situation in the Middle East means they have to use it sparingly.' Pausing, he looked at the frowning face opposite him. 'None of this gets us any nearer to solving your problem. My guess is that MI6 is acting on its own. If they can shut you up permanently, then the whole matter will go away. I take it you've threatened to go public with what you know?'

Richard looked uncomfortable for a moment or two and then nodded sheepishly. 'That's exactly what I said if they didn't take the dossier seriously. But I wanted to give them the opportunity of righting this huge wrong. Even if the information was made public for the world to acknowledge, that would be . . . something.'

'Indeed it would – the start of a global disaster. The clamour for revenge would ring out loud and clear and once the bandwagon started rolling it would be practically impossible to stop it. If sanctions are imposed on Iran and even more pressure is brought to bear on Afghanistan and Pakistan to give up bin Sydal, where will that lead? Gaza is ready to explode as it is. If we demand the arrest and extradition of the men involved we'll have an *intifadeh* across Europe. People will die. Remember, we are dealing with fanatics. If they die killing their enemies they go to heaven. A suicide bomber is a hero. And let me tell you there's almost no known defence against these people. We try and stop them beforehand, otherwise all we can do is sweep up afterwards.'

Richard was staring stone-faced at the surface of the table. Nick laid his hand on his arm. 'Are you all right?'

'I'll be better after I've had something to drink.'

Nick got out of his chair.

'Sure. I'll get us a menu too, shall I? My shout. Do you want another pint or will we have some wine?'

Nick took care of arranging steaks and a bottle of red wine before they returned to the matter in hand.

'My boss, General Macnair, is the only man I know who can get through to the Director-General of MI6 and get them off your back. But, Richard, you'll have to promise not to go public with the dossier.' Seeing the protest on his cousin's lips, Hunter raised his hand. 'I know that's a bitter pill to swallow but you have no choice. Otherwise they'll destroy you. The power of the establishment is awesome. I know. I've seen some of it in action. I'll ask the General to vouch for you. He may just manage to persuade them to leave you alone. He has a certain amount of clout. Especially with Six.' He looked at his cousin, the concern obvious in his eyes. 'Richard, you have to get on with life. Drop it, once and for all.'

Reluctantly, Richard nodded. His cousin was right. It *was* time to move on. Richard forced a smile, though it was more of a grimace but he nodded a second time. The remainder of the evening was spent exchanging family news and gossip. By the time he called for a taxi, Richard had regained his equilibrium. He was relieved to have involved Hunter. With luck, his cousin would be able to clear the decks for him.

He took the night sleeper south and by ten o'clock the following morning Richard was at his desk in his Southampton offices. Hunter phoned in the middle of the afternoon. It had been fixed. MI6 would put the situation on ice, as long as he "behaved himself". He thanked his cousin and broke the connection. The bitterness and anger swept through him once more. Analysing his feelings, he identified his primary emotion as frustration. The gutless West had given in – yet again. Well, not this time. In spite of what he had agreed with Hunter he intended taking action. His cousin had made it easier for him to operate – had given him breathing space. 'Sorry, Nick,' he said out loud.

Pennington-Prentice was feeling decidedly nervous as he put through the call. 'Richard Griffiths has agreed not to go public. I can't sanction another hit, he's too well connected.' He listened briefly. 'I'm more use to you alive than dead and if you want further information I suggest you keep a civil tongue in your head. Griffiths has been effectively silenced and we must content ourselves for the moment. Now, as soon as the verdict is in, it will appear on CNN. But it's a foregone conclusion at this stage. It's the appeal we have to worry about. Yes, I will keep you informed.' Breaking the connection he took out a handkerchief and mopped his brow. That had been close. He no longer had the money to return.

The court at Camp Zeist gave its verdict. Abdel Nazrallah from Libya Air Security was found not guilty and immediately set free. Lamen Al-Ghoul was found guilty and sentenced to life imprisonment in a British jail. An appeal was immediately lodged with the court.

The international press had a field day of speculation. Who had ordered the tragedy? Was Muammar Harwazi, the Libyan leader, the guilty one? And if so, why had he done it? Who else was involved? Had the Iranians been behind the outrage to divert attention from themselves? The verdict had opened up more questions than it had answered. But, as was often the case, the reporters came closer to the truth than anyone guessed.

Watching it all on television and surrounded by video tape and newspaper cuttings, Richard was one of only a handful of men in possession of the answers. He drew up a definitive list of the men responsible for the deaths of Ellen, Phillip and Lucy. It was a long list.

First came a cell of the military arm of the Palestinian

HAMAS – they would stop at nothing to further their aim of an independent Palestine. The cell involved had been made up of Afez Nidal and Abdullah Bashar. Killers and fanatics of the worst kind. Yet Richard reserved a special hatred for their leader, Jalal Chalabi. His greed and utter fanaticism had made the attack happen. One day, he hoped they would meet, face to face.

The list continued. Walid bin Sydal and his men – Jamal Al-Wadl, Ali Mohamed, Tawfik Kirawi, Massoud Talabani and Ahmed Al-Hakim. *Now based in Afghanistan, they had organised the whole conspiracy.*

And finally, the Libyans – Colonel Muammar Harwazi, Abdel Nazrallah, Lamen Al-Ghoul. *Harwazi – the Libyan ruler with a pathological hatred of the West and so paranoid he never slept in one place for more than a single night. So much for the self-styled Prince of the Desert.*

It was time, discreetly, to bring his contacts back into play. Orthodox methods of gaining justice had failed him. The Establishment had compromised, rather than avenge the dead. But Richard had other ideas. He was going to take a much-needed trip.

Like the rest of the Griffiths family, Richard was financially well off, thanks to his share holding in the company. He lived off his salary, while the dividends were paid into a savings account which had been accumulating for years. The money would be put to good use.

He spent his spare time with Vic and Matt on the new boat. He bought another caravan for use when he was on site, as it was easier than having to book into and then vacate a hotel every trip. It also meant he cooked his own meals. There was a limit to eating the rich food sold in restaurants and pubs.

In spite of his desire to move on with his life he decided, this time, to call the boat *The Lady Ellen*.

They had made numerous design improvements on the original *Ellen*. They had incorporated a constant turning shaft with a variable pitch propeller, which increased the speed of the boat from 10 knots to 14 knots without increasing fuel consumption. They also installed a bow-thruster and instead of the old-fashioned wheel of *The Ellen*, they had incorporated a modern joystick. Other changes were more cosmetic, like air-conditioning as well as central heating – although the intruder alarm system was the same as the previous one. Richard, however, regarded the most important additions to be the ingenious hiding places Vic and Matt had come up with.

Proudly, the two old men showed Richard what they had done. In spite of himself, he couldn't help smiling. If ever he went in for smuggling, *The Lady Ellen* would be ideal. He would defy any customs officer to find the hiding places they had designed. Even with sniffer dogs.

The rest of the boat was almost identical to the original – an MFV with a hull of 55ft and a beam of 17ft. Small differences made her appear far more spacious and allowed for an additional cabin to be incorporated up forward. The finish was to the same high quality and luxury, leaving her looking like a rich man's toy.

Richard's plan was in motion. He updated what he knew, paying bribes where required. He made the arrangements, fixed his leave dates from work and continued to refine his ideas. He purchased the necessary charts and guide books and finally had a yacht delivery firm quote him a price to pre-position the boat at Pescara on the eastern coast of Italy. He thought £1,500 excessive, but he accepted.

Since his return to the company, Richard had taken no leave, preferring to immerse himself in his work. At the beginning of June he announced he was taking a month off. As he was entitled to it nobody objected.

He flew to Rome. He had been updated on the boat's progress every evening and when he arrived in the picturesque harbour of Pescara *The Lady Ellen* was just entering the port. Disappointment was etched on the faces of the three-man delivery crew as he greeted them on the quay-side. They had hoped for a few days in port, partying. They knew a boat like *The Lady Ellen* was a big attraction to the opposite sex. Richard understood and paid them off with a bonus of a hundred pounds each.

The following morning, he spent time filling her diesel tanks, topping up the water and laying in stores. He had taken her to sea on two previous occasions back in Southampton but this would be his first long passage. As dawn broke, he slipped the berth and headed out past the breakwater. He travelled due east, straight for Dubrovnik in Croatia. If there was one place in Europe where he could buy what he needed, it was in the former Yugoslavian State. He even had a name and location for a man who could help him.

Richard set the autopilot, checked the radar and went below to make himself a cup of coffee. There was very little shipping about and it was too early for pleasure craft to be cluttering up the seaways. However, old habits die hard and it was totally alien to him not to have somebody on watch at all times. After barely ten minutes he returned to the wheelhouse.

There were just over 200 nautical miles to his destination. The weather was ideal – a gentle breeze from the south, a cloudless sky and a temperature that would reach a pleasant 80F by the middle of the afternoon.

At a steady 14 knots and all being well, he would arrive at Croatia in less than sixteen hours. The early morning mist quickly burned off and the day began to warm up. Changing into shorts and tee shirt he checked the boat from top to bottom. Even after her long sea voyage from England there was no water in her bilges. She was a dry ship, a testament to the refit she'd had at the hands of Vic and Matt. He had to admit, she was an improvement on the original *Ellen*.

Later that morning, he sat in the bows, lounging in a deck chair, enjoying the feel of the sun on his face and body. He had set the radar to warn him if any vessel came within 5 miles. There was a swell from the south and the boat rocked gently as she ploughed her way eastwards. Richard dozed lightly, to be awoken by an insistent buzzing. He immediately recognised the radar alarm and stood up. He looked first to starboard. If there were a vessel approaching from that direction it would be his duty to take avoiding action. Nothing. He looked to port and then astern. Coming behind was a fast moving pleasure craft, one of the very expensive plastic arrows commonly seen all over the Mediterranean.

It was doing at least 30 knots, maybe more. Richard knew it was his duty to stand on, not to confuse the over-taking boat with a sudden or unexpected alteration of course. He watched her gain rapidly on him. At half a mile, he reached for his klaxon and sounded five short blasts, the official warning sound meaning, "I am in doubt whether you are taking sufficient action to avert colli-sion". He sounded it again. The boat was now alarmingly near and did not appear to have anybody at the helm. He grabbed the receiver on the radio and transmitted in on channel 16.

'Unknown vessel approaching *The Lady Ellen*, wake up! You are on a collision course. I say again, wake up! You are on a collision course.' The pleasure craft was less than a cable astern and still coming straight at him. Richard tried to judge which way to turn. He could turn swiftly to starboard. But if whatever idiot was driving the other boat realised the danger they were in and turned to starboard simultaneously, then disaster could result. He sounded his klaxon again, hoping that the other craft would follow the Rules of the Road so strictly laid down. The other boat was now less than fifty yards away and bearing down on him.

10

STILL RICHARD COULD see no one at the helm or in the wheelhouse. He would have to wait until the last second, put the wheel hard over and pray the fool didn't follow. Suddenly he had a thought. What if the person driving the boat had suffered a heart attack or somehow been incapacitated? Damn! Richard watched in morbid fascination as the gap narrowed. At less than fifteen yards, he pushed the joystick to starboard and turned away from the speeding boat. On board the pleasure craft, 4 or 5 bikini and swimsuit clad figures leapt up and cheered. Richard was dumbfounded – of all the irresponsible, mindless idiots. He automatically noted the boat's name painted across her transom – *Slippery Eel*.

Out of the corner of his eye someone aboard the *Eel* caught his interest. A woman, tanned and blonde. She wasn't cheering and laughing with the others, in point of fact, she looked positively irate. Although she was dressed in a sarong and bikini, the uniform of the pneumatic beach babes who inhabited the Mediterranean, something told him she was no bimbo. Her face was shadowed by a large straw sun hat, but he could make out a small, pointed chin and a generous mouth. Fascinated, he watched her berate the tallest of the men on board the *Slippery Eel*. Through his binoculars, Richard could see that his only response to her anger was a gormless grin.

He didn't know what she was saying but he was glad not to be on the receiving end. And if he was honest, even at this distance, her allure was potent. His physical awareness of a woman was, as always, combined with a vague sense of unease.

Grabbing the receiver, he called the boat on Channel 16. '*Slippery Eel, Slippery Eel,* this is *The Lady Ellen*, come in, over.' He tried again and at the third attempt he was about to give up when he got a reply.

'What do you want, creep?'

'This is *The Lady Ellen*. Please confirm that this is the *Slippery Eel* and that you addressed that remark to me.'

'That's right, creep. I'm talking to you. Keep out of my way in future or I'll run you off the sea.' A further torrent of profanity followed before the transmission went dead.

Idiots, Richard thought. Initially seething, he quickly calmed down. The incident was best forgotten. He just hoped in the future that he might meet the driver of the boat on a dark night in a quiet place.

He put the matter behind him, reset his course and settled back in the bow. He watched the *Slippery Eel* quickly fade from sight and closed his eyes once more.

Forcing himself to relax, Richard took time to apply sun block before settling back in his chair. The sun was setting when he went below and changed. He switched on the navigation lights and sat down in the wheelhouse to look at his charts. He wanted to check the lighting arrangements for approaching Dubrovnik. The next time the alarm rang it was to warn him that he was approaching land.

By now, it was pitch dark. The sky was alight with a myriad number of stars and the heavens revealed themselves in a manner only seen by those at sea. Looking up, Richard saw a shooting star that was followed by a second only moments later. Taking his binoculars he searched the shoreline. The lights of Dubrovnik shone clearly across the water. Car headlights could be seen weaving up and down the hills behind the city and there, at sea level, he found the intermittently flashing green light he had been searching for. He passed the buoy close to starboard and made his turn for the entrance to Dubrovnik harbour.

The outer harbour was filled with merchant ships of all sizes. *The Lady Ellen* slowly passed into the inner harbour, where the pleasure craft and smaller boats were to be found. He stopped at the entrance and drifted for a few seconds while he took stock of the place. To port were bright lights, bars, cafes and restaurants. The boats were moored Mediterranean style all along the harbour, stern to the wall. To starboard, a number of fishing boats were berthed in the shadow of the outer wall. Here, there were no lights which suited Richard's purposes. Ten minutes later, he was secured alongside, stern to, with both the boat's anchors holding her at right angles to the wall.

A London contact had given him the name Nairi Demirchian, as well as the location of a bar which Demirchian and his henchmen frequented. Richard lost no time. Donning a leather jacket over his shirt and jeans, he checked his pockets to make sure he was not carrying any ID, credit cards or his wallet. Into the front pocket of his jeans he stuffed a few American dollars and to his right leg he strapped a fisherman's knife. Locking the boat, he set the alarm and went ashore.

He walked the hundred metres around the harbour and into the lights of the road and bars. Halfway along the harbour wall, he saw a white boat with a number of people on board enjoying a drink. When he got closer, he saw her name – *Slippery Eel*. Richard smiled. Perhaps there was a God after all.

The well lit bar he entered had very few customers. Asking the barman if he spoke English and receiving an affirmative nod, he enquired after the bar he wanted. He was met with a sullen shrug. He tried asking the question again, this time waving five dollars under the bartender's nose. In pidgin English, he was told it was one street behind, leading away from the harbour. Richard nodded his thanks and left. Walking up the cobbled street, he was struck by how quiet the town became away from the waterfront. He passed a few old women in black, but curiously, no men. He presumed they were in the bars, imbibing a glass or two of the local schnapps. Turning into the next narrow street, he followed the road as it wound up hill. The bar he was looking for was the only premises with a light on.

The shabby room was packed with men, all smoking, hunched over tables in earnest discussion. To a man they stopped talking and looked at Richard. Their eyes followed him as he approached the bar and leant forward to speak to the bartender.

He was aware of their stares on his back, the animosity. There must have been at least thirty men in there, unshaven, tough looking.

'Do you speak English?' The man looked back at him sullenly. He repeated the question. No response. The bar was still quiet, its occupants continuing to stare at him. Turning around he leant against the bar and asked loudly, 'Is there anybody here who speaks English?' He was met with the same hostile stares. Time for a different approach. 'I am looking for Nairi Demirchian. Does anybody know where I can find him?'

His question was met with a wall of silence. 'Tell him that I will be at the Hanover bar on the front at seven o'clock tomorrow night. Tell him to come and see me. I have a business proposition to put to him, but I leave in twenty-four hours.' Still no response. He walked out the door.

As soon as the door closed behind him, the talking started again. Richard passed in front of the taverna window and started back towards the harbour. A few metres took him out of the light. Darting across the road he hid in a doorway. No sooner had he stepped into the deeper darkness than the door of the bar opened and a man came out, headed in the same direction. The man hurried forward, almost running. Richard smiled. So somebody had understood him after all.

Staying hidden, he saw his pursuer return a few minutes later. When the man entered the bar Richard crossed the road and carefully looked inside. Through the grime on the window he saw the man approach a table of four. He spoke to one of them, who nodded. The man at the table appeared to be in his forties, stocky, unshaven, with a greasy moustache that curled around his mouth and down to his chin. Richard guessed he was Demirchian.

Richard started back to the waterfront. Approaching *The Lady Ellen* he took out his electronic security card and checked. It signalled an all clear. It was still early so he allowed himself a glass of cold white wine, a light Frascati and sat in the bow, deep in thought. He had a horrible feeling that his plan was so full of holes he would be lucky to survive the encounter, given the locals' reputation for banditry and bloody vendettas.

Half a cable across the water, he watched a group of people come out of a bar and noisily make their way along the front. They stopped at the *Slippery Eel* and clambered aboard. Raising his binoculars, Richard examined the boat and her occupants. There were six of them, three men and three women. He immediately recognised the woman who had berated the fool who had almost caused the collision. She appeared to be arguing with him again. Suddenly the disagreement became heated and the man raised his hand as though to hit her. Drunk though he was, he obviously thought better of it, for he lowered his arm without striking her. The young woman stormed away into the bows. Things quietened down and soon music drifted across the water. Richard watched the boat's occupants becoming more and more inebriated, apart from the woman who had walked away.

She was sitting quietly up front, her back to the party. She appeared to be upset. Somewhere in the nether recesses of his mind he had been contemplating doing the crew some mischief, to pay them back, but looking at her, he changed his mind. Anyway, he had a job to do. What he planned was dangerous enough without jeopardising its success before it had even begun and all for the sake of a stupid prank.

In spite of her friends calling to her to rejoin them, the girl stayed where she was. The man she had been arguing with approached her, trying to cajole her to return to the party. When she refused, he shouted at her again, before walking off in disgust. Something about the girl intrigued Richard. He guessed she was in her late twenties or early thirties. Her swathe of blonde hair, streaked by the sun, was tied casually in a knot at the back of her head and occasionally she would lift a tanned hand to brush back some wisps of hair which had escaped. He couldn't see her face well from this distance, but her cut-off jeans and figure hugging T-shirt left little about her figure to the imagination. Richard smiled. It had been a long time since he had noticed another woman. Ellen had been his whole life. His smile faded when the girl, hugging her slim knees to her body, lifted a finger to wipe her face. Richard realised she was crying. A natural instinct kicked in and he was half way out of his seat before reason reasserted itself. *Steady on, Sir Galahad, you can't just wade in there – you don't even know her. You could easily make matters worse. What if it's just a lover's tiff?*

Ill at ease, he went below. Checking the remote cameras, which would alert him to movement within fifty metres of *The Lady Ellen*, he hit his bunk and was soon asleep. At anchor, radar would warn him of an approaching vessel from as far away as 20 miles. In harbour they didn't work, but Richard had installed a little extra security. From the comfort of the wheelhouse he could view 360 degrees around the boat with the cameras.

He passed a peaceful night and early the next morning

completed his daily run along the foreshore before the sun was fully up. Back on board, he was visited by the assistant harbour master, paid his dues for a week and declined an offer of diesel or water. Both would probably be contaminated.

The Hanover bar lay roughly in the middle of the harbour front and boasted German beer and German food. It stood next door to the London bar which offered Guinness, Watney's Red Barrel and an English all-day breakfast. There were thousands of similar establishments scattered throughout the Mediterranean, monuments to the German and British desire to sample only their own culture, even when in a foreign land. *Especially* when in a foreign land!

Richard idled the morning away doing minor chores. The occupants of the *Slippery Eel* didn't appear until late in the afternoon. When they did, they looked much the worse for wear; with the exception of the blonde woman whose sadness had so intrigued him. From the wheel-house he used his binoculars to take a closer look at her. Her hair was now plaited into a thick golden rope, which hung down her back. The shade of her sun hat and the angle she was standing at made it difficult to see her face. The curves of her body and the narrowness of her waist made Richard suck in his breath. If anything, she appeared more attractive in the light of day than she had the previous evening.

At 19.00 the sun dropped below the horizon and Richard strolled across to the Hanover bar. Outside, the menu promised solid German food and German beers. Inside, the place was clean, the décor provided by pictures of old German movie stars hanging on the walls. Only three of the fifteen tables were occupied. At the bar there was standing room for a dozen people and half a dozen barstools. Richard stood in a corner, leaning against the bar with his back to the wall, nursing a bottle of Pilsner. He was dressed as he had been the previous evening, right down to the knife at his leg.

He bought dinner – German sausage, boiled potatoes and red cabbage. After the meal, he wandered down to the water's edge and looked at the boats. Some very expensive toys were moored there and idly he wondered why people came so far. If he was looking to bum around the Mediterranean this would be one of the last places he would choose. The only attraction he could see were the prices, for everything from diesel to booze and cigarettes were half what you would pay in the European Union. It was evident that some of the plastic arrows were capable of speeds from 30 to 50 knots. Such speed always seemed far too excessive to him. What was the point of dashing from one port to another without enjoying the pleasure of the trip?

He found himself standing next to the *Slippery Eel* and stared at her stern. She was about 40ft long with a 12ft beam. There was no doubting her luxury. In spite of his reasons for being in the port, he sat on a bollard a few metres away. He could not help speculating about the girl. As if in answer to his thoughts, she appeared at the stern-well and nimbly leapt ashore. He stood up and smiled at her.

'Good evening,' he said pleasantly.

'Hello.' He noticed she did not return his smile. Close up, he could see that she was extremely pretty. She had large eyes, a wide mouth and a determined air about her. She walked away from him.

'Nice evening,' he offered, falling into step beside her. He felt like an idiot, desperately trying to think of something to say, to engage her in conversation.

After a dozen paces she stopped and turned towards him, face on. Her eyes – an amazing blue, he noticed – locked with his. 'Listen bud, are you following me? Or just going my way?' Her accent was American. 'Or is this by any chance an attempt to pick me up?'

Richard smiled at her boldness. 'Which would you prefer?'

'None of the above. I would prefer you to go away and leave me in peace. I just want a quiet walk and time to think.' She spun around and carried on walking.

Richard, for reasons he couldn't quite fathom, continued alongside her.

After a few minutes she stopped, put her hands on her hips and rounded on him. 'What part of "Go away" don't you understand? I've had enough of men to last me a lifetime. I need to think about how I'm going to get out of this hellhole. Okay? So beat it!'

'Have you fallen out with your boyfriend?'

'That's none of your damn business. Now, please go away.' There was anger in her voice. Though, Richard hoped, not directed at him.

There was a shout from behind and a man ran towards them.

'Damn. Now look what you've done. This I need like a hole in the head.' She faced the man rushing towards them.

He was in his twenties, tall and thin, with lank hair, long and untidy, bleached by the sun. 'Where do you think you're going?' he asked angrily, stopping next to her, grabbing her arm.

Wrenching it free, she said, 'Go away, Freddie. I've had enough of you and your childish games.'

'You're coming back with me,' he took her arm again.

'I'm warning you, leave me alone.' She tried to pull her arm loose again but his grip tightened on her.

'You're coming back to the boat,' he yelled in her face.

'I'm not. If you don't let go I'll break your arm,' she said through clenched teeth.

'Leave her be,' said Richard, deciding it was time to intervene.

'Mind your own business,' said Freddie, barely glancing at him.

Before Richard could do anything the girl lifted her leg and stamped down hard on Freddie's foot. He gave a yelp of pain and let go of her arm. Stepping back from him, as he hopped on one foot, cursing her, she kicked him hard in the side of his other leg. He collapsed onto the ground.

'Now stay away from me. Or I'll kick you where it really hurts.' She took a step towards him and Freddie scrambled away, moaning. Turning around she began to walk away.

'Don't come back, you bitch! Do you hear? If you do, I'll kill you. You can rot here for all I care.' Getting to his feet Freddie limped away, cursing and muttering loudly.

Richard fell into step. 'That was pretty impressive.'

'No, it wasn't. I was aiming for his knee.'

Richard smiled. 'Where did you learn tricks like that?'

Stopping, she looked at him with a puzzled expression. 'Listen, I don't know who you are and I don't care. Now go away. Or do you want some of what I gave Freddie?'

Richard held up his hands in surrender. 'I can take a hint. But it seems to me you're in some sort of trouble and I want to help. Tell me about it.'

'There's nothing to tell. Somehow, I need to get out of here.'

'Where to?'

'Anywhere. I'm not particular.'

'So what's stopping you?'

'Freddie.'

'What's he got to do with it?'

'He owns the boat. Or at least his daddy does. He's taken my passport and won't give it back to me. He's hidden it somewhere. He says I can have it when we get back to Italy. That's what we were arguing about when I walked off. You delaying me gave him time to catch up. You saw the result. Now I'll never get my passport.'

'Do you want me to have a word with him?'

'You mean, please may I have Victoria's passport?'

She laughed mirthlessly. 'I'm afraid Freddie doesn't "do" reasonable. Thanks, but forget it. He'd as soon drown you. He's a vicious swine. He always gets his own way.'

'I can be very persuasive,' Richard replied with equanimity.

'I said, forget it. I'll sort this mess out for myself. It's been nice talking to you, Mr...' she held out her hand.

He took it, saying, 'Richard Griffiths.' Her hand was warm and dry and he held it for a few seconds longer than necessary, staring into her eyes. 'And you are?'

'Victoria Shand. Can I have my hand back?'

'I've got a better idea.' He changed his grip and held her hand by his side. Their shoulders were almost touching. 'Why don't we walk a little further and I'll try and help you with your problem?'

She walked a few paces with him before stopping and suddenly pulling her hand free.

'Look, Richard Griffiths, you seem a very nice man but I'll sort my problems out on my own.'

Richard guessed it was time for a tactical retreat but gave it one more try. 'You see that boat over there?' He pointed at *The Lady Ellen*. 'She's mine. Say the word and I'll give you a lift back to Italy. You can go to the police there and tell them Freddie has your passport or you can report it lost and get a new one at your embassy. Either way, you'll be out of the clutches of the odious Freddie.'

She chewed the side of her lower lip, thought for a few moments and then replied. 'Thanks, but no thanks.' She shook her head.

'Why not?'

'I've had enough of men.'

'You're going to need your passport as well as money. Do you know where the nearest American embassy is?'

'No, I don't. But I'll find it.'

'How will you get there?'

'I don't know, but I will.'

'You're angry and upset which I understand but you

aren't thinking straight. Where will you go tonight? Sleep on the beach?'

'If I have to,' she spoke defiantly.

Richard sighed. There was no doubting her courage and determination. 'Okay, have it your own way. 'Well, you know where to find me. The offer stands.' He turned away.

Victoria said, 'Wait. You may be right. I need to think about it.'

Richard paused, seeing the uncertainty on her face. Taking a deep breath Victoria appeared about to say something but changed her mind.

Richard decided to give it one more try. 'I was on the boat Freddie nearly ran into yesterday. You all thought it was such a wonderful game of chicken. So believe me when I say there is no love lost between Freddie and me.'

'I thought it was you. I told Freddie. He just shrugged and said, who cares? If you tried anything he'd take care of you. I know he carries a gun because I've seen him firing at seagulls often enough. And I'm sure he's not afraid to use it.'

'What led to your fight in the first place?'

She hesitated a moment before saying, 'If I tell you, you must promise not to tell a soul.'

'Who can I tell?' It appeared a ridiculous thing to say.

'Freddie's father is rich. He lets him play with all the toys you can think of – the boat, cars, a two-seater aeroplane. According to Freddie though, his father keeps him short of money. Plenty of credit cards and accounts, but no ready cash. So a few months ago Freddie came over here and set up a deal with a local thug. He took some heroin back to Italy and sold it. He's made three other trips so far and each time he's carried more heroin. This time he's planning to take back ten kilos. It's worth a fortune on the street.'

'How did you get mixed up in all this?'

'I didn't know what he was up to. I'd spent months

around the art museums of Italy and ended up at Pescara.
I met Freddie and some of the others in a bar. We got
talking. He invited me along and I agreed on certain
conditions.'

'Which were?'

Victoria held up her fingers. 'One, no hanky panky.
Meaning I wasn't going to sleep with him. Two, I'd do
the cooking to pay for my passage and three,' she touched
her index finger, 'I'd have time to visit the sites.'

'What sites?'

'Sites from the times of the Ancient Greeks and Romans.'

'Here in Croatia?' Richard couldn't keep the surprise
from his voice.

'The entire region is littered with them. One of the
tragedies of the troubles a decade or so ago was the Serbs
bombing the fourth century Diocletian palace in Split.
Since then, the palace has become the focus of attention
in academic circles across Europe and America. And there
are beautiful medieval paintings and frescoes all over
Croatia. The Serbs stole thousands of works of art when
they looted the country and still haven't returned them.
Don't be fooled by what you see. There's a lot more to
Croatia than meets the eye. Have you heard of Antun
Augistincic?'

'What is it? A virulent disease?' he grinned at her.

'No, you pleb. He was a Croatian sculptor. He carved
the wonderful monument made from local marble known
as "The Horsewoman" which is outside the main United
Nations building in New York.'

'You mean that one with the woman astride a galloping
horse with her hair flowing behind her? I am impressed.'
Richard changed the subject. 'What went wrong with
Freddie?'

'He ignored my conditions. When I refused to go to
bed with him he went through my bag and took my passport. On the way over here, he told me about the heroin.
He bragged about the previous trips, how easy it was.

He even showed me where he hides the stuff in a special safe. He says that makes me an accessory to the crime. He says if we get caught I'll go to prison for twenty years.' Anger welled up as she added, 'The injustice of it makes me so mad.'

'You may not get caught. You let him take you back to Italy and you do a bunk.'

She sighed. 'I know. I've thought of that. But look at the risk. This is his fourth trip. The authorities aren't that stupid. Each time he's made the journey increases the odds of him being found out. Besides, I don't hold with drug smuggling. Especially heroin. Drug dealers are the lowest scum on earth. Well,' she paused, 'now you know.'

'I'm glad you trusted me. Look, no strings attached – I still want to help. I've also got some business to take care of but, as soon as I'm done, I can take you back to Italy. What have you to lose? A few days with me or twenty years in prison?'

She smiled and he was astonished to feel his heart miss a beat. 'I should probably elect for prison but something tells me you're for real.'

'I've an idea. Why not use the satellite phone I have on board and tell somebody where you are and who you're with. My credentials can easily be checked.'

'You wouldn't mind?'

'Not if it'll reassure you.'

She thought about it for a few seconds. The fact was, there were very few options available to her. 'And no strings?'

He sighed inwardly. 'No strings.' He held out his hand and she shook it.

'Will you do me another favour?' she asked.

'Sure, if I can,' was the prompt reply.

'I need to keep a watch on the boat. They're planning to go ashore for dinner. As soon as they do I'll sneak back on board and get my things. Will you keep watch while I do? Just in case Freddie turns up.'

'Certainly. Why don't we sit on this bench,' Richard pointed at a seat a few metres away, 'and wait until they leave?'

They sat in silence for a few minutes, Richard thinking furiously for something to say. He was impressed with her. She had guts, beauty and she was smart. He wondered how well he could get to know her over the next few days.

After only a few minutes she said, 'Here they come.'

They watched Freddie and the others climb down from the boat. They were laughing and joking though Freddie didn't seem too happy. He was still limping a little. They walked around a corner and out of sight.

'Good. Let's go,' said Victoria, standing up.'

Returning to the *Slippery Eel* she leapt nimbly onto the deck and went below. Richard could hear her rummaging around. She took a lot longer than he'd been expecting. Finally, she appeared carrying two holdalls. She threw them onto the ground and quickly followed.

'Sorry. I was looking for my passport.'

'Did you find it?'

'No,' she said bitterly. 'Damn Freddie.'

'We can sort it.' Richard picked up the bags and hefted them in his hands. 'You travel light.'

'I always do. If I need something I buy it. I can carry those.' She held out her hands for the bags.

'It's all right. I've got them. Let's go.'

Falling into step beside him, Victoria asked, 'When are you planning to leave?'

'I'm not sure. It depends how long it takes me to complete some business.'

She looked at him in a calculating manner before saying, 'Not drugs?'

'No, not drugs.' *Just guns and explosives*. Somehow, he thought that was too much information to impart.

11

WALKING ALONG THE quayside, Richard began to wonder if he was compromising his own mission. Hell! He couldn't just leave her to Freddie. If she was caught on board a boat carrying so much heroin she would spend a very long time in an Italian jail. Now that he knew about her plight there was no way he could abandon her.

Approaching *The Lady Ellen* he surreptitiously checked the security system. A quick glance showed the lights were green. Nobody had been near her. They climbed aboard and he showed her the forward guest cabin.

'Make yourself comfortable. Come back to the salon for a drink when you're ready.'

Closing her door behind him, he went aft and up the companionway to the wheelhouse. As he did so, he glanced at the jetty. There were two men walking purposefully towards his boat. They stopped alongside and one of them made as though to climb aboard. Neither of them had seen him.

Opening the wheelhouse door he stepped onto the deck and put his foot on the fingers of the first man who was about to pull himself up. 'Stay where you are.'

Reaching behind him onto the roof of the wheelhouse Richard unclipped a three metre long wooden boat hook with a heavy steel end.

'Who are you and what do you want?'

Neither of the men had been in the bar the previous evening.

The second man spoke. 'We come take you to Demirchian.'

Richard took a torn piece of paper from his pocket and handed it to the man. 'Give Demirchian this. Tell him if he comes here in one hour I will give him the other half.'

The man looked at the paper and goggled. It was half of a thousand dollar bill.

'But Nairi said…'

'Never mind what he said. I'm paying the piper so I call the tune. One hour and he comes here alone.'

'He not be happy.'

'Then explain to him that I'll pay another thousand dollars for ten minutes of his time. Understood?' He indicated 10 minutes on his watch and held up the $1,000 bill. All the time he had kept his foot on the first man's hand but had not pressed down. Now he removed his foot. 'And tell Mr. Demirchian that it is polite to hail a boat before coming on board.'

Standing in the shadow of the wheelhouse he watched the men climb inside a battered car and leave. Things were beginning to progress.

He felt a presence beside him and turned to Victoria. 'The phone's over there. Just dial in the usual way and you should get through. The country codes are in the directory in the drawer.'

'Thanks, Richard. What do I need to know about you?'

'Well the boat is *The Lady Ellen* and I own her. She's registered at Lloyd's and her registration certificate and number are also in the drawer. I'll give you my business address and telephone number and whoever you call can check it out.' He knelt down to a cupboard under the chart table where he opened a small wall safe and reached inside for his passport and a business card. 'Here. Give whoever you talk to all the details.'

She handed the passport back to him. 'I guess you're

kosher if you're prepared to let me go to all that much trouble.'

'I could be bluffing.'

'You could be, but I don't think so. I'm not that bad a judge of men.'

'Freddie being the famous exception to the rule?'

'Ouch, that's not fair! That was below the belt. Isn't everybody entitled to a mistake or two?'

'Two?'

Victoria looked at him, seeming to make a decision. 'I was planning to get married once, a long time ago. Straight out of university. Commonsense prevailed and I called it off. I started travelling. First of all across America and then Europe. Been moving on ever since.'

'What went wrong?' He caught her look and held up his hands. 'It's okay, you don't need to tell me.'

'Good. I won't,' was the tart reply.

He grinned. 'Would you like a drink? The bar is on the starboard side forward in the salon. There's white wine in the fridge.'

'Sure. Can I get you a glass?'

'No, thanks. I need to keep a clear head. I'm expecting a visitor.'

An hour later the same battered car returned. This time only one man alighted and he walked steadily towards the boat. Richard recognised him from the bar the night before. Stepping onto the deck, Richard waited for the man to draw nearer.

'I come for the other half of this,' he said, holding up the torn bill.

'Let me come ashore and we can talk.' Richard stepped on to the quay and approached the other. They did not shake hands. Richard offered the other half of the bill and it was taken without a word.

'Let's walk along a bit.'

'What do you want? You said you have business deal for me.'

'You are Nairi Demirchian?' Shorter than Richard, he looked strong but had the beginnings of a gut. He stank of tobacco, stale wine and garlic.

'Why else I come?'

'Can you prove it?'

'Me? Why?'

'For the second thousand dollars I'm prepared to pay you.'

Demirchian glared at him before reaching into his pocket. He held out a tatty piece of what Richard assumed to be an identity card. Taking it, he could not understand the writing but he recognised the photo and the name. He handed it back.

'Okay. I was given your name by a contact of mine.'

'Who?'

'Abdul Majid of Egypt.'

The name was greeted with a smile. 'I know him. I do business with him.'

'I know. He's bought guns and explosives from you and sold them to the Palestinians.'

'I not know where they go.'

Richard didn't believe him but that was of no consequence. 'I have a list here. I spoke to Abdul before I made it. He assures me you can complete the order.'

'Let me see.' He scanned down the list. 'Three, perhaps four days. What are these numbers?'

'The price I am willing to pay.'

Demirchian handed back the list. 'Not possible. Double this and we do deal.'

'Then we need to talk.'

Both were skilled negotiators. Even so, Richard was aware that the price he finally agreed was over the odds. In return, Demirchian had agreed to fulfil the order in two days. When they parted, they shook hands.

Victoria was standing in the wheelhouse as he reboarded *The Lady Ellen*. Her voice was strained. 'Do you know who that man is?'

'A local gangster by the name of Nairi Demirchian.'

'What the hell are you doing? He's the man who's supplying Freddie with the heroin. Well, Mr. Griffiths, I think I will take you up on that offer of a phone call, because my first impression of you has changed drastically.'

'You know where everything is. Feel free. I'm going below.' In the salon Richard poured himself a whisky and soda. More doubts about helping her whirled around his head. Damnation! He had barely started on his plan and he was messing things up. After all he had been through, all the money he had paid and the angst he had suffered here he was making a dog's dinner of things. He'd complete his business with Demirchian and take Victoria to Italy if she wanted him to. If she didn't, then that was up to her. He could hear her murmuring on the phone. He had refreshed his drink twice before she came below.

'Satisfied?'

'Maybe. I've got a friend of mine checking. He'll call back in the morning.'

'Good. In the meantime I'm going to bed. I'll be setting security alarms so please don't wander further than this deck. Goodnight.'

In his cabin he checked the camera coverage, set the alarms and crawled under the duvet. His head full of Victoria, he had a fitful night. His morning run was longer and faster than usual as he worked off his frustration. He arrived back at *The Lady Ellen* to hear an argument raging below. Slipping quietly on board he stepped down into the salon. Freddie was there, his back to Richard, yelling at Victoria. He raised his arm to strike her and Richard decided that it was time to intervene.

When he stepped across the salon Victoria cast a glance his way. Either the glance or some instinct warned Freddie, who turned, as fast as a cat. In his hand he was holding a wicked looking stiletto.

'Keep out of this, creep. She's coming with me.'

'No, she isn't. Now get off my boat.'

Freddie started waving the knife in front of him in what he presumably thought was a menacing manner. Although by no means in the same league as his cousin when it came to hand-to-hand fighting, Richard was no slouch. Against a member of the special forces he might not have stood a chance, but against a yob and a civilian he could easily hold his own.

Disarmingly he held out his hands to either side, palms up and smiled. Stepping closer, he looked Freddie in the eyes and lashed out with his right foot. Wearing trainers, he remembered to curl up his toes. He kicked Freddie just below the kneecap, hitting him where Victoria had aimed the night before. Screaming in pain, Freddie collapsed to the deck, dropping the knife and clutching his leg.

Richard bent down, picked up the knife and put it safely out of Freddie's reach. Grabbing him by the collar he dragged him across the deck and up the companionway. Although he was tall, Freddie was skin and bone. On deck he held Freddie by the throat. Their noses were inches apart.

'Understand this, if you come back here again, I'll break your legs. Stay away from Victoria. You got it? And this is for trying to run me down when we were at sea.' Pulling back his fist, he hit Freddie as hard as he could in the guts and then pushed him over the guard rails into the harbour.

Freddie came to the surface, spluttering. Awkwardly, he swam away from *The Lady Ellen*, not looking back. Richard stood and watched him go, aware that Victoria was standing nearby. When he reached the other side, Freddie crawled up the harbour steps. For a few seconds he stayed on his hands and knees, getting back his breath and strength. Finally, he got to his feet and glared back at Richard. Shaking his fist, he bellowed in fury. 'I'll get you, you bastard. One day, I'll get you.'

Giving him a cheery wave, Richard went below, followed by Victoria. She said, 'You didn't have to do that. I was getting ready to take care of him.'

Richard smiled. 'I'm sure you were. But it's all part of the service. On board this boat you come under my protection.'

Victoria smiled back. 'Thanks.'

'What happened? How did he come along?'

'The phone rang and I went up to the wheelhouse to answer it. It was my friend in the States.' She stopped and Richard nodded. He didn't ask her what her friend had said, figuring she would tell him if she thought it was appropriate. If it wasn't about him, he had no right to enquire. 'I came back down here and the next thing I knew he was coming on board. I thought at first it was you. He had the knife. He threatened to cut me up if I didn't return with him. Said I had showed him up in front of his friends. He was about to hit me when you arrived.'

'Would he have succeeded?'

Victoria shook her head. 'No. You got to him about a second before I did.'

'That's what I thought. I think we've seen the last of him.'

'You don't know him like I do. He's a viscious little rat. If he can do the dirty on you, he will. And don't forget, he's got a gun.'

'I hadn't forgotten. Which is why I intend to get my retaliation in first. Now he knows you're here you don't have to worry about being seen. We've a couple of days to kill, so let's enjoy the sun.'

Later that morning, Richard went into the forward workshop and checked his diving gear. He topped up his set of ordinary compressed air bottles and inspected his re-breather set. The CDBA – Clearance Diver's Breathing Apparatus – was used in the Royal Navy for clandestine operations. He had specialised as a diving officer and using the equipment was second nature to him. The set was now obsolete, but he had been able to buy one, with its ancillary equipment, from the Ministry of Defence.

He had already used it once, to make sure it was in working order and now he checked the bottle pressures. When diving, the main bottle was carried horizontally across the back, while an emergency bottle sat in the front. Oxygen slowly passed into a black lung that covered the diver's chest. As the oxygen was used up, the exhaled carbon dioxide passed through a canister containing a chemical filter that absorbed the exhaled gas. The oxygen continued to circulate until depleted. It could be replenished either by cracking open a valve and letting in more gas on the setting known as on demand, or by an automatic flow of 1.5 litres per minute. The CDBA's main advantage was the lack of telltale bubbles in the water. Its main disadvantage was its inability to function below a depth of ten metres, where oxygen became narcotic.

That afternoon he and Victoria lay in companionable silence on sun beds on the deck. After a while, Richard leant on his elbow and gazed down at her. She was wearing a deliciously skimpy bikini, her skin brown and tantalising. There was a small scar at the corner of her mouth, on the left side, hardly noticeable unless you looked closely.

To take his mind off his thoughts he asked, 'How did you get the scar?'

Victoria tensed for a moment and then relaxed, rolling onto her side, gazing at him. She sighed. 'A car crash. I was lucky, I was left with this.' She touched the side of her mouth. 'The two people in the other car were killed.'

'How did it happen?'

'No one really knows. They were in a car coming towards me, swerved across the white lines in the middle of the road and straight into me. They were driving some old banger while I had a new Audi I'd rented for the weekend. The airbag saved me. They didn't have one.'

'That's awful.'

Victoria shrugged. 'No, it's life. And I don't mean to sound callous. Sheer bad luck all round, I guess.' She sighed. 'I spent nearly a month being fixed up. The cops were happy that it hadn't been my fault and that was that.'

'Where did it happen?'

'In France, four years ago.'

'You said you've been travelling. What do you do for money?'

'You just cut to the chase with your questions, don't you? I had a small trust fund left to me by my grandmother. I used some of it for college though I also did various odd jobs to supplement the trust. There's still some left. I keep adding to it whenever I can. I've tended bar, worked as a guide in a number of art museums and spent frugally.' She sighed. 'Now it's time to go home and find a proper job. I can't keep doing this for the rest of my life. Woman with a suitcase, that's been me. Or two bags. Now you. Are you married?'

'No.'

'Divorced?'

'No. My family . . . I lost them.'

Victoria narrowed her eyes and said, 'I'm so sorry.'

'It was two and a half years ago so let's drop it. I earn a living by working for an offshore shipping company. Right now I'm on leave. That's about it.'

She looked at him thoughtfully. 'I know about Griffiths and Buchanan. But I think there's a lot more to you than that.'

'You know about the company I work for? Is that what your friend's telephone call had been about? What else were you told about me?'

'Let's just say that I'm still here and I no longer fear for either my life or my virtue.'

'What a pity,' he mumbled.

'Sorry?' she asked sleepily, her head cradled in her arms, her eyes shut.

'Nothing,' he sighed and lay back down, closing his

eyes. He missed the smile she was trying to suppress.

That evening, they decided to eat on board. Victoria fried a steak, baked potatoes and tossed a salad. Richard's contribution was to make a dressing of olive oil, wine vinegar, honey and mustard. In spite of his determination not to drink too much, between them they saw off two bottles of Californian red wine and finished by nursing large brandies, sitting in the stern. For the first time since Ellen's death, Richard realised he felt comfortable talking with a woman – this woman, which was all the more surprising, considering the short time he had known her. They talked animatedly, getting to know each other better, constantly aware of the underlying current between them. When it eventually became time to say goodnight it was with a good deal of regret. He had a problem resisting the temptation to kiss her.

The following day was also spent on board. The occupants of the *Slippery Eel* came and went but did not take any notice of them. In the afternoon Victoria said, 'You know, I really want my passport back and I don't see why I can't get it.'

'What do you suggest?'

'Going over there and demanding it.'

'So he tells us he hasn't got it. Then he tells us to get lost. We retreat empty-handed and he gloats over his victory. I have another idea. I hope to conclude my business tomorrow, so we can leave then. From what you said about his timetable, he's probably already collected his heroin. So what's he waiting for? Just absorbing the local culture? I doubt it. I think he's planning to get revenge. I don't relish the prospect of defending myself from that madman at sea, especially not against a gun. However, I have my own ideas.' Briefly he explained his intentions.

After an initial frown, Victoria smiled and nodded. 'I like it.'

Around 22.00, he and Victoria were standing in the

stern. Richard had on a pair of swim shorts and a black tee shirt. He slung the CDBA over his shoulders, adjusted the strap until it was comfortable and then put the mouthpiece between his teeth. Breathing down the contents of the lung he cracked open the valve and flooded it with oxygen. He breathed steadily for two minutes, removing the nitrogen from his body. Richard was well aware of the danger of hypoxia, especially in the shallow depths he would be swimming in.

Richard gave the OK sign and slid over the side into the water. Victoria handed down a large adjustable spanner which he tied to his belt. He carried a dive-board to which was strapped a compass, a depth gauge and a watch. He took a sighting of the target and slipped beneath the surface. Immediately, he was lost to sight. He was using the board because experience had taught him how easy to was to become disorientated even over such a short swim.

The water shimmied in the gentle breeze, ruffling the reflected lights from the street on the other side of the harbour. Looking down there was nothing to be seen from the surface. Victoria sat in the stern, impatiently awaiting his return.

Under the water it was pitch dark, unless he looked up, where he could see the lights quivering across the surface. He checked his course and followed the needle. In minutes he was across the harbour. Slowly he surfaced, his hand above his head. He touched the underside of a boat and looked up. It was white. But so were many of the other boats berthed there, so he had to double check. He followed the hull to the stone wall and quietly surfaced. Glancing up he saw the painted characters of the name *Slippery Eel* and left the surface again.

He swam down to the propellers and checked the arrangement on the end of the shaft. At such a shallow depth some reflected light penetrated the water and he could just make out the port shaft. A large boss nut held the propeller in place while a split pin prevented it from rotating off the end when the prop spun round. Richard took a pair of pliers from his belt and removed the pin. Next, he fitted the large wrench and tried turning it. Nothing happened. He readjusted the position of the spanner and this time braced himself with his feet on the other shaft. He took a firm grip and began pulling. He continued to increase the pressure until his muscles were bulging and his eyes were popping with the strain. Suddenly he shot away and because of the angle he had been working at went down into the soft, silted bottom of the harbour. Luckily, he had enough of his wits about him to keep a firm grip on the spanner. Regaining his bearings, he swam back to the hull. He felt for the boss nut. He was sure it had moved. Fitting the wrench he tried again. The nut moved freely and he quickly wound it all the way off. He also removed the nut on the other shaft, this time more easily than the first one. Following the hull until he was at the bow, he set the reciprocal bearing on the compass and returned the way he had come. Halfway across the harbour, he dropped the nuts into the soft silt.

Surfacing at the stern of *The Lady Ellen,* he waited for a few minutes to make sure there was nobody about. Satisfied, he took off his fins and pushed them on board. As he did so Victoria appeared at the rail and reached down. He slipped the two buckles on the right side of the set and passed it up to her. Minutes later he was under the shower, highly satisfied with events.

Sitting in the wheelhouse with a whisky and soda he gave Victoria the details. Her smile told him it had been worth it. When he said goodnight to her his regrets were greater than ever. He fell asleep wishing he had not given his word to behave like a gentleman.

In the middle of the following afternoon a young boy brought Richard a message. Demirchian was ready to do the transaction.

'I have to go ashore. I'm meeting someone.'

'Demirchian?'

He nodded. 'I've some business to finish and then we can get away.'

'I don't understand. What can he possibly have that you want? The friend of mine who checked you out works for the American State Department. She told me a lot about you and the company you work for. So what on earth are you up to?'

'Business. Please, just leave it at that. We can meet up afterwards, if you like. I know I said I'd take you to Italy but I've been looking at the chart. Let me show you.' He got the chart from the wheelhouse and spread it on the deck.

'I'm headed for Tunisia. That means sailing south of Sicily and north of Malta.' He indicated their track with a pencil. 'I could drop you at Valletta. You can go to the American Consul there, report your passport lost, get a replacement. I'd prefer to do that as it would save me going all the way to Italy.'

Victoria shrugged. 'Okay, if that's what you want.'

'You don't mind?'

'Me? Why should I mind? I'll have escaped the odious Freddie and with a passport I can go anywhere.'

'Good. That's settled then.' Richard reached into his hip pocket and took out a wad of notes which he offered to Victoria. 'Why don't you go shopping, get some food for the next few days, buy something nice for yourself.' As soon as the words were out of his mouth he knew he had said the wrong thing.

'I don't want your money!' she blazed. 'I can buy a bit of food and I certainly don't want something nice as you put it.' She was livid.

'Victoria, it wasn't meant that way. I'll be away for at least four or five hours and I don't trust Freddie. I thought you might be safer if you weren't here.'

Her temper vanished as quickly as it had risen. 'I guess I'm not used to a man thinking about me. I have money. I'll do some window-shopping and buy some food. All right?'

'Good enough. I'll see you later.'

On the other side of the quay Richard waited only a few minutes before a car pulled up alongside him. He climbed inside. The interior reeked of unwashed bodies, stale cigarette smoke and God alone knew what else. He opened the window and tried to get some fresh air. There was only the driver with him and he didn't speak. They passed quickly through the town and were soon climbing the shallow hills to the east on the road to Martinovici. They pulled onto a side road and then a dirt track that led them into a forest of pine trees. They came to a stop in a large glade. When he climbed from the car, Richard was hit by the heady perfume of shrubs, herbs and wild-flowers. It made a pleasant change from the atmosphere he'd been sitting in. In the middle of the glade was Demirchian, sitting on a crate, smoking a cigarette.

'My friend, I have all you ask for. Have you the money?'

'I intend to check the merchandise first. Do you mind?'

Making a magnanimous gesture, Demirchian stood and waved at the crate he had been sitting on. 'It's all there.'

Richard walked across the grass and looked down at the box. It was a green wooden crate, about 1.5m long, 1m wide and 0.5m deep. Richard lifted up the lid. He took each item out and placed it on the ground.

'Is it okay if I check these out?'

'No problem. No one will hear us here.'

Richard stripped and checked each of the guns before firing a single round. The Glock 19 he shoved in his waistband. If he thought anything of it, Demirchian didn't show it. Finally, Richard took a small amount of plastic explosive, detonating cord, safety fuze, an ignitor and a detonator. He quickly assembled them, pulled the pin on the ignitor and walked away. The safety fuze burnt for approximately 30 seconds, the detonating cord was instantaneous and the detonator set off the PE. The explosion was not much louder than the gunshots.

Demirchian was looking at him with more respect. 'You work good,' he waved at the gear.

'Believe it. Like I told you, this is only the beginning. If my buyers are happy, I'll be back for a very large consignment. Will you be able to handle it?'

'Certainly. My NATO contacts can get good stuff. When you come again?'

'In a month. I have the number to call you. This could be the start of a very profitable alliance.' Reaching into his pocket he withdrew ten thousand dollars in used dollar bills. 'I am paying well over the odds on this trip, to show my good intentions. When I return, I will, of course, expect a far better deal. After all, there has to be plenty of profit in this for us all.'

Richard watched Demirchian closely. The driver was at the periphery of his vision. There was nothing to stop the Croatian shooting him, keeping the weapons and the money. The suggestion of a lot more money to be made in the future didn't guarantee his safety, but greed was always a strong motivating factor. After all, it would be stupid to kill the goose that laid the golden eggs. He hoped Demirchian had been told the same fairy tales as a child. It had been the best ploy Richard could come up with. He guessed that if there was to be any funny business, it would be about then. After all, there was plenty of space to get rid of a body.

Demirchian nodded, then he smiled. 'Relax. I am businessman. Make money. I not kill my customers. And what about the, how you say? The end users?'

'They work for *Allah*.'

'It is just as I thought. I go this way,' he pointed along the track. 'The driver will take you back.'

They shook hands and Demirchian walked further into the forest. For his part, Richard placed the box inside a large canvas bag and stowed it in the trunk. The car journey back was uneventful and made in silence, which suited Richard. He was dropped on the street running along the harbour. He lifted out the bag, slammed the trunk shut and waved to the driver who immediately took off.

He ambled towards the boat, his eyes everywhere. This was the first time in his life that he had done anything so far outside the law. To say he wasn't comfortable was an understatement off the scale of understatements. As he approached *The Lady Ellen* he checked the intruder alarm. Nobody was on board. Good, Victoria was still ashore somewhere. It made things a lot easier. Once on board, he set about stowing the gear in the special places Vic and Matt had designed. The Glock 19 he hid in a small cupboard in the wheelhouse, behind the shelf holding his seamanship manuals. If Customs and Excise in any European country found what he was carrying he would go to prison for a very long time. Richard was now operating outside the law.

12

A SHORT WHILE later a taxi dropped Victoria at the harbour and she came on board, bearing two carrier bags of food.

'I found the most marvellous market and got everything we needed. Look.' She began unpacking the bags and showing him the fresh fruit and vegetables she had bought. 'Here, have a peach, they're delicious.' She handed one to him.

He bit deeply into the fruit, feeling the juice running down his chin. 'Superb. I've checked over the boat, the engine is warming through and all we need do is cast off. Care to help?'

'Understatement. I can't wait to get out of here.'

On deck, he let go the stern ropes and started the windlass. He allowed the port anchor to drag them across the harbour until the chain was up and down. The anchor broke free of the bottom and was quickly raised and secured. *The Lady Ellen* swung to the starboard anchor and he engaged the windlass again. Victoria was nervously watching him from the wheelhouse. When the anchor broke free of the mud and they started drifting slowly across the harbour he signalled to her. She engaged the gears ahead and turned the wheel to point seawards while he secured the second anchor.

Stepping into the wheelhouse, he took over from Victoria and manoeuvred the boat until she was at right angles to the *Slippery Eel*. He called the boat's name. Freddie came on deck with a scowl. He immediately realised that they were getting set to leave and yelled for the others.

'Have a nice trip,' said Richard. 'Think you'll catch us?'

'Listen, you jackass, I'll be right behind you.' He made a pantomime of pointing two fingers and cocking his thumb.

'Freddie, do yourself a favour and stay in harbour. If you come after me you'll regret it.'

His words of caution were met with a mouthful of abuse. Richard shrugged. 'Don't say I didn't warn you.' Setting the autopilot he steered very slowly away, giving the *Slippery Eel* plenty of time to catch up. He turned a dial to steer the appropriate course, freeing himself from the necessity to continually adjust their heading as they approached the outer harbour. Following the correct procedures, he informed the port authorities that he was leaving and requested warning of any shipping movements. In the background he heard the deep, throaty roar of the *Slippery Eel's* engines starting and looked back. The crew was desperately running around, being yelled at by Freddie. They had raised the anchors and were edging out of the berth. The *Eel* turned towards the entrance and followed.

Increasing speed, Richard steered *The Lady Ellen* into the outer harbour. Approaching the main entrance, they continued to pick up speed. Freddie was coming up fast behind them, paying scant attention to the Rule of the Road, or to his navigation. He was half a cable astern when both of the *Eel's* propellers flew off simultaneously. The results were awesome. One of the propellers flew upwards and smashed a hole in the hull. The *Slippery Eel* began to take on water and a battle began between the damaged stern and the bilge pumps. The second propeller shot straight off and dropped into the mud. With no resistance, the shafts' rate of rotation increased alarmingly. Freddie had neither the wits nor the experience to understand what was happening. First the port and then the starboard shaft buckled, the latter snapping in half. The port shaft bent, smashed into the hull and drove through it. Within seconds it had dug a hole greater than the first and the battle with the pumps was over. The *Slippery Eel* began to sink.

Stopping *The Lady Ellen,* Richard couldn't resist. He turned the boat around and went back just as the crew was leaping into the water. Freddie was still standing on the fly-bridge paralysed with fear, looking down at the boat. Turning alongside her, Richard called, 'Hey, Freddie! Who's the jackass now? What's daddy going to say?'

Freddie looked across at him, tears of fury streaming down his cheeks. With an enraged snarl he reached into his pocket and withdrew a revolver. Realising he was about to be shot at, Richard shoved the joystick fully ahead and ducked.

The Slippery Eel lurched suddenly and vanished beneath the water. Freddie was thrown off balance backwards and fired into the air. By the time he spluttered to the surface, *The Lady Ellen* was leaving the harbour behind.

Throughout the debacle, Victoria had been standing in the stern, watching the turn of events in fascinated horror. She turned to Richard. 'Shouldn't we get someone to help them?'

He radioed the port authorities, reporting the *Slippery Eel's* situation. He added a final piece of information. 'You may be interested to know that there may be heroin on board. It might be worth checking out.'

'Thank you *Lady Ellen*. You can leave it to us. Out.'

They spent the day sunning themselves, reading and stealing covert glances at each other. When Victoria closed her eyes and lay on the deck, her head pillowed on her arm, Richard watched the rise and fall of her breathing. Everytime she stirred a longing shot through him. How could the mere fact of her being beside him disturb him so greatly?

That evening, as the sun was setting, they sat companionably in the wheelhouse.

The next few days were idyllic. The weather remained sunny and bright, the wind stayed away and not a cloud appeared on the horizon. They spent blissful hours, slumped on deck, reading or gazing out to sea. In a cupboard in the salon, Victoria found his small collection of old videos and exclaimed with delight when she recognised *Casablanca* amongst them.

'It's my favourite film of all time,' she enthused. 'Rick's selflessness is so . . . romantic. "Of all the gin joints in all the towns in all the world, she had to come into mine",' she parodied. 'Want to watch it later?'

That evening Victoria sat with a glass of wine and a box of tissues, enjoying every minute of the classic film. 'I feel tears welling up every time I watch the scene where she asks Sam to play their song and she starts to hum along.' At odd moments over the next few days, Richard was aware of her dreamily humming the tune to herself.

Three days later Malta appeared on the radar. Suddenly there was so little time left. Richard realised that all the things he had wanted to say to her would have to wait. Assuming he had the opportunity to say them sometime in the future. He was sure that if he had made the slightest move they would have slept together. Which would have really complicated matters. Because of what he intended doing he didn't dare involve Victoria. But, he admitted to himself, there was another reason as well. There was a chance that he might not make it back. Doubts about his plans played heavily on his mind but he managed to quell them. If they had slept together, getting her to leave would have been even more difficult without some sort of explanation. And his problem was, he couldn't think of one. No, it was better this way. If they met up later then it could all be different. Maybe.

'Richard, why don't I come with you? I can sort out a passport in Tunisia.'

Richard shook his head. 'It's just not an option, Victoria. I'm sorry.'

'If it's to do with some boring business deal, fine. I'll shop in the bazaars and let you go to work. Please, Richard.'

He shook his head. 'I'm sorry, Victoria, honestly I am.'

Richard was adamant. Victoria nodded and went below to pack her bags. A short while later, when they finally entered Grand Harbour, they were barely on speaking terms. Victoria said a stiff goodbye and walked away, her back stiff, her anger evident.

With a great deal of regret Richard backed *The Lady Ellen* away from the harbour wall and headed out to sea. He had work to do and, where he intended going, there was no room for passengers. He looked back to see her turn around, drop her bags and glare at the boat, her hands on her hips.

The following day, Richard carried the guns up onto the deck. Again, he stripped each one, checking the action. Throwing one of the boxes over the side, he backed the boat away. At about 15 metres he screwed a silencer on the end of the Austrian Glock 19, took aim and fired. There was a gentle cough and a piece of the box flew off, leaving a white gash in the green paint. He fired again. Satisfied, he put on the safety, pressed the magazine catch on the left side of the butt and slid out the mag. He pulled back the slide to eject the round in the chamber and placed the gun on the deck. The automatic, partly made of plastic, was relatively light. The 19 was the compact form of the Glock 17. It measured 174mm and weighed 595g. It fired 9mm Parabellum cartridges, standard throughout NATO. The gun was used extensively by police forces throughout the world and had been adapted for use by numerous armies. The serial number stamped on the right side of the slide had been erased.

The only time he had fired a Zastava M85 submachine

gun had been back in the forest glade, watched by Demirchian. The Croatian had told him it was a 1987 Yugoslavian copy of a Soviet AKSU-74. It had been chambered to fire Western 5.56mm cartridges instead of Russian 5.45mm. Weighing the gun in his hands, Richard knew it was one of many in circulation illegally. The Balkan conflict meant that the actual number of guns in the region was unknown. NATO estimated the figure at between two hundred and fifty and three hundred thousand firearms. This Zastava had a capacity of 30 rounds and fired at a rate of 700 rounds per minute.

Feeding bullets into the magazine he checked the safety. It lay in the top position, locking the trigger and blocking any movement of the cocking handle. He rammed home the magazine, slid the safety down two positions pulled back the cocking handle, aimed and fired. There was a loud crack and the box leapt in the water. As soon as the box began settling in the sea he flicked the switch up one and fired on fully automatic. He emptied the magazine into the box just as it vanished beneath the waves. Satisfied, he put the safety to the off position, refilled the magazine and placed the gun beside the Glock.

Throwing the other empty box overboard, he examined the Italian Beretta Sniper he had acquired. Based on the Mauser-type bolt action, its heavy barrel was fitted with a harmonic balancer contained in a tube and concealed by a wooden fore-end, ensuring accuracy. The rifle was fitted with iron sights, but also carried a NATO standard telescope and electro-optical sights. Like the other guns, its serial number had been erased.

He threw an empty wine bottle as far as he could and fired at the target. The bottle shattered. He threw a second bottle and backed away about a cable. He fired a second round and was gratified to see that he had lost none of his shooting ability since leaving the navy. The bottle blew apart. Stowing the weapons in their secret compartments he turned the boat west and continued towards Tunisia.

Without Victoria, he was forced to admit to himself that he was lonely. He thought of her constantly. He acknowledged to himself that the thing he had feared and protected himself from had come to pass. He had met a woman with whom he could imagine . . . he couldn't bring himself to complete the thought but then he did. Spending his life with her? Fear clenched the pit of his stomach. What could he offer her? Loving someone meant being afraid of losing them. He thought of Ellen and the twins. His eyes filled with tears. Was this how it felt to betray their memory?

Richard passed a restless night. The following morning, he sailed between the two islands that made up the Isles de Kerkenah and began his approach into Sfax.

The Tunisian harbour was beginning to attract the adventurous European holidaymaker who wanted more than just the bland version of northern Africa available from Cairo to Casablanca. The airport had recently been extended to take international flights and now a daily service operated from various European cities. The local economy had also greatly benefited from oil, which had been found only a few dozen miles away on the edge of the semi-desert. The area had long been the province of nomadic herdsmen, who scratched a living from the soil with their flocks of goats and sheep. Not all the locals, however, had welcomed the oil and frequently there was trouble. The wealth being generated was not finding its way down to the poorest people in the region. However, tourists still visited, boasting of their adventures on their return home to civilisation. Attracted by the air of danger, those same tourists quickly demanded protection in the face of any actual threat.

Using his credentials as the Operations Director of Griffiths & Buchanan Offshore, Richard had carefully considered his cover. He was to attend a bona-fide meeting to discuss the possibility of searching for oil between the mainland and the Isles de Kerkenah. In reality, his primary

interest lay in a very different meeting. A meeting he had
learnt would be attended by Walid bin Sydal in Tunisia.

Nine months earlier, Richard had attended a meeting
at the G & B Offshore offices in Oman, to discuss a rig
towing contract. He had been completely taken aback
when Al-Wadl introduced himself and requested his help
in getting to America. Al-Wadl was a Sudanese who had
spent two years in the US before joining the *mujahedin,*
fighting the Soviets in Afghanistan in the middle of the
1980s. For years he had been secretly siphoning off funds
from *al Qaeda*. He was about to be exposed, he told him
and feared for his life. Aware of Richard's interest in the
plane disaster and in exchange for his aid and connections, Al-Wadl had been more than willing to share what
he knew. He had given Richard several useful contacts.

Richard had arranged to smuggle the man out of the
Middle East on board a tug. Al-Wadl had been deposited
safely aboard an American warship patrolling the area.
Since then he had been giving testimony to the Americans about bin Sydal, *al Qaeda* and the workings of the
organisation.

Over the next few months, Richard had cultivated the
contacts he had been given by Al-Wadl. He paid cash for
low grade information. Finally, he hit paydirt. For fifty
thousand dollars Richard had leant about the desert
meeting. A second source had told him much the same
thing, albeit for a lot less money. This was the reason he
was now approaching Sfax.

Standing at the helm of *The Lady Ellen*, Richard
regarded Sfax harbour with a jaundiced eye. This was
the capital of the south, a lively and industrious place
and Tunisia's most important port. Exports included phos-
phates, esparto grass – used for weaving and making a
grade of paper – cuttle-fish bones, sponges and olive oil.
The harbour was a melting pot for their various odours
and perfumes and the entire city was testament to the
Arab laissez-faire attitude to pollution. In short, a dump.

Slowly, he motored past the rust heaps that passed for merchant shipping lining the dockside. *The Lady Ellen's* doors and windows remained firmly shut, with the air conditioning battling against the heat and the smell. Staying well over to the starboard side of the channel, Richard was alert for any moving traffic. A few bumboats and dilapidated *dhows* were moving slowly across the scum-covered water, but on the whole it was quiet. The port authority told him to continue past the merchant ships and berth at the western end of the docks. Rounding a bend, he saw a narrow entrance with numerous masts sticking up, their hulls hidden by the harbour wall. Once he was opposite the entrance he checked there was no other traffic and turned to port. Sounding five short blasts on the horn to warn anyone on the other side of the wall that he was nearby, *The Lady Ellen* nosed slowly through the entrance. There were about a dozen small craft tied to buoys and a few alongside the wall. None were pleasure craft, just working boats, fishing boats and one lone rubbish barge. The Tunisians still dumped their rubbish in the middle of the Mediterranean Sea, despite international agreements to the contrary.

It was hardly a secure place to leave *The Lady Ellen*. Richard guessed that within ten minutes of him going ashore she would be stripped of everything portable. Using the bow-thrusters he turned the boat around and went back into the main harbour. Continuing towards the harbour entrance he finally eased the boat between two merchant vessels. He had seen offices proclaiming to be Customs. Richard tied her up to the wall and leapt ashore. After so many days at sea, even on calm water, he swayed a little while he got his land-legs back. Stepping across the quayside he entered the Customs office. Already his shirt was sticking to his back.

Behind a battered desk sat a man in uniform – albeit without his tie and with his jacket undone. He was unshaven and a cigarette dangled from the corner of his mouth. Squinting against the rising smoke he tapped slowly at an old-fashioned typewriter.

'Do you speak English?' asked Richard, trying hard not to wrinkle his nose against the smell of the harsh tobacco and the body odour filling the room.

The man looked at him, removed the cigarette and said, '*Oui*. I speak English.' His accent was a curious mixture of French and Arabic, harsh and grating.

'I was told to take my boat into the inner harbour.'

'Then why do you not do so, *Monsieur*?'

'I want my boat where it can be seen and possibly guarded.'

'That is not my affair, *mon vieux*. Talk to the harbour master.'

'Agreed. In the meantime I would like to remain berthed in the outer harbour where I am and ask you to keep an eye on her.'

The man shrugged. '*Impossible, mon ami*. You see how busy I am. I have not time to keep watch on your precious boat.'

'I appreciate that you're a busy man, so I'm prepared to make it worth your while. Twenty dollars if you watch her while I am away. I shan't be more than an hour.'

Dropping the note into the out-stretched hand, Richard nodded his thanks and left. His first port of call was the harbour master's office, where, for another $20, it was agreed that *The Lady Ellen* could stay where she was. Using the harbour master's telephone he contacted the regional Governor's office and made an appointment for later that day. Such a meeting with a local dignitary quickly improved the harbour master's attitude to Richard. He also suggested that for a mere $20 a day he could send his nephew to guard the boat. The youngster could be trusted. They shook hands on the arrangement and Richard returned to *The Lady Ellen*. His appointment with the local Governor was scheduled for after the siesta that stretched from 13.00 until 17.00. Stepping outside, he barely reacted to the smells infesting the area. He was becoming acclimatised.

Expecting to be in port for at least ten days, Richard spent the next hour rigging awnings across the fore deck and the afterdeck. At least they offered some shade when moving about outside. He went below, turned the air-conditioning down to one-quarter strength and fell into a fitful doze on the couch in the main salon. He woke with a heavy head and a sour taste in his mouth. Shaving, showering and brushing his teeth made him feel better and he was ready to go when the taxi he had ordered drew up alongside.

On deck he was surprised to find a young lad about ten years old, waiting patiently. Richard presumed it was the harbour master's nephew. He ascertained his name was Javod and giving him a couple of cans of coke, Richard told him what he expected. His orders were acknowledged with a wide grin and a nod of the head.

The taxi dropped him at the town hall, a large white neo-Moorish building on the Boulevard Habib Bourguiba, halfway between the Medina – a ninth century fort and the harbour. Richard knew that the real power in any area of Tunisia rested with its Governor. The country was split into twenty-three governorships, each bearing the name of its main town or city. Although elections were held every five years there was still plenty of opportunity for a corrupt man to prosper. Governors retired rich.

The rooms inside were high with slow moving fans feebly attempting to circulate the air and keep the temperature in the realms of the bearable. An obsequious man who turned out to be the Governor's secretary, greeted him. Richard was immediately shown into the large, well-furnished offices of the Governor, where he was given a glass of thick, sweet coffee and abandoned.

He scrutinised his surroundings. The floor was an ornate pattern of blue and white tiles. In one corner stood a large desk, next to bay windows that stretched the height of the room and opened onto a balcony. Leather sofas lined one wall and a conference table, capable of seating a dozen people, stood in the middle of the room. The walls boasted pictures of various dignitaries. The most impressive showed Habib Bourguiba, Tunisia's President, first elected in 1959, who, after three terms in office, had been made President for Life.

A map of the region hung on one wall alongside an old calendar from the 1950s. Incongruously, it hung open at a page showing Marilyn Monroe lounging seductively in a white bathing costume. He was staring at it unseeingly, thinking of Victoria, when a door in the far wall opened.

'Ah, Mr. Griffiths. I apologise for keeping you waiting. I see you are admiring my favourite picture. The most beautiful woman of this century, I'm sure you'll agree.' The man walking towards Richard with his hand outstretched stood about 5ft 6ins tall. His fat stomach strained against the buttons of his dark suit jacket. He had a thick, black moustache and wore his ample hair slicked-back and held in place by a fragrant unguent. His handshake was firm and dry and it occurred to Richard that there was a toughness about the man, which was not to be underestimated.

The Governor offered Richard more refreshments, obviously using the delaying tactic as an opportunity to size up his visitor. Richard cringed inwardly at the thought of another cup of the syrupy sweet drink but said he'd be delighted. While the coffee was served they chatted about the world markets and in particular, the price of oil.

'I thought we should have this initial meeting alone. To establish the ground rules as it were, should we move forward.'

'I understand.' After years of dealing with corrupt officials all over Africa and the Middle East, Richard understood the rules only too well. In some countries he had visited it was referred to as *baksheesh* or *bakhshish*, in others it went under the name of *dash*. In Britain and America it was called bribery or a back-hander.

They discussed the running of a supply vessel from Sfax to various oilrigs off-shore. That was where the Governor would make his *baksheesh*. His mark-up on the products would make him a great deal of money for virtually no effort. The Governor couldn't hide his smile. Like similar situations in virtually every other country where oil was at the core, men would become rich. All Richard needed was a letter stating that he was acting on behalf of the Governor and that every courtesy was to be shown to him. The letter was quickly forthcoming.

Richard stood to leave.

'How long will you be staying in Tunisia?'

'At least ten days, maybe more. I was glad of an excuse to travel here and visit your country. It's like an all-expenses paid holiday for me. The arrangements – berthing, crew changes and the like – I could wrap up in two days but, as I said, I'll take a lot longer than that.'

The Governor appeared satisfied with this explanation and, shaking hands, Richard took his leave. There had been no invitation to dine or to meet socially. With bribery in play, it was best to keep personal contact to a minimum. Richard wondered how long it would be before the Governor learnt that there would be no supply vessel sailing from Sfax or any other port in his territory. When he did, he would be a very disappointed man.

13

NEXT, HE NEEDED to hire a car. The rental office was a few hundred metres along the Boulevard from the town hall. There were various types of cars available. The local drivers, however, appeared to have a collective death wish. Accidents were the will of God, pre-ordained before time began and hence unavoidable. Richard settled on a dented and scratched Land Rover Discovery. With less than 150,000kms on the clock he knew that at least the engine would be OK. He might not actually be any safer than in an ordinary car but at least he would feel it. Besides which, the 4-wheel drive would come in handy for what he had in mind. Richard was glad when he finally turned off Rue Ali Bach Hamba and into the port where *The Lady Ellen* was berthed without hitting another vehicle.

Javod was still on duty. He gave the boy twenty dollars and told him to return the following day.

'No, sir. I sleep here.' He indicated the bows where he had made himself a bed of a rolled carpet and a sleeping rug. 'I guard all night.'

He offered Javod something to eat but the lad declined. He had brought his own food from home. However he did accept another two cans of coke.

He couldn't stop shaking. Life imprisonment in some forsaken British jail. In the name of *Allah*! He would never see the outside world again.

The metal door opened and a stranger entered. He crossed the small cell and sat opposite the prisoner. He greeted the Libyan with the words: 'Al-Ghoul, you will die behind bars in a prison far from home.'

Al-Ghoul's thinning curly hair now bore strands of grey. Behind his glasses he forced back his tears. He said nothing.

Conversationally, the man continued. 'We've built a special jail for you. It's a part of Wormwood Scrubs. It's all ready and waiting. You'll be kept isolated from the other prisoners. Not for your own good you understand, but for theirs. Some of the boys would take great delight in harming you, would even kill you. Some will just spit in your food or force feed you pork. The trouble is, they would get into trouble and lose their remission. Not something Her Majesty's Government wants to see happen. Of course, some of the warders will also take great pleasure in the odd attack or two. Still, at least you'll live. Don't worry, you'll have all the comforts of home. We aren't totally barbaric. You can have television and your beloved *Koran* to read.'

Al-Ghoul interlaced his fingers tightly but the shakes wouldn't stop. He stared at his visitor, mesmerised, like a rabbit hypnotised by a snake. He was paralysed with fear and couldn't take his eyes off the other man's face.

'I just thought I'd let you know what you're in for.' The man stood, stepped to the door and paused. 'Oh, I forgot. In one year you will be transferred to Guantanamo Bay. You know, the American Naval Base at the south eastern end of Cuba? They aren't as civilised as us.'

If it was possible Al-Ghoul went a sicklier green.

'Ah, I see you've heard of it. Well, don't believe all you've heard. It is, in fact, a great deal worse than its reputation.'

'What is it you want from me?' His voice was a croak.

His visitor smiled and walked slowly back towards the table. 'That's better. Much better.' He sat down, waiting patiently.

'What?'

The reply came as a shock. 'We want to put you into a witness protection programme in America. We will give you a new life, one you can live in peace. Are you interested?'

Taking a deep breath, he finally managed to get his shaking limbs under control. 'And what do I have to do for this new life?'

'Tell us all you know. All the details of this and other acts you've committed. We are aware that you were obeying orders. The men responsible are leaving you to rot. Without further evidence we will be forced to draw a line under the incident and continue with business as usual. We will move on to other matters. You, in the meantime, will be forgotten about. Except, of course, by the families of your victims. They will ensure you never get parole and that you stay in prison for the rest of your life. Quite literally. There will be no exchange. You will not be sent back to Libya. Not once you are at Guantanamo. Family members wishing to visit you will have to travel thousands of miles. That is, assuming Colonel Harwazi will let them. If you co-operate with us, the reality would be very different.'

'*Aiwa*. Oh yes, very different. My mother and younger sister will die a terrible death. Instead, they will live a happy life, knowing that I have taken care of them. I have been promised.'

'And you believe the promises?'

Shrugging, Al-Ghoul reached for a cigarette. 'As much as I believe yours.' He inhaled deeply and blew out a lung full of smoke. 'I am a little cog in a big machine. Two years ago I thought I was an important man. I had been given orders by the highest in the land. He trusted me. Now I am nothing. It is the way of the world, decided by *Allah*, long before I was born. *Qisma*.'

'We in the West don't believe in fate. We believe that every man has control over his own destiny. You can take control of yours.'

'You do not understand. What I have just said about my mother and . . .'

'I understood. Here's a picture that was taken yesterday and sent to me. You can see your mother sitting in the street with a begging bowl at her feet. Here is one of your sister. She is working in a small bar for tips.'

'It cannot be.' The voice was barely a whisper. 'It cannot be! I gave them the money. The money I was paid. The Fifty thousand dollars. What happened to that?'

'It was taken back. Two days ago.'

Al-Ghoul bent forward and knocked his forehead on the table. Hard. Once. Twice. Three times. 'My sister. A whore!' For that was the reality of a girl doing the kind of work his sister had been given.

'Stop it! What if I told you we have a solution to your problem? What if I told you that approaches have already been made to your mother and a proposition made to her?'

'What sort of proposition?'

'We will arrange to have them taken to America.'

'What do you mean?'

'Just what I said. We will arrange for them to leave Gaza and go to America.'

'I hate America.'

'Then die in jail and let your mother and sister suffer for your crimes.' There was no mistaking the contempt in his voice.

'How will you do it?'

'That we can do and do easily. We have our ways.'

Al-Ghoul looked up from the table and said, 'I do not understand. If you want to learn things from me why don't you fill me with drugs? Torture me?'

'Your human rights for one thing. Don't misunderstand. That is exactly what I would like to do to you.' The level tone, the reasonable voice, added to the menace in the words. 'But we can't. You will live in a British prison, mostly in isolation for one year and then you will be handed over to the Americans. They, I can assure you, will not be so magnanimous as far as your human rights are concerned. By then, of course, the information you have will be mostly out of date. Always a problem in our business, don't you think?'

'*In-sha'a-llah.*'

'You may be right. It may be the will of God. But there's a hell of a lot we can do to influence it. Even in a year, a little of what you tell us will be useful. But we want the information now. We can get it if you agree to the protection program. Your mother and sister will be safe in America. So will you. Or you can rot in jail for the rest of your life. What's it to be?'

There was no reply.

The man stood up and said, 'You have until I reach the door. Then you're on your own.'

As his hand touched the door handle the Libyan said, 'Yes. I will do it.'

The man from MI6 nodded, satisfied. It was what he wanted to hear.

The following morning, before the sun was up, Richard was driving along P1, the major road that led to Gabès, over 130kms south of Sfax. The road followed the curve of the Gulf of Gabès, a two-lane, modern highway with sufficient traffic to justify its existence. It was still dark when he passed the Sfax Thyna Airport, 8kms from the town and soon he was driving in the untamed beauty of the countryside, his headlights cutting a swathe of light in the darkness. A signpost announced that the next town was Gabès, still 120kms away. He fiddled with the radio, but the reception was poor. Switching it off, he contented himself with the drive and the landscape that was slowly unfolding as the dawn broke. The sun came up in a blaze of glory and began to heat up the car after the cool of the night. He turned on the air-conditioning.

An image of Victoria brought a smile to his lips – an

oil-smudged cheek when she had greased the windlass and wiped the sweat off the side of her face. And always, the last vision he had of her, so small and sad when they said goodbye.

Weaving past slow moving trucks he overtook a camel train plodding slowly south. He wondered where they were headed, what they were carrying. The remaining ride was smooth and fast. Two hours later he arrived at Gabès, the centre of the local Governorship. Approaching the town he came to the Avenue de la République and passed the taxi and bus stations on the right. Locally a filling station was known as a kiosk. Finding one he filled up with diesel, although he had only used a quarter tank. He was surprised to discover how cheap it was.

It was now nearly eight o'clock and the roads were busy. Richard was glad to reach the southern edge of the town. Here the road forked, right to Matmata and left to Medenine and Jerba. He veered left.

At Medenine the P1 continued along the coast. The road branched right at this point, the P19 going south for Tataouine. Richard took it. By now, he had the air-conditioning turned up full. The pyramid shaped peaks of the Dahar Mountains loomed ahead. In times gone by, villagers, desperate to escape the terrible heat, had hewn their homes from the living rock there. Most were abandoned now and had been replaced by more modern housing, but several had been turned into tourist attractions.

Soon he could see the impressive rock face that marked the town of Tataouine. For many people this was a name that conjured up the end of the world. Here the French convicts who had made up the African light infantry battalions had been stationed. For them, brutality and hardship had been the order of the day, lived under the glare of a pitiless sun.

He was now on the road to Remada, another hour's drive south. The landscape was unbelievably harsh, with a succession of high peaks topped by great slabs of rock.

It was beyond his imagination that people eked out an existence there and had done for thousands of years.

Just before he reached Remada, the road branched left and deteriorated. Now a single track, the tarmac was breaking up in places. There was virtually no traffic other than a number of solitary camels with their owners. He stopped in the early afternoon to stretch his legs. Within seconds he was sweating and he climbed gratefully back into the Land Rover.

For two more hours he bumped and twisted south until at long last he reached the abandoned village of Bir Zar. He stopped the car but left the engine idling, the air-conditioning working flat out. This was a desolate place surrounded by low hills of rock. The houses were dilapidated, their roofs falling in and doors long decayed. A sign on the left of the road was written in Arabic. Underneath was the translation in English. Libyan Border.

The sun was setting towards the west. Donning a wide-rimmed khaki hat to ward off the evening sun, he set out to recce the place. The village was about a kilometre long with houses on both sides. It had once been a prosperous trading place, a crossroads and oasis. When the only well had dried up the people had left.

At the furthest end of the village he came across a wide-open space. Walking across to the other side he looked towards Libya. A road had been built, stretching east to west. A road, he was sure, that led nowhere. Returning to the Land Rover, he drove through the village and onto the road. It proved to be in surprisingly good condition. Sure enough it ended after about a kilometre. *A road to nowhere*, he thought, *but a runway to many places*.

According to his information, a meeting was to take place in five days time. This particular site had been used on three other occasions. An advance party would appear to erect tents before the main body arrived. The meeting would last one day.

He stayed the night, camping out under a clear sky. The

temperature had dropped quickly once the sun had set and he sat gazing pensively into the flames of a small fire. What on earth was he doing here? He pulled out the dog-eared photo of Ellen and the twins he always carried and gazed at it. Only a matter of a few weeks ago he hadn't cared whether he lived or died. Now, he couldn't get Victoria out of his head. A feeling of guilt welled up in him. Could he once again enjoy the happiness he had known with Ellen? One thing he did acknowledge to himself, Victoria had touched him in a way he had not expected.

Watching the flames, doubts began to envelope him. Perhaps he should just quit now. Fold up his tent and slink away into the night. Leave what he was planning to the experts, like his cousin Nick.

Lucy and Phillip would have been eight now, nearly nine. The fire crackled and a piece of wood fell inwards with a burst of sparks. It was enough to snap him out of his morbid mood and back to reality. He had come this far and he had no intention of stopping.

He woke to a stiff back and a cold fire. Dawn was breaking and the shadows of the land were beginning to take shape. He lit a Primus stove and made a cup of coffee before starting the day with a traditional Tunisian breakfast called laglabi, a puree of chickpeas. He followed this delicacy with harissa, semolina soaked in honey and flavoured with orange-flowers. He managed to swallow it wishing he had opted for bread, butter and jam instead. The coffee washed the taste from his mouth and left him feeling more or less human.

Stowing the gear away he began measuring distances.

By the time the sun was up and he was beginning to feel its effects, he was finished. He climbed behind the wheel of the Land Rover and started north. No, there was no going back.

'If he talks, we will be the worlds' lepers for many more decades to come. We need to silence him once and for all. I have therefore made the necessary arrangements. The details need not concern you.'

'Yes, my Colonel.'

Harwazi nodded his dismissal. Once known as the "godfather of terrorism" he was now considered an elder statesman of Africa. He had been rehabilitated as far as the world was concerned. Which was why he kept such a low profile when it came to supporting those who attacked the West.

When the man had gone Harwazi smiled wolfishly. Greed and failed ambitions made a man vulnerable. To have someone so high in the British secret service on his payroll brought joy to his heart. The money had been well spent.

14

'Come in, Commander, take a seat.'

'Thank you, sir.' Hunter crossed the General's office and sat down opposite him.

'A job has come up which I want you to deal with.'

'What kind of job, sir?'

'A lift and shift.'

'Not our usual kind of operation,' Hunter frowned.

'I know, but there are extenuating circumstances. It's highly sensitive, speed is of the essence and, quite frankly, we are about the only force with the right mixture of skills available.'

'You have my attention, sir. Who, where and why?'

'Ah, The where is easy. Gaza.'

Whatever he'd been expecting, it wasn't that. 'Gaza? Who in hell am I getting from that godforsaken hole? Is he one of ours? Or someone coming over? And if he is, why doesn't he come the usual way?'

'Actually, you'll be bringing out two women . . .'

'Two women? Sir, you're joking!'

'I never joke about operational matters, Commander, as you know only too well.'

Hunter nodded, accepting the mild rebuke. 'Sorry, sir. So who are they?'

'Al-Ghoul's mother and sister.'

'Why am I bringing them out? Al-Ghoul will never see outside of prison . . .' he trailed off.

'Precisely. Al-Ghoul will be put into a witness protection programme in America. He'll sing his head off. He'll confirm what we want to know with regards to the BA flight as well as give us details about many other atrocities they've committed. He will also name the names of his so-called brothers-in-arms.'

Hunter frowned. 'But why, sir? It makes no sense. These people are fanatics. They just don't . . . don't turn state's evidence. Ever. At least, not to my knowledge.'

'What you say is true. However, the circumstances this time are somewhat different. Al-Ghoul thinks he's been betrayed. His mother has been forced to beg in the streets, his sister working in a bar as a prostitute.'

Hunter sat back and crossed his legs. 'I don't like it. In view of what he did to my family, I'd let the bastard rot.'

'I know. I appreciate that. But there's too much at stake. Al-Ghoul's information will be priceless. Information is the most vital weapon we have.'

'I always thought,' Hunter looked puzzled, 'that provided a HAMAS member said nothing, kept quiet, his family was looked after.'

'They are.'

'But in this case?'

'But in this case, nothing. They are being looked after. Al-Ghoul was shown photographs that were fake. They'd been very cleverly produced.'

'And he fell for it?'

'Don't forget, he'd just been sentenced to life imprisonment. He was off balance. Not thinking straight. It was easily done.'

'So why are his mother and sister agreeing to being brought out, if they are being looked after?'

'It's a relative term. Looked after in Gaza is not the same as being looked after in the West.'

'I can go along with that.' Hunter sighed. 'Okay, why the hurry?'

'Two reasons. The most important one by far is that we know the West is being targeted. What we don't know is by whom, where and when. Anything he knows we need. It means saving lives. They only need to get lucky once to cause massive damage and many lives to be lost.'

'I know. Whereas we have to be lucky all of the time. I appreciate that, sir. And the second reason?'

'He won't talk until he sees his mother and sister. In the flesh.'

There was nothing for it. 'When do I leave? And what about a briefing?'

It was a day for surprises. Macnair looked at his watch and said, 'You just have time to make your flight. You'll be briefed en-route to Edinburgh Airport. You'll take a BA flight to Heathrow and from there to Cyprus. You'll be kitted out once you reach *The Victoria*.'

'What about back-up?'

'None, I'm afraid. One, we're stretched to breaking right now and two, the fewer people who know about it the better. But it should be relatively simple. One of Israel's finest will be meeting you on the beach with your charges.'

'You mean Mossad?'

'The same. Nick, all you need is a passport and civvie clothes.'

'Right, sir. In that case, I'd better get moving.'

By early afternoon he was on Cyprus. The trip, Hunter acknowledged, had been painless, if boring. He didn't go through Customs. Instead, he was escorted to a military helicopter on the other side of the airfield. It was sitting with its engines warmed through ready to go. As soon as Hunter was strapped in, it took off and headed out to sea.

It was a glorious day, which wasn't lost on Hunter. Due to the dangerous nature of his job, he had learnt to enjoy each day as it came. This was no exception.

The *Fort Victoria* was an RFA – Royal Fleet Auxiliary ship. In short, a supermarket at sea for the Royal Navy. She supplied everything from fuel and water, to tinned, powdered and dried food. She had been detached from a fleet exercise that had been taking place off-shore Cyprus. She was now ploughing her way at top speed towards Israel.

An RAF aircraft lifted off from the Dutch Air Force base near Nijmegen. Al-Ghoul sat handcuffed to two Military Policemen. So far, he had been treated courteously and correctly. Nevertheless, his mouth was dry with fear at the thought of what lay ahead. He'd simply been obeying orders. For the first time since the trial, he put the blame for his predicament firmly where it belonged. The Colonel, he sneered. *Al Aqid, The Great One.*

He made himself think of America. The witness protection program. Could he trust the Americans? But that was idiotic. Why go to so much trouble to get his family out of Libya? In one year, instead of being sent to Guantanamo Bay, he would be set free. He *had* to believe that. A feeling of despair washed over him. He barely heard the warning that the aircraft was approaching RAF High Wycombe and only realised it when the plane hit the runway with a bump. When the doors opened he saw it was raining hard. A shiver ran up his spine as he was helped to his feet and towards the exit.

The RAF VC10 was the last plane to land that day. It was midnight.

The Vicky, as she was affectionately known, was just outside the 3 mile limit steaming at a speed that just about gave her steerage way. Hunter was ready to go. The inflatable was lifted off the deck and lowered towards the sea. As it hit the water, Hunter started the engine, slipped the carrying sling and steered away from the hull. A few hundred yards away he established radio contact and was given a heading to steer.

This was the tricky bit. Any danger was still ahead. The Mossad agent was sitting on the beach with a radio beacon beamed at the RFA giving pinpoint accuracy. An operator on board the ship was in contact with Hunter, directing him towards the target.

'Come left, ten degrees.'

Hunter repeated the order and moved the steering wheel, watching the compass carefully.

'Come right, five degrees.'

And so it went on. Finally, he heard, 'Distance to go, two cables. On track.'

'Roger that. Going in now.' Hunter flicked off the safety on his automatic pistol. In this close, a handgun was more useful than a rifle or machine gun. Any trouble, he'd discourage his attackers and get the hell out of there.

'Is everything ready?' he asked the driver.

'Fer crying out loud. How many more frigging times? Yes. They'll come on the frigging M40 then down the A40. Everything's been fixed.'

'What if they go by a different road?'

'If they change the frigging route we'll know. Whatever happens, they have to take the A40. If they use the back streets we'll be frigging ready for them. The hit either goes down at junction 1 or at Du sodding Cane Road by the prison. The bastards won't get away.'

Their Glaswegian accents were harsh, from the East End of the city. They had been recruited especially. Unknown in the south, these were six hard men who had been in and out of prison most of their lives. For them, this was the big one. They were being paid six million pounds to kill one man and God help anybody who got in the way. Whether they were pigs or army, it wouldn't make any difference. They had never had so many guns and so much firepower. As soon as the job was over they would retire to Spain. It was all arranged.

The sound of the mobile phone shattered their jangled nerves.

There was no greeting. 'Just as they said. One car in front and one behind. The van is Securicor.'

'How many in the cars?'

'Just the driver and one. London filth saving money as usual.'

'Aye, well they're in for a frigging surprise, aren't they?' He broke the connection and turned to his accomplice. 'Two cars with two bobbies in each. And the van.'

Both men dragged on their cigarettes. If they were nervous, neither showed it. After tonight they would be amongst the most wanted men in the world. With a million apiece it wouldn't worry them too much. The phone rang again.

'We're on the motorway.'

'Right, stay behind. Right behind. But watch them. They can still come off the motorway before junction 1. Close up, as soon as you pass junction 2.'

The rain pounded down. It suited them. It would deaden the noise. Affect the cameras. Give them the time they needed to escape.

The phone rang for the third and final time. 'Okay. It's junction 1. We're closing up now.' In the black car following the police convoy the man in the passenger seat reached behind him and lifted up two Uzi machine guns. He checked they were loaded and pulled the cocking handles. Pushing the combined safety catch and fire selector forward he primed both weapons to fire on automatic. The magazine could hold 25, 32 or 40 rounds. They had the full 40.

All three cars moved into position. Two of them parked in lay-byes, either side of the roundabout, about a hundred metres away. The car following the convoy closed up. The driver of the second police car had noticed the black car following but dismissed it. Nobody knew that Al-Ghoul was arriving that night. It had been put about that he would be leaving in the morning. A low-key oper-ation. Just two cars and a van with two guards. A nice quiet job. The police car in front of the van approached the roundabout and slowed down. The van and car behind did the same. All three vehicles were now close together.

The two cars screeched to a halt in front of the convoy blocking it. Four men wearing balaclavas leapt out from the two cars. There was no finesse. They opened up with their machine guns and killed the two policemen in the front car instantly. The car behind rammed the back of the second police car hard. The two men jumped out. Even as the officer in the police car was radioing for help a hail of bullets killed him and his partner.

The van transporting Al-Ghoul was an ordinary Ford Transit with bars on the rear windows and a lock that a child could open. Even that was too much trouble for the Glasgow hard men. They sprayed the sides of the van with bullets until a mixture of blood and petrol poured out the bottom. The hole cut in the side was big enough to take a hand grenade and one was forced through. A second hand grenade was lobbed inside the car used to ram the police car. The six men ran for the two remaining vehicles. Jumping into the cars, they were already moving when the grenades exploded, sending two balls of fire high into the sky.

The cars hit the M40 north bound and went like crazy. They intended leaving the motorway at junction 2 and hiding in a safe house in Slough. At speeds approaching 90 mph they were followed by the cameras on the motorway. A police patrol car which was racing to the scene of the incident and was at Junction 1 was diverted in pursuit. With its blues and twos going they began to gain on the other cars. One of the gangsters smashed the back window of the black car and began shooting at the pursuing police vehicle. It slowed abruptly. The first car came off the motorway at the slip road and sped towards the roundabout. The second followed. The driver barely slowed down as they reached the roundabout and he turned the wheel sharply to the left, the tyres screaming and sliding on the wet road. The machine gunner was not a trained soldier. He still had his finger inside the trigger guard, though he wasn't shooting – the police car was too far away. He fell backwards, into the driver's seat and his trigger finger involuntarily clamped tight. The gun began firing inside the car. Three bullets and the magazine was empty. The bullets went through the back seat and into the floor. One severed the brake fuel line and hit the petrol tank. The black car exploded in a ball of fire and smashed into the hedge on the side of the road. The three men inside were incinerated in seconds.

The constable in the police car radioed HQ and told Control what had happened and that they were now giving chase to the first car. They were on the A355, near Farnham Common and the car was vanishing into the distance. More than anything they wanted the occupants alive. The car slewed left and headed for the sleepy village of Stoke Poges. The order to scramble helicopters had already been given and armed police were being ferried to the scene. Other cars were closing in from all directions.

'Christ all bloody mighty! Can't this heap go no faster?'

'Shut yer gob. We're doing a hundred and frigging twenty. Where's that frigging police car?'

'We lost it,' said the man in the back.

'Don't be so sure.' He turned sharp right, barely retaining control of the car and sped towards the A412. He knew the M4 motorway was nearby. He wanted on it where he'd race the bastards to Wales if he had to.

Suddenly, ahead, a beam of light flooded down and then held them in its grip. They heard the clatter of the helicopter blades and a voice over a loudhailer telling them to stop and give themselves up.

By way of response the man in the front passenger's seat opened his window and fired his Uzi up at the sky. He missed, but it was enough to make the helicopter sheer away.

'Oh, Jesus. Sweet Mary, Mother of God. There are cars all over the place.'

Police vehicles blocked the road, lights were flashing from the roofs of at least 6 cars. Armed police stood behind the vehicles. The fleeing car screeched to a halt just as another half a dozen police cars raced up behind and blocked the road. Checkmate. The three men in the car sat there in utter fear and panic. They had never faced anything like this in their lives before. There was nowhere to go. Except to prison. It was all over. Life inside would be sheer hell. The police would see to that.

The driver got out, raised his hands above his head and started walking forward. All his dreams of a privileged life in Spain were washing away with the rain that was still belting down and soaking him to the skin.

'Get down! Get down! Now! Down or we open fire!' The driver was bombarded with orders. He sank to his knees with a moan and lay face down on the wet road.

'Now the next one. Out! Out! Out! Come on! Move it! Drop your weapon! I said, drop your weapon or we fire!'

The second man kept coming. Suddenly he raised the gun and ran forward, his finger curling around the trigger. He got off two rounds before he was cut to pieces in a hail of bullets. Minimum force. Let internal affairs make what they liked of that one.

The third man came out of the car with his hands raised. 'Don't shoot! Don't shoot! Please don't shoot!'

When the cuffs were put on, the circulation was cut from their hands. Both men sustained injuries in the car as they were taken to the nearest police station. None of them were particularly life threatening.

A news blackout was imposed on the whole incident, giving the police time to investigate what had happened. Al-Ghoul's death was a huge embarrassment, to say nothing of the tragic deaths of four policemen and a Securicor guard and driver. Heads would roll. Luckily, the Assistant Commissioner of Police knew to telephone TIFAT at Rosyth and spoke to Macnair.

* * *

'Commander, this is the Captain. Do not go ashore. I repeat, do not go ashore.'

The order startled Hunter. He was merely a few yards from the beach and he could see three people. A man and two women. No one else was in sight.

'Say again, over.'

'I say again. Do not go ashore. The operation in cancelled. I repeat, cancelled. Return to ship. Over.'

'Roger that. I am on my way.' He twisted the wheel as far as it would do and opened the throttle. In seconds the boat was up on the plane and speeding towards the big gray hull of the RFA. What the hell was going on?

It only took a few minutes before he was alongside and hooking onto the lifting gear. As the boat came out of the water he saw the Captain leaning over the rail.

'What's up, sir?'

'I was just told to recall you. I have the General on a secure line on the bridge.'

Hunter followed the Captain to the bridge where he was given a handset.

'Sir?'

'Nick, I have just learned that Al-Ghoul was ambushed and killed a short while ago. It was bloody carnage.'

Following the events, one thing was certain. There was a traitor in the midst of the British Establishment.

15

RICHARD SPENT TWO days working on his cover story around the port of Sfax. Then, once again, leaving young Javod guarding the boat, he headed south. He had enough explosives with him to start a small war. In an area known for its paranoia against so-called freedom fighters, he knew it would be best not to get stopped. Were it to happen, then he hoped that the Governor's letter would get him past any problems. However, just as the first time, the journey passed uneventfully and by the evening he was at Bir Zar.

According to his information, the advance party would be arriving late the following day.

At the end of the village stood a shallow, indented amphitheatre, one hundred metres in diameter. Here the hard rocky surface of the earth was covered in a thin layer of sand about a foot deep. The houses started about fifty metres back, on both sides of the street, leading away in a gentle curve. Backing the Land Rover into one of the dilapidated houses he unloaded his stores. From the upper floor of the house he had an excellent view of the amphitheatre and beyond. It was very hot although he was in the shade, but he put all thought of discomfort out of his mind. He began to unwrap the plastic explosive from its brown greaseproof paper. The PE was a little brittle, but with kneading it quickly became pliant again. It was PE4, made mainly of RDX – or cyclo-trimethylene-trinitramine – with a thirteen-percent mixture of liquid paraffin and lithium stearate. The plasticiser made the RDX less sensitive and more stable but also more powerful and violent than TNT, it was one-and-a-half times more powerful than RDX alone.

Richard fashioned ten round balls of PE, six inches in diameter. The sooner he buried the explosives, the longer the wind would have to hide any telltale marks he made in the sand. Reluctantly, he lifted out a spade and a pickaxe, threw them over his shoulder and went out into the blisteringly hot sun. Using the spade, he scraped away the sand and then swung the pickaxe into the ground. The sandstone broke away easily. He dug a hole twelve inches deep and the same around. Satisfied, he started on a second. Completing five holes he returned to the Land Rover to drink a can of cold mineral water and swallow a salt tablet.

Back in the sun he worked quickly, finishing the remainder of the holes. Ten holes were now scattered across the surface of the amphitheatre. He rewarded himself with another can of water.

Next, he scraped away the sand, digging a trench from each hole to a position on the lip of the amphitheatre nearest the village. This time, he rewarded himself with something to eat as well as drink. Sitting in the shade, between mouthfuls of bread and cheese, he threaded detonating cord into a garden hose. The white plastic cordtex came on reels of 500ft and had a tensile strength of 130lbs. Its explosive filling, PETN – or Pentaerythritol Tetranitrate – had a detonation rate of 22,000ft per second. Finishing his simple meal, he drank a couple of pints of water and once more stepped out into the blazing sunshine. He couldn't help thinking of the Noel Coward classic, "*Mad dogs and Englishmen go out in the noon-day sun.*"

Back at the amphitheatre, he ran the hose and cordtex along each trench. Shovelling the sand back into the trenches, he covered the hose.

At each hole he located the end of the cordtex and fitted a detonator, an aluminium tube known as an L1A1.

It was 2.35 inches long and 0.256 inches in diameter and fitted exactly over the cordtex. Each time he pushed the detonator on, he pulled it off again and checked the end of the cordtex. A few yellow grains of explosive could be seen, proving contact. Richard refitted the detonator and crimped it into place, using a pair of specially designed pliers.

With a screwdriver he made holes in the lumps of plastic explosive. He inserted the detonators into the holes and squeezed the holes closed. Placing the PE into the ground he carefully covered the plastic with a layer of nuts and bolts he had brought along for the purpose. Working doggedly he finished all ten. Carefully, he covered each hole with sand and placed a rock on top. He stood back and looked at his handiwork. Already, the ceaseless wind was having its effect and his traces over the areas he had been working and walking on were being obliterated.

At the lip of the amphitheatre he used the pickaxe to dig a shallow, narrow trench. He made it the width of the pick and 3 inches deep. The hose was used to protect the cordtex in the event of somebody hammering a tent peg into the ground and accidentally hitting the explosive trail. The hose would bend but not break whereas the cordtex on its own could easily be pinched so that the explosion failed to travel along it. In this way, he reduced the likelihood of a misfire.

He dug the trench to the house where he had hidden the Land Rover. Laying cordtex along the trench, he connected it to the ten ends of cordtex at the amphitheatre. Sweating profusely, Richard began filling in the trench. First, he covered the cordtex with sand to protect it and then finished the job using the chunks of sandstone he had dug out.

Standing in the entrance to the house and knowing what he was looking for, he could easily recognise the seam he had made across the rock. He hoped nobody else would be looking that hard. Darkness was falling. He drank his fill of fruit drinks, forced down a sandwich and swallowed two salt tablets. Tomorrow would be a busy day. He laid out a sleeping bag, climbed wearily into it and fell into an uneasy sleep.

Waking with the dawn, he lit the Primus and put on a kettle of water to make coffee. While he did so, he contemplated his plans. The house he had selected to hide the car in was eighth along from the amphitheatre. It had two rooms downstairs and two upstairs. He had driven in through an opening in the end wall where the stones had broken loose and lay scattered across the ground. With his coffee in hand, he examined the wall more closely. With a sigh, he got to his feet, throwing away the dregs in his mug.

He began to rebuild the wall, hiding the Land Rover from prying eyes. It was backbreaking work, but by mid-morning he had built the wall as high as his head. Next, he started work on the front door and single window. By the time he had finished, the openings were filled with stone. It would take a determined individual to bother to open them up again. Standing outside, his hands on top of his head, he examined the results. He hoped the stone work was a sufficient deterrent to anyone thinking of looking inside.

Climbing over the wall he had built, he went back into the house. His final task was to set up the Beretta Sniper in the upstairs front room.

He was both relieved and apprehensive when, in the late afternoon, he saw a convoy of lorries arriving. A small army of men climbed out of the trucks and began pitching a tent in the middle of the amphitheatre. The tent covered three of the stones he had placed showing him the position of the explosives. When the tent had been erected he saw the three stones being thrown out. Other, smaller tents were pitched around the large one. He watched as steel pegs were driven into the rock and he tried in vain to decide whether they were anywhere near the cordtex. If a peg were driven into the plastic explosive, nothing would happen. If it hit a detonator then it would probably explode with devastating results.

When the men had finished putting up the tents, piles of carpets and rugs, along with cushions and small tables, were carried inside. The whole operation took less than an hour. Richard was impressed by the efficient manner in which it was executed.

As dusk was falling, the men began to relax. He estimated that there were fifty or sixty of them, each with a rifle or a machine gun slung across his back. In spite of the work not one man had put his gun down. A generator was started and electric lights came on. Richard realised that one of the trucks was a mobile kitchen and, soon after sunset, the men stopped to eat. They broke up into small groups and sat around talking, eating and smoking. He was gratified to see that no sentries were posted. This sign of sloppiness encouraged him.

Headlights appeared across the border, approaching fast. The men were suddenly alert and extinguished their cigarettes. When the first car in a convoy of six came to a stop a few of the men began firing their guns into the air in greeting. Richard took a deep breath as he watched Colonel Harwazi step into the light, arms raised, a wide smile on his face. Cheers and yells filled the air. "Al Aqid!" He had known of Harwazi's dislike of flying.

Aiming his Beretta directly onto the face of the Libyan ruler Richard curled his finger around the trigger. 'Bang, you're dead,' he said softly. Overhead, a helicopter appeared and landed, creating a mini sandstorm. The tall, turbaned, bearded figure of Walid bin Sydal emerged. He walked sedately across the sand to greet Harwazi. The two embraced warmly. Bin Sydal turned to two men who were standing beside him. Both wore the black and white chequered kaffiyeh favoured by Palestinians. With a quickening heartbeat Richard tried to recognise them. Even at this distance they looked very similar in appearance. One could, he thought dispassionately, be Jalal Chalabi, but he wasn't sure.

With the arrival of Harwazi the attitude of the soldiers underwent a radical change. Now they stood guard around the perimeter of the camp or patrolled in groups of two, appearing alert and business like. One patrol began to walk along the street of the village houses, looking inside doors and windows with a flashlight. It was sloppy work but came as no surprise to Richard. There was no attempt to search properly, to secure the area. As usual, it was all show with no substance.

Watching two men approach, Richard was not unduly concerned, but nevertheless he readied his silenced automatic. They passed noisily beneath his window without so much as a glance in his direction. Continuing to the end of the street they turned around and started back. Walking on the other side of the narrow, dusty street they continued straight to the campsite.

The newcomers settled around a fire and began to talk. Not, Richard realised with a grimace, anywhere near where he had set the explosives.

Harwazi and bin Sydal talked well into the night, occasionally interrupted by one of the Palestinians. The second Palestinian seemed contented to merely nod. The remainder of the entourage sat listening, saying nothing. Harwazi was waving his hands, obviously indulging himself in the rhetoric for which he was famous.

Hours later, the meeting finally broke up. Checking his watch, Richard saw that it was nearly 03.00. He wondered if the men were preparing to depart and got ready to open fire. Two shots, two targets – Harwazi and bin Sydal. He would blow the camp, shoot up the helicopter and break out through the wall. His mouth was dry. He took up the slack on the trigger, the crosshairs on Harwazi's face.

Suddenly, Harwazi turned and walked towards the main tent followed by the others. They disappeared inside.

The guards were no longer patrolling. Some had wrapped themselves in blankets and gone to sleep while others sat looking in at the camp, not outwards where any potential danger lay. It was now or never.

The cordtex ended next to the Land Rover. Attached to it the black safety fuse was long enough to burn for one minute. To the end of the safety fuse he had attached a Mk3 igniter. Richard removed the split pin and pulled the main pin. There was a small bang and the fuse lit. Pressing his stopwatch button, he bounded up the stairs and settled behind the Beretta. The second hand hit fifty-four seconds and he began firing.

His target was the helicopter. He emptied the magazine. He was surprised it didn't explode, the bullets failing to ignite the helo's fuel. How much damage he'd done was impossible to tell. Pandemonium broke out in the camp, with guards leaping up and firing their guns aimlessly into the night. At that moment the cordtex ignited.

Inside the tent, when the firing had started, Harwazi's bodyguards, who had been awake and alert, threw themselves on their leader to shield him. Bin Sydal had thrown himself flat, trying to worm into the sand. The others in the tent had jumped to their feet, grabbing for their guns. The Palestinian Jalal Chalabi, lay still. Seeing his brother leap up he screamed a warning.

The explosion's journey through the cordtex across a distance of a few hundred metres was nano seconds. At each location of the plastic explosive a chemical miracle took place. Energy was released in four forms – heat between three to four thousand degrees centigrade, pressure at two to three million pounds per square inch, a flash of light and a huge bang, destructive in itself. The gas produced was ten to fifteen thousand times the volume of the original explosive. This deadly combination of energies swept the nuts and bolts covering the plastic in a deadly scythe across the amphitheatre. Men sitting on cushions in the main tent were cut in half. Those guards around the perimeter were annihilated, dead before they knew what had happened. Those who had been sleeping awoke to a world gone mad.

Several of the trucks exploded when petrol leaked across the ground. Richard reloaded, saw some guards running towards the village and changed his aim. He shot three of them. The remainder fell to the ground and returned fire. Chips of stone erupted from the wall around him and he decided it was time to go.

Running down the stairs, he threw the rifle into the back of the Land Rover. Turning to the wall he had built, he put his shoulder to it and shoved. Nothing happened. He had done too good a job and he was trapped. He fought to hold down the panic that was welling up inside. Climbing into the Land Rover, he started the engine and inched forward until the bumper touched the wall. He kept going as stones fell outwards and the wall collapsed. Slowly he drove over the stones, terrified of getting a puncture. He reached smooth ground without mishap and twisted the wheel hard left, away from the devastation he had caused. He stopped, he climbed out of the car, pulled the pin on another safety fuse igniter and scrambled back into the vehicle. Accelerating, he sped away. Two minutes later there was a huge explosion in the derelict house. Half a dozen Libyans who had been closing in on the place, were killed by the falling masonry.

Without headlights, he drove on to the road and gunned the engine, speeding away towards the main road.

'I want them. I want them alive!' Harwazi screamed at the officer in charge.

'Yes, my Colonel. Only . . .'

'Only what?'

'We have no trucks. The pilot is checking the helicopter and we are checking the cars.'

'Where did they come from? Was the area not secured?'

'I promise you it was, *Al Aqid*. On my life.'

'On your life and on the lives of your family!' Again he yelled his frenzied rhetoric, threatening death and destruction to those responsible. 'What of Sheikh Walid bin Sydal? Did the cowards kill him?'

'No, my Colonel. Several of his men are dead, but, *al ham dulillah*, all praise to *Allah*, the Sheikh was only slightly injured. It is nothing. A mere cut across the brow.' The officer flinched under his leader's thunderous expression.

'Is it nothing that a man who is an honoured guest in my camp is injured in this way? Is it nothing that his devoted followers are killed when under my protection? Is there nowhere safe in this land for *Al Aqid*? Find them! Find them now, you sons of whores. And don't come back without them. I will make them suffer for what they did.'

'Sir, they are headed into Tunisia. If we follow them there we will be arrested.'

'Better to rot in a Tunisian jail than to let those men escape,' came the hissed reply. 'What of the Palestinians?' They were an afterthought.

'I will find out, sir.' The man ran across the amphitheatre to the devastated tent. Already some order was being imposed and the wounded and dead sorted. He found one of the Palestinians sitting on the ground weeping. He cradled something in his hands. The Libyan nearly threw up when he saw what it was. Jalal Chalabi was cradling the head of his brother, completely severed from its body. Hot tears dripped down onto the sightless eyes of the younger man.

Chalabi bent and kissed the blood covered lips before looking up. 'I will,' he said harshly, hate and anguish in every word, 'have the heads of the men who did this. I swear it on the grave of my brother.'

The helicopter was ready to fly. It was an old, venerable Wessex. The shots Richard had fired had broken the glass on the co-pilot's side and studded the cabin and tail with holes, but there didn't appear to be any serious damage. Whether there was or not, they would have flown regardless. Better to risk crashing than to face their leader's wrath.

While the helicopter was starting up, two carloads of men chased after Richard. In the distance the men in the lead car could see the loom of headlights and bright red tail lights.

Richard floored the accelerator, glanced in the mirror and winced. Christ, but they were closing fast. The road cut through a narrow defile bordered by low rock on both sides. Less than 50 metres into it there was a ninety degrees turn to the right and Richard slammed on the brakes, switching off his lights. Throwing open the door, he grabbed the Zastava M85 sub-machine gun and ran as fast as he could back the way he had come. Just as he reached the bend the first car appeared. Richard opened fire with the gun set to fully automatic. The driver died instantly and the car careered off the road, hitting the cliff rock face. The petrol tank burst and the car erupted in a ball of fire.

Seeing what had happened the driver of the second car slammed on the brakes. With tyres screeching, the car swerved from side to side and one of the front tyres burst. The wheel bucked in the driver's hand and the car slid to a halt jammed hard against the rock on the passenger's side. The driver's door opened and a man fell onto the road, dazed. Simultaneously, the back door opened and this time a man stepped out an AK74 in his hands. Richard reacted first and killed him with a short burst from his M85. He reached the car, switched aim and shot the driver through the head and then sent a cascade of bullets into the other two passengers who were trying to claw their way across the seats.

Turning, he ran back towards the Land Rover. He heard

the helicopter and looked over his shoulder. Damn, he thought, he had hoped he had put the sodding thing out of commission at least. It was approaching fast with its searchlight on. Frantically, he fumbled with the magazine and changed it for a full one. He was about to turn around and shoot the helo when he was hit a huge blow in his right shoulder and he fell to the ground with a bone-jarring, wind expunging crash. He expected more shots. He knew he was about to die.

It didn't happen. Sheer bloody-mindedness gave him the strength to roll over. He was pinned like a butterfly on the end of the searchlight. The light passed over him and Richard saw that the helicopter was preparing to land on the right side of the defile.

Even as the realisation came to him that they wanted him alive, Richard pulled the trigger and held it, hosing the helicopter from front to back. The helo hung motionless for a few seconds then it smashed down into the defile and exploded. Miraculously, the flying shards and bits of helo missed Richard, the two wrecked cars affording him some protection. He lay still for a few minutes, summoning the strength to stand. It was the thought that there might be others following that got him to his feet. He swayed for a few seconds and then managed to walk towards the Land Rover.

Before he did anything, he knew he had to see to his wound. He grabbed the first aid kit he had had the presence of mind to buy. He saw he had been lucky. If it could be called luck. The bullet had nicked the bone next to the joint. It hurt like hell and was bleeding, but at least he could move his arm. He dusted the wound with antiseptic powder and awkwardly fixed a bandage around his shoulder, strapping it as best he could. He took four painkillers, drank deeply from his store of water and started the engine.

He drove with his mind on automatic. The painkillers helped to reduce the pain to a sort of numb ache. But as each kilometre passed and the pills wore off, it got worse, the wound seeming to throb in time to his heartbeat. The road continued to be deserted and he put his foot down to the floorboards. The speedometer hit 100mph and he did his best to keep it there. Fleeing the unknown, he was prey to his wildest fears at the thought of being caught by the Libyans. The fear leant recklessness to his driving and he took bends dangerously. Without any special driving training only luck prevented him from crashing.

Dawn was breaking. The harsh landscape began to harden on either side and he was able to make out the hills surrounding him. At the stop sign for the P19 he turned onto the main carriageway. To his right lay Remada less than 10kms away, while to his left and north was Ksar Ouled Soltane. He considered holing up in Remada for a few days, but instinct drove him north to *The Lady Ellen* and escape. Loss of blood and a deep weariness muddled his thinking and he had only one plan – to get to the boat and safety.

The road was again a two-lane highway and other vehicles were beginning to appear. The last thing he needed was to be stopped by the police. They were notorious for identifying the blue licence plates of rented cars and pulling the drivers over. He eased his foot on the accelerator and slowed to 60mph. By the time he arrived at Medenine his vision was blurring and he had difficulty in staying awake. He had no choice. He had to stop.

Exhaustion made him careless. He missed seeing two Libyan cars less than a hundred metres behind when he indicated left and pulled off the road. He came to a halt under the shade of some palm trees. He switched off the engine, lowered his seat and closed his eyes. The Libyans swept past.

When he awoke Richard was bathed in sweat and he felt as weak as a kitten. He groaned as the pain in his shoulder bit deeply. His head was throbbing in the terrible heat. He felt as though he was being cooked alive. Opening the door he stumbled out into the searing sunshine. The shadow cast by the palm trees had long passed and the car had been baking under the sun, which was now reaching its zenith. Cars and lorries sped by. Opening the back door he fumbled for the cool box. There was one can of juice left. Eagerly he pulled the tab and then, tilting back his head, luxuriated in the taste and feel of the cold liquid pouring down his throat. All too soon it was finished. He felt only slightly refreshed and with hours of driving still ahead of him he knew he needed to buy more.

Reaching into the cab, he turned on the engine and put the air-conditioning up full. He sat on the step on the passenger's side, the cold air hitting his back. With both doors open, he was shielded from the gaze of people in passing vehicles. Laboriously, he took off his shirt. He removed the bandage and looked critically at the wound. Both entrance and exit were the about the size of a pencil. He adjusted the wing mirror to look at his back and was relieved to see that the bleeding had stopped and a scab was already forming. The hole in the front was slightly smaller but still seeping a little.

He wiped the blood away as best he could. Gritting his teeth, he wrapped a clean bandage around his shoulder. The ordeal finally over, he sat for a few moments to regain his strength. He was bone weary, tired beyond coherent thought. Rummaging in the first aid kit he found the bottle of painkillers and swallowed another four pills. He pushed himself to his feet and staggered around to the back of the car. From a holdall he took a clean shirt and khaki trousers. Gritting his teeth, he put on the shirt and awkwardly changed his trousers. The bloodied items he ditched on the side of the road.

Back in the Land Rover he sat still for a few seconds, savouring the coolness. Then, reluctantly, he engaged the gears and drove away. Having travelled the road three times now, he was surprised when he hit a long tailback of vehicles just to the south of the Gabès Canal, where the road crossed the bridge and narrowed to become the Avenue de la République. In an instant Richard realised that Harwazi's long arm was already reaching out, tentacle-like, across the country. He could envisage the threats, bribes and powers of persuasion adopted by Harwazi in order to find the men who had bombed his peaceful camp. No doubt, similar roadblocks were being set up all across the country. There was a petrol station a few hundred metres ahead and he drove up to it. Climbing out he told the attendant to fill the car with diesel. In his mediocre French he asked what was going on. Richard received confirmation that there was a road-block ahead. That terrorists had struck in the south of the country. Nodding his thanks, he paid for the diesel and bought a handful of cokes from a mercifully efficient refrigerator. Sitting in the car he drank two of them, pondering his next move.

During his frantic drive, Richard had consoled himself with the thought that the Libyans would not have expected so much damage to be wreaked by one man. They would be looking for a car full at least. Possibly even more than one car.

There was one problem though. If the car was searched and the guns found, it would all be over. He turned the car and headed back the way he'd come. About 3 miles along the road he arrived at a dirt track and turned down it, rounding a bend. Once out of sight, he pulled up. The ground around him was rock and scrub, with scree scattered along one side of a steep hill. Removing the firing pins within minutes he had buried the rifle and sub-machine gun under a pile of rocks. The pins he threw away. The PE, cordtex and safety fuse were all gone, but he did have plenty of ammunition. This he buried separately. He kept only the Glock and the ammunition for it.

Wrapping the gun inside a plastic carrier bag he sealed it with masking tape. Then he opened the bonnet and began to cut the top off the windscreen-washer bottle.

With a slit about ten inches long, he was able to force the gun inside the bottle, where it sank to the bottom. The ammunition quickly followed. He sealed the hole by wrapping the tape around the bottle. He tried the washer and found it still worked.

He was relieved to see that no more blood had seeped from his wound. Back inside the car he looked at his bloodshot eyes in the rear-view mirror. He had done what he could but with stubble on his cheeks and the gaunt look on his face, Richard thought he looked as guilty as sin. Before driving off he opened the glove compartment and located the Governor's letter.

16

HE WAS OVER an hour in the traffic queue. Nearing the front he became more nervous. He didn't like the look of the armed men standing with the police who were conducting the stop and search. Eventually, his turn came. Opening the window he stuck out his head, cheerily asking what was going on.

He was answered in Arabic and he shrugged. A policeman grabbed his door, opened it and indicated that he should step down. With an insouciance he didn't feel, he complied. Other policemen opened the doors of the Land Rover and began to search inside. An officer wandered across from another stopped car.

'You are British or American?'

'British.'

'Passport.' He held out his hand and as he did so, he asked, 'Where have you come from?'

Richard decided it was time to use his authority. 'That, constable, is none of your damned business. Now tell your men to stop what they're doing or there'll be trouble.'

'My rank is lieutenant and the only person in trouble will be you if you do not keep a civil tongue in your head.'

Richard yelled at the men who were opening his holdall and about to rummage inside. Turning back to the officer, he said, 'I suggest you read this letter, lieutenant.' He emphasised the title, putting scorn into his voice.

The officer took the letter while his men stood silently, watching. Pursing his lips, he frowned. Obviously, this damned Britisher had a great deal of influence if he carried such a letter from a regional Governor. 'Stop what you're doing,' he ordered. Standing up straight he threw a salute to Richard. '*Min fadlak*, my apologies. You may proceed.'

Magnanimous in victory, Richard thanked the lieutenant warmly. Climbing back into the Land Rover, he was aware of an argument going on between one of the armed civilians and the officer. The civilian held up a piece of brown paper that Richard recognised as the type used to wrap plastic explosives in. How in hell had he been so careless? He put the gears into first and got out of there. In the mirror he saw the man was still looking his way.

Passing the taxi and bus stations, Richard crossed over the Oued Gabès and drove along the P19. He swallowed more painkillers and continually sipped at the cans of drink. Aware that he was running on adrenaline and close to collapse, his relief at seeing a sign for Sfax airport 20kms away was tremendous. He was nearly back at *The Lady Ellen*.

He entered the harbour. Unusually for the time of year, a thunderstorm was brewing and as he pulled up at the boat the heavens opened and rain began to fall. Richard sat for a few seconds looking at the boat, summoning the energy to get out.

His young watchman was standing under the awning looking solemnly at him. From somewhere Richard summoned the energy to smile at the boy. It was time to make a move in spite of the downpour.

He climbed down, locked the car and shuffled across to *The Lady Ellen*. He asked Javod if he was all right, received a nod and stumbled below. Taking another handful of painkillers, he staggered into his bedroom and passed out on the bed. He slept the remainder of the day and into the evening. It was midnight when he finally awoke. His head was throbbing, his body was stiff and his mouth tasted like the bottom of the proverbial birds' cage.

Getting groggily to his feet, Richard used the heads, brushed his teeth and swallowed yet more painkillers. Luxuriating under a hot shower, wasting water, he washed away the last couple of days of hardship and fear. The wound opened up again but by now it was merely an oozing trickle of blood down his front. He put on a new dressing, T-shirt and shorts and went into the galley to make a sandwich. With cheese, bread and a handful of olives inside him he felt his strength returning. A mug of coffee also helped. It was, he figured, time to leave.

He'd go first thing in the morning. Switching off the lights he realised that the rain had stopped and that the moon was rising. He felt the boat move as though a wave had washed against her hull and heard a thud from up on deck. His heart racing he moved forward, towards the bows, wishing he'd collected the gun from the Land Rover.

Above his head he could hear feet scuffling along the deck. Opening the door to the cabin where he kept his diving gear he found a diver's knife which he quickly strapped to his bare leg. He grabbed a spear gun, checked the compressed air pressure and fitted a bolt.

Silently he went to the forward hatch, unclipped it and eased it up a fraction. In the shadows he could see a figure lying on the deck and realised it was Javod. He was crumpled over in an unnatural position. There was a sound at the stern like someone moving but the bows seemed as silent as the grave. Pushing the hatch further up he slid over the combing, closing it silently behind him. He checked the boy, relieved to find a pulse, although the poor lad was deeply unconscious. Anger replaced the fear he had been feeling. The way to the Land Rover was clear and he was about to take it when he stopped with a stifled groan. He didn't have the bloody keys!

He could smash the side window, open the bonnet, rip off the top of the washer bottle and grab the gun. He could then unwrap it, put a bullet up the spout and shoot the men who had climbed onto *The Lady Ellen*. As long as they were prepared to give him at least five minutes and ignore the car alarm system that would be making enough noise to wake the dead.

Instead, he would grab the kid and hide. Reaching for the boy he swung him over his shoulder. He weighed hardly anything and Richard quickly crossed the deck to the guard-rail. Climbing onto the top of the rail he stepped down onto the quay. He was halfway to the Land Rover when a man stepped out from behind it, pointing a gun.

Richard couldn't understand the words but the jerking of the gun indicated that he wanted him to raise his hands. Richard was holding the spear gun alongside his right leg. The man was less than fifteen feet away.

'What?'

The man jerked the gun up again, just as Richard hoped he would. He didn't hesitate. He swung the spear gun up and, with less noise than a silenced revolver, fired the weapon. The spear hit the man in the chest and drove him back against the wall behind him, the shaft of the spear sticking out of his back. The man threw his arms wide, dropping his gun. He looked down at the shaft, looked back at Richard and collapsed to the ground.

Richard's first thought was *Christ, who have I killed?* If it was a local policeman he was in far more trouble than it was possible to imagine. Now he really needed to get the hell out of there. He looked over his shoulder, whoever was on the boat hadn't heard anything.

Placing the boy gently on the ground behind the car, he took a closer look at the corpse. Richard gave a tentative pull on the spear, but it wasn't going to budge. The flesh had tightened around the shaft and he would never get it past its triangular head. Where was the gun? He couldn't see it anywhere until he checked under the Land Rover. There it was. He scrambled underneath and grabbed the weapon by the barrel.

It was an old-fashioned looking thing. Careful examination showed him the safety catch. It was off. Grabbing the slide on the top of the automatic, he pulled it back. A cartridge ejected into the night and he let the slide spring forward. There had already been a bullet in the chamber.

He darted along the quayside until he was well astern of the boat. He approached *The Lady Ellen* keeping below the gunwale, out of sight. How many men were on board? At least two, he was sure. Maybe more.

He sneaked over the side and onto the after deck. Whoever had come on board had used the starboard entrance to the wheelhouse. He could hear somebody moving around below. There was a crash as something was thrown to the deck. A voice suddenly came from up forward, loud in the stillness of the night. It sounded like an oath and a man's head appeared in the bow. He jumped onto the quay and Richard was about to shoot him in the back when something hard pressed into his spine.

The meaning of the words was clear enough. He raised his hands the gun dangling from his right index finger. His mind had gone numb with terror. What in hell could he do? The man standing behind him spoke harshly to his accomplice ashore. The man replied in a loud voice. He had just found the body of their colleague.

A blow to the head sent Richard reeling to the deck. He was on his knees shaking his head when he heard the tinkle of breaking glass and the Land Rover's alarm sounded, activating its flashing orange indicators. All three of them were momentarily distracted, but it was Richard who reacted quickest. Fear gave him an edge. He pushed off the deck ignoring the excruciating pain in his shoulder and launched himself at the man with the gun. Grabbing him around the waist Richard received a second blow to his head. Taking the man with him he went over the side with his arms and legs locked around his assailant. Richard took a deep breath as they plunged into the water. The man struggled frantically in Richard's grasp dropping his gun, desperate to get to the surface. Richard kept driving them down, conserving his air, oblivious to the blows on his back and injured shoulder. The man grabbed Richard's hair and wrenched his head back. Richard ignored everything but the necessity to conserve his air. He could sense the other man was growing feebler. Richard squeezed with every ounce of strength that he could muster and forced the last of the air out of the other man's lungs. Instinct made the man inhale the foul water of the harbour. Suddenly he went limp and Richard let him go. Although his chest was burning, he kept his wits about him, swimming underneath the hull to surface by the wall, gasping in air. He knew there was a set of steps about ten yards away and swam silently towards them.

When he reached them, he began to crawl up the slime-covered, concrete steps. The alarm was still going on the Land Rover, but somehow the sound was fading in and out. His wounds had opened up again and he was losing blood. One thought was uppermost in his mind. There was still another one of the bastards to deal with and somehow he had to find the strength to do so.

Before he reached the quay he drew his diver's knife. Lurching towards the Land Rover, with its flashing lights and baying alarm, he searched for the man. A sudden movement on the boat caught his eye and he saw the man straighten up and look at him. He had been searching the water for his friend. With a snarl, the man leapt onto the quay and pointed his gun at Richard. He shouted something that Richard didn't understand. If he was telling him to raise his hands that was too bad. Richard didn't have the strength. The man came towards him and stopped three paces away. This time he spoke in French, apparently telling Richard to prepare to die.

A shadow passed between the car and the flashing lights, distracting the man. This was Richard's one and only chance but before he could act the shadow hardened into a body and a heavy piece of metal smashed down across the gunman's arm. The cracking of the bone was unmistakable in the still night. The man screamed in pain, dropped the gun and turning, he blundered away in a shuffling run.

Richard knew he was dying because from far away he could hear Victoria's voice calling his name.

He awoke lying in the master bedroom. Groggy beyond belief, he tried to sit up. Cool hands pushed him down.

'Stay where you are.'

'Victoria?' he croaked.

Her beautiful face peered down at him and she smiled. 'Hi.'

He looked up at her, her blonde hair framing her wide mouth, the small scar an invitation to be kissed. Memory returned. Christ, they had to get out of there. He tried to sit up again but she pushed him back. 'Lay still or you'll open your wounds again. You need to rest.'

He groaned. 'No time for that now. We need to set sail before the police arrive.'

'Too late, Richard. There's a police guard on the boat and a senior officer will be here to interview you shortly.'

'Jesus wept.' He groaned again. 'Get me some water, will you? And tell me what's happened.'

'I think you're the one who needs to be forthcoming with the explanations.'

'All in good time. Please, some water and some painkillers.'

Victoria helped him to sit up and swallow them. Leaning back wearily, he said, 'What's happening? What the hell are you doing here?'

'Well, the last part is easy. After you dumped me ashore on Malta . . .' Ignoring his interruption she continued, raising a hand to reject his protests. 'Yes, dumped, I was really angry. I've never felt so angry in my life. I decided to head straight back to the States and put you down as history. But I changed my mind. I knew I wanted to see you again and it would be stupid to let my pride get in the way. And anyway, I was curious. I had an itching desire to know what you were up to, so I decided to scratch it.'

He grinned at the fierce scowl on her face. 'Best decision you ever made,' he croaked. 'But how did you know where I was?'

'I'm not stupid. I saw the chart. I knew where you were likely to be and more or less when.'

Richard smiled.

'It took me a few days to sort out my passport and to get some money wired to me. Then the detective work began. There were only certain places you could be so I rang the harbour masters in a few of the ports, starting with Tabarka. Sfax was the fourth place I tried. And bingo, there you were. That was two days ago.'

'What took you so long to get here?'

'I changed my mind. Pride reared its ugly head and I had second thoughts.' She shrugged. 'But then I thought, what the hell. I've located you so I may as well find out what you were up to. I had nothing better to do for a few days.' Her concerned smile belied her words.

He reached for her hand, giving it a gentle squeeze.

'I caught a flight yesterday from Malta to Tunis and a connecting flight to Sfax. It was late departing so I arrived just before midnight. I thought about going to a hotel but I decided to come straight here. I saw *The Lady Ellen* from the other side of the harbour. I was literally walking around when I saw those men attacking you. I ran as quickly as I could and when I got here I saw the body.' Victoria's voice caught and she paused for a second. 'And then I saw the little boy lying unconscious. I didn't have a clue what was going on. I just felt sure you were in trouble. I smashed the Land Rover's window to distract those men. You went over the side and the other man jumped back onto the boat to look for you. You were submerged so long I was sure you were dead.' Victoria paused. 'Then suddenly you appeared crawling up the steps. I saw the man pointing his gun at you. I had picked up a piece of iron piping to protect myself and instead used it to hit him across the arm. Do you remember him running away?'

Richard nodded. 'It's all coming back to me now.'

'I disconnected the battery in the Land Rover and stopped the lights and horn before I dragged you back here. Getting you on board took some doing, believe me. I'd only just done so when the police arrived with their ruddy lights flashing and horns blaring. I was absolutely petrified. I told them that you had been attacked. They took the boy to hospital and the bodies to the morgue. I also told them about the one who'd run away.'

'What did they say?'

'They've posted guards and warned me to tell you to stay put. The Chief of Police is coming back to talk to you.'

Richard groaned. 'What a sodding mess.'

'You got that right, buster. So what's going on?'

'I'll tell you later. We need to get away.'

'No, what you need to do is start thinking straight. Forget getting off the boat. Right now there are two armed policemen sitting in the wheelhouse. We aren't going anywhere. Use what few brains you've still got left to come up with a credible story. Are you any good at making up fairy tales?'

He lay back with a groan and closed his eyes. One thing was certain, he couldn't tell the truth. Victoria fed him yet more painkillers and cooked a Spanish omelette. She cut up his food while he fed himself one handed.

'Okay, here's what we'll do. You stay with the absolute truth. Tell them we had a row in Malta and you walked off. That you changed your mind and came here looking for me. All right?'

Victoria shrugged. 'Sure. That's no problem. What about you?'

'I'll plead total ignorance. I have no idea why they attacked me. I'll surmise they were crooks trying to rob me and stick with the truth about the attack itself. After all, I can prove that they were armed and I wasn't.'

After a few seconds Victoria said, 'I think it would be a good idea to have a lawyer with you. Just in case. The Chief of Police thought so too.'

Alarmed, Richard asked, 'Did he say why I needed one?'

'No. Just that it would be a good idea.'

'In that case, I'd better take his advice. What time is it?'

She looked at her watch. 'Coming up to six o'clock.'

'Okay, wait until nine and contact the Governor's office. His phone number is on the table. Ask if he can recommend someone. Suggest that I'd like to keep it in the family, so to speak.'

'In the family?'

'Have you ever heard of a politician who didn't have a tame lawyer in tow?'

'Cynical point taken.'

'Any news about the boy?'

'No. I'll try and find out. Why don't you get some sleep? You look dreadful.'

Richard managed a weak smile and a nod before he drifted off again. When he next awoke, he was alone. A glance at the bedside clock showed it was a few minutes after 09.30. He struggled out of bed and began to dress.

Victoria heard him and entered the cabin. 'How are you feeling?'

'Like hell. How's the boy?'

'Virtually recovered. He's a tough mite. He's been insisting that he return to the boat. I think he feels bad he didn't guard you better.'

'Tell him from me he did a great job but his services are no longer required. Give him a hundred dollars bonus and my gratitude. That should make up for the headache

he suffered. On second thoughts, make that two hundred.
There's a few hundred dollars hidden at the back of the
cutlery drawer. Any news about a lawyer?'

'Yes. I spoke to the Governor. He's sending someone.
Also, the Chief of Police is his cousin.'

'Ah! Good! I think. Thanks for your help. Especially
last night. And thanks for contacting the Governor. I'm
sorry to put you to so much trouble.'

'Don't be stupid. It's no trouble. But I want to know
what's going on. You can tell me later once we get out
of this mess. Okay?'

He nodded without making any commitment. He
wasn't sure if she was ready to hear it.

Mid-morning, the Chief of Police, the advocate, named
Mr. Mustapha, Richard and Victoria met in the salon. In
impeccable English the Chief of Police introduced
himself, while Mr. Mustapha spoke in heavily accented
English.

'*Monsieur* Griffiths, let us go over your story once
more. These men brutally attacked you, after attacking
the boy. Is that correct?'

Richard nodded.

'One of them shots you here.' Mr. Mustapha points at
his own shoulder. 'You cannot be certain but you think
it was the man who fell into the water with you. I suggest
that you were shot by the man who later died of a spear
gun wound.' There was a rapid exchange in Arabic
between the Chief of Police and the lawyer.

Mr. Mustapha turned to Richard and said in English.
'Self-defence. You were shot and had to defend yourself.'

Richard nodded. If that was what they wanted to hear
then that was what they would hear.

The interview continued. Whenever either the
policeman or the lawyer was unhappy they corrected
Richard's story until it was to the Chief of Police's satisfaction. Finally, they were finished. A stenographer was

waiting outside. He was called down, the story quickly told again, this time without any necessary corrections and the stenographer was dismissed.

The Chief of Police made himself more comfortable, opening his coat and slackening his tie. 'Now we can get down to business. Mr. Griffiths, I do believe the incident was merely one of self-defence. But allow me to tell you a little story. By the way, I would like a large scotch.'

The lawyer asked for fruit juice, Richard wanted water. Victoria stood up to get the drinks.

While they waited, in the silence, Richard asked, 'What happens now?'

'The stenographer will type up your statement and be back within the hour. We shall both sign it and our business will be concluded. Thank you.' He broke off to accept the whisky. 'Cheers.'

'You speak excellent English,' said Richard.

'I was up at Oxford for three years. Now, shall I begin my little story? Two days ago a meeting took place between some Libyans and a Saudi Sheikh. Do you know anything about it?'

Richard shook his head.

'It seems that Colonel Harwazi met with Walid bin Sydal and two Palestinians. Apparently, a gang of terrorists attacked them in the middle of the night. Mortar bombs rained down, killing many of them.'

'Including Harwazi and bin Sydal?'

'Thanks be to *Allah* the glorious leader of Libya was spared.' There was no mistaking the irony in the Police Chief's voice.

'And bin Sydal?'

'Again, *Allah* was merciful.'

'What about the Palestinians?'

If the Police Chief was surprised by the question, he gave no sign. 'One died. Decapitated. The other, by the name of Jalal Chalabi, escaped.'

'I see.' Somehow, Richard managed to keep the disappointment out of his voice. He knew the idiosyncrasies of an explosion. There were hundreds, even thousands of anecdotes about bombs and explosives going off, some killing and maiming, others, as if by a miracle, missing their target. He knew of people who'd had their clothes blown off without sustaining as much as a scratch. At the mine warfare school in Ostende, Belgium, there hung a photograph of a huge Second World War bomb found fifteen years after the war had ended. Sitting on top of the bomb were half a dozen soldiers. For no apparent reason, a second after the picture was taken, the bomb had exploded killing all of the men, including the photographer. Other men standing next to the photographer hadn't even been blown off their feet.

'However, many of those with bin Sydal were killed, as were many of Harwazi's bodyguards and senior aides.' He took a mouthful of whisky. 'The perpetrators escaped and were chased by the Libyans. Further Libyan casualties ensued and a helicopter was shot down, causing more deaths. It was all very tragic. Unfortunately, pressure was brought to bear on my government. My country was coerced into helping our Libyan brothers find the culprits. Not a situation we enjoyed, but we felt that we must show solidarity with our neighbours. May I?' He held up his glass for a refill and Victoria duly obliged. There was another silence while the drink was poured.

'Thank you,' said the Chief of Police. 'At one of the roadblocks, a piece of paper was found in the back of a vehicle. It was identified as wrapping found around PE4, the plastic explosive. How are you enjoying my little tale so far, Mr. Griffiths?'

Richard shrugged. 'Fascinating.'

'It gets better. The vehicle was traced as your Land Rover. Of course, that's impossible, wouldn't you say?'

'Definitely. Somebody made a mistake.'

'Yes, that is my thinking too. The men who attacked you appear to be Libyans, although they were not carrying any identity papers. The man who escaped has not been found and nobody has gone to a doctor or a hospital for treatment.'

Victoria, though listening to the Police Chief, had been looking at Richard. 'How did you identify them as Libyans?' she asked in a low voice.

'We have our methods, Miss Shand. I don't like the Libyans. I do not like dictatorships and I particularly don't like Colonel Harwazi. Further, I do not like the fact that he had the effrontery to meet in my country.'

'Why did he choose Tunisia?' asked Victoria.

'I can answer that,' replied Richard, looking directly at the Police Chief. 'Satellites passing overhead. There is no interest in Tunisia and so they aren't looking here. Bir Zar is an obvious location for a clandestine meeting to take place.'

'Who said anything about Bir Zar?' The Chief of Police smiled, reminding Richard in that instant of a shark that has spotted its prey.

'I thought you did.'

'No matter. But you're right. That is why Bir Zar was chosen. An interesting tale, don't you think?'

'Thank you for sharing it with me.'

'It has been my pleasure. I trust you will be leaving Tunisia soon?'

Taking the hint, Richard said, 'I shall be topping up the fuel tanks later today. Will tomorrow be early enough?'

'Yes, that will do fine. In the meantime I shall leave two of my men to watch over things. Even so, I cannot guarantee your safety. We have made it clear to Colonel Harwazi that you are well connected to our local Governor and that you cannot possibly have had anything to do with the attack. That you are an important businessman. He appears to believe us.' The policeman stood up.

Richard struggled to his feet and held out his hand. 'I hope whoever carried out the attack escapes.'

'I hope so, too. But take care. Colonel Harwazi is a

lunatic with periods of lucidity. It makes him a very dangerous man.'

'Thank you for all you have done.'

'You have yet to see your advocate's bill.' He smiled and left the boat.

Victoria saw him off and returned below to see Richard signing a cheque for the lawyer. He thanked the advocate for his help and said goodbye.

'Well that was one hell of a lawyer's bill but worth the price.'

'How much was it?' Victoria asked, pouring herself a glass of red wine.

'A mere bagatelle. Twenty thousand bucks.'

She spilt the wine on the deck.

17

RICHARD LAY IN bed, wide awake, staring up at the overhead bulkhead. The clock showed it was coming up to 03.00. After the Chief of Police had left he had taken more painkillers and gone to bed. He'd woken to drink fruit juice and take yet more pills before going back to sleep. His sleep pattern was shot to hell and now he was wide awake. He was wondering how he was going to explain the Police Chief's story to Victoria. He had known her such a short while, but he desperately wanted to get to know her better. She was the first woman who had made him feel the way Ellen had. Whether or not she could replace Ellen in his affections he wasn't sure, but one thing was certain – it was time he moved on with his life. He was physically exhausted and mentally disturbed by the events that had taken place. Continuing to plot against bin Sydal and Harwazi he now realised was totally unrealistic. He'd almost been killed twice and had a bullet hole to prove it. A few more inches and he'd have been dead. It was a sobering thought.

Wasn't it time to let go? Richard waited for the familiar flames of hate to course through him. He felt nothing. The dawn was breaking when he climbed out of bed and got dressed.

He went up top and nodded to the two policemen sitting in the wheelhouse. Standing at the guard-rail Richard watched the beauty of the sunrise. Suddenly he felt liberated, as if a door had been opened, offering him a glimpse of the future. For the first time since losing his family he felt hopeful. He was going to build a new life and consign the past to where it belonged. He flexed his stiff and sore arm. It was a reminder to how close he had come to dying.

Richard went ashore and tidied up the Land Rover, removing the broken glass and re-attaching the battery. He also recovered the gun from the water bottle and slipped it under his shirt. The two policemen sitting in the wheelhouse ignored him.

Back on *The Lady Ellen* he said to the policemen, 'I am leaving.' He held up a $20 note and the car keys. 'If I give you this will you return the car to the hire place?'

The two men exchanged glances and one of them shrugged. 'Yes, *Monsieur. Merci.*' He took the keys and the money and they left.

Richard started the engine, the noise bringing Victoria to the wheelhouse.

'It's only six o'clock,' she complained.

'I know. I couldn't sleep. Will you make us some coffee while I get us the hell out of here?'

They anchored in a bay off Chergui Island, 15 miles east of Sfax. Richard got out a small barbecue set and prepared to cook pieces of chicken he'd had marinading in home-made sauce all afternoon. With a glass of red wine in his hand he turned the succulent pieces of meat. Victoria sat nearby. Both were aware that they had a good deal to talk about, yet neither seemed ready to begin.

'How's your shoulder?'

'It hurts. But it's mending.'

'Good. Richard, I've been patient long enough. Are you going to tell me what it's all about?'

Shrugging, he looked steadily at her before resuming his aimless turning of the chicken.

'Well?'

'I don't know where to begin.'

'Did you do what the Chief of Police said you did? I mean, are you some sort of terrorist or a homicidal monster? Richard, I know we've only known each other a short while but I can't believe that I misjudged you that badly.'

Still he said nothing, much to her exasperation.

'Listen, Richard, if you can't trust me then whatever is going on between us is over before it's begun. We can't have a relationship based on lies and deceit. I have to know.'

Richard nodded. She was right, of course. But he had never told anybody the full story before. He wasn't even sure any more what the full story was. All day he had been haunted with the thought that grief had turned his wits. Had he turned into some sort of madman who had lost control? How many of those men he had killed had deserved to die? The reality – the stupidity – of what he'd done, threatened to overwhelm him.

'I want something stronger than a glass of red wine if I'm going to try and explain everything to you.' He went below and helped himself to a single malt whisky, throwing in a couple of ice cubes. Back on deck, he swirled the cubes around in the glass, watching the amber liquid catch the last of the sunlight. It was wonderfully peaceful. There was no wind, the sea was flat calm. He took a sip.

'It began,' he said, 'a couple of years ago. Nearly three, to be precise. It started with a storm in the Gulf of Mexico . . .' While he related the story and the events that had led up to him bombing the encampment, Victoria sat quietly. While he spoke, he sipped his whisky, refilling his glass numerous times. Though he removed the chicken from the barbecue and placed it on plates, they forgot to eat.

Sitting under the awning in the stern, Richard rambled on, sometimes speaking so softly she could hardly hear him, at other times with such animation in his voice that she could see the passion that had driven him. If Victoria was shocked by his account of what he'd done in Tunisia, she didn't show it.

The hardest part was to explain his present conflicting emotions. His whole *raison d'être* for the last few years was a sham; the outcome a Pyrrhic victory. Speaking in a way he had never been able to before, he peeled back the layers of his soul. She listened quietly as he revealed his pain and confusion, his fear of letting someone become close again. Perhaps, he told her, this was the biggest fear of all. With gentle wisdom she took him in her arms.

That night they became lovers.

Richard was recovering quickly, his natural fitness and stamina helping his body to heal. When the scabs on his shoulder began to itch he started taking exercise and went swimming. There was something particularly sensuous in diving overboard into the deep blue sea and swimming naked around the boat. The activity always led to further exercise, usually under the awning down aft.

The journey to Gibraltar took over a week. Richard quickly discovered the intelligence behind the beautiful façade that Victoria presented to the world. She proved herself to be more than just another academic working on her PhD. They had many interesting discussions late into the night. They covered topics from politics to religion to war to economics to terrorism – and back again. When they weren't discussing world affairs, they played Scrabble. Usually, Richard lost.

'Remember when we shot down the Iranian Airbus?' Victoria asked.

'I remember.'

'That was an act of incredible barbarism. Unjustifiable.'

'You can't say that. The Iranians violated the airspace around one of America's warships. It was warned off, but it chose to ignore the warning. The ship opened fire, thinking it was under attack.'

'What would be your reaction to the Americans if your family had been on board?'

'I've asked myself the same question many times over

the past few years. The truth is, I would want to have the American captain in my sights and pull the trigger. And if I could sink his ship I'd do that as well. But it can't be denied, the Americans did have a legitimate reason for their actions.'

'Sure, but we're still capable of putting a spin on the story. Ask yourself this. If you were an Iranian would you believe the Americans?'

'As an Iranian I wouldn't believe my own government, so why would I believe the Great Satan?'

'Exactly. It just keeps going round and round. I hit you, you hit me. I kill one of yours, you kill two of mine. It's a circle. A circle of revenge that has to be broken.'

He acknowledged this last parry in the cut and thrust of their discussion with a grim nod. Looking at her, her hair freshly braided after their swim, the soft colours of the late afternoon reflected in her eyes, he smiled. 'Well, for my part, it's time for me to step out of the vicious circle.'

Victoria spoke carefully, searching for the right phrase. 'Life does move on for those who let it.' She smiled in return and then changed the subject back to something they had been discussing earlier. 'I still disagree with you about our politicians. They have to deal with a grave new crisis practically every day. As each one passes, they get on with the next. They have to be pragmatic. Does that make any sense?'

Richard sighed. 'Political point scoring and ancient rivalries. Despite everything, I even have sympathy for the Palestinians. Did you know that there are Palestinians living in refugee camps still with the keys to their houses in their pockets? Houses that are now occupied by the Israelis? Most of them are more sinned against than sinners. Except HAMAS. Those evil swine need wiping off the face of the earth.'

'But Richard Griffiths will no longer be the one to do it?'

He smiled ruefully. 'Count me out. I've done enough.

Besides,' he smiled, pulling her to him, 'I've decided that I prefer the snap of your bikini elastic to the snap of a body bag.'

In Gibraltar they stocked up with food and drink, filled up the diesel tanks and topped off the water. The weather forecast was for fine weather and the following day Richard decided it was time to hit the Atlantic. They had a run of 800 nautical miles to A Coruña in Northern Spain. On the afternoon of the third day they reached their destination. Life on board had settled into one of a relaxed and enjoyable routine. They shared the watch at night and dozed during the day. The radar alarm only buzzed a few times and they watched as merchant ships further offshore passed them by.

It wasn't until they were half way across the Bay of Biscay that the weather broke. In the early hours of the morning a sudden storm swept in from the west and quickly turned a flat calm sea into a state 5 with waves as high as twelve and fourteen feet. *The Lady Ellen* rocked badly and a few dishes were broken but she rode the weather like the thoroughbred she was. Richard eased her back to 8 knots while the storm lasted. It passed as quickly as it had arisen and the sea settled down to an uneasy choppiness that lasted into the afternoon. At sunset the sea returned to flat calm and Richard increased their speed to 14 knots. The following afternoon they saw Lizard Point in Cornwall painting in the top left hand corner of the radar. Altering course to starboard they headed straight for the Isle of Wight.

Wistfulness settled over them as they realised that they were coming to the end of their voyage and that real life was about to intrude once more. They had not talked about the future but Richard was beginning to dwell on it.

From time to time unwelcome thoughts intruded. He wondered what Chalabi had been doing at Bir Zar. What were they plotting? It had to be something, as why would they meet there? Whatever the reason for it one thing he had learnt. He was ill equipped to deal with men such as them. He had been lucky. The itch in his shoulder was a reminder of how lucky he'd been. Now the future beckoned. It was over. Finished.

Victoria appeared from the galley with a mug of soup. Richard was sitting in the chair on the starboard side of the wheelhouse, watching as the lighthouse at The Needles took shape in the distance. It was a pleasant summer's day and quite a number of sails could be seen ploughing through the Channel.

Placing the mug in the holder in front of him, she smiled quizzically and said, 'Penny for them.'

Putting his arm around her waist he drew her to him. 'I was thinking of the future.'

'Big subject. Any particular area?'

He looked up at her and smiled. 'You. Me. Us.'

'Contrary to popular belief, not all women are looking for a good man to settle down with and raise a family.'

'They're not?' He spoke with a mixture of mock surprise and horror.

'Idiot.' Victoria thumped his arm, none too gently.

'Hey! Watch my shoulder.'

'That's the other side. And don't change the subject. What were you saying about futures?'

He floundered momentarily, unsure how to go on. It was suddenly very important to him to say the right thing. He found refuge in humour. 'If you won't settle down with a good man, then how about a bad one?'

'We'll see,' was the enigmatic reply. 'Let's take our time. It's one thing to get to know each other during a cruise and quite another to live together in real life.'

'Do you think you'll miss being in the midst of heroin smuggling, sinking boats, terrorists, explosions, saving my worthless hide?'

'That's my worry. With you, there'll never be a dull moment.' Her smile took the sting out of her words. 'Let's give it time,' she repeated.

Relieved, he nodded. It was the response he had been hoping for.

They berthed at the boatyard and were welcomed back by Vic and Matt. Richard had decided to move into a marina where he and Victoria would have access to more facilities such as shops and restaurants. He made the necessary arrangements with Ocean Village Marina, Southampton. When he broke the news to the two brothers they looked decidedly relieved. They had been looking for a way to tell him that they had been made an offer for the yard, one they couldn't refuse. It was, they said, time to retire.

When he steered *The Lady Ellen* from the yard for the last time it was with a good deal of regret. For the next few weeks life settled down to a quiet routine. Victoria enrolled successfully in a PhD course, supervised by a lecturer at Southampton University. Richard immersed himself in his work happier than he had been since Ellen and the children had died.

Finally, he made up his mind and over dinner one night asked, 'Will you marry me?'

Simms knocked and waited until he heard an abrupt, 'Enter.' He wondered again why he had been called back from his duties at the embassy.

Opening the door, he stepped into the room and closed it quietly behind him. If he was in any way perturbed he didn't show it. He had been passed over for promotion to lieutenant colonel so there was not a great deal they could do to him.

'You sent for me, sir?' He stood at ease, gazing at the grey haired man sitting behind the desk. The return look was frosty, tainted by what, to a more perceptive man, would have seemed like hatred.

A piece of paper was thrust towards him. 'Sign this and go.'

'What is it?' Simms frowned, a puzzled expression on his face, as he took the paper.

He began to read – Sir, I have the honour to request that my resignation be accepted forthwith – 'What the hell is this?' Simms demanded.

'Your resignation,' came the blunt reply.

'But I've no intention of resigning.'

'Indeed you do, Major Simms. Otherwise I'll have you court-martialled.'

'On what charge?' he blustered.

The Colonel bit back the retort that had sprung to his lips. 'Embezzlement of mess funds in excess of ten thousand pounds. It's been audited twice, checked three times. We know how you did it and where. We have a confession from the suppliers. They have been invoicing us for wines we have not received over a period of nearly two years. You split the profits. They were so grateful for our agreement not to press charges that they gave us your name and that of the wine steward. He's been sacked. You may resign.'

'But . . .'

'Silence,' the Colonel said loudly. 'You're a disgrace to your uniform. You sold your honour for a pittance. You have dishonoured the regiment and yourself. The only reason I don't have you court-martialled is to avoid a scandal for the Black Watch. Be thankful you can leave with your pension. Now sign it and get out.'

'But sir, it's a tissue of lies.' Simms was mustering his arguments ready to fight for his career. He wouldn't go quietly, that was sure.

'Major Simms,' thundered the Colonel. 'Damn it, man! We know! We have signed affidavits detailing every rotten transaction. The money you stole barely covered your mess bill. Even as a crook you're small minded and ineffectual. Now sign it and get out. If you are still on the premises in one hour I'll have you arrested.'

Simms was about to protest again but one look at the Colonel's face and he knew better. Picking a pen up from the desk he scrawled his signature. 'Here,' he said bitterly, 'you've wanted me out of the regiment for a long time.'

'I've never trusted you, Simms. I've never been able to put my finger on it but there's something about you that's rotten. Now get out. Inform the Paymaster by letter where you want your pension sent to.'

The Colonel watched as Simms left. Good riddance to bad rubbish. He comforted himself with the notion that Simms would come to a bad end one day.

Outside, Simms was shaking with rage and self-pity. Then he thought it through. He'd get his pension and his lump sum. He'd be all right for a year at least. He had time to get himself organised. Suddenly, he grinned. He knew just the man who would appreciate his talents.

18

'How do you do, Mrs. Shand?' Richard shook his future mother-in-law's hand. They had just arrived at the home of Victoria's parents.

'Oh, do call me Joyce. And this is Bill.' Victoria got her looks and her colouring from her mother. Richard guessed that she was in her mid fifties but looked a lot younger.

'How do you do, sir?' They shook hands. He was a few inches shorter than Richard, dark haired with a touch of grey at the sides. His handshake was firm and dry and he seemed genuinely pleased to meet Richard.

'Welcome to the family, son,' he said.

'Thank you, sir, that's very kind.'

'Don't call me sir, call me Bill. I'm delighted somebody has finally thrown a line around my girl and is putting his brand on her.'

Richard was thrown for a second but nodded.

'Come, Richard,' said Joyce taking him by the arm, 'you must tell me all about yourself.'

She led him away, around the side of the house, leaving Victoria and Bill to follow. He just caught Bill saying, 'Seems a nice enough fellow. A bit old, though.'

'Dad! There are only eight years between us. He makes me very . . .'

He didn't catch the rest of it as he answered another of Joyce's subtle questions about his family.

The Shand home was in La Jolla, a pleasant suburb of San Diego, California. It was early evening, a barbecue was fired up and a glass of excellent local red wine was thrust into Richard's hand. Bill was busy cooking while Joyce and Richard sat comfortably in chairs on the wide porch. Victoria stood close to her father, casting furtive eyes at Richard, a smile hovering around her mouth. By the time he was drinking his second glass Richard felt as though he had been through the Spanish Inquisition. Joyce knew just about the entire history of the Griffiths dynasty.

As Victoria's father approached the porch with a platter full of meat, his wife said, 'My, Bill, did you know that Richard has an Earl and a knight in his family?'

'Actually,' Victoria corrected her mother, 'two knights and a dame. That's enough, mother, you've been asking Richard too many questions about his family.'

'But,' Joyce began to protest but her daughter shook her head at her.

'Mom, you'll meet his family when they get here next week.'

'But where can they stay? They'll be used to castles and things. Oh my, Victoria, what have you gotten yourself into?'

'Don't mind my wife,' said Bill, 'but after the last time, she's very protective of our only child. Please, help yourself to some food.'

'Yes, do,' said Joyce. 'I hope you like barbecued steak.'

'I love it.' Richard forked a succulent piece of meat and added, 'Please be assured that I love Victoria very much and wouldn't do anything to hurt her. I'll give her the best life I can.'

Bill Shand nodded, looking intently at Richard, liking what he saw. 'I think you will too. A man can't ask more than that for his daughter. Here, let me top you up.' He picked up the wine bottle.

Richard held out his glass, saying, 'This is a nice place.'

Now it was time for Richard to get the Shand family story. The house was wooden colonial and was part of

Bill Shand's sinecure with the University of California, where he was the Head of the Archaeology Department. Here, Richard realised, was the root of Victoria's love of antiquity. Bill's job required him to give twenty hours of lectures a week. The rest of the time he spent writing books on the subject. He'd had two best sellers that had made the Shand family comfortable but not rich. They employed a Mexican woman to cook and clean. Otherwise the four-bedroom house would have been too much for Joyce. Being the wife of a professor who was also the Dean of his Faculty she had duties to perform and was often busy around the university. That semester she had involved herself with the dramatics society. They were putting on a Neil Simon play.

The patio overlooked a small wood and behind it were the campus grounds. In the distance some of the beautiful buildings of the university could be seen.

When they'd finished eating, the women cleared away the table.

Bill asked, 'Will you stay with the wine or would you prefer something stronger?'

'No, thanks, wine is okay with me.'

It was very pleasant sitting in the evening sun, a sharp contrast to the early spring weather back in Britain.

When Victoria and her mother rejoined them they were arguing. 'I'm sure Richard will agree, won't you?' Joyce said to him.

'About what?'

Victoria stood behind her mother shaking her head and mouthing NO.

'About the fact that you should stay in a hotel until the wedding. It will be so much nicer for you both on the big day.'

Richard didn't understand what she meant by that, nor did he want to find out. He merely nodded and said, 'Why, of course. I don't see that as being a problem.'

Victoria glowered at him and turned her scowl to a

smile when her mother turned triumphantly to her daughter. 'You see! I told you Richard wouldn't mind. You were fussing for nothing. Now all we need to do is to find a suitable hotel.'

'That won't be necessary,' said Richard. 'I've already booked a room at the Hotel del Coronado. I've always wanted to see the place where they filmed *Some Like It Hot.*'

He wasn't sure who looked the most surprised, Victoria or her mother.

'The Coronado?' said Joyce. 'My, how very nice. And how very thoughtful of you.'

'Yes, wasn't it,' said Victoria icily. 'Would you like a drink, Mom? A cocktail, perhaps? Instead of the wine?'

'Why yes, dear, that'll be lovely. A weak gin and dry martini. The olives are in the fridge.'

Catching Victoria's gesture with her head, Richard said, 'I'll give you a hand.'

He followed his fiancée into the kitchen. 'Traitor,' she hissed at him. 'Leaving me here alone.'

'If you think for one minute,' he whispered back, 'that I was going to sleep with you in your parents' house then think again.'

'Of course not. We'd have separate bedrooms but I'd be able to sneak along and see you.'

'That's what I figured.' He put his arms around her and gave her a kiss. 'So I removed myself from temptation. Besides, the hotel is much better. You can leave some clothes there and we can spend as much time in the hotel as we like. It's a far more sensible arrangement.'

'I suppose,' she said doubtfully.

'And anyway,' he added, 'you're going to be terribly busy with your mother making all the arrangements, aren't you?'

Victoria giggled. 'Hardly. What do you think she's been doing since the new year? Arranging my wedding or anybody else's come to that, is right up my mother's alley. All we have to do is turn up wearing the right clothes.'

'Sounds about right.' Richard stifled a yawn. 'Actually jet lag is catching up on me.'

'Me too. I tell you what. I'll take you down to the Coronado in Mom's car. We might have time . . .' she left the thought dangling between them.

'Forget it. I need my beauty sleep.'

'Spoilsport.'

The hotel room was large, with two double beds, two comfortable chairs and an occasional table. Lying on the bed together Richard smiled at a rather dishevelled Victoria. 'This is not quite what I had in mind when I suggested you help me to unpack.'

Victoria giggled. 'Perhaps not, but it's exactly what I had in mind.' She sighed. 'I'd better go before they send the cops to look for me.'

Richard nodded. Now he was really feeling the jet lag.

The wedding was to be at the church in the university. Without doubt one of the most beautiful cities in the world, San Diego lent itself to the romanticism of a wedding. The forthcoming nuptials, ten days away, were headlines in the "future events" section of The San Diego Union-Tribune.

It was sheer co-incidence – but then, events great and small often occurred because of it – ex-major Simms was in San Diego, enjoying his early retirement. He was finishing his breakfast, lingering over a final cup of coffee, idly looking through the newspaper when he saw the photograph of the happy couple. He recognised Richard immediately. He couldn't help smiling. He was about to enhance his pension fund quite considerably.

Simms spent the day carrying out a reconnaissance. Once he was satisfied he returned to his hotel where he e-mailed the information, along with the website of the newspaper, to a contact in London. The recipient, in turn, forwarded it to an address in the Gaza strip.

Jalal Chalabi was a fanatic. Nothing was allowed to stand in the way of his objective which was the total annihilation of Israel. He had proven that when he had killed his brother's fiancee, blaming it on Mossad. Now his brother was dead. Killed by an Englishman. One day he would have his revenge. The thought haunted him. Was with him almost every day of his life. But not today. Today he had other work to do. Chalabi had a dream. He dreamt that one day Palestinians would be free. To that end he never stopped planning and with each passing day he thought the time was drawing nearer when he would achieve his ambition.

From the age of eleven onwards many Palestinian children were taken to HAMAS training camps for their weekends, learning to fight and kill their enemies. Abdel had been one of them. Now he was back in his village, near the border with Israel. His parents knew nothing about his mission and although he was unusually quiet and withdrawn that Monday morning, they assumed he was feeling unwell. Assuring them that he was not ill, he picked up his school bag and walked along the dusty street. Abdel wasn't sick, he was scared. He had heard what the Jews did to terrorists, even young ones. They roasted them alive over a fire and ate their flesh. Tears welled up and he fought against them, wiping his eyes dry. He was honoured and he knew it. To die a martyr was the path to great glory. He had been told so many times.

It was then that he saw the man from the camp. The one who had chosen him.

Chalabi could see that the boy was close to tears. He knew that he had to put some backbone into him if his orders were to be carried out.

'Remember, Abdel, this is a wonderful thing that you

do. You will die revered by everyone and go to paradise. You will kill many filthy Jews and be blessed in the eyes of *Allah*. Your mother and your father will be proud of what you have done.'

The thirteen-year-old straightened his shoulders and nodded acceptance. It was a great thing to die for the cause. He just wished that he did not have to die so soon. He would have liked to do many things. Especially he would have liked to do *it* to a girl. Just once. He'd heard the other boys boasting about doing *it*. He wondered where and when they had found the opportunity but he did not doubt that they had done so. Still, in heaven he would have a continual supply of virgins. It was written in the Koran.

Chalabi, the fearsome and famous HAMAS commander, knelt and gave the boy a hug. 'Go with *Allah*.' He could feel the skinny body trembling in his hands and he wondered if the boy would be able to go through with it. It would be just as well to take precautions.

Abdel nodded and started towards the checkpoint. The plan was simple enough. It had been explained to him that as he was going to school he would not be stopped. He was to take the bus as usual, with the other children, who on this day would all be Jewish. The Palestinians had been warned to keep their children at home. No reason was given – it never was.

When the bus reached the square where the shops were, he was to press the button. *Allah*, he had been told, would bless him for his courage.

Abdel passed through the checkpoint without any problems. There was an irony in the fact that the children were being educated less than a hundred metres apart, Jews at one school, Moslems at another. Apart from academic subjects each group were also taught to hate the other.

The school was 3kms inside what was now occupied territory. As a gesture of goodwill, the Palestinian children were allowed to travel to a school they had used in the past for decades. The Israelis considered it magnanimous of them to allow it.

Abdel dragged his feet to the bus stop. The morning was cool but a bead of sweat suddenly broke out on his brow. He stood near the other children, saying nothing. The Israeli boys and girls, ranging in age from ten to sixteen laughed and joked while they waited for the bus. They ignored the small Palestinian boy standing alone.

The bus appeared and the children surged forward. At that moment Abdel's nerve broke and he turned to run. He had taken three paces before a bullet hit him in his skinny chest flinging him backwards. A second bullet hit his school bag and it exploded.

As usual, Jalal Chalabi had left nothing to chance.

The children at the bus stop were flung to the ground, many hurt, two killed outright. The windows in the bus were blown out but by some miracle none of the children on the bus were killed.

Two Palestinian sisters, whose parents had not received the message not to send their children to school, were sitting in the front seat. They were wounded. Within minutes, the emergency services arrived with the police right behind them. Ambulances rushed the two girls, along with the other wounded, to an Israeli hospital. There, two Jewish doctors fought to save the sight of one little girl and the arm of the other. Both operations were successful. When their parents came to collect them there were tears of joy, but no thanks. The hatred was too deep even when acts of kindness were performed.

The Israelis responded to the shooting by blowing up a nearby house they were convinced the shots had been fired from. The occupiers of the house had denied it but they had been told by HAMAS what would happen if they said anything else.

Abdel's parents were utterly grief stricken in private,

forced to be proud of their son in public. The Palestinian anger and hatred, as always, was directed at Israel.

Chalabi was at his home, a squalid building, with a small kitchen and public room downstairs, two small bedrooms and a shower room with toilet upstairs. The water supply was intermittent at best and like food, always in short supply. He sat in the shade outside his door. All morning men came to talk to him, reporting on events across the country, as well as other parts of the Middle East. Support for the Palestinians was as great as ever.

His thoughts once more turned to his brother. Sorrow and thirst for revenge, always there, ready to blossom in his breast, did so now. At that moment, his laptop pinged. Reluctantly he went inside. He noticed the e-mail was dated 3 days earlier. It had only just arrived because the electricity had been cut off as part of Israel's reaction to the bombing. As always, the violence continued round and round, stoking up hatred on both sides.

He read the e-mail. It had come sooner than he had expected, sooner than he'd wished. But it had come. There was even an offer of a plan of operation from the good major. One that Chalabi could implement. He would arrange payment to Simms in the next twenty-four hours. The money had been well earned. Looking at the picture of Victoria, a fresh wave of hatred seethed through him so virulently that he shook. He e-mailed back his response.

Richard spent the week being a tourist. Victoria was justly proud of the city she had been born in and took great pleasure in showing him around. She took him to the famous Presidio Hill, where on 16th July 1769 California began when Father Junípero Serra conducted a mass, dedicating the Mission San Diega de Alcalá. The sprawling park at Presidio Hill proved to be an oasis of peace in a sea of traffic flowing north on I5 and west on I8.

At the bottom of the Hill was the six-block area known as Old Town. Here there were old adobes and restored Victorian houses incorporating shops, museums and many bars and restaurants. They ate there on numerous occasions. They visited Sea World in the Mission Bay area where parkland, beaches and inner lagoons allowed for extensive outdoor leisure pursuits. It was a wonderfully happy and relaxing time for them both.

'I don't think I've ever been anywhere,' said Richard, 'that was so ... so pleasant. It's the only word. Perhaps Geneva but I wouldn't bet on it. This really is a wonderful city.'

'Don't be fooled,' said Victoria. 'Like all American cities it has its underbelly of crime. We have a huge drug problem with cocaine from South America coming over the Mexican border. And turf wars are always breaking out between the gangs. I haven't shown you the squalid areas we call downtown. If I did you might change your mind. On the whole though, it is a wonderful place to live. The city is lovely in the right places and the weather is usually glorious. But we have massive problems of deprivation that are hidden most of the time. And the amount of violence is horrific. We have more gun related deaths in this city in one year than you have in the whole of the UK. Paradise has its fair share of serpents.' Changing the subject, she asked, 'When are your family starting to arrive?'

'In a few more days. We've practically taken over the Coronado. I'm surprised and delighted how many of them are coming, but then the Griffiths clan are a gregarious lot who enjoy a good party.'

Chalabi arranged to meet the leader of HAMAS. He explained what he wanted and was given the assurance that all arrangements would be met. Twenty-four hours later he got the message. The FATAH delegation didn't like it, but he would be added to the list of those going to the UN.

'How did you do it?'

'I told that buffoon Kaddoumi,' he was referring to the leader of FATAH, 'that as we are the government then we had the right to have a representative along. He argued that it was a FATAH initiative, not HAMAS but, let us say, I persuaded him.'

Chalabi had no need to ask what threats were made. It was ever thus in the Gaza Strip.

'Are you sure you want to continue with this?'

'It could be my only chance. I must take it. I must avenge Ismael. If I do not, my life will be nothing.'

'Then be careful, my friend.'

'I will. But we know the Americans will honour my diplomatic immunity. Their observance of such idiocy plays into our hands.'

Farouk Kaddoumi, with a small delegation, had arranged to travel to the United Nations to plead for help. They wanted the UN to put pressure on Israel to stop them cutting off their water and electricity supplies whenever they wished. Also to allow more food into the country. It was little enough to ask for. Of course, the hidden agenda was that if the FATAH party could achieve their objectives, then at the next election they would have a better chance of regaining power. It was an outcome the West desired. Hence their co-operation. The indications were that Israel would agree to it as they also preferred to deal with FATAH. The necessity to go through the UN was for domestic Israeli consumption. Right-wingers and Jewish fundamentalists wanted to clear the holy land for their use.

'There is another advantage if you succeed.'

Chalabi smiled. 'I know. If we let the West know what we have done, using the delegation as cover, then the agreement will be torn up.'

His leader nodded. 'Precisely.'

Just like in Israel, the Palestinians were split when it came to doing a deal with their enemy. In public HAMAS was forced to accept what FATAH was attempting, in private they were virulently opposed.

As it had been for centuries, nothing was simple when it came to the Middle East.

Chalabi decided who would go with him. Afez Nidal, Abdullah Bashar and Hosni Farid were all made from the same mould. All three were of average height and weight, sported designer stubble, had bad teeth and smoked incessantly. Nidal and Bashar had been responsible for many of the acts of violence committed against Israel in the past decade and had been with Chalabi when they had planned the explosion on the British Airways plane. Farid was a relative newcomer to HAMAS.

'You will shave,' ordered Chalabi, 'and you will buy new clothes in Damascus. You will be travelling on Syrian passports. In San Diego you will contact our people there. They will arrange weapons. Remember, we are not only getting our revenge for the cowardly attack by this man on our comrades but we will be paid a great deal of money for doing so. That money will be used against Israel.'

All three were excited by the prospect of going to America. It may have been the great Satan, but it was so full of riches, so opulent, that they knew it would be a wonder to see.

Their journey to Damascus was straight forward. There they bought western style suits, shirts and ties. Their transformation into businessmen was amazing, as they each admired themselves, staring at their reflections in a mirror. They travelled separately to the airport, each man ignoring the others. If any one of them were recognised, stopped and arrested the others could continue with the plan. Their flight to London was uneventful. Because they were catching a connecting flight they had no need to pass through immigration and passport control a second time.

Due to strong head winds, the Virgin Airways flight arrived at Los Angeles International Airport 30 minutes behind schedule. Now was the time of maximum danger. At passport control they were each questioned closely. Their answers must have satisfied the immigration officers as they had their passports stamped and were allowed through.

It was left to Nidal to present his passport and driving licence at the Hertz counter. It only took minutes to complete the paperwork and be told where to collect the Ford Explorer 4X4. While he did so, the other two took taxis into the city, still travelling separately. They were dropped at the railway station. Nidal arrived an hour later, picked them up and then headed south towards San Diego.

'There is so much here. Look at the cars. Look how well fed the people are.' Abdullah Bashar voiced the age old Palestinian lament for the unfairness of it.

Afez Nidal added bitterly, 'And we have so little.'

'Yes, but that's true of many other countries,' argued Hosni Farid. 'Look at the wealth in Saudi Arabia and Kuwait. Our people work there as servants to send home a pittance to feed us.'

'Perhaps, but they are Moslems. These are infidels.' Nidal's argument was illogical but common throughout his part of the world. 'We should take it away from them. Then they won't be able to support Israel.' He spoke with emphatic bitterness.

'My friend,' said Bashar, 'that is impossible. America will always be here and will always be strong. Our attempts at hurting them are nothing more than the attacks of a flea against the hide of an elephant.'

They had gone about 40 miles down Interstate 5 when a police car appeared behind them and turned on its flashing red lights. Nidal was driving and for a second he panicked. The car swerved before he regained control and pulled over.

'What do we do?' asked Bashar.

'Keep quiet and let me do the talking,' Nidal said. He opened the window and put his head out, trying to smile. 'Is there something wrong?'

'Kindly keep your hands where I can see them and step out of the car, please sir.' Although he stood with his hand on his gun it was still holstered. With a note-book in his other hand, the deputy sheriff did not strike a menacing pose.

Nidal looked at his friends and said in Arabic, 'We will all get out. If we have to, we'll jump him.'

'And the other one?' asked Farid.

A second deputy was sitting in the car, watching as events unfolded. He did not seem overly concerned.

Bashar continued, 'Just keep calm. It makes no sense that we have come this far. If it was serious, if they knew who we were, there would be many more of them.'

Nidal opened his door and stepped out. The other two did likewise. The deputy stepped back in alarm. 'Stay where you are,' he ordered in a loud voice. Seeing what was happening, his partner quickly climbed out of the car and drew his weapon.

'What is the problem, officer?' asked Nidal nervously.

'We clocked you travelling at 15mph above the speed limit, sir. It is my duty to give you a ticket and a fine.'

Relief flooded through Nidal and he smiled. 'I am so sorry, officer. Where I come from the speed limit is much higher. I simply wasn't paying any attention.'

'And where might that be, sir?'

'Syria. We are Syrian businessmen. We came to America to discuss opening a McDonald's burger bar in my country. The first of many, we hope. Our meeting is next week and we thought we would spend a few days here on your famous West Coast. To see all the beautiful sights. I am very, very sorry.'

The words soothed the deputy's nerves and he relaxed. 'In that case, sir, I'll let you off with a caution. Be on your way, but please, keep your speed down.'

'Thank you, thank you. You are very kind.'

They climbed back into the car with alacrity, Nidal waved and quickly pulled away leaving the two deputy sheriffs to resume their patrol. 'Pigs! Filthy rotten pigs! May they rot in hell.'

'Afez, they are not of the true faith. It is inevitable that they will rot in hell,' said Farid, the most devout of them.

The others relaxed and they laughed out loud, the release of tension between them palpable.

'That was an important lesson,' said Bashar. 'We must be vigilant at all times. We are in enemy territory. It was a sign from *Allah*, telling us we must never let our guard down.'

There were murmurs of agreement and Nidal eased his foot off the accelerator although they weren't breaking the speed limit. The deputies' car appeared alongside, the nearest officer gave a friendly wave and the car accelerated quickly away. Nidal managed to wave back.

They stayed on the I5 all the way to San Diego. At a gas station, they filled up, bought cold drinks and a map of the city. Soon, they were at the downtown area and the interchange for Harbour Drive. Shortly after that, they drove onto Market Street and stopped outside the house they had been told to go to. They were approaching the front door when it suddenly opened. A man stood in the doorway. Even through the door mesh they could see he was of Middle Eastern extraction. In his right hand he held an automatic at his side.

'*Allah* be with you,' Nidal began.

'And with you,' came the expected reply.

'It is filthy weather.' It was a beautiful, sunny day.

'May the sun always shine.' With that out of the way the mesh door was opened. 'Please enter. My house is your house,' he used the Islamic greeting. Then he added, 'Here, I am known as Joe Farandi.' He was short, fat and bald. A cigarette hung from the corner of his mouth.

They followed the man through the house and into the kitchen. He wasted no time on the usual hospitality shown to visitors. Instead, he placed the gun next to the sink before he dragged a table across the floor and pushed it against the wall. Kneeling down, he scrabbled at the edge of the oilcloth covering the floor and began to roll it back. Nidal squatted beside him to help.

Underneath was a trapdoor. It was heavy and took both men to pull it open. Reaching under the floor, the man flicked on a light switch to expose a set of wooden stairs. 'Wait a moment.' Farandi lay down and put his head and arms through the opening. Reaching under the top step he fiddled with another switch. 'It is now safe to proceed.' He stood up with a smile.

'What did you just do?' Farid was intrigued.

'Any person who is not invited and who treads on the top step would go no further. Or perhaps I should say, he would take his longest journey ever. To hell.' Farandi chuckled at his own wit and indicated for Farid to lead the way. He declined and Farandi chuckled again before starting down the stairs.

The others followed cautiously. At the bottom of the stairs another light switch was turned on and strip lighting flickered into life. The cellar was a long and narrow room with an aisle stretching down one wall. Along the other wall were racks of weapons, ammunition and explosives. The Palestinians were impressed.

'Where did all this come from?' Nidal asked, wonder in his voice.

'Over many years, my friends, we have been amassing what you see now. There are many such sites all across America, waiting for the day *holy Jihad* is declared. Then we will rise up and kill as many of the infidels as we can.'

The others nodded, awe on their faces.

'I even have a bullet proof vest.'

'We'll take it,' said Nidal.

'Nick, thanks for agreeing to be my best man. I wasn't sure you'd be able to make it.'

'I have an excuse. I'm visiting The Pacific SEAL teams

at Coronado Beach. We've had a couple of requests by some of them to join TIFAT and so I'm going to take this opportunity to meet them. I'll probably work out with them as well.'

Richard smiled. 'Rather you than me. I still remember the mud runs with a twinge of pain.' While on a year's long-course to become a naval diving and explosive specialist Richard had taken part in the notorious exercise. Dressed in a diver's dry suit they would run for miles across thick oozing mud. The effort of pulling feet out of the mud helped to strengthen muscles far more quickly than merely running or jogging. Many divers collapsed from heat stroke and exhaustion during that time of their training. It was the Royal Navy's equivalent of the SEAL's hell week. 'One thing, just remember to keep the jokes clean.'

'You can rely on me,' Hunter grinned.

'For your ears only and please don't make any innuendoes or obscure references to the fact, but Victoria is pregnant.'

Hunter's smile broadened. 'That's great news, Richard. Congratulations. I couldn't be happier for you.'

'Thanks.'

'How far gone is she?'

'About two months, she thinks. She's going for a check-up after the wedding, so we've delayed our departure to Mauritius by a week.'

Hunter nodded. 'Turning to other matters, I take it you've really stopped looking for revenge over the bombing.'

Richard's smile faded and he nodded. 'I have. Now that I've got Victoria and with a sprog on the way,' he shrugged. 'It's time to move on. Permanently.'

'Good. I know it's not much consolation but we aren't leaving it. TIFAT, that is. If we get the evidence we need, then we'll go after whoever's involved.'

'With all due respect but you won't. Not with Harwazi

trying to rehabilitate himself in the eyes of the world with this United States of Africa business. Even Iran is beginning to come in from the cold. Pragmatism is the order of the day. One man's terrorist is another man's freedom fighter and all that crap. And every other cliché you can think of applies. The West needs to stop bin Sydal but that's about as far as it goes. After that, I suspect the real problems will be with China. And they'll be economic.'

Victoria joined them and as Hunter stood to kiss her cheek he congratulated her on the baby. 'I thought we agreed we wouldn't tell anybody?' she said to Richard in exasperation.

'I haven't,' Richard protested nonsensically, 'only Nick.'

'Less of the only Nick,' Hunter thumped his cousin's shoulder.

They ordered pre-dinner drinks. The wedding was only five days away.

The FBI agent was leaning back in his chair with a cup of hot, freshly poured coffee in his hand. He was idly checking the names of the Palestinian delegation to the United Nations. It was routine, as they would be travelling with diplomatic immunity. Still, it paid to know these things. When he saw the fourth name on the list he suddenly sat forward, spilt coffee onto his lap and said, 'Jesus. Catherine, you'd better see this.'

Special Agent Catherine Demarco crossed the room and peered at the screen. 'Oh boy, I don't believe it. Jalal Chalabi. That scumbag! Are the Palestinians off their cotton-picking heads? This will be a red rag to a bull when the Israelis find out. Christ, our lot aren't going to be too thrilled with it either.'

'What do we do?' Special Agent Tony Carpenter asked, mopping at his lap with a paper tissue.

'We'd better give Zak a heads-up and let him pass it on to the Director. This will have to go all the way.'

Special Agent Zak Zakowski was the bureau chief in charge of the local FBI office. The duties of the FBI had changed over the years as the nature of crime had changed. Originally, the force was created to fight criminals, unhampered by state boundaries. Today, its first task was to protect the USA against terrorism and its second was to stop foreign intelligence operations and espionage.

Checking who came into the country was routine under certain circumstances. For years, the United Nations had used its unique position to bring in people who were at best, undesirable and, at worst, enemies of America. Of course, many of the accredited dignitaries were also enemies of their host country. Which was why the FBI kept an eye on things. On this occasion it was a close eye. They had been tasked with supplying the protection detail sometimes required by UN personnel.

The Palestinians had many friends in the world, but they also had a great number of enemies. They did not have permanent representation at the UN and so a visit by the Palestinians was a rare event. The USA was not prepared to risk anything happening to them whilst they were on American soil. The Secret Service would normally have carried out the protection detail but it was stretched to breaking point due to other commitments and lack of manpower. So on this occasion the task had fallen to the FBI.

There was one oddity when it came to the United Nations. Once they entered the grounds and buildings that comprised the UN, they were no longer technically on American soil and hence no longer subject to American laws and protection. However, whenever they left the UN they were subject to those laws and entitled to protection once more. One of the most irksome tasks the FBI and the Secret Service had was to protect people who were dedicated to the destruction of the American way of life. Be that as it may, being the professionals they were, they got on with the job. The Palestinians had been faxed explicit instructions about what they could and could not do. It was not possible to assign a team of agents to protect each individual and therefore they were to stay together at all times and not just when they wanted to. It was pointed out to them that the strong Jewish community in New York had more than its fair share of people who would like to see them dead. They were also told not to take the warning lightly.

Catherine picked up the phone to her boss. 'Zak? Have you seen the list of Palestinian delegates? No? Then you'd better log on.' She broke the connection and waited. She didn't wait long for a reaction.

The door flew open. 'Are they crazy? Totally one hundred percent nuts?'

'That's more or less what I said,' replied Catherine calmly. 'They must have a reason for bringing him along.'

'Well I can't think of one.' In his agitation Zakowski reached for a cigarette before remembering that, like all government buildings, it was non smoking. Besides which he was trying to quit. He took his empty hand out of his pocket and paced the floor instead. A big, raging bull of a man in his mid thirties, his size concealed a sharp brain.

Catherine Demarco was petite, dark-haired and slim. She wasn't pretty in the conventional sense but her energy and sparkle made all who knew her attracted to her. Zak had been in love with her for about two years but hadn't the courage to tell her or even ask her out.

Agent Tony Carpenter was of average height, average weight and average looks. He could get lost in a crowd of two. This anonymous quality he had used to his advantage on many occasions. He was highly effective and had often made arrests while in disguise and in the damnedest places. Stories about him were legion. Like the time he dressed as a waiter in an Italian restaurant. Presenting a wine list to a Mafia boss he was pointing out a particular vintage even as he was slipping handcuffs on the target. It was rumoured that on another occasion he had dressed like an old beggar woman and got up close to two members of a particularly violent cocaine smuggling gang. He had them lying on the walkway with cuffs on before they knew what was happening. Both crooks had been armed and known to be highly dangerous.

The only good thing about the protection detail the team would be working was that round the clock surveillance wouldn't be necessary. The Palestinians would be going into the UN, allowing the agents plenty of respite. It was still a thankless task that none of the twelve men and women detailed to the job relished.

'I'll pass this to Quantico. The Director will have to take it further. The message has to be loud and clear. This man is not wanted in this country. Period. All right, leave it with me.'

Back in his office Zakowski watched the sun passing behind the corner of 3rd Avenue as he reached for the phone. He called the Director of the FBI, Dr Lou Murray. His reaction was completely predictable. Dr Murray, in his turn, telephoned the White House.

'Sarah?' the Director addressed the National Security Adviser's secretary, 'I need to see him urgently.' He listened a moment. 'I said urgently, Sarah. And when the Director of the Federal Bureau of Investigation asks for an audience he means *now*. It isn't a request, it only sounds like one out of politeness. I'll be coming by helicopter. Thank you.' He replaced the phone, resisting the urge to slam it down.

He was kept waiting for twenty minutes, cooling his heels in an anteroom until Dan Flynn granted him an audience. When he got inside, the National Security Adviser was slipping into a tuxedo jacket.

'Make this quick, Lou, I've got a dinner to go to.'

Murray looked at the overweight, over-bearing NSA and resisted the urge to kick him up the pants. 'We have a problem,' he began.

'Then solve it,' was the sharp reply. Flynn was glaring

at his unwanted guest from the other side of his desk. 'I thought that's what you were paid for.' He sat down in his leather, swivel chair.

Murray leaned on the desk, using his knuckles. 'Don't,' he said, 'tell me what I'm paid to do. I've done this job for five years and I've had no complaints so far. When I come running to you it's because I need political clout that I don't have. Now are you ready for this?'

'Shoot.' Flynn glared at the man from the FBI with loathing. Neither man could help it. There was total antipathy between them for no discernible reason and had been from the day Flynn got into office.

'Farouk Kaddoumi is coming with a delegation of five others for a meeting at the UN.'

'We know that. What's your problem? Surely you've known as long as I have?'

Flynn was being deliberately obtuse and Murray knew it. 'That isn't the problem. One of the men who is coming is Jalal Chalabi.'

'I know.'

'What do you mean, you know?'

'I approved his application. Well, not quite that exactly, but I did indicate that we would have no problem with anybody Kaddoumi brought with him. I seem to remember that we did ask that the delegation did not exceed six people and that request has been complied with.'

Murray stood up from his leaning position and sat down in a chair. 'Have you any idea who Chalabi is?' He didn't add "you idiot" though he was solely tempted.

Flynn shook his head. 'No. Why should I?'

'Did it never occur to you to check the names with us?' He could see from the other's face that it hadn't. 'Chalabi is one of the most wanted terrorists in the Middle East. We are certain he was connected to the BA bombing a few years ago and to the U.S.S. *Cole* attack.'

'The *Cole*?'

'Yes! Do you have any idea what I'm talking about?'

'Of course I do. Don't patronise me, Dr Murray. The *Cole* was blown up while in Aden Harbour in the Yemen. A dozen of our people were killed.'

'Seventeen. Not a dozen.'

'Whatever. These are service men and women who are paid to risk their lives. So what? The Palestinians are here trying to get the UN to get Israel to stop imposing sanctions. It's in everyone's interests. If FATAH were to be re-elected then tensions in the Middle East will doubtless ease. The Israelis can make some concessions, the Palestinians can be brought to heel . . .'

'Yeah and peace and good will breaks out all over.'

'Not that. But it might ease tensions, save lives. You know. The stuff we're both hired to do.'

'You're missing the point, like you always do,' said Murray with feeling. Before the other man could retort he held up his hand. 'I'm not here to bandy words. I haven't got time. I cannot guarantee Chalabi's safety. It's as simple as that. I won't put my agents' lives on the line for this piece of scum. If Chalabi is in New York we'll have Mossad and MI6 to name just two of our allies willing to take him out.'

'Preposterous. They wouldn't dare.'

'Indeed they would. You need to get on the phone and stop Chalabi coming now. Tell them we are withdrawing his diplomatic immunity. Christ! Tell them anything you like. Just stop him.'

'I can't.'

'What do you mean, you can't? Or do you mean, you won't?'

'No, I mean I can't. For a number of reasons. First, it's too late. He's already on his way. Second, the visa has been issued and I can't cancel it and third, I won't embarrass this Administration by making us look like idiots. Anybody would think the right hand doesn't know what the left is doing.'

'That's precisely because it doesn't,' Murray spoke

harshly. 'God Almighty! Right,' he pointed his finger at Flynn, his anger taking him outside the bounds of good manners. 'Here's what you do instead.'

'Don't come in here telling me what to do,' Flynn thundered. 'I've had enough. We should have retired you when we first came into office.'

'Yeah, well you didn't and you missed your chance. As I recall, you had other problems like getting nominees past various select committees. You get on the phone to Britain and Israel and tell them in no uncertain terms to lay off. In exchange we'll supply as many photographs and as much information about the man as we can. But he is not, repeat not, to be harmed by either country while he's on American soil. Please make that absolutely clear to them.'

'Perfectly. Is that all?'

Murray sighed, weariness washing over him. 'Yeah, for now. If I think of anything else I'll let you know.' He slammed his hand on the desk. 'What a complete balls-up.' Standing up, he left abruptly.

As the door slammed behind the Director of the FBI, the National Security Adviser said, 'Dickhead.' He never made the calls.

19

In Tel Aviv the CNN film footage of the Palestinian UN delegation arriving in New York was watched avidly. There, smiling for the cameras, was Farouk Kaddoumi wearing a traditional black and white kaffiyeh held in place by a double corded agal. Following him down the airline staircase came the five other members of his delegation, each wearing a different coloured head cloth, with the same double stranded black cord holding it in place. To some Israelis watching their televisions it was a betrayal. Men such as those should not be allowed amongst civilised people. To others it was the only hope. Israel had to find peace.

General Moshe Sher was only half listening to the commentary, enjoying a cold beer at the end of the day. A slight movement of the head of a delegation member caught his eye and he froze in disbelief. He had sufficient mental agility to press the record button on his video remote control before the image changed back to the presenter.

Grabbing his phone he pressed a memory button. 'Shimon? Moshe. Have you seen the CNN coverage of FATAH arriving in America?'

'No. I've just walked in.'

'Check the internet. Call me as soon as you've seen it.' The most senior officer in the Israeli army put the phone down on the Director of Mossad, Israel's renowned and feared secret service.

Ten minutes later his phone rang. 'Was that who I

think it was?' Shimon Mazkoret's incredulity was apparent in every syllable.

'I'm sure of it. Can we check?'

'I can ask Langley.'

'Do it and do it now.'

'Calm yourself, Moshe.' There was alarm in the Mossad Director's voice. He knew how hot-tempered the General could be sometimes.

'Just do it and get back to me.' Hanging up the phone, the General began to pace the room of his small flat. He was a tall, thickset man with a shock of white hair. A widower for nearly fifteen years, the sixty-five year old hated the Palestinians not just politically, but on very personal grounds. His wife had died in an explosion caused by a Palestinian bomb. The General was sure that Jalal Chalabi had been involved. He had been looking for an opportunity to get him ever since.

His phone rang and he swept it up in his great paw of a hand. 'Sher.'

'Langley confirmed, Moshe. He was added to the delegation at the last minute. Under the circumstances, there were no objections.'

'The son-of-a-bitch. What do you think he's he up to?' It was a rhetorical question and treated as such. 'We know that he no more wants the UN to interfere than we do.' Both men were from the right wing of Israeli politics and as such hated any involvement by the United Nations. It was inevitably on the side of the Palestinians. 'If we could show that he was behind the suicide bombing of the kids at the bus-stop then world wide condemnation would stop them before they got to the UN.'

'We know it was him. That's why I was late getting home. Our informants told us that it was Chalabi's faction of HAMAS that caused the explosion. Apparently, the boy they used tried to run and Chalabi shot him.'

'Can we prove it? Is the evidence good enough to stand up in a court of law?'

There was a pause. 'No,' was the sad reply. 'It never is.'

'That's what I thought. I want a plan by midnight of how we can get him.'

'Chalabi?' came the shocked response.

'Of course Chalabi. I've been thinking about this ever since I saw him on the news. He'll be protected by the American Secret Service or FBI while he's in New York.'

'Right. So we wait until we get another opportunity.'

'No! I've waited fifteen years for the bastard to make a mistake and he's made a big one now.'

'But we can't risk American lives to get him. Moshe, the repercussions are too horrendous to contemplate. If anything goes wrong and you know it so easily can, innocent bystanders could get hurt. We'll be vilified not just by the Arabs for not honouring his diplomatic immunity but by our closest and greatest ally.'

'Shimon, I may be getting old but I'm not senile. We cannot, dare not, upset the Americans. They are all that stands between us and oblivion. But two can play at the Palestinian game. The United Nations is a large place. A sovereign territory. Every delegate behaves with the utmost civility to other delegates, even when they hate each other's guts. Our people do it all the time with half the Arab world.'

'What is your point, Moshe?'

'I'm suggesting we send somebody in as part of our delegation with the specific aim of taking Chalabi out.'

The Director of Mossad considered the idea. His protest was only half-hearted. 'I'm not so sure, Moshe. It takes time to get somebody accredited to the UN.'

'Get one of our lot sent home and in his place we put in an agent. We've enough of them in America.'

Israel's paranoia was so great, they even distrusted their American friends. Hence Mossad agents were to be found in all the major cities, watching out for those who were too sympathetic to the Arab cause.

'I'll see what I can do. Moshe, whatever happens, we mustn't tell the Prime Minister.'

'That left wing bastard? Of course not. This will be strictly between us. If Chalabi dies before the agreement is signed the whole thing will have to be called off. Put on hold. Delayed. Anything, while an investigation into his death is carried out. It's our only hope. I don't want to deal with the Palestinians any more than you do. How many times have we said that they only understand one thing? Force and retaliation.'

For all their commitment to their country, which could not be questioned, the two men were dinosaurs. Effective in the past, they're ideas were out of date in a modern world.

'The talks are in three days,' Mazkoret said thoughtfully.

'So we have twenty-four hours. You had better get on with it.'

The three-man HAMAS cell, still posing as Syrian business men, had booked into a motel that had seen better days. The pool was covered in scum, the sheets on the bed were a uniform grey and the carpets were threadbare. The place had its advantages. They had paid with cash and no questions were asked.

The Palestinians were so accustomed to hardship that they barely registered their surroundings.

Aware of the importance of the mission, the three men were tense, fretful. They snapped at each other fearful that they would be discovered with the weapons they'd collected. That the mission would be over before it had properly began.

The television bulletin of their leader accompanying the Palestinian delegation arriving in New York helped to relieve their tension a little.

The following morning, Nidal and Farid went to a local travel agent. They explained that they were in San Diego on business but would like to spend a few days away, somewhere in the mountains or the desert. They wanted a place that was quiet. They were assured that there was a wide range of remote, restful areas within driving distance and were given details on dozens of so-called shacks for hire. To the HAMAS warriors each cabin appeared palatial, very different from the tumble-down shacks they were used to. Clearly, the American idea of roughing it had faded about the time the last covered wagon came west. They were shown photographs of many properties and after careful questioning they settled on a place in the Chocolate Mountains, about 110 miles to the east.

Thanks to Major Simms they knew the whereabouts of Victoria's parents' house. Whilst one of them sat around a corner in the car the other two took it in turns to wander past the end of the driveway. After only a few hours they recognised Richard from his picture in the paper. They followed him to the Hotel del Coronado. Nidal went into the huge foyer and sat in an easy chair that gave him a view of the bank of elevators. The other two men sat in the shade near the pool and ordered coffee. Shortly afterwards Richard emerged and also sat in some shade a short distance away. They saw a tall, dark haired man join him.

Nidal wandered out of the hotel and joined them. 'With a gun,' hissed Nidal, 'we could walk over there and kill him. It would be over in seconds.'

'Jalal has forbidden it. He wants to make the man suffer. We follow his plan,' Farid argued with his scowling companion.

'Afez likes things simple,' offered Bashar.

'Just like you, eh, Abdullah?'

Farid could sense the tension building in Nidal. 'Let us order some more coffee.' Farid beckoned over a waiter.

Dressed in suits and ties they did not look out of place. Similarly dressed men were holding business meetings all across the splendid grounds of the hotel.

As the waiter was returning with the coffee, Nidal reached into a pocket, took out a packet of cigarettes and lit one.

'Excuse me, sir,' the waiter said, 'but there is no

smoking here. We have a specially designated area on the other side of the hotel you can use. So I must ask you to extinguish your cigarette.'

Nidal drew in a deep lung-full of smoke and exhaled a long cloudy stream. 'I will smoke where I like. Leave us.'

'I am sorry, sir, but I must insist. Or I'll have to ask you to leave the hotel.'

'I said go. I will smoke if I please. This is the land of the so-called free. If I cannot smoke when I wish then where is the freedom?' Nidal's voice was rising and one or two occupants at other tables were beginning to take notice.

'You can smoke when you wish, sir,' said the waiter, 'but not where. I must insist.'

'Afez, please, people are looking,' Farid was almost begging.

Behind his calm exterior Nidal's nerves were stretched taut. A cigarette was all that kept them from snapping.

Farid noticed the man at Richard's table looking their way, frowning. It made him uneasy. He spoke harshly in Arabic to Nidal. '*Subhaa-nullah*, Afez, you're making a terrible mistake. People at the table over there are looking this way. Must I tell Jalal how you jeopardise the mission?'

Nidal ground out the cigarette in a saucer, all the time staring at the waiter.

'Take it away,' he said coldly to the man.

Seething with resentment at such treatment the waiter did as he was ordered.

Farid tried to placate Nidal. 'Only a few more days, Afez.'

'Hold your tongue.' Nidal spoke in a cold furious whisper.

Farid dropped the subject. He knew better than to argue when Nidal was in one of his rages.

Director Mazkoret dialled his direct line to General Sher. 'I think I have found a solution. Please meet me at HQ in half an hour.'

Although the General rated a driver he often drove himself and this night was no exception. It was almost midnight and the streets were still busy with people leaving bars and restaurants. Tel Aviv was renowned as a city of great hospitality. Sher loved it with a passion, but was constantly aware that his wife was no longer there to share it with him. At the thought of her, his hands gripped the steering wheel more tightly and acid erupted in his stomach. He wanted Chalabi dead.

In the office he met with his old comrade-in-arms. Both men had served Israel for over 30 years. They had reached the pinnacle of their chosen professions.

General Sher came straight to the point. 'What do you have for me?'

Shimon Mazkoret was an immigrant from Eastern Germany who had crossed the border back in the late 1950's. He had been a boy at the time, a boy whose parents had dreamt of a life in Israel. He had embraced the country with all his heart and, at an early age, had dedicated himself to its survival. He had never married, claiming that he was wedded to his country. He was short, wiry and completely bald. His response was equally direct.

'Just as we said. One of our delegates will become ill. He'll be taken to hospital and we'll insist on a replacement.'

'He will have to be a good actor to fool the medical staff.'

'No acting required. He really will be sick. We're going to poison him. Moshe, if you let me run through this without interruption, we'll get done a lot sooner.'

The General nodded and kept silent. When Mazkoret finished, Sher sat for a few moments pondering the plan. Finally, he nodded. 'I like it. Who do you intend sending in?'

'Michael Rinski.'

'An excellent choice. Where's Rinski now?'

'He's in London. He's attached to our embassy there.

However, he has diplomatic status in Britain, so we ought to be able to get the UN to play ball.'

'What about our government?'

Mazkoret shrugged. 'They'll know nothing about what we're up to. We'll have members of the party insisting that our man be replaced. That we can't allow the Palestinians to have more delegates than we do. You know the usual rubbish. Point scoring in a meaningless fashion. Rinski is the obvious man to send at such short notice.

General Sher nodded. 'It should work. Thank goodness Mordecai is the Ambassador.'

The Israeli members of the United Nations were sitting in the UN Ambassador's office.

He had personally handed out cups of coffee. He watched one of the men, Simon Schute, with interest. The direct e-mail he had received a few hours earlier had contained the ingredients and recipe for a mild poison. He had sent his secretary to purchase what he required and had her make up the concoction. The cup he had handed Schute contained the liquid which was practically odourless and tasteless. The coffee masked what smell there was and added sugar took away any taste.

The men were discussing the forthcoming meeting and what the Palestinians hoped to gain from it. Opinion as to whether or not they should get what they wanted was as divided as it was across Israel. The Ambassador kept his own counsel. He was virulently opposed. It was because of his attitude that he was the Israeli Ambassador to the UN

Schute sipped the hot coffee. 'I think the Palestinians should get the concessions. If FATAH gets back in power there's a chance we can negotiate a proper peace. That won't happen as long as HAMAS is in control.'

The argument went back and forth, round and round.

Suddenly, unexpectedly, Schute gagged. Nausea rose within him.

'Are you alright?' The Ambassador asked, concern in his voice.

'No. I . . . I . . .' he rushed from the room, his hand over his mouth.

Shortly after that he was examined by a UN doctor. Due to the virulence of Schute's symptoms of vomiting, sweating and diarrhoea it was decided that he be taken to hospital immediately. He went in an ambulance with lights flashing and a siren blaring.

The Israeli Ambassador contacted the UN security council immediately and insisted on a replacement. When told it would be an accredited diplomat from London, surprisingly, no one objected. It was a first for the UN. Usually, somebody liked to make mischief, especially where the Israelis were concerned.

Zak Zakowski was not a happy man. The Palestinians had been difficult from the start, insisting that they be allowed to sightsee should they wish. The Special Agent-in-Charge pointed out that there was a good deal of bad feeling towards them in the country, but to no avail.

With no firm threat against them, Zakowski did not have the authority to stop the delegates going wherever they wished. Besides which, their diplomatic immunity should and did count for something. But as the Secret Service and the FBI knew, it wasn't the vast majority they had to worry about, just the fanatical few. Chalabi's plan was working. Establishing a pattern of freedom around New York was an integral part of his scheme.

'They want to visit Saks now. What the hell do we do?' Catherine Demarco asked.

'We let them,' Zakowski replied. 'We'll just have to be extra vigilant.'

'How many are going on this outing?' Catherine asked.

'Just two. Chalabi is one of them.'

'Why don't we take them on a sight-seeing tour,' said Carpenter, 'and lose them downtown? Then we let one of the gangs know. They'd kill them just for the kicks. We can claim that we'd warned them but they gave us the slip and must have wandered into one of the gang's territories by mistake.'

'Nice going, Tony, but no cigar,' said Zak.

'So what's the agenda?' Catherine asked.

'You pick them up at the hotel. The other team will take Kaddoumi and the others to the UN building. You four stay with Chalabi and the other guy. When they've finished shopping take them back to the UN and come back here. Okay?'

There were nods from his agents.

From the hotel to Saks by car took longer than if they'd walked. Catherine and another agent climbed out of the car first. It was mid-morning, the streets were packed with cars and delivery vans which frequently double parked as they dropped off one item or another. Tempers frayed, horns blew and voices were raised. Pedestrians ignored it all. It was part of the daily routine mirrored in any city in the world, though none quite like New York.

Chalabi got out of the car, rudely pushing past Catherine. 'Hey,' she called, 'wait until I tell you to move.'

Looking at her disdainfully Chalabi walked towards the store's main entrance.

Catherine hurried forward and grabbed his arm. 'I told you to wait until I said it was safe to get out.' She spoke through gritted teeth.

He shrugged his arm free. 'Don't ever touch me again,' he said coldly.

Catherine had had enough of the man. He was rude, arrogant and downright obnoxious to all the agents. 'Or else what?' It was as if he didn't want their protection.

'Or else,' the little man glared at Catherine, 'I will break your arms.'

The words were said with such venom, such passion, that Catherine stepped back in surprise. Tony Carpenter joined her and asked, 'Is everything all right?'

Catherine was about to complain when she saw the Palestinian hide some facial expression. What was it? A smirk? There was something going on and she was damned if she wasn't going to find out what. Looking coolly at Chalabi she said, 'Everything's fine, Tony.'

'Mr. Chalabi,' said Carpenter, 'if you would kindly remember that we are here to protect you, we'll get on a lot better.'

The Palestinian glowered at the agent and walked towards the door of the store. His colleague joined him, nervously looking around as though he expected a bullet at any moment.

There was no apparent pattern to their meandering through the shop. They spent some time in the music department but made no purchases. In the menswear department Chalabi tried on a number of jackets. One he appeared to like. He searched for a pair of trousers to go with it. With four pairs slung over his arm he headed for the changing rooms. He ignored the sign saying only one item at a time could be tried on.

Opening the door he saw a corridor with cubicles on both sides and at the far end a door marked "Staff Only". Each cubicle had a curtain across it. Chalabi turned to the FBI agents, 'If you don't mind, I'll go in here alone. As you can see, there is no danger.'

Carpenter hesitated and nodded. 'All right. But please hurry up.'

Chalabi did not acknowledge the agent and closed the door in his face. He crossed quickly to the staff door. It was closed, the entry lock a numerical one. Without much hope he tried the door. To his surprise, it opened. He put his head through. Typical of departmental stores all over the world, the customers' side of the door was clean and tidy, while behind the scenes it was shoddy. It was ideal for his purposes. He returned along the corridor and went into the first cubicle. He waited a few seconds before rejoining the FBI agents.

'I'm not sure about the trousers. I'll take the jacket,' he announced.

Michael Rinski didn't appear to be Jewish. For a start, he was blonde, tall and athletic looking. Secondly, he had been educated at Harvard. He had, in fact, married into the faith before converting and emigrating with his wife to Jerusalem. As an ex-marine he had no difficulty in joining the Israeli army, where he had quickly earned promotion to captain. He came to the attention of Mossad and they offered him a job. He took it with alacrity and now, fifteen years later, he was a senior member of the organisation in the field. A further promotion would see him in an office in Tel Aviv. He didn't relish the thought. Killing Chalabi would be the icing on the cake of his so-far, distinguished career.

'Chalabi's death,' said the Israeli Ambassador, 'must look like an accident.'

Rinski nodded. 'Yes, sir. I know. It's imperative.'

'How will you do it?' The Ambassador was curious.

Rinski held up the palm of his hand. 'With this ring.' A silver ring with a minute snake's head motif adorned the little finger of his left hand. He pressed the band with his thumb. A tiny needle shot out. It was less than a tenth of an inch long and barely discernible. 'It has taken years to develop,' Rinski continued. 'The needle and band is hollow and contains a powerful narcotic. The poison takes anything from twelve to fifteen hours to be effective depending on the target. When it does kick in the target's respiratory system stops. It's an unpleasant death. However, there's nothing to show how it's happened. It's a highly refined derivative of sparteine but a million times more potent.'

The Ambassador nodded his approval. 'And it's been tested?'

'Affirmative.'

The Ambassador did not ask on whom. 'How will you get close enough to administer it?'

'I've been discussing that with my boss. The obvious way is before the debate we will wish the Palestinians luck and offer them our hands. They will not be able to refuse. We would like you to arrange it.'

The Ambassador nodded. 'I will be delighted.'

Tomorrow, Chalabi thought, just for a change, he'd be nice to the FBI. That would confuse them. He would ask if he could go back to Saks in the afternoon because he had changed his mind about buying the trousers. They were so easy to manipulate. Tomorrow would be a great day. Chalabi went to sleep dreaming of holding Richard Griffiths' neck in his hands and slowly squeezing.

'He's up to something,' said Catherine dispiritedly, looking at the condensation on the side of her glass of cold beer. She was sitting with Zak, Tony and Pete, another member of the detail. 'I can feel it in my bones.'

'You may be right, but there's nothing we can do except keep him alive.'

'I've been checking the records,' said Carpenter, sipping an iced tea. 'If he's responsible for only half of what Mossad think he's done then he's a piece of dog turd that should be wiped off the face of the earth.'

'Amen to that,' said Zakowski. 'But it's out of our hands. Look at what history tells us about terrorists.'

'Yeah, yeah,' said Catherine. 'But history all depends on who writes it.'

'That's very philosophical of you so early in the evening,' said Carpenter.

'What this guy has done is so awful it can't possibly be justified. He gives me the creeps. I just wish I could find out what's going on in his sick little mind,' Catherine replied.

'Let's drop it,' said Zakowski, 'and call it a night. You're on tomorrow morning. But we should be free in the afternoon until the evening because of the debate beginning in the chamber.'

The others nodded and Catherine and Pete left, leaving Zak and Tony nursing half-empty glasses.

'Isn't it time you told her how you felt?' Carpenter asked his boss.

'I'm not with you.' He would have blushed if he'd known how.

'Come on, Zak, it sticks out a mile. You're crazy about her. Ask her out and have done with it.'

'What are you talking about, man?'

'Zak, it beggars belief that an agent with Catherine's acute observational powers hasn't noticed the way you look at her.'

'That's because I've looked at her that way from the moment I met her.'

'Hardly. However, ask her on a date, for crying out loud.'

'What if she says no?'

Tony Carpenter grinned at his friend. 'Zak, I've been watching you two for months. Believe me, old buddy, she won't say no.'

'I'll do it – as soon as this assignment is over.'

On that note, both agents left for their respective apartments.

It was mid-morning the following day when Zakowski took the call. 'He wants to do what?' he yelled down the phone.

'Go back to Saks, sir. He says he won't take long. An hour at the most. If we could meet him outside at one thirty he'd be, get this, grateful.'

'Grateful? That little turd? We're FBI not Secret Service. We investigate crime not bodyguard..' he paused. 'Okay, okay. Leave it to me. So much for our free time. I'll tell Catherine. What about the goddamn vote?'

'When I asked he shrugged and said politics bored him.'

'I bet they do. You know, I think Catherine's right. He's up to something. Watch him like a hawk.'

Hanging up the phone, Zakowski called Catherine into

his office. Remembering his conversation with Tony the night before he wondered for a second whether he should ask her out to dinner. No, after the Palestinians were safely off American soil. Then they could celebrate.

Chalabi stood in the huge foyer of the UN building at 13.28 precisely, waiting for his escort. They arrived a few seconds later. Good. One of them was the woman. He smiled politely.

'Thank you for your patience. I promise I won't be long. I should have bought those trousers I tried on yesterday.' Chalabi's pleasant manner caught the two agents off-guard.

Minutes later they had reached the underground car park and were heading out. When they arrived at Saks, Chalabi even waited in the car until Catherine gave him the all clear.

In the men's clothing department the Palestinian grabbed a handful of trousers and headed for the changing rooms. Catherine, a noted observer of human nature, thought that he was acting nervously. The two agents stood outside the door to the corridor and waited. Catherine leant against the wall opposite the door.

'I don't get it,' she said. 'The son of a bitch is even being nice to us. And with the vote this afternoon it's really an odd time to want to go shopping.' She shook her head and then suddenly snapped upright. 'Unless . . . Hell!' Drawing her weapon she ordered, 'Follow me.'

Carpenter didn't hesitate. Slamming open the door, a quick glance into the nearest cubicle revealed the pairs of trousers thrown carelessly over a chair. Both agents sprinted down the corridor and threw the Staff Only door open. Nobody!

20

CHALABI HAD NO idea of the store layout. He ran along another corridor and yanked the handle of the door facing him. It opened straight onto the shopping area. He hurried to the nearest exit. Outside he hailed a cab ordering the driver to take him to Newark Airport. Staring through the window behind him, he began to relax. The plan had worked. He had lost his FBI minders.

At the airport he had a reservation in a different name. At the check-in desk he showed his Syrian passport as proof of ID. He wasn't carrying any luggage and quickly went through to departures. The American Airlines 15.20 flight to Los Angeles was on time. He settled back in his seat, relishing what lay ahead.

Landing on time in Los Angeles he was met by Afez Nidal. On seeing Nidal's scruffy appearance a boiling rage erupted within Chalabi, which he had to keep under control until they were in the car.

'Cretin! Look at you! You are a pig! When did you last shave? You smell even worse! Can you do nothing without me?'

'Forgive us, Jalal. We didn't think . . .'

Chalabi interrupted him. 'Is that what we put on your coffin? Here lies Afez Nidal who died because he did not think! I see I have arrived not a moment too soon!'

'What the hell is Chalabi up to?' Zakowski asked. It was a rhetorical question. None of them knew the answer. 'It has to be something big to go to all this trouble. What in hell is happening here that warrants all this?'

'Maybe we should check the internet. See if there are any significant Jewish activities going on that a bomb or two could disrupt.'

'Or even a single shot. He could be going after one man. I'd better talk to the Director. This is way over my head.' Sighing with exasperation he picked up the receiver and dialled. 'Sir? I'm sorry but I have some bad news. Chalabi's done a runner.' Briefly Zakowski told his boss what had happened. 'I would like to put out an all points and have him arrested, sir.'

Lou Murray sighed. 'I have to go higher with this. He has diplomatic immunity. In theory, he hasn't broken any law. What can he be arrested for? Ducking away from his protection detail? When did that become a crime?'

'But sir, he's up to something. I know he is.'

'I don't doubt it for a second. But unless we catch him in the act there's nothing we can do about it.'

'What about an all points? Find him. Stop him without shooting the bastard. Although that would be my preference. We could argue the niceties of the law afterwards.'

'Do nothing for now. That's an order. To my knowledge this is unprecedented.'

The FBI Director picked up the telephone to the White House. He learned that the National Security Adviser was in with the President and not to be disturbed. He left a message. Flynn was to call him the second his meeting was over. Please.

One reason Lou Murray had been successful as the Director of the FBI was that he always knew when he needed help. A second reason was that he was never too proud to ask for it. This was such an occasion. He telephoned his opposite number at Langley.

'Director's office.'

'Margot, it's Lou Murray. Can I talk to Mr. O'Brian?'

'Certainly, sir, wait one moment please. You're through now.'

'George?'

'Hi, Lou. I take it this isn't a social call.'

'You're darned right. What do you know about a Palestinian named Jalal Chalabi?'

'You mean the scumbag the Palestinians brought with them? A hell of a lot but not as much as I'd like. I'd give half my pension to get my hands on him.'

'What about the other half?'

'I'm holding it in reserve for bin Sydal. Do you have something new on Chalabi?'

'He's given my agents the slip.'

'You'd better tell me what's going on and I'll see if I can help.'

Briefly Murray told the CIA Director all that he knew. 'So the situation is, we have a terrorist at large whose whereabouts, motivation and target are unknown. Jesus, George, what a mess!'

'Amen to that. I don't get it. The Palestinians have too much to lose if Chalabi does anything stupid. What's happening over in the UN right now is too important to them, both for the immediate future and the long term. One thing though, I don't believe for a moment that Chalabi is acting alone. I've pulled up the file on him while we've been talking. He usually has others to help him with the dirty work. Unless he's killing kids, that is. He doesn't appear to mind doing that himself.' O'Brian found himself grinding his teeth. 'Look, I'll have my people trawl the records and see if they can come up with anything. You never know.'

'Thanks, George. Oh and one day I might just surprise you with a social call.'

Chuckling at the thought, O'Brian hung up the receiver.

The hand shaking had taken place. The Palestinians did not volunteer an explanation as to why Chalabi wasn't present and the Israelis didn't ask for one. Michael Rinski was a true professional and would try again. He went down to the foyer to check if there was any sign of his target's return. Wandering outside, he looked up at the row of white flagpoles, each carrying the flag of every nation represented at the UN. Instinctively he searched for the Star of David with the two blue stripes top and bottom and felt pride welling up within him. Such a small country to have achieved so much, he thought.

He wandered along the sidewalk and onto American soil. Trained to be observant, he immediately noticed the extra activity around the perimeter. Seeing agents coming and going, talking into their personal radios, he wondered what was happening. His instincts told him the activity was somehow connected with Chalabi. He weighed the possibilities. Perhaps his obsession with the Palestinian was clouding his judgement. Still it would be worth checking out. He turned around and went back into the UN building and up to the Israeli offices.

On a secure line to Tel Aviv he reported to Mossad what he had seen and asked if they could investigate.

'Certainly, Michael, wait ten minutes. I'll speak to the Director.'

The call came back in six. To his surprise it was Mazkoret himself on the line.

'It seems your instincts are correct, as usual. Chalabi has gone missing.'

'He's gone to ground?'

'Disappeared completely. Our contact said that there's a Bureau-only alert for him. They don't want the press to get hold of it.'

Rinski didn't need to ask how Mossad had got the information so quickly. Supporters of the Israeli cause were spread all over the world, in all walks of life. Few things happened which directly or indirectly affected Israel without Mossad finding out.

'We could use the information we have and leak it to the press,' said Rinski, thinking out loud. 'That could stop the Palestinians.'

'What do we have? A delegate absences himself from a UN conference? Hardly of much significance, is it?'

'You're probably right, sir. I'll see what I can learn.'

After hanging up the phone Rinski hurried out the door and along the corridor. Within minutes he was outside the Palestinians' office. It had been loaned to the Palestinians who did not have an Ambassador at the UN.

He knocked. There was no answer. He knocked again, only louder. Finally, looking both ways, he bent to examine the lock. Reaching into his pocket he took out a state-of-the-art key gun, thought capable of opening ninety-nine percent of all known locks. It had certainly served Rinski well on many occasions. He inserted the thin blade and pressed the trigger while at the same time twisting the gun. Electronically the gun examined the lock and fired minuscule blades of tungsten, which fitted the lock exactly. Two seconds after inserting the blade the lock turned. He opened the door and entered. Expertly and quickly he tossed down the room. Filing cabinets and desk drawers were empty. The few files he did find contained nothing of interest. Out of thoroughness rather than anything else he looked in the wastepaper bins. Two were empty but a third one contained a torn scrap from a newspaper cutting. Reaching for it, he slipped it into his pocket. Minutes after opening the door he was back outside, locking it again.

Back in the Israeli offices he examined the scrap of torn newspaper but it told him very little. The original article had been torn to shreds. This one piece alone survived. He could make out the word "wedding" and across the top was the name of the newspaper and a date. Damn it! The scrap of paper wasn't a lot to show for his efforts. But looking at the recent date he thought it just might be significant.

When the National Security Adviser telephoned Dr Lou Murray he was already in a foul temper. Murray's revelation of Chalabi's disappearance did little to improve it.

'Just how incompetent are your agents,' he stormed, 'to lose a high profile terrorist like Chalabi?'

There was no answer possible so Murray wisely said nothing.

'You're making too many mistakes, Murray. I want this sorted out immediately.'

The FBI Director almost choked on a string of expletives. The man was a complete cretin. 'We are looking for him right now. If he has a false passport or other form of ID he could be anywhere. If we do find him and there's no other crime attributable to him he'll fly home with the rest of the Palestinians. Also, may I remind you, he has diplomatic immunity. Any suggestions?'

The NSA was silent for a few seconds. 'We have it revoked,' he said weakly.

'How? You ever done it? And it's UN backed, don't forget that.'

'Damnation! I've just finished speaking with the President. We're backing the Palestinians. We have to get some sort of stability in the region. There's been enough killings over the years.'

'Not to mention the need to keep a lid on things. For the sake of oil.'

The irony was lost on Flynn. 'That too, of course. The Israelis won't like it, but tough. It's time they toed the line. The damn country only exists and survives thanks to us.' As the biggest donor of aid to the region there was no doubt that Israel would have collapsed decades earlier without American largesse. The justification for that aid was the fact it was the only true democracy in the whole of the Middle East.

'If the news about Chalabi leaks out the talks could blow up in Kaddoumi's face.'

'Maybe, maybe not. Irrespective, we need to find him and find him soon.' Flynn sighed. It was as though he had forgotten to whom he was speaking. He almost sounded pleasant. The he switched back to type. 'If you don't find him I'll be demanding your resignation.'

Murray lost it and threw caution to the wind. 'Listen Mr. NSA my agents are currently trawling our sources for the smallest snippet of information. So far we've drawn a blank.'

'I'd better go and update the President.'

'Hang on a minute. Before you do, I think it would be a good idea to warn the Israelis not to use this information in some way. Particularly not to scupper the talks.'

'How would the Israelis know what's happened?'

'Believe me, they usually know what's going on five minutes before we do. Anyway, Chalabi being absent is pretty obvious, wouldn't you say?'

Murray, having slammed the receiver down on Flynn, immediately picked it up again. 'Zak, have you found anything that could have enticed Chalabi from his hole and brought him to the US?'

'No, sir, not a thing.'

'Okay, keep looking. So far we've kept this to New York. It's time to widen the net. I'll pass the word nationwide that we want him. Also get on to the airports. Send the latest photos we have.'

'What about the press getting hold of the story?

'The fact that we're looking for one unnamed man won't be noticed. And there's no point in using the name Chalabi. He's not stupid enough to be using it. Just the photos will do.'

'Right, sir. What about Kaddoumi? Is anybody going to have a word with him?'

'I don't know. That's a political decision. I've passed this to the White House.' He hung up thinking about his budget. It was being shot to hell once again.

Michael Rinski was frustrated. In desperation he looked up the web-site for the San Diego newspapers on the date he had found on the scrap of paper. He keyed in the word "wedding". Browsing through the announcements of the forthcoming nuptials he found the details of the wedding between Richard L. Griffiths and Victoria Louise Shand. They matched the scant information on the newspaper scrap. Nothing about them seemed relevant. Neither were Jewish – they were both Protestant. So why have a scrap of paper in a wastepaper bucket? Another thought occurred to him. It probably had nothing to do with them. The article about the wedding just happened to be on the same page as one that did interest Chalabi. Or on the other side of the page. The web-site contained the whole newspaper as separate articles. He printed off the lot and tried again. Still nothing that made sense. Maybe he had found exactly what it seemed to be – a scrap of newspaper bearing no relationship to Chalabi's plans. Although it seemed like the logical conclusion, somehow he just didn't believe it. He sent what precious little he knew to Tel Aviv. He would let Mossad's analysts take a look. Perhaps they could work out a connection.

Victoria tried on her wedding dress and twirled around in front of the mirror.

'Vicky, darling, you look lovely.' The only person ever to call her Vicky had been her high-school friend, Valerie Sinclair. Vicky and Val had been inseparable until Victoria had begun to travel the world. They had stayed in contact by letter, phone, postcard and e-mail. Using whichever was convenient at the time.

Vicky had returned to the States for Val's wedding when she had been her bridesmaid. Val now had two children, both boys, who were going to be pageboys while Val was maid of honour.

Victoria smiled at her friend in the mirror. 'Thanks. Although white is a tiny bit, shall we say, hypocritical?'

'From what you've been telling me about Richard you should be wearing scarlet.'

Victoria giggled and gazed fondly at her friend. Val was several inches shorter than Victoria. In fact, with her raven hair, she could not have been physically more different. Yet the two women still shared the same effervescent personalities that had attracted them to each other as children. 'And you, Val, are you happy with Luke?'

'What can I tell you? He's an accountant. Seriously, Vicky, he's a great husband and father. I think I can safely say I'm happy.'

'No regrets?'

'What is this? Twenty questions?'

Victoria shook her head. 'I hope I'm not making a mistake.'

'You aren't! Listen, if you don't want him I'll get rid of Luke somehow, get custody of the kids and run away with Richard.'

Victoria laughed out loud. 'Val, you're incorrigible.'

'Vicky, he's a good guy. Handsome, smart and one day – from what you tell me about the Griffiths family – he'll be loaded. What more can a girl ask for?'

'How about love and happiness?'

'In your case they're thrown in for good measure as well. Sweetheart, count your blessings. It doesn't get any better. Now, let's check out the veil.'

'I'm too old for a stag do,' Richard protested to Hunter.

'You're never too old,' his cousin contradicted him. 'Besides I'm not suggesting a night of drunken debauchery, just a few beers. A couple of the lads from the SEAL team who know you want to come along too.'

Richard looked blank.

'A Commander Rory Calhoun and Lieutenant Pete Redman. Rory met you at Chattenden when you were doing the explosives training for your long course.'

'Good grief! Rory! I remember! He was a lieutenant j.g. in those days.'

'We were talking about the wedding and I learnt that he'd been there at the same time as you. He showed me a course photograph and there you were, as large as life.'

'It'll be great to see him again. And Pete. He did a midshipman's exchange to HMS Towey when I was the First Lieutenant. Did Rory tell you about the mess dinner we attended together?' His cousin shook his head. 'As you know only too well, naval dinners are highly civilised affairs.'

'Are you by any chance about to disparage the noble traditions of army dinners?'

'Would I? This dinner was for a class of royal engineer officers, all second lieutenants. After we finished eating the mess president hit his gavel and announced a pee-break. The whole room erupted and the officers dived out of their chairs for the heads. Honestly, Nick, doors were torn from their hinges. There were seven of us and we followed right behind them. Nobody was allowed to return to the table until everyone was ready. When the word was given they fought their way back to the tables wreaking yet more havoc. We didn't have a clue what was going on until the name of the last person back was announced. He was fined a round of port for everybody there.'

'Expensive.'

'At sixty-six glasses of port it wasn't cheap. Every man paid his share of the damage except us, as we were guests. It was a lot cheaper to pay your share of the destruction than pay for a round of port. That was my first and only army mess dinner. When did Rory join the SEALs?'

'A while back. He's now in command of SEAL Team Six. I went diving with them. I used one of their new closed-circuit breathing sets. It's computer controlled and allows for diving down to two hundred feet with very good endurance but without stops. They've got some gear I want TIFAT to take a close look at. If it's okay with you they'll come over tonight and we can hit the high spots.'

Richard chuckled. 'Let's do it as long as we keep things reasonably civilised. Did you interview the guys who want to join your outfit?'

'Yes. Two of them have skills we could use. I need to talk to Rory about them before I speak to General Macnair.'

Later that night, after too many beers and beer chasers, Richard had a terrible urge to speak to Victoria. The phone rang out at her number. She had also planned a batchelorette party for that evening, a non-riotous affair of dinner and a nightclub with a few family friends. Frowning, he stared blearily at his wristwatch and wondered what she could be up to at 01.30. Thankfully they had opted to celebrate their last day of freedom two days before the wedding. After all, they'd both agreed, where was the enjoyment of attending your own wedding with a hang-over?

21

'JALAL, WE'VE BEEN over every detail a dozen times.'

The look Chalabi gave Nidal was frosted with contempt. 'And we will go over it another dozen times if we need to. Until I am sure you understand. I want this man Griffiths but equally importantly we want the money. We use the girl as bait. If the girl is dead he won't pay the ransom. First we get the money. Then we kill him. We do so quietly and we leave no trace.'

'Twenty-four hours. Is the time scale not too tight?' Farid asked.

'I think not.' Chalabi approved of Farid. He was the youngest member of the cell but he was totally reliable and could think for himself. He asked sensible questions and wasn't afraid to do so, unlike Nidal and Bashar. One day, he would make a good HAMAS leader.

'Let us go over everything once more. She is at her parents' house . . .'

The briefing took another ten minutes. 'Is everything clearly understood? Abdullah, you will go to the cabin and wait for us there.'

Bashar left in the middle of the afternoon. He was dressed for the outdoors. After all, it was cold in the mountains at night.

The other three showered and shaved and put on their suits and ties. Smart business attire was essential. Policemen all over the world were more inclined to treat a person favourably if he looked respectable. The only difference was these particular businessmen would be travelling armed with silenced automatics.

They had driven the route half a dozen times and knew precisely where to go. The freeway was almost deserted and they completed the journey quicker than planned. Parking directly opposite the house they sat listening to the quiet of the night. 'We move in now. To wait any longer is too risky.' Until Chalabi spoke, the loudest sound was the ticking of their cooling engine. The interior light had been turned off and climbing out of the car they silently closed the doors. Moving up the drive, they spread out. They carried their guns hidden inside their jackets, ready to be drawn in an instant. Chalabi, bringing up the rear, also carried a slim briefcase.

It was a warm night without a cloud in the sky. Somewhere they heard the shrill screech of a cat, followed by the barking of an excited dog. The men froze until the noise ceased. Chalabi and Nidal went to the front door while Farid went around to the back.

Hiding behind a large oleander, Chalabi opened the case and extracted what looked like an aerosol canister with a long length of thin plastic tubing attached to the nozzle. Threading the tubing through the door he turned the handle on the canister which began to emit a faint hiss. He waited the best part of two minutes before switching it off. The powerful knock-out gas would drift through the house and render unconscious anyone who inhaled it. It took the smallest amount to be effective. Farid's job was to pick the lock on the back door. Recovering the tubing Chalabi and Nidal moved around the side of the house, intending to join their colleague. They disappeared just as a car drew up.

The secret warriors of Mossad had been up all night researching the scraps of information transmitted by Michael Rinski from the United Nations. Amongst all the intelligence services in the world they were renowned to be the most effective, the best. They specialised in creativity and lateral thinking. But the true secret to their phenomenal success was their persistence. Mossad left no stone unturned.

All night they worked on the Chalabi newspaper fragments, weighing the arguments, seeking out possible connections, mutual enemies, potential clues. In this particular case, *not* to find the connection could quite literally mean someone's death. Finding it represented a step closer to Chalabi. The opportunity to kill the Palestinian should not be lost under any circumstances.

As a third level analyst Albert Roszak had access to almost every secret his country possessed. He was a mathematician by training and a computer freak by choice. In any other country in the world he would have been the chief executive of a successful software company and a multimillionaire. In Israel he applied his many talents to the protection of his country and her people. Pushing himself away from the monitor on his desk he rolled his office chair round to face his assistant, a jubilant smile on his tanned face. 'Lillian, I found him. I know who he is. I've just made the connection.'

Roszak's fingers flew across his computer keyboard. A picture of Richard Griffiths appeared along with an array of details. 'Do you remember when Harwazi's camp was attacked in Tunisia?'

Lillian smiled, her fat face becoming cherubic. 'I'd like to shake the hand of whoever did it.'

Roszak nodded. Her positive attitude was one of the things he liked about his assistant. She had no scruples about helping to kill their country's enemies. Her one regret was that she was unable to do so herself. 'Take a look at this. Do you remember when the BA flight was blown up a few years ago?'

'I remember. They never did find out who did it.'

'Well, this man's family was on the flight. He lost a wife and two children. Twins, to be precise. We know that he has spent time and money trying to find out who was responsible.'

'And did he?'

'We don't know. What we do know is that he *thought* he knew who had been responsible. He passed a report about it to MI6.'

'What did they do?'

'Nothing. NFA.'

'No further action? Why? Was the information wrong?' Roszak shook his head. 'I'd say not.'

'What has this to do with what's going on now?'

'We've checked up on Griffiths. Apart from writing the report he also took an extended boating holiday in the Med. We know he went to Tunisia and that he was there about the time of the bombing.'

'You think he could have done it?'

'Griffiths' background is very interesting. He was a minewarfare and clearance diving officer in the RN.'

'An explosives expert.'

'Precisely. We know Chalabi's brother was killed in the desert bombing. What if Chalabi is out for his revenge?'

'It fits.'

'That's what I thought. I need to pass this information to the Director. He'll have to decide.'

Lillian may have been his assistant, but she was highly intelligent as well as analytical. 'If we let Chalabi kill Griffiths we'll win a propaganda coup and stop the Palestinians getting their aid. Even if we're too late and the resolution is voted through, we'll probably be able to get it rescinded afterwards. On the other hand, if we warn them now and Chalabi is stopped before he does something, he could deny he was planning to do anything and claim it's all a mistake. The Director will have to decide.'

Mazkoret was finishing his breakfast when Roszak telephoned him. After he was briefed, he thanked the analyst for a job well done and thoughtfully replaced the receiver.

He had hours yet to decide what he was going to do. The West was still sleeping.

Victoria and Val climbed out of the cab with some difficulty and paid the fare. Giggling and walking none too straight they started up the garden path until Victoria became aware of footsteps. Thinking perhaps Richard had come over to surprise her she turned around, ready to stretch her arms out wide. She was the first to see the two strangers walk around the side of the house towards them.

'Which one of you lovely ladies is Miss Victoria Shand?'

The man appeared polite and well dressed. Without thinking Victoria replied, 'That's me.'

'Thank you, Miss Shand.' Without another word, Chalabi drew his gun and shot Val through the forehead.

Victoria stood paralysed in total shock, staring at Chalabi, aware only of his eyes and the terrible silence. Before she had any thought of reacting, Nidal darted forward and clamped a hand over her mouth. The assault brought her to her senses. Victoria began to kick and struggle. She opened her mouth and bit down on Nidal's hand as hard as she could, forcing him to let go. She was drawing a deep breath to scream when he hit her across the back of the neck and she fell unconscious.

'Stupid bitch,' Nidal said with feeling, blood dripping from his finger. 'Let me kill her now, Jalal.'

'All in good time, my friend,' Chalabi whispered. 'Go and fetch Hosni.' Chalabi knelt beside Victoria and quickly opened his case. From it, he extracted a hypodermic filled with a powerful narcotic and injected it into Victoria's arm. She moaned softly as the needle went in. Farid rejoined them.

'What do we do with the dead woman?' he asked.

'We take her with us. Hurry up.'

Farid helped Nidal throw Val's body over his shoulders then he and Chalabi carried Victoria between them to the car. They bundled the two women in the back of the Ford and covered them with a blanket. Climbing into the car, Nidal gunned the engine and they pulled away with a squeal of tyres.

'Slow down, you fool,' Chalabi ordered. 'We don't want to draw attention to ourselves.'

'*Assif*, Jalal,' Nidal apologised. He eased his foot on the accelerator but was still breaking the speed limit.

'Slow down!' Chalabi yelled this time. 'If the police stop us now we'll have to shoot our way free. Everything will be lost.'

Nidal slowed down further, fighting his animal instinct to flee a dangerous environment. He turned onto Highway Fifteen. He wanted to floor the gas pedal and get as far away as possible. Within minutes they saw the sign for Highway Eighteen and turned left along Mission Freeway. They had a 118 miles to go to the El Centro turnoff and the start of the Chocolate Mountain range.

'Put the car on cruise control,' Chalabi ordered.

'What?' Nidal wasn't listening. He was too busy looking out for police cars.

'Put the car on cruise control and take your foot off the accelerator. That way you won't break the speed limit. Then we won't attract any attention to ourselves.'

Doing as he was told, Nidal began to relax a little.

'Afez, Hosni. When we get to the cabin I want you to take the dead woman in the boat and drop her into the lake. Make sure she is weighted.' In his mind's eye he could see an image of the woman's body slipping into the depths of the Salton Sea where she could lie undisturbed possibly for decades, while water skiers and swimmers enjoyed their activities above. Salton Sea was unique. An inland lake of saline water, its maximum depth was only 51ft.

Two hours later they turned left off the highway for El Centro and drove past a signpost for Brawley town

10 miles away. The place was small, hardly more than an extended village through which they quickly passed. There was a hint of dawn in the eastern sky with the promise of another lovely day ahead. The last 5 miles were spent travelling over a dirt track that wound around the hills on the eastern side of the lake. The beautiful inland waters of royal blue made the area a favourite summer vacation spot. All around, the hills and shores were dotted with private houses with large keep-out signs. When they finally pulled up outside the luxury cabin the sun had risen.

The property stood a 100m from the foreshore. Its nearest neighbours lay a mile away in either direction and the other side of the lake could just be discerned in the morning haze, 11 miles away. There was a motor boat tied up at the end of a 30m long wooden jetty. Nidal and Farid picked up Val's body to go down to the boat.

'No, wait.' Chalabi had a smile on his face. 'Take the dead woman inside. We will put her with her friend.'

What they were about to do and how it would affect Victoria when she regained consciousness was not lost on the others. To a man, they grinned.

Chalabi and Bashar picked up Victoria and followed the other two into the cabin where they dropped her onto the floor. Chalabi explored the pine cabin. Its sheer luxury sickened him. The living room was huge and stretched the length of the building, overlooking the lake. Behind it was a large kitchen and dining room. He could hear Bashar demonstrating the marvels of the jacuzzi and steam room to Nidal, who was laughing with relief and excitement at having pulled off the job. Walking out onto the huge patio in front of the cabin Chalabi steeled himself against the beauty of the lake, the clean air and the opulence. Comparisons with the filth and squalor of his homeland were facile. Soon Palestine would free herself from the grip of poverty, *in Shallah*.

Farid disturbed his thoughts. 'Where shall we put the woman and the body?'

'Put her in the wash room. Handcuff her. She must not escape.'

Nidal and Bashar carried Victoria to the utility room where Nidal handcuffed her right wrist to the cold water pipe. Farid was left to drag Val's body after them. Unable to resist, Farid ripped off Victoria's knickers and took a good look at her. Lust rose in his throat. 'Soon, Hosni, soon. Come, my friend, it is time for food.'

In the kitchen, Farid and Chalabi were having coffee and smoking. Eggs were frying in a pan.

'I want somebody patrolling at all times, 100m around the house. I want you armed. If anybody approaches ask them to leave. If they refuse, you have my permission to shoot. We will be here less than twenty-four hours. Anybody killed we can drop out there.' He gestured towards the deep blue water. 'Abdullah, did you check the boat?'

'Yes, Jalal. It is fuelled and the key is in the ignition. I have also started the engine.'

'Good. We should not be needing it, but just in case we need to get away and can't go down the track we can cross the water and steal a car.'

'You think of everything,' said Farid, deep respect in his voice.

Chalabi was pleased with the compliment but chose to ignore it. It helped to maintain his status as a planner, a thinker, a man to be trusted. 'Now let us eat.'

Fried eggs and bread was all they had. When they had finished Chalabi lit another cigarette and said, 'Afez, go and administer the drug. She should be awake in ten minutes.' He then sat with Victoria's mobile phone in his hands. He scrolled down to Richard's number. He would be calling it soon.

Nidal nodded and stood up, grabbing the briefcase. In the utility room he took out the hypodermic and injected

Victoria in the arm. Sitting back on his haunches he began to run his hands over her naked thighs and the tops of her legs. He decided to take her quickly before the others appeared and was moving his leg over her inert body when Bashar appeared at the door.

'We have drawn lots, Afez and you have lost. You have the first two hours of guard duty.' He grinned at spoiling Nidal's fun. He went back into the kitchen for another coffee.

Victoria's screams told them that she had returned to consciousness. Chalabi was walking into the utility room when he pressed the auto-dial on the phone.

22

IN HIS LAVISH hotel bedroom Richard was sleeping off the excesses of the evening. He awoke to the ringing tone of his mobile phone. Who the hell could be calling him at this ungodly hour? If this was Nick's idea of a joke he'd kill him, best man or not.

The heavily accented voice he heard snapped him wide-awake, his hangover forgotten.

'Richard Griffiths? My name is Jalal Chalabi.'

Fear dried his already dehydrated mouth.

'Say again, this is a bad connection,' he croaked.

'You know who I am, so don't play games with me.'

Richard was thinking furiously. He needed time. His thought processes were blocked on a single word. Danger. Danger. Danger.

Chalabi misinterpreted Richard's silence. Struggling to keep his emotions under control he hissed between clenched teeth. 'So you want to play games, do you? Well listen to this.'

Victoria had finally stopped screaming. She was struggling against the handcuffs, at the same time staring into the face of her dead friend, feeling on the brink of madness. She vomited all over herself and the floor.

'Say something nice to your boyfriend, bitch,' he yelled at her.

Victoria's overwhelming terror left her bereft of speech. In a towering rage Chalabi grabbed her by the hair. 'Speak, you bitch, or else I'll kill you.'

The pain jerked her back to her senses. 'Stop it!' she yelled. 'You're hurting me.'

Chalabi put the phone to his ear. 'Did you hear that? Did you hear the bitch?'

Richard's heart was hammering and sweat had broken out all over his body. 'Yes,' he croaked. He coughed and said again, 'Tell me what you want.'

'We'll come to that later,' said the Palestinian. 'Listen to me and listen well. You will not contact the police. You will tell no one what has happened. I have your woman here and I will kill her if you do not do exactly what I tell you. Do you understand?' There was silence. 'Do you understand or do you need another demonstration?'

Before Richard could reply, Chalabi kicked Victoria in the side and she screamed. 'Do you understand?' he yelled into the phone.

'Yes! Yes! Don't hurt her anymore. I understand. What do you want?'

'I want one million dollars and I want it today.'

'But . . . but that's impossible,' Richard protested.

'If you say it can't be done I shall be forced to post the lovely Miss Shand back to you in little pieces. Is that what you want to happen?'

'No! For God's sake leave her alone. Look, let her go. I'll get the money somehow. It'll take time but I can do it.'

'Time is a commodity you do not have, Mr. Griffiths. You have until the banks close today. After that, she dies. Having already lost your young family, *sediq,* it would be a tragedy indeed if you were to also lose this lovely, nubile young woman.'

Richard experienced each syllable as a branding iron to his soul. His voice, when he finally answered, was sepulchral. 'Touch her, Chalabi and you sign your own death warrant.'

'Hosni!' Chalabi yelled for Farid. When he appeared at the door he shouted, 'Take your knife. Cut off her little finger. Now! Do it!'

'Wait!' Richard screamed down the phone.

Chalabi gestured to Farid to stop. He was kneeling next to Victoria and had her right hand pressed flat on the floor. He held a knife to her little finger. It had cut the skin, drawing blood.

'Mr. Griffiths?' Chalabi spoke softly enjoying his feeling of power.

'I said wait, damn you. I'll get the money somehow.'

'You have until five o'clock this evening. At that time I will give you your new instructions. If you try any tricks, she will die. Did I tell you that we have wired her with explosives? If there is even a hint of police or FBI involvement, I will kill her. You do believe me, don't you?'

'Let me talk to her.'

'The money first. Then you can talk to her.'

'Listen, Chalabi, I just want to reassure her, that's all. There can be no harm in that, can there?'

The terrorist thought for a second. 'All right. But make it quick.' He thrust the phone down to Victoria's ear.

'Richard?' she whispered. 'Richard?'

'Yes, my love, it's me. Don't worry I'll get you out. They want money which I'll get in time. So be brave.'

'He killed Val.' The horror and desolation in her voice chilled Richard to the bone.

Victoria tried to speak again, but Chalabi wrenched the phone away.

'You have until five.'

'You bastard! Why kill her friend?'

'So you know my threats are not idle ones. That I have not mellowed over the years.'

'If you lay a finger on her I'll hunt you down like an animal. Even if it takes me the rest of my life.'

'Be careful, Mr. Griffiths. That might not be as long as you think.'

Breaking the connection, Chalabi looked down at Victoria without emotion. She glared back at him for a few seconds and then looked away. Her fear was palpable. 'Don't take this personally, Miss Shand. This is business. A money raising initiative for our holy *jihad* against Israel.'

'A Holy War? Killing innocent men, women and children?'

He knelt beside her. 'Do not condemn us when you know nothing of our struggle. You Americans support the fascist regime of Israel. You allow them to steal our land and kill our people and expect us to do nothing? Should we emulate Christ and simply turn the other cheek? Was that the motivation behind Griffiths' actions in Tunisia? He killed innocent men, Miss Shand. Among them my brother and for that he will die.'

'So the ransom money – it's just a charade?'

He laughed. 'Indeed no. It will bring me another million for my holy war on top of the ten million I will receive for killing your future husband. A lucrative day's work, I'm sure you'll agree. And here's the bonus. I want him to feel the agony of watching you die. If I had more time it would be a long and painful death for you both but unfortunately I have to deny myself the pleasure. Instead, I am going to take you out into the middle of the lake and drop you over the side. They do say that death by drowning is a terrible way to die. You hold your breath, you struggle and pray and then you breath in. I leave you with that thought.' Turning on his heels, he walked away satisfied at the look of utter desolation and fear on Victoria's face. Behind him he heard Victoria sobbing.

Back in the living room, Chalabi said to Nidal, 'Burn the car I came in. We only need one car to leave here and we don't want to leave any evidence.' He nodded to Bashar. 'Plant the explosives and incendiaries.'

Richard sat on the side of the bed with his head in his hands and cursed. He could feel the black mist descending. Despair and hatred fought one another within him. He had thought his depression a defeated enemy.

After a few minutes the mist rolled away and Richard began thinking with clarity and purpose. His emotions underwent a paradigm shift from frantic fear to the purely practical. Chalabi had killed his family. He would not steal this second chance at happiness.

Richard considered his options while he made himself a cup of coffee. He thought about the dossier he had compiled on Chalabi. He could easily remember it – he'd read it so often. He knew that the man was totally amoral. He would kill without compunction. Any sex and any age. He was fanatical to the core in his desire for two things – the complete destruction of Israel and the establishment of a Palestinian state. To achieve those ends he needed money. He obviously knew that Richard either had his own money or access to it through the family. A million dollars were neither here nor there. With his own money tied up in investments, mainly in the company, with the family in town, he could have the cash in no time.

What were his options? One thing he was sure of. Giving Chalabi the money wouldn't save Victoria. Her life was forfeit, regardless. He knew the Palestinian intended to kill them both.

What about help? Richard thought of Nick but instantly dismissed the idea. He couldn't risk it. If he could deal with this alone he might get away with it. Chalabi needed only an inkling that outside forces were involved and Victoria would be killed without a second thought. Staring at himself in the bathroom mirror, Richard barely recognised the grey face with the gaunt lines running vertically from cheek to chin, bleak anguish reflected in his eyes.

It was only just after 06.00. The next three hours were the longest in his life. Finally it was time to make a move. He shaved and showered before he took a taxi to the nearest Wells Fargo bank. A hole-in-the-wall wouldn't give him as much as he wanted so he entered the bank where he showed his passport to a teller.

'Can I use my AMEX card and withdraw some cash, please?'

'Certainly, sir. How much?'

'How much can I have?'

She swiped the card along the back of a keyboard. 'Ten thousand dollars.'

'I'll take it.'

'Please enter your card there and your PIN.'

He did as he was told. 'Thank you. That seems in order. How would you like the cash?'

'In one thousand dollar bills?'

The teller smiled and shook her head. 'There's no such thing. The largest bills we have are five hundreds. Will that do?'

Richard nodded. It didn't really matter. Outside, he hailed a taxi. 'Can you take me to an instant print shop?'

'Sure, no problem. There's one down on Chatsworth.'

The shop was large and busy. In the back, he saw the offset litho presses going flat out. Reaching the counter he put a five hundred-dollar bill on the surface. 'Can you make up fake copies of this?'

The proprietor looked at Richard suspiciously. 'Sure. But they won't pass inspection. It'll just be on ordinary paper. You can't use them.'

'Of course not. I want to use it in a board game I'm devising. You've heard of Monopoly?'

'Sure. Who hasn't?'

'Well, I've invented something similar. Except it's a sort of war game with property and money. I need some printed in a hurry.'

'Okay. That's no problem. Tomorrow suit you?'

Richard shook his head. 'No, I need them today. In a few hours. I'll pay you double your normal price.'

There was a short silence. 'All right. How about four hours?'

Richard nodded.

'I don't need the bill. We have the image on our software.'

'Let me ask you something. Can you print one thousand dollar bills?'

'Sure. Companies use them as gift vouchers. They aren't legal tender but it's amazing how many people think one thousand dollar bills exist.'

'Okay. Print me one million dollars worth of thousand dollar bills.'

'You got it, fellah. Leave it with us.'

Outside the shop, he was about to hail another taxi when he looked along the boulevard. Five doors away he spotted premises that looked like Fort Knox. The windows were barred and the door looked like it was made of solid steel. In the window there were clearly displayed signs that the place was wired for CCTV and alarmed to the nearest police station. It was just what he was looking for.

Inside, the room stretched back the full width of the building. There were rows upon rows of glass-topped cabinets, six-foot-long by four-foot-wide. Underneath the glass were weapons of all sizes and calibre. A short, middle-aged man approached and asked if he could be of any assistance.

'I'd like to buy a gun, please.'

'Certainly, sir. What sort?'

'An automatic. Can I get one with a silencer?'

'Yes, sir, provided it is for use at a particular range. Some of them like silenced weapons.'

'A particular range? I'm sorry, but I don't understand.'

'You need to belong to a particular shooting club. One that uses silenced guns.' The man paused and then asked, 'Are you a resident here, sir?'

'No, I'm just visiting.'

The man was shaking his head. 'Then I'm sorry, sir. I can't help you. You have to be a resident to purchase a gun in California. I would need to see your driver's licence and your resident's permit. You would be able to purchase the gun but then you'd have to wait fourteen days before you can collect it. That gives the police time to check you out.'

'There's no way around it?' Richard rubbed his thumb along his fingertips.

'No, sir!' The owner was adamant, though it was obvious he wasn't answering the question for the first time.

Leaving the shop, Richard again felt the panic welling up inside him. He couldn't fight Chalabi unarmed, dammit.

23

MOSSAD PASSED THE information they had to The International Force Against Terrorism. General Macnair read it as a matter of routine with the rest of his signals. A glance at his watch showed that it was 08.30 and he was running late for his meeting. The Heads of Departments met twice a week, once on Monday to discuss the week ahead and again on Friday to discuss what had actually happened. Often, as was the nature of things, something had gone wrong.

The staff room was down the corridor from his own office. He was outside the door when an agitated Isobel rushed in. 'Sir, I need to see you right away.'

'Can't it wait until after the meeting?

'No, sir, it can't.'

Knowing his head of IT he knew better than to argue. 'What's the matter?'

'The Mossad signal, sir. We have to do something about it.'

'We do? Why?'

'Richard Griffiths, sir. He's Nick's cousin. Nick is in America right now for the wedding.'

'Good Lord, I remember now. Wasn't Griffiths the man who put the MI6 file together?'

'That's the one, sir. We're pretty sure he was involved in Tunisia. Though nothing was proven.'

'That's right. Thank you for bringing it to my attention. We'd better warn Lieutenant Commander Hunter.'

'I've tried his mobile, but it goes straight to answering

machine. I've left a message and sent a text telling him to call.'

'Good. In the meantime I'll telephone Admiral Christchurch at SPECWARCOM and have a word with him.'

'It's pretty late, sir, you may not get him. Early weekend and all that.'

Macnair nodded.

'What about the Heads of Department meeting?'

'Tell them I'll be there in ten minutes.' Returning to his office, the General put through a call on a secure line to SPECWARCOM in San Diego. Admiral Bartholomew Christchurch was the officer commanding all SEAL units in America – both West Coast and East Coast teams. As Isobel had pointed out and Macnair suspected, the Admiral had left for the weekend.

'Can you give me his mobile number?'

'Yes, sir. But can't the duty officer help?'

'Who is he?'

'Commander Calhoun, sir. He's here right now.'

'Put him on. Commander Calhoun? This is General Macnair. I'm the commanding officer of . . .'

'Yes, sir, I know. TIFAT. Two of my men have applied to join you.'

'Right. Commander, we've received a heads-up from Mossad. According to them, a Palestinian terrorist by the name of Jalal Chalabi could and I stress the word could, be planning to disrupt a wedding that's taking place tomorrow in San Diego.'

'The Griffiths-Shand wedding? Sir, I know Richard. We served together a lifetime ago. I went with him on his stag run-ashore last night.'

'Good. Then you know what's happening over there. The wedding arrangements and everything?'

'Yes, sir. I'll be there.'

'All right. I don't want to alarm anyone, least of all the bride and groom, but I think we need some cover.

This man Chalabi is one of the most wanted terrorists in the world. He entered the States as part of the Palestinian delegation to the United Nations but he appears to have gone missing. Mossad is convinced he's up to something and I can't say I blame them. Anything you can do?'

'Sure, sir. I'll need permission, but let me talk to the Admiral. I'll alert the FBI and we'll see about sniffer dogs. Leave it to me, sir.'

'Good. By the way, have you seen Commander Hunter?'

'Yes, sir. He's just left the base. We were going over some equipment together. If you were ringing his mobile it might have been switched off. We were playing around with some explosives and a ringing phone at the wrong moment can be a bit tricky.'

'Thank you. I'll call him again.' The General broke the connection and again tried to phone Hunter. This time it was engaged.

Richard went to Avis and hired a BMW Z3. It was fast and small and just what he needed. He collected the fake dollars, which wouldn't have fooled anybody up close and stuffed them in a plastic briefcase he had bought from a Woolworth store. He made ten bundles of the fake money. Next door was a shop selling items for the "great outdoors".

Richard spent half an hour buying gear he thought might be useful. When he was about to leave the shop he noticed a glass topped table like the ones in the gunsmith's. Approaching it, he saw that it contained cross-bows and arrows.

Beckoning over the sales assistant, he asked, 'Do these things come under the same regulations as for firearms?' The assistant assured him that there was no two week wait or proof of residency required.

'Good. In that case I'll buy one. How do you carry the arrows?'

'You clip that sheath to your belt. As you see, the bolts are only eight inches long.'

'What's the effective range for killing a, em,' he hesitated a moment and said, 'a deer?'

'Sir, you have to get a lot closer than with a rifle. The effective range of the bolt is one hundred metres. But,' the assistant smiled, 'you have to be an exceptionally good shot to kill a deer at that range.'

Richard nodded. He intended to get a great deal nearer than that.

He borrowed a copy of Yellow Pages and found the section headed *Surveillance Equipment – bought, sold and installed,* followed by a page of detailed information. He was about to ask the way to Garnet Street when he thought better of it. The less anybody knew about his business the better. He had a map in the car. Dumping his purchases in the trunk he pulled out the map. Garnet Street ran at right angles to the coast from Pacific Beach to Highway Fifteen. He'd be there in minutes.

The shop boasted just about every form of electronic gadget imaginable. Just weeks earlier Richard had bought Victoria a new satnav mobile phone to match his own. It meant that they could use them anywhere in the world, even at sea and miles from land. Victoria had joked there would be no excuse for not contacting each other. They would never be able to claim to be in a no-signal area.

'Do you sell satnav mobile phone scanners?'

'Sure do, buddy. Five hundred bucks.'

'Thanks, I'll take one.' The scanner had been one of Richard's priorities. He knew it could pick up a signal from a satnav mobile telephone and give its location to within 100m.

'Do you also have a directional microphone?'

'Sure, which type? There are a few on the market.'

'One which I can aim at the side of a building and hear what's being said.'

'We've got the very latest bit of equipment. We call

it a microwave phone. It's this little beauty here.' The gadget was surprisingly small, no larger than a paperback book. 'You clip this in here and aim it like a gun.' A red laser spot appeared on the wall opposite. 'Slip on this earphone and adjust it here.' The salesman was obviously an expert on the equipment that he had in his well stocked shop. Richard selected what he wanted and paid with cash. In the United Kingdom every item he'd bought either needed a special licence or was downright illegal. *Thank God for the land of the free.*

He drove down to Ocean Beach and parked in a shady spot away from other cars. He now had a solution to his biggest problem – how to find Chalabi. Originally he had intended going along with the terrorists' instructions and turning the situation to his advantage at the last minute or die trying. Act fast and hard and turn the tables on them had been his master plan. Now he possibly had a distinct advantage. Taking out his mobile he checked the in-coming calls memory. There it was – Victoria's phone number.

He switched on the scanner and watched as a row of tiny red lights came on. The scanner self tested and each light turned to green. With six greens, the device was ready to go. He dialled in his own phone number and pressed the on-station button. His phone was now locked into the scanner. Pressing the speed dialling button, his hands were suddenly slippery with sweat. Constant activity had kept thoughts of Victoria at bay but now they were back with a vengeance. Was she even still alive?

The phone at the other end kept ringing. The scanner was already at work, tracking down the signal as clearly as if it was a landline. The beam hit the nearest aerial and bounced along another four until it hit the phone. Bingo! Fifteen seconds later the latitude and longitude of the receiving phone was displayed on the screen. For a second he considered hanging up but he wanted Chalabi to answer.

The ringing stopped. 'Griffiths, I hope you are calling with good news. Otherwise . . .' he let the threat hang in the air.

'Otherwise nothing. If you lay a finger on her, you won't see a cent of the money. Is a million dollars worth leaving her alone for? I've wired my family and will have the money around five to five thirty guaranteed before the banks shut. So allow whatever time it takes for me to drive from here and I will be with you then.'

There was a pause. 'When you have the money telephone me. I will give you directions. And Mr. Griffiths, you had better be alone, or she will die a slow and painful death.' Chalabi broke the connection.

Richard sat still for a few minutes, marshalling his thoughts, trying to calm his beating heart. He'd never been so scared in his life, terrified of what might happen to Victoria.

Using the map he converted the latitude and longitude on the scanner to a location to the east of Salton Sea. He drove down Ingraham Street and hit the Ocean Beach Freeway, also known as Interstate Eight. The road was busy with convoys of cars, all travelling at or just under the speed limit. Now the Z3 would come into its own. Although it was an automatic he could put the car into first, second and then automatic, which was where most people left it. He slammed it into second and floored the accelerator. The little car took off like a rocket. Richard put the gears into automatic and began dodging around the traffic reaching 70 to 75mph, braking down to 40mph when he had to. He drove like a man possessed. The faster he drove the greater his time advantage at Chilabi's hideout would be. It was now 15.30. They wouldn't expect him until 20.30 at the earliest.

A car in front braked and he shot round to the left and back in front. A horn blew behind him but he ignored it. There was a quiet stretch and he gunned the car up to over 100mph before being forced to drop back when a

lorry suddenly pulled out in front of him. Richard caught
the reflection of the driver's face in the lorry's side mirror
and knew that the driver had acted deliberately. Flooring
the accelerator he shot around the huge truck, ignoring
the klaxon blaring at him. Already the lorry was fading
in his rear-view mirror. The little car was eating up the
miles and soon he was passing the sign for La Mesa. The
sheer concentration he was forced to bring to his driving
kept the fear away. Speed. It was all that mattered.

He was right behind and about to pass a black and
white car when he realised it was a police vehicle. Hitting
the brakes he slowed to a respectable fifty-five. After a
few minutes of intense frustration the police car's indicator began flashing, then the red roof lights started and
the car pulled quickly away. Richard increased speed as
well, staying a few cars behind, dodging through the traffic
on the police car's tail. About 5 miles down the road the
other car pulled off the highway and Richard carried on.
He passed the signs for the Anza-Borrego Desert State
Park and realised that he was more than halfway along
the highway to his turn off.

The traffic thinned. There were fewer irate drivers to
sound their horns at him but he did see a few indignant
shakes of the head as he zoomed past. The high-pitched
beeping he heard took him by surprise until he realised
that it was the radar-warning device he'd purchased. He
slammed on the brakes and dropped from 115mph to a
respectable 55mph in seconds. The policemen up ahead
stood and watched him driving sedately past. He was
relieved to see in the mirror that they took no notice of
him and he began to accelerate. A sign warned him that
El Centro was 10 miles ahead. He glanced at the map to
confirm his turnoff. An hour and twenty minutes to travel
100 miles was not bad going. Just as he was turning off
the highway his mobile phone rang.

Picking it up, he pressed receive and put it to his ear.
'Griffiths.'

'Richard? It's Nick. Where are you?'

'Sightseeing,' he said evasively.

'Richard, we've had a warning from TIFAT. Chalabi is on the loose here in the States. We think he's coming after you.'

He and Nick had always been straight with each other. 'You're too late, Nick. I know.'

'Jesus, are you all right? What's happened? Richard, you have to tell me. Listen to me, I know you. Don't do anything stupid or rash. You aren't equipped for it. You're not trained. Let me help.'

Knowing his cousin's abilities Richard was tempted. If anybody could pull off a rescue it was Nick. But this was his responsibility. Nick had no resources to call on in the States. Besides, there was no time. He glanced at the clock on the dashboard. It was now 16.58.

'Nick, I'm sorry, but I have to do this myself.'

'Where are you?'

'Going into the Chocolate Mountains.'

'Where the hell is that?'

'Nick, never mind. I've got to go.' He broke the connection.

Hunter stood in his hotel room thinking hard. One thing he knew above all else – special forces stuck together. When the chips were down you couldn't rely on the politicians or civilian forces. They were hamstrung by the law – but you could rely on your own.

He dialled again. 'Rory? It's Nick. I need a big favour.'

'Anything, Nick, just name it.'

'I need equipment and possibly transport.'

'What have you got in mind?'

'Tracking gear. Weapons.'

'Would you like to tell me what's going on?'

'Sure. But it needs to be at SPECWARCOM.'

'Okay. I'll leave word at the gate. Meet me in the ops room.'

Hunter broke the connection and phoned Macnair on the General's mobile.

'Sir? Things have already happened this end. My cousin appears to be chasing after Chalabi. I've an idea to go after him but I wondered where I stood asking the SEALs for help.'

There was a pause before Macnair replied. 'All right, here's what I can do. As of now TIFAT has an operation to take out Chalabi. Our mandate is world-wide so we don't need to ask anyone for permission. We inform host countries as a matter of courtesy if we're operating on their territory. That should prevent the politicians from interfering. I'll ask Admiral Christchurch to extend every facility short of manpower. We can't use non-TIFAT personnel. If we have a problem legally I'll get back to you. What are you going to do?'

Hunter told the General briefly what he had in mind.

'Right! I can go with that. Let me make my calls.'

When Hunter arrived at the base Commander Rory Calhoun was waiting for him at the main gate. 'Admiral's compliments, Nick, whatever you want, you get.'

'I have to hand it to the General,' said Hunter, 'when he does things he does them fast. First of all, I need to track the whereabouts of a mobile phone.'

'Nick, if we triangulate the signal we can get to within about 20 miles.'

'Richard has the new satnav phone.'

'Then that's easy. We can place one of those to within a few metres. Let's go to the communications centre. The scanner we use is in there.'

Looking at his watch Hunter said, 'No, let's go and sort out the gear first. I want to give Richard more time to get where he's going. Then I'll phone him.'

24

RICHARD PARKED THE car on a dirt track about 5 miles short of the latitude and longitude he'd got from the scanner. He made the phone call.

'Chalabi? I have the money. Where do I come to?'

'You drive down Highway Eighteen to El Centro. Stop there and phone again. I expect you to call in two hours.'

'Wait a minute, Chalabi. Have you seen the traffic? I'm stopped on the freeway right now. It's the rush hour when every car in San Diego is on the move. I need more time than that.'

'Let me put it this way. For every minute you do not ring me past eight o'clock I will cut off one of Miss Shand's fingers.'

'Now look, Chalabi…'

'No! No, you look,' Chalabi screamed down the phone. 'No more tricks. No more delays.'

The phone went dead. *Bastard*! Still, he had over two hours in hand. He looked at the scanner. There was a slight change in the seconds of longitude. In San Diego he had taken the precaution of buying a local Ordnance Survey map of the area and he plotted the position again. It was close to an isolated property near the water's edge at Salton Sea. He was almost there. Driving further along the track the bottom of the little car scraped loudly when it hit deep ruts and low stones. The fifth time it happened he decided it was time to abandon the car.

Driving off the track Richard pushed the nose of the car through some bushes. He emerged into a clearing and stopped. Climbing out he changed his clothes into an American Ranger's suit. The disruptive pattern of green and grey blended in well with the forest. He strapped a black-handled knife to his side and slid another into the special sheath sewn into the right leg of the suit. Each of the bolts for the crossbow was individually held in a leather sheath like a cigar case. Even the flights were green and grey. He hoisted out the briefcase and a small knapsack that he slung over his shoulder and left the car. For what it was worth, he was ready for action.

He'd barely gone a dozen paces when his phone rang. He didn't recognise the number so he answered it, in case it was Chalabi on a different phone.

'Richard? It's Nick. Don't hang up, I just want to help.'

'You can't, Nick. It's too late. Chalabi has Victoria. It's a ransom job. I've got the money here to pay him.'

'Richard, you can't trust Chalabi. He doesn't want money.'

'No kidding, Sherlock.'

'So wait for me to come and help.'

'No time, Nick. I've got a few surprises for Chalabi.' Richard severed the connection. He was now on the track and broke into a fast jog. As he did he switched the phone off. He didn't want it ringing at an awkward moment. He'd switch it on again when he wanted to contact Chalabi. In the meantime, if Chalabi tried calling him, it was too bad. There was nothing he could do about it.

'Did you get it?' Hunter asked.

'Sure, sir, no problem. Here are the co-ordinates.' The communications operator handed the information to Hunter.

'I'll take those,' said Calhoun plucking the paper from Hunter's hand. 'Let's have a look at what we've got.' He typed them into a computer terminal and stood back to watch. 'There you go. Salton Sea. Let's take a closer look, shall we?' He typed instructions into the keyboard. 'This is it. That's where he is. Is the subject moving, sergeant?'

The communications operator checked his console. 'Sorry, sir, he's switched off the phone. I can give you the last known co-ordinates.'

Calhoun typed them in. Richard had moved about fifty metres. The SEAL commander pointed at his screen. 'He's on this track, heading that way.'

'Where does the track lead?'

'There are two possibilities. This cabin here or that one,' Calhoun indicated with a pencil.

'Any way of checking them? Who they belong to?'

'Easy. What then?'

'Then we telephone the owners and find out if either of them are rented out or being used.'

'Leave it to me.'

'Rory, I'll go and get kitted up. I want to leave as soon as we know the target. By the way, do you have a file with names and photographs of Palestinian terrorists?'

'Sure. It's on the computer. We update it regularly, usually with details supplied by Mossad. You know the sort of thing. Delete those killed, add the following. The additions have been far greater than those deleted of late.' While he talked, Rory was busy with his computer terminal. 'Okay. What do you have in mind?'

'Let's see Chalabi first.'

The Palestinian's picture appeared, a full head shot and side view, obviously taken in a street somewhere in the Middle East. An update due to his arrival in the States had yet to be posted.

'What about known associates?' Hunter asked.

Calhoun pressed more buttons. 'Just photos or histories as well?'

'Just photos will do.'

The screen filled with photographs two inches square. Hunter pointed at one. 'Can you enlarge that one and call up his history?' He read out the details. 'Afez Nidal. Definitely involved with the plane bombing. His first operation. He started in the big time,' commented Hunter. 'But I see he's been busy since.' He scrolled down the list of incidents that Nidal was suspected of being involved in. 'Hell and my cousin is going up against him! The sooner I get there the better.'

'How do you know Nidal is there?'

'I saw him at the Hotel Del Coronado.'

Richard moved off the track about a mile from the house. In the forest he walked slowly and cautiously. The sun was setting and it would be dusk soon. For all his caution he knew he wasn't being silent but when he stopped and listened there was plenty of noise. A slight breeze had picked up and the leaves and lighter branches rustled constantly. Animals were on the move. He thought he caught a glimpse of a deer, but wasn't sure in the dim light of the dense forest.

Although he had never trained with special forces, Richard had done escape and evasion exercises when he had completed his specialist training as a bomb and mine disposal diving officer. As he tramped through the forest he remembered his unit being dumped in woods in Southern England, strip searched for food and money, given a sack full of old clothing and told to travel the best part of a 100 miles across country. They had been instructed to live off the land and treat everybody they came across as an enemy. All the while they had been pursued by the army and the local constabulary, who also found the exercise effective training. They had done well to avoid capture and get to their destination in the time allocated. That experience, he realised grimly, had not prepared him for this. For one thing, he was more than a little afraid – afraid of failure.

For the umpteenth time he looked at his watch. 19.25. Sniffing the air, he stopped. He could smell smoke. It was coming from ahead. He sniffed again and recognised that it was from burning wood. The cabin had to be nearby. He bent over and walked very carefully, the crossbow held in front of him ready to shoot, trying to present as small a target as possible.

The sun finally set but it was still some time to full darkness. Stopping at the edge of a clearing, he saw the red roof of the cabin stark against the clear sky. Richard froze. His mouth was dry and his mind was suddenly fogged with fear. He couldn't understand it. He had never felt like this before. And then he understood why. Now he had too much to lose. The fear of that loss was paralysing him. He mentally took a grip of himself.

A red glow moving in the gloom caught his eye and he studied it for a few seconds. The tip of a cigarette. Stepping backwards very slowly Richard vanished into the trees. Once he was out of sight he put the briefcase and knapsack down by a tree. He began to walk slowly to the left, around the clearing.

Taking his time he was about halfway to his target when he realised the man was moving. The smell of tobacco smoke came strongly to his nostrils and simultaneously the terrorist walked around the bole of a tree straight in front of him. The young man stopped in utter shock an automatic dangling in one hand, a cigarette in the other. Richard didn't hesitate. Snatching the crossbow to his shoulder he barely bothered to aim before he fired. At a distance of about 4m he couldn't miss. The bolt smashed into the man's chest, pierced the heart and threw Farid into the tree with a crash. The Uzi he was carrying fell from his lifeless hands.

With a shaking hand, Richard fumbled for another bolt. His heart was racing and he was breathing in shallow gasps, like an asthmatic. He was in no condition to continue. He stopped for a few minutes, breathing steadily. When he felt composed enough he bent down to search the man. In his pockets he found a packet of cigarettes, a book of matches from the Hotel del Coronado and a Syrian passport in the name of Hosni Farid.

Picking up the gun he examined it. The safety was off and he flicked it on before he slung the weapon over his shoulder. He'd stick with the crossbow for close work. The bolt he had fired had all but vanished through the body. There was no doubt that at short range it was a highly effective weapon. Lifting Farid over his shoulders, he went deeper into the forest until he found a dense bush. Unceremoniously, he shoved the body underneath and rearranged the branches to hide it. One target down. How many to go?

Locating the briefcase and knapsack, he returned to the clearing and worked his way around to the other side. There were about 15m of forest between him and the house and he moved as quietly as he could. Hopefully, any noise he made would be put down to the man he had just killed.

Crouching at the edge of the trees and hidden by the foliage he opened the rucksack and took out the infrared directional microphone. Switching it on he aimed it at the side of the house and listened. He could hear nothing. He switched it off, replaced it in the bag and moved further around to the side. He tried again. In the background, he heard a faint rumbling of voices. He was now at the very edge of the trees. He could see that he had moved closer to the water and if he went any further there was a possibility of being seen from the shack. One thing was now in his favour. It was rapidly growing dark. He checked his watch. Another twenty minutes until he needed to phone Chalabi.

Adjusting the setting on the microphone he listened again. This time the voices were clearer. He recognised the language as Arabic although he didn't understand what was being said. Concentrating intently he decided there were two voices at least, perhaps more but it was hard to tell.

He gave himself another ten minutes when it was finally fully dark. Flicking the Uzi's safety to fully automatic he adjusted the strap and slung it across his chest. With the bow in his hands he crouched low and headed for the corner of the house between the front and the side. Reaching there without any difficulty he paused. He tried the microphone again. He was so close that the voices within almost blew his eardrums. He adjusted the volume and aimed it along the front of the house. Although the red light struck the wall at an angle he was able to discern three distinctly different voices. Where was Victoria? He needed to find her before he did anything else. The side of the house had curtained windows and he ducked low as he walked alongside. Now he held the microphone up close to the wall, listening intently. Nothing.

The wall at the rear of the house was solid wood except for two average sized windows with a door in between. There were no lights showing from this side and he cautiously approached the first widow and placed the microphone against it. Silence.

At the door he paused and tried the handle. It turned and when he gently pushed the door moved. It could be the way in – or the way out. He reached the second window, placed the mike against it and listened intently. Was that something? He concentrated. There. He turned up the volume. Quite distinctly he heard the rustling of cloth and a soft thumping sound. In surprise, he recognised it as a heartbeat. He prayed it was Victoria's.

25

'YOU'VE GOT EVERYTHING?'

'Yes, thanks Rory. We're agreed on what we'll do?'

'Sure. I'll tell the FBI as soon as you jump. It'll take them hours to get there and the action will be all over, one way or another.'

'Good. And many thanks.'

'Are you sure I can't come and help? I'd be pleased to.'

'I know you would. But we're on dubious legal ground. The General will protect me if he has to, but he doesn't have any way of protecting you. Like you said, it takes permission from the Commander-in-Chief to mount an operation like this. And that's the President. Somehow, with what's going on in New York right now, I doubt he'll give that permission. Besides which, it's far too late. Richard needs help right now.' Hunter touched his earphone. 'I'll stay in contact. And if General Macnair gets anything out of New York let me know.'

'One thing has just occurred to me.' Calhoun frowned at Hunter's face, already darkened with camouflage cream.

'What's that?'

'If Chalabi is with the Palestinian UN delegation he'll have diplomatic immunity. Presumably that's how he was able to get into the country.'

Hunter looked grim when he said, 'Have you ever heard of Police Constable Yvonne Fletcher? There's a plaque to her memory in London. In April 1984 there was an anti-Harwazi demonstration outside the Libyan embassy in London. In typical British fashion we had only a few constables patrolling, making sure the demonstration stayed peaceful. Which it did, until somebody in the embassy opened up with a machine gun and killed her. The British government asked the Libyans to waive the diplomatic immunity of the man who had committed the murder but they refused. The Government's response was to throw the lot of them out and close the embassy. What would you have done?'

'Stormed the place and killed the lot,' was the passionate answer.

'Me too. That poor young constable's family received no justice – just pious platitudes. I don't want the FBI or any other law-enforcement agency near there until I've dealt with Chalabi and whoever's with him.'

The two men shook hands and Hunter climbed into an AH-1W Super Cobra helicopter. The chopper was used as a support machine in time of ex-filtration when stealth was no longer the order of the day. It carried a great deal of firepower including an M-197 three-barrel 20mm cannon, AIM-9L Sidewinder, Hellfire or eight TOW-II missiles, a new radar warning system and an infrared jammer. Plugging in his headset Hunter told the pilot he was ready to go. They lifted as smoothly into the air as an express elevator.

Richard continued around the house. Should he go in and try and get Victoria out, or try and deal with Chalabi and his men first? He needed more information before he could make a decision. He was now at the front wall. The windows here ran the full height of the living space and stretched across the entire width of the house. The curtains were drawn but chinks of light shone through. He put an eye up to the window. Through a narrow gap he could see a few feet of room. While he stood there a figure crossed in front of him and he caught a fleeting glimpse of one of them. Moving further along he tried other gaps in the curtains but saw nothing of interest. The microphone gave the same message as before. There were three different voices inside. Checking his watch he saw it was time to make another phone call.

From the corner of the house he darted back into the relative safety of the trees and speed dialled.

'Chalabi? I'm at El Centro.'

He listened to his instructions before saying, 'All right, I've got it. But before I come any further I want to talk to Victoria.' An agitated Chalabi began to protest loudly. Richard cut him off. 'I'm bringing a million dollars, Chalabi. My mother didn't raise a fool. I want to know she's still alive. Otherwise I turn around and go back.'

'Wait. You will speak to her.'

Richard could hear Chalabi's footsteps on the wooden floor. Moving quickly through the trees, he positioned himself opposite the backdoor and waited. A light came on in the left-hand window.

He heard Chalabi say, 'Speak,' as he thrust the phone to Victoria's face.

'Victoria? It's Richard? Are you all right?'

'Richard? Oh, Richard, help me,' she began and started to sob.

'Satisfied?' Chalabi asked him.

'You bastard. If you've done anything to her, I'll kill you.'

'No more empty threats. If you want to see your woman alive again then you must do precisely as I tell you. Do you understand?'

'I understand.' Richard forced himself to introduce as much fear and anguish into his voice as possible. It wasn't difficult.

When they broke contact, Richard, crouching low, ran across the lawn to the rear of the house. He saw the light go out and heard a door open and close.

Knowing Chalabi he guessed that any further instructions would be to lead him straight into a trap. Gathering up his briefcase and rucksack, he quickly went around the clearing until he could see the front of the house. He arrived in time to see the door open and an armed man appear. Slinging a gun over his shoulder, Bashar stopped to light a cigarette before walking towards the forest.

As stealthily as he could Richard worked his way back through the trees, calculating the angle where the terrorist would reach cover.

'Hosni!' Bashar called out in a loud whisper and then cursed. Reaching the trees he said again, 'Hosni!'

Richard stepped out from behind a tree and took a pace towards him. Bashar said in Arabic, 'Hosni! Where have you been? I've been calling you.'

He got no further. Richard raised the crossbow and fired from a distance of less than 3m. Richard aimed the bolt at the terrorist's chest but it flew upwards and went straight through Bashar's throat. Dropping his gun, he fell backwards with a gurgle, his hands around his neck.

Stepping forward from the shadows Richard stared down at the man who was still alive, gasping for breath, blood oozing around his fingers. His voice box was shattered. Bashar gargled and tried to speak while Richard knelt and watched. They stared at each other, only feet apart, their eyes gleaming in the darkness.

'*Tatakalam Inglesi*?' Richard whispered.

From his expression, it was clear that he did understand English. 'When you die I shall bury you. Here in these woods. Your mother will never look on the face of her dead son. And when I do I want you to know that I will put a pig in your grave.'

The man convulsed in horror at the thought. He would be damned forever. Letting go of his throat he reached for Richard with a feeble gesture, trying to sit up. Richard slammed the top of the bow into the man's face and he collapsed back. With a deep-throated rattle Bashar exhaled for the last time. A search of his pockets provided a few dollars, cigarettes and lighter and a Syrian passport in the name of Abdullah Bashar.

Crossing the lawn to the rear of the house Richard silently opened the back door and listened intently. Apart from the noise of the forest behind him there was silence. Immediately behind the door was a dark corridor. A strip

of light ran under the door at the far end. Richard felt
his way slowly along until he came to a door on his left.
He found the handle, turned it and pushed the door open.
There was a patch of starry sky in the corner of the
window, but otherwise the room was pitch black. His
eyes were accustomed to the dark and he could see
Victoria, slumped against the far wall.

Darting across the room he whispered urgently to her,
'Victoria, wake up. It's me.'

Snapping awake Victoria peered through the darkness.
'Richard!' she gasped loudly.

'Shshsh. They'll hear you.' He knelt next to her. 'Have
they hurt you?' He waited, in dread of the answer.

She put her hands on him, touching his arms and face
as though to convince herself that he was really with her.
'No, just . . . just get me out of here.'

'Chalabi told me you were wired to explosives.' He was
whispering, his eyes darting around the room but they kept
being drawn back to Val. In death she looked ghoulish.
What torture it must have been for Victoria, lying face to
face with her once vibrant, loving childhood friend.

'It's not true,' Victoria whispered.

Quickly patting her down Richard satisfied himself
that the explosives had merely been a bluff. 'Let's get
out of here.'

'I'm chained,' Victoria whispered. 'Look.' She shook
her handcuffed wrist. The handcuffs were fixed to a water
pipe that came through the wall at that point and led to
a washing machine.

Richard felt along the pipe for a possible weak spot or
a join but found nothing. He tugged hard at the pipe and
felt it move at the machine end. Following the pipe with
his hands he felt around the back of the washing machine.
It was a tight squeeze but by stretching his fingertips he
found where it connected to a plastic hose.

'Richard, what are you doing?' Victoria whispered.

'Finding a way to get you free.' Following the pipe

back again he found a tap and checked it was turned off. Taking his knife he searched for the hose connection once more and sawed through it. Grabbing the end of the pipe he bent it towards him. When the pipe was far enough across to get his other hand in he took hold with both hands and pulled hard. The screws holding the bottom wall bracket in place tore loose and the pipe came away. He worked his way along the wall, pulling the brackets free until he reached Victoria.

'Can you get to your knees?' He knelt beside her. She did so, stiff from the many hours she had spent on the cold floor.

'Let's go.' Helping her move along the pipe Richard had to force the handcuff past the tap where it became jammed for a few heart-stopping moments. Victoria threw her arms around him, dry sobs wracking her body. 'We've got to get out of here,' he whispered in her ear. 'Before one of them comes to check on you.' He felt her nodding against his shoulder. 'Now listen. Outside we turn right and down the corridor. Don't run! Stealth is what we need now. Are there only four of them?'

'Yes, I think so.'

'Come on.' Opening the door, he listened. 'Off you go!'

Victoria stepped into the corridor with Richard close behind. He had the Uzi ready. Now that he had Victoria, if they were spotted, he'd use the gun and she could make a run for it. Outside the house he put his hand on her arm to stop her. Looking left and right they listened intently. Apart from the background noises of the live forest the night was peaceful.

Pointing across the lawn at the woods, he said, 'You first. I'll cover you.'

Victoria crouched down and hurried across to the trees with Richard a few paces behind. Catching up with her he led her to a large tree in the clearing where he had stashed the briefcase.

'What's in there?'

Richard grinned at her. 'A trap. I'll explain later, sweet-heart. Right now we need to get away.'

The cool night air was rent by a terrible cry of rage from the house followed by loud, angry instructions in Arabic.

'Damn! It looks like we could get caught up in a fire-fight which was the last thing I wanted.'

'Richard we can't,' she gasped. 'There are four of them. All with guns. What chance do we have?'

'A pretty good one. I've killed two of the bastards.' Richard spoke matter of factly. 'I guess Chalabi is yelling for them now.' He looked around. 'Here, quick. Hide under this bush.' Pulling back the overhanging foliage he urged her underneath, out of sight. 'I need you somewhere safe.'

Victoria got down on her knees and crawled in. When she was out of sight Richard darted across the clearing towards the house, taking the briefcase with him. Chalabi and the other man were outside, calling the names of the dead men. Chalabi, angry to the point of madness, pointed towards the track. The other man ran in that direction.

Richard stayed just in the tree line and went parallel to the track, staying as quiet as he could. He paused to look back across the clearing and drew a deep breath. Chalabi had just ran across the lawn and into the trees. Taking his phone from his pocket he pressed the speed dial. He imagined he could hear the phone ringing.

'Chalabi?' Richard spoke in a loud whisper. 'Is that you?'

'Griffiths! Where are you?'

'My car is stuck in the dirt track and I'm having to walk. Phone me in two minutes.'

'Wait!' But Chalabi was speaking into a dead phone. Exasperated, he rang Richard only to be told that the number was unavailable and to try again or leave a message on the voice mail.

Opening the case with the dummy money, Richard dumped the bundles in the middle of the track. To him, the cash looked real. He could hear Nidal running back towards the house presumably to report that he had been unable to find the other two. Switching on his phone again he placed it on top of the pile of fake money and crouched down nearby, next to a tree. He held the crossbow ready.

Chalabi had pressed the speed dial button again, rage coursing through him. Again no connection. And again. And again. And . . . finally it rang.

Nidal was panting when he rounded the bend. He stopped at the sight of the pile of money on the track. Coming clearly from the middle was the ringing of a mobile phone. He stared at it for a second.

Standing up Richard shot him from close range. The bolt hit Nidal in the arm just above the elbow. It passed straight through smashing the bone and pinning the arm to his side. With a scream of agony Nidal flew sideways and struck a tree. His gun fell from his hands and lay in the track next to the money.

Nidal saw Richard approaching and whimpered. 'No . . . please . . . no! Don't shoot!'

Stopping, Richard retrieved his phone. With distaste he regarded Nidal, curled up in agony at the base of the tree, tears rolling down his cheeks. 'Please, don't shoot,' he begged. 'Get help. Get police.'

How many innocent men, women and children . . . he left the thought unfinished. Kneeling beside him, Richard grabbed hold of the man's hair and pulled him up until their faces were inches apart. 'You're scum. Remember your part in the plane bombing?' Richard saw the man tense. 'This is for my family.' Nidal didn't see the knife in Richard's other hand, but he tensed in agony as it slowly entered his throat, through his palate and into his brain. The sensation lasted agonising seconds.

Now there was only Chalabi left. Richard's phone rang and Chalabi's number glowed green in the tiny window. He hesitated and then decided to answer it. But on pressing receive the voice he heard was not Chalabi's.

26

THIRTY MINUTES AFTER take off Hunter was told to standby. He checked his gear and waited patiently. Glancing at the two altimeters he wore, one on each wrist, he ensured that they matched. Pin-point accuracy in his height above land was mandatory. The pilot's voice squawked over his headset. 'Go!' and the crewman beside him tapped his arm. Shoving his drop-bag through the door he followed it out. The bag hung below him as he fell through the air and clear of the helicopter.

He had jumped from 10,000ft. He adjusted his position, his arms and legs spread out, his belly pointing downwards. The night vision goggles he wore were state-of-the-art. It was the first time Hunter had worn them, courtesy of the SEALs. The built in binoculars, he was glad to discover, worked incredibly well. He was able to focus effortlessly on the house containing his target.

By the simple expedient of telephoning the owners of the two houses in the area they had learned which one had been rented to a group of Syrian businessmen.

Hunter could see a jetty protruding into the lake, close to the cabin. Adjusting his fall, he aimed at the clearing. Seconds later a low buzzing began in his ears. He pulled the cord and the canopy opened with a muted thud above his head. It was only moments before he felt the weight come off the bag that was dangling 6ft beneath him. The aerofoil had been in action for less than fifteen seconds. Just enough to ensure a safe landing. Only the most expert of jumpers could use the gear. This was Hunter's third time.

* * *

'Richard, I'm sorry, I thought he was you . . .' Richard heard the muffled sound of a smack and a yell of pain from Victoria.

Chalabi screamed down the phone. 'Griffiths! Where are my men?'

'Lost your little friends?' Richard prevaricated, cocking the Uzi as he ran along the track, heading for the place he had left Victoria. He knew exactly where Chalabi and Victoria would be. He made no effort to be quiet. Now speed was of the essence.

Down the phone he heard Chalabi yelling. 'If you don't bring me my men I will kill her! Do you hear me?'

Richard threw the phone into the undergrowth. He entered the trees and slowed down. Nearing the clearing he crouched low and stealthily inched his way forward. He stopped at the forest edge and looked around. They were gone! Where were they?

He heard a shout, Chalabi's voice carrying on the night air. 'Griffiths! If you want the girl bring me my men and the money! You have three minutes to bring them to the jetty on the sea. If you don't show, I'll put bullets in her knees and throw her into the water.'

As he ran through the trees branches whipped across Richard's hands and face, scratching him and snagging at his clothes. On the track he found the dummy money and threw it back into the briefcase. He then ran back down the track towards the house. Approaching the building he slowed down.

'Your time is running out, Griffiths!' Chalabi yelled loudly, hysteria evident in his voice.

Where were they? There! Next to the jetty. Near a picnic table. Chalabi was standing over Victoria pointing a gun at her head. The jetty's lights had been turned on and half a dozen lampposts ran out to the end. Chalabi and Victoria were just in front of the first of them. It was a stupid place to be. Chalabi's eyesight was bound to be affected by the loom of the lights behind him. Richard glanced at the end of the jetty and saw the boat berthed there. That, he guessed was the way the Palestinian intended to escape. The reason he was by the jetty.

The forest ended almost at the water's edge, about 10m from the jetty. As quietly as possible, Richard moved along, just inside the tree-line.

'Hurry up, Griffiths, or I swear I will begin to put bullets into the bitch. First her knees, then her elbows.'

Richard said nothing. He knew that if he showed himself, Chalabi could shoot Victoria and then start firing at him. Their chances of survival would be next to zero. He reached the water's edge. He placed the case of money on the ground. It was no use to him. Slowly, carefully, he walked along the shore towards the jetty. Chalabi didn't see him as he was concentrating on the open ground up to the shack and Richard was still protected by the darkness. Suddenly Chalabi kneeled down and rammed his gun into Victoria's mouth, breaking a tooth. She screamed.

'Show yourself or I will kill her!' Chalabi was partially hidden by Victoria, the shot more difficult but not impossible.

Richard had the Uzi ready, on automatic, aimed at Chalabi who was now about 20m away. Before he opened fire he wanted to distract Chalabi. He wanted Chalabi to look up.

Hunter landed as lightly as gossamer, collapsed the wing and got ready to move out.

The bay where the house was situated was a deep indentation in the valley. He had studied a map of the area and made his decisions. He'd been given a choice of weapons and in the end selected a modified Colt Commando. Not only did it fire single shots as well as fully automatic but he knew it was one of the few submachine guns with a built in silencer, a modification added for special forces. He had a thirty round magazine with two spares. Strapped to his thigh was the matt-black killing knife favoured by special forces the world over.

'Moving out,' he said softly into his throat mike. The helicopter that had dropped him was now hovering 5 miles away and acting as a relay to Rory Calhoun. There was no acknowledgement of his message. None was expected.

The sound of a single shot sounded clearly in the night.

'Chalabi!' Richard yelled. Chalabi's head jerked around towards where Richard was standing. He was raising his weapon when Richard opened fire with the gun on fully automatic. A single shot hit Chalabi in the chest and then the gun jammed. Chalabi was thrown backwards, his arms outstretched, his pistol spinning into the lake.

Richard ran towards the two of them. Much to his surprise Chalabi got to his feet and staggered along the jetty. Richard ejected a cartridge and pulled the trigger again but still nothing happened. He had reached Victoria and was going after Chalabi when she called out.

'Richard! Don't go! I beg you! Please stay! Oh, God, Richard.' She began sobbing.

Richard hesitated, heard the sound of a boat's engine start up and knew it was too late. He knelt beside Victoria and cradled her in his arms. He felt his own tears trickling down his cheeks as he held her tight. Thank you, God, thank you, he said softly. Thank you for letting her live.

The explosion was huge. The cabin blew apart and incendiary devices took hold. The conflagration was fierce and brief.

'Richard! It's me, Nick!' He saw his cousin silhouetted against the jetty lights.

'Jesus H. Christ! You scared the life out of me. Where did you come from?'

'Tell you later. In the meantime, I'll send for the cavalry. 'Sentinel, this is Quaker. Sentinel I've got the pigeons.

One man escaped by boat across the lake. Can you come for me and give hot-pursuit?' He listened to the reply. 'Roger that. I'll be at the end of the jetty. Two minutes.'

They looked at what was left of the house.

'Oh my God,' said Victoria, her hand over her mouth. 'Val! Val!' she screamed.

Richard looked at Hunter. 'She was dead,' he said softly.

Hunter nodded. 'Wait here. The FBI are on their way, but God knows when they'll get here. Who was in the boat? Chalabi?'

'Yes.' The bitterness was clear in Richard's voice.

'Right. I'm going after him.'

Hunter ran along the jetty. The helicopter came to a hover thirty feet above him and winched down a strop. Slipping it over his head and under his shoulders Hunter transmitted he was ready. Even as the helicopter shot into the sky he was being winched upwards. Seconds later he was being helped inboard by a crewman and plugged into the helicopter communications system.

'The boat headed straight across the lake. Can you see anything?'

'Negative,' the pilot replied. The moon appeared slowly from behind a mountain and cast its white light across the water. 'I see his wake. Got him.'

The helicopter swooped down like an eagle dropping onto a rabbit. The pilot hit the searchlight. The boat was centred in the middle of its beam. Chalabi looked up, swung his Uzi and emptied the contents at the helicopter. The pilot didn't even bother taking evasive action.

'You handled one of these before, sir?' the crewman asked Hunter.

'Not exactly. I've used the British GPMG.'

'That's nothing to this baby, sir.' The American fiddled with the M-197 20mm cannon and said, 'Ready to fire, sir.'

Hunter looked along the sights, fixed on the rear of the boat and squeezed the trigger. The shells flashed into the night in a solid stream of steel. Moving the gun left and right he fired along the length of the boat. After a few seconds the petrol on board caught light. There was an explosion as the tank went up. A few moments later the boat hit the beach.

'Nice shooting, sir. You got him.'

'Maybe. Can you drop me?' he asked the pilot.

The helicopter stopped two feet above the ground and Hunter jumped out. Drawing his Colt Commando he ran down to the boat where the fire was already dying. The boat was sinking in a few feet of water. He could see there was no sign of a body. Cautiously he moved down the pebble beach. There was a patch of sand and as clear as a signpost, he saw a set of footprints.

Hunter ran after them until he hit grass. Slowly now he continued across the open ground. He could see picnic tables with combined bench seats scattered around the area but there was no sign of anybody. Suddenly the night was ripped apart by two shots and a scream of terror. The scream came from up ahead and Hunter sprinted towards it.

Car headlights swept the area in an arc when a car turned and sped away. Hunter knelt, took aim and fired at the red lights fading into the distance. 'Sentinel this is Quaker. He's in the car heading for Highway Twenty-Six.'

'I see him. Shall I pursue, over?'

'You know the rules of engagement, over.'

'That's affirmative, Quaker. Which is why we're glad to have you on board.'

That was the advantage of working with special forces. Every man could think for himself. Hunter grinned mirthlessly. The pilot knew very well what was required. RoEs were the bane of every military commander in the civilised world. The enemy could act anyway it liked, while the West kept itself hamstrung with its rules. Everyone was aware that Hunter alone could shoot Chalabi because of TIFAT's mandate. If the Americans killed Chalabi, technically they could be arrested for murder. That wasn't likely to happen, but it obscured the lines of the moral high-ground. Which were obscure enough as it was. Or they could give the credit to Hunter. SF personnel weren't in it for the glory but for the results.

'Glad to be aboard,' said Hunter running to where he had first seen the car. 'Damn. Sentinel this is Quaker. Get back here fast. We've two injured kids. They need to get to a hospital, fast.'

The boy had been shot between the eyes but the girl, although she was covered in blood, was still breathing. After checking her over, Hunter found a bullet hole in the top of her leg which was pumping dark arterial blood. Placing his hand on the hole he pressed hard. The girl moaned but remained unconscious. The helicopter landed and a crewman jumped out carrying a first aid kit.

He assessed the injury instantly. Puncturing a plasma bottle he put a drip into the girl's arm within seconds. The young crewman placed the bottle in its specially designed holder alongside the body. He took a pressure pad from the kit and placed it over Hunter's thumbs. 'Now.'

Sliding his hands away, Hunter allowed the pressure pad to take the place of his thumbs and the crewman held it tightly in place. Hunter grabbed a bandage and wrapped it around the wound.

'Ready, sir?'

'Let's go.' Carefully, they picked up the young girl and hurried back to the helicopter. Placing her on a stretcher the helicopter was back in the air less than three minutes after it had landed.

'How bad is she?' The pilot asked over the intercom.

'Bad,' was the crewman's simple answer. Already he was changing the plasma drip for a fresh one.

'Okay. I'll see what I can do.'

The helicopter accelerated until the engine was howling. The chopper screamed across the sky at a speed that it wasn't designed for while Hunter alerted the FBI.

The pilot had already contacted Air Traffic Control at San Diego and told them that he was bringing in an emergency gunshot wound and that he was heading for the Naval Air Station at Coronado Island. It had one of the best medical facilities in the country with the best surgeons. The pilot radioed ahead to the centre and when he came in to land a gurney was already waiting. It didn't have far to travel. He had landed only metres from the hospital entrance.

When the girl had been trolleyed inside the pilot turned to Hunter. 'Now what, Nick?'

'We've no chance of catching Chalabi. Christ, that man must have been cradled with Satan. We'd better get back up there and see what's to be done. Before we do though, I'll get out of this kit and back into civvies.'

With the camouflage cream washed off and dressed in civilian clothes, Hunter was taken back to Salton Sea. Even as the helicopter was landing, cars arrived from which poured FBI agents with guns drawn. They froze in position while Hunter climbed down from the helicopter and stood quietly, watching it fly away again. They didn't know who he was and until they learnt otherwise they'd treat him with the utmost caution. It wasn't normal for a military helicopter to land in the middle of what had been reported as a kidnapping and shooting.

'Who's in charge?' Hunter asked, when the noise of the chopper blades had faded.

'I am.' The agent was about 5ft 10ins, slim and fit looking. He had brown wavy hair and was clean-shaven. His FBI badge hung over the breast pocket of his dark suit jacket. The two men shook hands. 'Who are you?'

'My name is Hunter. I was sent to get the men responsible for the kidnapping.'

'Special Agent Robson. Sent by whom? And by "get" do you mean kill? Because I have to tell you right now that isn't the way we do things around here.'

Hunter shrugged and walked towards Richard and

Victoria. The agent had no choice but to follow. He looked over his shoulder, 'Secure the area,' he yelled to the twenty or so agents, men and women, who were standing around, waiting for orders.

Richard and Victoria were seated at the picnic table. Neither said anything, just sat there eyeing the activity around them, watching Hunter and the agent approach.

'Hey buster, Hunter or whatever your name is, will you tell me what's going down?'

'What were you told?' Hunter countered the question.

'That some terrorist, one that's on our "most wanted" was to be found here. That he'd kidnapped somebody and we were to get here straightaway.'

Victoria had stopped weeping and now sat huddled next to Richard.

'Are you two all right?' Hunter asked.

Victoria didn't reply and Richard shrugged.

Hunter made the introductions. 'This is Richard Griffiths and the lady is Miss Victoria Shand. They were to be married tomorrow. Miss Shand was kidnapped by a group of Palestinians and held for ransom. Richard, do you feel able to tell the special agent what's been happening?'

Richard nodded.

'Before you do,' Hunter continued, 'I want to tell you what happened across the lake.'

Succinctly Hunter explained what had transpired, describing Chalabi's brutal means of escape. The special agent listened to the story. He looked sceptical initially, but called his office and then the local police. An all points had already been put out for Chalabi. He was described as armed and highly dangerous.

'Now, Mr. Griffiths, perhaps you'll be good enough to tell me what's been going on here?'

'Certainly.' Richard began his story. When Richard described shooting Farid the agent became outraged.

'That's murder, Mr. Griffiths. I'll have you...'

Hunter broke in. 'Get real, Special Agent Robson. It was self-defence. The man had a gun and was about to shoot Richard. Isn't that right?' He looked at his cousin warningly.

An FBI agent approached and said, 'That's the perimeter secured.'

'You'll find the body of a dead woman in there,' Richard pointed at the burnt out wreckage, 'Or what's left of her remains.' Victoria began to shake and Richard put his arm around her, pulling her tightly against him. He continued his story. When he finished, he said, 'That's all.'

'And where do you fit in?' Robson glared at Hunter.

'I work for an organisation known as The International Force Against Terrorism.'

'And who the hell are they?'

'You'd better check it with Quantico. If you haven't heard of us then you obviously don't have the right sort of clearance. You're too junior to be in charge here.'

The agent was shot through with indignation. 'Listen, buster...'

His opinion was lost amid the sound of another helicopter arriving. They watched it land. Along the fuselage in large yellow letters was the legend – FBI. A tall, distinguished looking man with grey hair alighted and came forward with his hand outstretched.

'Commander Hunter?'

'Yes, sir.'

'I'm Jake Atwood. I'm the Deputy Director for the FBI in California. Sorry I'm late getting here. I've been getting briefed about what's been going on from General Macnair and Admiral Christchurch. What's happened?'

Richard and Hunter related their stories once more. This time Richard emphasised his need to defend himself from the Palestinians.

Atwood waved his hand. 'They deserved to die. You saved the taxpayer a ton of money, Mr. Griffiths. Pity about Chalabi though.'

'What's the chances of getting him?' Richard asked.

'It all depends on what he does. I'd have crossed into Mexico by now if it were me. After all, the border is only a spit away. But somehow I don't think that's what he'll do. We'll see. Miss Shand, I am so sorry about your friend. Do you know who killed her?'

'Yes,' She spoke barely above a whisper. 'It was Chalabi.'

Atwood took out a photograph of Chalabi from his breast pocket. 'Is this the man? I just want to be sure.'

'Yes.' Victoria whispered. Seeing his face again turned her stomach.

'That's Chalabi,' said the Deputy Director. 'I'll get this written up and I want you to sign a statement to the effect that he killed your friend. It's possible that Chalabi is going back to New York. Maybe he thinks his diplomatic immunity will save him. If he does, he's got a hell of a shock coming to him.'

Richard nodded. Now it was all over he looked drained and exhausted. 'Can we get out of here?'

Hunter looked at Atwood who nodded. 'That's okay by me.'

'Come on,' said Hunter. 'The sooner we get Victoria to a hospital the better.'

'I've got a car hidden some way down the track,' said Richard.

'Give me the keys,' said Atwood. 'We'll find it.'

'Thanks. It's about a couple of miles or so. On the left as you walk down the hill.'

Victoria was given a sedative and strapped into a seat.

'You were bloody lucky,' said Hunter speaking to Richard, as they strapped themselves in.

The engine began to start and Richard leaned over towards his cousin and yelled in his ear, 'I know.'

From Victoria's hospital bed they contacted her parents and cancelled the wedding. It would be another two days before Victoria miscarried.

27

CHALABI DROVE LIKE a maniac. Halfway to L. A. he forced himself to slow down. Even so, he was fortunate not to be stopped by the Highway Patrol. He broke the speed limit all the way. So great was his fury at losing his men that he was halfway along Highway 15 before he cooled down enough to think clearly. He would have earned ten million dollars with the death of the man Griffiths. If it hadn't been for the bullet proof vest taken from the house with the arms cache he would have died as well. He knew that there were many more caches like it across the country. It was time to rise. Time to hurt America and hurt it badly. He, Jalal Chalabi, would see that it happened. The thought sustained him.

It wasn't until he was passing the turnoff for San Clemente that he began thinking about his immediate problem – how to get back to New York. He understood the politics of the situation as well as the Americans. They would have to let him go if they wanted the aid deal to go through. They saw it as a first step towards peace in the Middle East. Or so they thought. Little did they know, or even comprehend that there would never be peace as long as Israel existed. Furthermore, he would scream diplomatic immunity. Deny everything! Claim it was an Israeli conspiracy.

He carried on to Harbor Freeway. Within minutes he was in a maze of streets in downtown Los Angeles, not far from Union Station. Here, there was a mixture of renovated buildings and empty lots. Much of the area was run down, dilapidated. These were the homes of people who had been born with no hope or who'd had hope ground out of them. Down a side street he found what he was looking for. The walls of the buildings were daubed with gang colours and threats to other gangs to stay away. The streets were still busy with people hurrying about their business. He liked the neighbourhood he was in. He liked the way the pedestrians kept their heads down, avoiding eye contact. *This was fear country, where people said don't bother me, don't look at me. I'm not looking at you, so leave me alone.* It was still a few minutes shy of midnight.

He left the Uzi in the trunk, the keys in the ignition and the driver's door unlocked. Climbing out, he walked away. This was the sort of area the police didn't enter unless trouble was reported. Here, law-abiding citizens acted like the three monkeys – saw no evil, heard no evil and definitely didn't go telling the police about any evil. He figured the car wouldn't be there more than twenty minutes. One of the local gangs would think all their Christmases had come at once – especially when they found the gun and ammunition.

The majesty of Union Station was totally lost on him. The station was busy and he saw on the huge departures board that there was a train leaving at 00.15 for Las Vegas. The journey of nearly 300 miles would take five hours. An early morning arrival into Vegas suited his purposes. He paid cash for a one-way ticket and caught the train with minutes to spare. Sitting in a corner of the carriage he kept his head down and feigned sleep. He wasn't pretending for long. Exhaustion finally swept through him and he fell into a troubled doze. The conductor, checking tickets, woke him some time later. After being disturbed he couldn't get back to sleep. Whenever the train stopped and passengers climbed aboard he wondered if they were federal agents or police.

Through the dark night the train crossed the Mojave Desert, over some of the most splendid and spectacular scenery in the world. Even if it had been daylight most of the passengers would have been oblivious to the beauty around them. They were travelling to get an early start in Vegas. They were looking forward to a rushed breakfast followed by slots, craps, roulette and virtually every other game they could bet on. This was the big one. They could feel it in their bones.

Half drunk with fatigue, Chalabi disembarked at Henderson. He thought about what he would do. The only way his diplomatic immunity could be revoked was if his Palestinian President agreed to it. And that would never happen. He took comfort in the thought.

Outside the railway station were buses departing regularly for the airport and a few minutes later he was at the terminal. Even though it was early, the place was already coming to life. Chalabi sought out a washroom. Looking in a mirror his reflection was as he had expected. His eyes were red-rimmed, he had a day's stubble and his clothes looked as though he'd been sleeping in them for days.

On the concourse he read that the next flight to New York was Continental Airways. Approaching the ticket counter he was served immediately.

'One way to New York,' he said to the woman behind the counter. 'Every year I swear I'm not coming back and every year . . . well, here I am.'

'Yes, sir.' She gave a mechanical smile. 'How will you be paying, sir?'

'Cash. It's my last dollars. I never bring credit cards with me. Otherwise I'd be going home poorer than I am now. Three days to clean me out. That was all it took.' He took the proffered ticket and turned to leave.

'Gate twenty-one, sir.'

He didn't bother acknowledging her, sure that his explanation of his appearance had convinced her. How many fools there were in this world, sitting at gaming tables, chasing their dreams, he thought savagely.

At some stage during his escape he had lost his mobile phone and so he stopped to make a call to New York.

The receptionist at the hotel quickly connected him to the room he asked for. Everything was as planned.

Nervously, he passed through airport security. Everywhere he looked it seemed to him there was an FBI agent. Even on the plane he couldn't relax. What if they were waiting for him at Newark? Given more time he would have taken the Greyhound and swapped buses all the way across America. Mentally, he shook himself. It would have taken days by bus. This was the only way. The risk was worth it.

Arriving at Newark Airport he disembarked and headed for the exits. Being an internal flight it was as simple as getting on or off a train or bus. He was outside and diving into a taxi within minutes.

'The Excelsior in Brooklyn,' he ordered.

He had never stayed at this particular hotel before, but he walked in as though he was a regular. He knew the room number and went straight up. Tapping three times, pausing and tapping three more he looked up and down the corridor. Come on, hurry up. The door opened.

'*Gir! Ya hala!*' After the Arabic welcome, her next words were, 'Jalal, you look awful.'

'While you, Jasmina, have never looked more beautiful.' Jasmina Khaled was twenty-two, tall and slim, with black wavy hair. She had dark eyes, a straight thin nose and a wide generous mouth. Yes, she was beautiful, but Chalabi knew she took more pride in being one of HAMAS' agents rather than how she looked. For the last few days she had been staying at the hotel.

'Did everything go like we planned?'

'To the letter. When I arrived, I let it be known that I was here to meet my lover. Casually, of course. I was talking in the bar, flirting with one of the barmen. He dropped hints about taking me out and I said I was waiting for you.'

'You mentioned my name?'

'Of course, Jalal. When I saw you arriving on TV I pointed you out to the bar staff. Telling them how you hoped to be able to get away to join me. I kept up the pretence with the room staff, hanging a "Do Not Disturb" sign and meeting them at the door, letting them see the drawn curtains and me in my bathrobe. See your photograph?' She pointed to a huge framed photograph twelve inches by twelve, standing prominently on the table. It was a portrait of Chalabi, dressed in a white shirt, smart suit and wearing a black and white kaffiyeh. 'I drew the maid's attention to it and I would say things to her like, "Oh, he's getting away from the UN this afternoon to be with me" or "We're going to the ballet." We did that last night.'

'I hate the ballet.'

'Well, it's more romantic than dog-racing, Jalal. I bought two tickets. I've kept them, as well as the programme, as souvenirs. We've been to Staten Island and to a few art galleries. Every time I've been anywhere I've bought two tickets. I've had room service bring up two breakfasts and I've had you taking a shower while I've tipped the waitress.' She pointed at the hand held Dictaphone. 'I have switched that on twice while the shower was running, just like you said. I've done everything exactly like we discussed.' If she was expecting a modicum of praise she was to be sorely disappointed.

'First, I need a shave and then a shower. Throw these clothes away, including the shoes.'

'Is there anything else you require?' She smiled coquettishly.

'Later,' he croaked. 'I have much to do.'

If they tried to arrest him he would argue he had been at the hotel the whole time. The staff would be called, the evidence produced. Enough anyway, to cause confusion. To give him time to leave with the delegation. A change of clothes was hanging up in the closet.

It was two hours later when a taxi dropped him outside the UN complex. He ran up the steps and was inside the building before the FBI agents watching for him outside realised what had happened.

Special Agent-in-Charge Zak Zakowski replaced the receiver. Stunned, he looked at Catherine De Marco and said, 'He's back. Chalabi's back.'

'What? You're kidding!'

'That was the stakeout at the UN on the phone. He walked in as though he didn't have a care in the world.'

Tony Carpenter looked up from his computer screen. 'What do we do now?'

Zak shook his head. 'I don't know. I'm out of my depth here and I don't mind admitting it. We can't just walk in and arrest him. He's got diplomatic immunity. Any judge would have our guts for garters. I'd better phone Quantico.'

'No he hasn't,' said Catherine.

'What?' Zakowski froze with his hand on the telephone.

'He hasn't. If a diplomat commits a crime as heinous as murder he can be arrested. I've checked. The American Supreme Court ruled years ago. Since then, through the UN, most of the other countries have agreed. The few that haven't are of no consequence.'

'That changes things,' said Zakowski thoughtfully. He stood, wandered across to the coffee machine and topped up his mug. He added milk and sugar. This put a different slant on things. He returned to his desk, picked up the receiver and pressed the stowed number.

A secretary answered. 'This is Special Agent Zakowski. The Director please.' A few seconds went by. 'Sir?'

'Hello, Zak,' Lou Murray greeted him. 'What can I do for you?'

'Sir, Jalal Chalabi has just walked into the UN.'

The Director sat up straighter in his chair. 'Has he, by God?'

'What do we do? Go in and arrest him?'

'No!' There was a pause. 'Actually, we can't. We don't have the jurisdiction.'

'Because of his diplomatic immunity? I thought that didn't apply in the case of murder.'

'It doesn't.'

'I don't understand. What's preventing us from arresting him?'

'The talks. We've been told to keep a lid on things. Believe it or not, the agreement for the Palestinians is deemed more important. With it, many lives will be saved. Food aid, water supplies, electricity,' he paused and repeated, 'It will save a lot of lives.'

'But sir, we can't let Chalabi get away with it.'

'He's not going to. Here's what we're going to do.'

The Director replaced the receiver. With a smile, Zakowski replaced his. He told the others what had been said.

Michael Rinski was as surprised as the FBI to learn that Chalabi was back in the building. 'Are you sure?' he asked one of the Israeli delegates.

'I'm sure.'

'What the hell is going on? I can't find out anything. Either nobody knows what's been happening or no one's saying anything.'

'That's because of the talks.'

'I know it is. But the motion carried thirty minutes ago. They have already announced that more aid is going immediately into the region, as a gesture of good will by the West. And we've agreed that the water and electricity supplies will be sacrosanct. Under no circumstances can we cut either off as a collective punishment. It's all signed, sealed and delivered.'

The other agent made no comment. He didn't believe in collective responsibility. Targeting terrorists and murderers was one thing, hurting women and children quite another. However, he had always had the good sense not to say so out loud.

Rinski sat frowning when his phone rang. Would he take a phone call from Commander Nick Hunter of TIFAT? Rinski had met Hunter on a few occasions in the past. He told the operator to put him through. 'Nick! What can I do for you?' He listened for a few seconds. 'I might have guessed this wasn't a social call. Yes, of course I'll meet with you.'

The coffee bar they met in wasn't busy. Hunter sat at a table, watching the door. When Rinski walked in Hunter gave a wave and the Israeli nodded. He collected a coffee from the counter and joined Hunter at the back of the room. They shook hands. Hunter noticed the Israeli's discomfort at sitting with his back to the door. He understood. Paranoia kept you alive.

There was no small talk.

'You were sent here to take out Chalabi,' Hunter began.

'Wow, Nick, take it easy. I can't tell you that,' Rinski paused with his cup halfway to his mouth.

'Mike, you don't have to. The General told me. He's been in talks with your boss and your Prime Minister.'

Rinski shrugged. 'So why are we meeting?'

'I want to borrow your ring.'

If he wasn't such a good actor, virtually a pre-requisite for a successful Mossad agent, his jaw would have dropped and the surprise would have registered on his face. As it was, he had the presence of mind to say, 'What ring?'

'The one that kills.'

'Oh, that ring. Why?'

'The General and your boss came up with the idea. You want Chalabi, we want him and you can be damned sure the Yanks want him.'

'What on earth do they want him for? What's he done to the Yanks?'

'He kidnapped a woman and killed her friend. While escaping he killed a young man and badly wounded a girl. She'll live but it was touch and go.'

'So why is there no mention of it in the news?'

'There's a news blackout because of the talks. The Palestinian agreement needs time to bed in. If news of what Chalabi did leaked out the Americans would have to pull the plug. The people would go nuts otherwise. There would be no aid from the States. What Israel does about it we don't know. There's one possibility that could save the agreement.'

Rinski shook his head. 'Now he has to die to *save* the talks.'

'You got it.'

Rinski took a deep breath and exhaled, blowing out his cheeks. 'I can't keep up.'

'That's politics. But I know what you mean. Mike, you were sent to kill Chalabi before the agreement was signed in the hope that there would be no agreement.'

'I didn't know that. I was just told to do it.' It was the lament of foot soldiers across the world – I was only following orders.

'Yeah, sure Mike. I've seen you in action. I know you well enough to guess that you'd worked it out.'

Rinski looked at Hunter, poker faced, said nothing. Then after a few seconds, he asked, 'So why did Chalabi do what he did?'

'Two reasons. He and some other people wanted revenge on my cousin and HAMAS wants the agreement stopped as well.'

'How will that be achieved?'

Hunter looked at the other man. It was his turn to say nothing.

After a few moments Rinski nodded. 'I get it. By admitting what they'd done. By suggesting that the whole thing at the UN was a sham to get him into the country.'

Hunter nodded. 'That's the way we figure it as well. Actually, it's worse than that. What if HAMAS claim that FATAH had been privy to the whole thing? That it had been done with their sanction?'

'They wouldn't be able to prove otherwise. FATAH would become as much of a pariah as HAMAS.'

'That's what we figure.'

'Have you ever seen such a convoluted mess?' Rinski shook his head, 'It can only happen in the Middle East. Is that why Chalabi isn't being arrested?'

'It's why he has to die.'

'But what's to stop HAMAS issuing a statement about what happened? It could still scupper the agreement.'

'Chalabi was determined he wouldn't spend the rest of his life in an American jail. So he arranged an alibi. He's claiming that he was at a hotel with a woman throughout the period. The FBI have been to the hotel and questioned her and the staff. It appears he really was there.'

Rinski's cynical look said it all. 'I've done that. Meals in the room for two. Bed slept in on both sides. Men's clothing scattered around the place. Shower running. No second person actually seen.'

'Precisely.'

'What about DNA?'

'There's none to be found. The chalet the women were in has burnt to the ground, the boat he used likewise and the car he stole can't be found anywhere. Also there was another burnt out car which was assumed he arrived in. Chalabi is a very cautious man and not to be underestimated. So, no DNA.'

'Why don't the Yanks arrest him for terrorist crimes?'

'I asked the same question. We know what Chalabi has done. However, there's no proof about any of it. He's never claimed personal responsibility.'

Rinski nodded. 'I guess you're right. HAMAS always made the claims.'

'Precisely. They've even claimed for things they haven't done. Welcome to the mad world of terrorism.'

'But if he's on the most wanted list . . .' he tailed off.

'Mike, that's our list. That's for TIFAT, Mossad, the CIA and the rest of the West's alphabetic soup in fighting terrorism. We find him, we kill him. He's off the list. There's no evidence that will stand up in a court of law. Look at Northern Ireland. People who are known terrorists are now in government. Known but never with the sort of proof good enough to make an arrest. And we as sure as hell aren't taking any other action. Not in the UK against British citizens.'

'You're right. So what now?'

'What if Chalabi gets back safely to Gaza and tells his story? The Islamic world would lap it up. And there'd be little we could do about it. After all, he's posted as one of the most wanted terrorists in the world. He can't go any higher on the lists. And what's the chance of getting him in Gaza?'

'None. Getting in and out safely is next to impossible. Everyone knows everyone. A stranger would quickly be noticed. It's one of the reasons we've never managed to get him.' Rinski finished his coffee. 'And once he's dead the Americans stick with the story that he was at the hotel.'

'You got it. Very few people know what actually happened. With luck we'll be able to keep the whole thing under wraps.'

'What about justice for the families of the woman and the boy?'

'I said the same thing. They'll be informed in a year or so. Meanwhile, I'm afraid they'll suffer like all families who have to face a bereavement. I don't like it. It's harsh, I know, but can't be helped.'

Rinski nodded. He'd seen enough death to understand. 'Irrespective of the agreement, his death is what we want for the crimes he's committed against Israel.'

'The same goes for us,' said Hunter.

Rinski reached into a special waistcoat pocket and extracted the ring. It looked innocuous enough. He showed Hunter how it worked.

28

CHALABI STOOD ON the plaza in front of the UN building with the other delegates. A wall of television cameras and journalists stood filming the speeches or taking notes. Chalabi wasn't listening. The historic nature of the agreement reached would be destroyed as soon as he returned to Gaza and told what he had done.

He was as nervous as hell, even though the FBI had spoken to him and said that he was free to go. That his story had checked out. Just like that. There had been nothing in the papers or on the TV about what had happened. But then, he rationalised, the death by shooting of a woman and some kids in California was hardly likely to be headline news in New York. With no DNA there was nothing the Americans could do about it. His explanation that he had deliberately lost his bodyguards to spend time with the woman in the hotel had been accepted.

He may have failed to kill Griffiths but he had achieved one major objective. The agreement would be finished. And as far as Griffiths was concerned, he would have another opportunity. He would make sure to have his revenge one day. He told himself that he was a patient man. Besides, the death of the woman would cause a great deal of grief to all who had known her. Let them suffer like he had suffered. Griffiths' and his woman's death would have been too easy. It was what he would be telling the Saudis. He would tell them it had been his plan. That he would return soon and carry out his mission. Perhaps they would pay the ten million dollars after all.

The more he thought about it, the more he convinced himself he could pull it off. Self delusion had always been one of Chalabi's traits.

At last, the press conference was over and Kaddoumi waved goodbye to the cameras. This was the time Chalabi had feared the most. Once away from the UN would they arrest him? Would his diplomatic immunity protect him?

He had a moment of panic when the FBI closed up as they reached the cars. The journey to the JFK Airport was uneventful. There, they were escorted through to departures taking the staff route.

In the departure lounge the man in charge of the FBI turned to Kaddoumi and held out his hand.

'Sir,' said Zakowski, 'good luck. I hope all goes well.'

'Thank you,' Kaddoumi shook Zak's hand.

'It is customary on these occasions to shake hands goodbye,' Zak continued, offering his hand to the other delegates, 'as a celebration that nothing has gone wrong. That you are safely leaving our country.'

Instinctively, each man shook his hand. The other three agents with him did the same. Chalabi didn't notice the fact that the tall, dark haired agent gave him a double handed clasp. He didn't even notice the drop of blood on the back of his hand. The fact was he was too strung out, desperate to leave America.

The flight was called and an attendant appeared to escort them to the plane.

Zakowski turned to Hunter. 'Okay?'

Hunter nodded. 'Thanks for your co-operation.'

Zak smiled. 'One, I had no choice. Orders. Two, I was delighted. Earlier today I had the details of what happened at Salton Sea. What I don't understand, is why you?'

As they left the airport Hunter explained about TIFAT's mandate.

* * *

In London, the Palestinians were kept waiting for nearly three hours. They sat in virtual silence. On the plane their talk had been animated, excited. It was an historic agreement. Perhaps, at last, life could be improved for the Palestinian people. Praise be to *Allah*. The television in the corner of the lounge showed the crowds in Gaza celebrating. The excitement of the people was palpable. FATAH was being talked about as the next government. HAMAS' days as the ruling party were numbered.

Chalabi knew better. The fools.

Their flight was called and the delegation gathered up their possessions and proceeded to board. The safety briefing was given and the plane took off. Sitting in a window seat, Chalabi looked out at the clear blue sky. A fine perspiration began to bead along his forehead as he broke out into a sweat. He adjusted the overhead blower and directed it at his face. A dizzy feeling swept through him. He reached for the sick bag in the pocket in front of him and held it to his mouth. Nothing happened even though the feeling of nausea remained. What was wrong with him? A shaft of pain struck him and he arched his back. He'd never felt anything like it before.

'Are you all right, sir?' A stewardess leant over him. 'Can I get you something? A glass of water? A pain killer?'

'Water,' Chalabi croaked. He then added, 'For the love of *Allah*, something for the pain.'

'Right away, sir.' She hurried away.

His body began to react more violently. What was happening? His back arched, the seatbelt holding him in his seat. His hands clamped more tightly around the armrests while his jaw dropped open and his eyes began to bulge. All the agonies of hell coursed through his veins. He tried to scream but couldn't. He could no longer breath. Time stopped but the pain continued. In the last agonising seconds of his wretched life a name flashed through his mind. *Richard Griffiths*.

* * *

Following Chalabi's death, events unfolded as predicted. From time to time his name was associated with the deaths in California. This was refuted and his presence at the Excelsior hotel, witnessed by the staff, was trundled out whenever it was required. Reference to his possible involvement faded. Other, more pressing and topical matters, needed reporting. Thanks to the agreement, an uneasy peace had settled across the Middle East. The pundits were even suggesting that a lasting peace was possible. The cynics doubted it.

29

THREE MONTHS AFTER the events at Salton Sea Vicky had a complete nervous breakdown. The memory of her dead friend's face had haunted her every day. Richard felt desperately guilty and did his best to give her all the love and support she needed. He rarely left her alone. Victoria lost weight, her beautiful shank of blonde hair lost its shine and her personality lost its sparkle. She took pills to put her to sleep, pills to wake her up, pills for a never-ending headache, pills to help her eat. He knew what she was going through. He had been there.

Time passed slowly. Six months after the wedding had been cancelled Victoria began experiencing violent mood swings, an emotional yo-yo, swinging from happy to suicidal. Sometimes her moods lasted for hours and sometimes for days. The miscarriage was a blur in the distant past, fading in and out of reality in her memory.

Richard knew that unless he managed to turn their lives around Chalabi would have won. In spite of the satisfaction he had derived from knowing he was dead, the bastard was ruining their lives just as effectively as if he had killed them both.

He had *The Lady Ellen* brought to America by a professional delivery crew and prepared her for a long cruise. Perhaps being on the boat, just the two of them, would help her to recover. He would do anything to get the old Victoria back.

They left Miami on a warm, sunny day. Victoria seemed happy enough and professed to be looking forward to the voyage. She was on a high. Richard decided to head east towards the Bahamas. The forecast was good, with a high pressure over the Gulf of Mexico keeping the weather stable at least for the next few days. The objective was simply to be alone to try and rekindle their relationship. Victoria insisted on sleeping in the forward cabin, claiming her incessant headache kept her awake and that she would disturb his rest as well. He went along with it.

On the evening of the first day just as the Bimini Islands began to paint on the radar, he turned the boat to starboard onto a heading of east-south-east. He knew that the following morning they would see Andorra Island, the biggest landmass in the Bahamas, but he intended skirting around it. They had provisions for two weeks and he had no intention of hitting land before then.

Richard kept watch that night, dozing on the bench seat in the wheelhouse, waking up whenever the radar buzzer sounded. In the morning, Victoria didn't appear until nearly 10.00 and when she did she was happy and playful. Richard, noticing that her eyes were unnaturally bright, tried to match her mood. But his heart was heavy with the knowledge of what he was about to do. One fear he had been nursing for some weeks appeared to have been correct. Kissing the smooth nape of her neck, he asked her to keep an eye out for other vessels while he had a shower and a shave. She nodded happily.

Below, he went into the forward shower compartment and turned on a radio. Above the music coming from a Bahamian radio station he could hear Victoria's agitated pacing. He didn't hesitate. Inside her cabin it only took him moments to find the drugs she'd been prescribed and another two minutes to find the cocaine. Opening a porthole he emptied the whole lot into the sea. He was going for broke. He had to help her kick her habit. When he met her she had been so warm, so completely without artifice. Now the coke filled her brain, making her brittle and paranoid. If he didn't help her to get clean and stay clean he'd never forgive himself. He would have destroyed her life.

He shaved and showered quickly. Wearing a fresh T-shirt and shorts he went into the wheelhouse carrying two mugs of coffee. He wondered how long she would stay high. It lasted about as long as it took to drink the coffee. Putting down her empty mug, Victoria became restless. She fidgeted, flicking her braid, picking up pencils, the roller-rule used for plotting a course and a book on local tides. She looked through the binoculars, put them down, put her head to the radar and twisted the knobs on it. As the minutes passed her agitation increased. Then she smiled. Here it comes, he thought.

'I need to go below.'

'Sure,' Richard nodded. He stood waiting. It didn't take long. He could hear her movements becoming more frantic.

She suddenly yelled his name the sound a curious mixture of hate, anger and fear. Rushing up the steps from the salon she faced him and screamed, 'Where is it?' Victoria was panting, sweat breaking out along her forehead, her lips pulled back in a snarl. 'My medicine. All my pills. Where are they?'

'Cocaine can hardly be classed as medicine, Victoria.'

She used language he had never heard from her before. Picking up the heavy metal rule from the chart table she smashed it onto the surface. The sharp corner cut a deep groove through the chart and into the wood.

'Give me it, you bastard.'

'I can't do that, Victoria. I threw it over the side.'

She cowered back and then sank to her knees, sobbing.

Richard knelt by her side and took her in his arms. 'Darling, darling, please let me help.' He pulled her close. She rested against him for a few seconds and then struggled frantically but he held her easily. She had grown so thin she was like a rag doll. She suddenly stopped moving. Richard kept his arms wrapped tightly around her while he reached behind to open a drawer in the chart table and grab the hypodermic he had prepared earlier. He jammed the needle into her buttock and pressed the plunger. She squirmed for a second and then collapsed as the powerful drug took hold.

There were tears in his eyes when he bent to pick her up. She weighed nothing. She would sleep for at least twenty-four hours. He carried her below and placed her on his bed. He knew from his research that he needed to give her time to get the coke out of her system. For serious addicts, ones who rarely, if ever, came down very far from their high, it was vitally important. It was the start of the cleansing process. Once she was physically clean Richard had to get inside her head and make her want to stay that way.

He had timed it all deliberately. Increasing speed he headed for a cove near Andros Island. An hour later they were anchored and he lay down to rest in the salon. Sleep was difficult but eventually he dozed off and slept most of the day. In the evening he checked on Victoria. She was still out cold. Kneeling alongside her he kissed her cheek and whispered, 'I'm not going to lose you, my darling. I'm not.'

He checked the anchor, set the alarms and began emptying the master bedroom and en-suite bathroom of everything portable. When he had finished, all that was left was a mattress, two sheets and a blanket. There was nothing she could use as a weapon, nothing with which she could harm herself. He removed the light bulbs and even cut the power to the room. Finally, he locked the hatch to the after deck and the door between the salon and the bedroom. All he had to do now was wait.

It was a long night.

Victoria awoke with a throbbing head and a mouth that felt as though she had been sucking on sawdust. Light was streaming through the uncurtained portholes and she wondered for a moment where she was. Then memory returned. She tried calling out for Richard but all she managed was a croak. Looking around her in confusion it took a few seconds for her to realise that she was in the master bedroom. Weakly, she stood up and went to the door and tried to open it.

'Richard! Richard! Open the door!' Her voice started as a whisper but grew in strength. She was becoming angry.

'Get away from the door,' Richard called, 'and sit on the bed.'

She stayed where she was. She'd force him to let her out. His voice came clearly from behind her and startled, she whirled around, her heart hammering wildly. He was hanging over the edge of the deck, his face in the open porthole.

'I said, get away from the door.'

She broke down in tears. 'Why Richard? Why are you doing this? Haven't I been through enough? Please, please let me out.'

Fighting back his own tears, Richard said, 'I can't, Victoria. We have to get you clean or our lives will be ruined. Sit down on the bed and I'll get you something to drink and eat.'

'I'm not hungry.'

'You must be thirsty.'

'Yes,' she spoke in a small voice. 'Yes, I am thirsty.'

'I'll hand you in a carton of orange juice.' Reaching behind him he plucked a litre carton off the deck and awkwardly pushed it through the porthole. He flicked it onto the bed. 'Shout if you need anything else.'

Pulling himself upright, he returned to the wheelhouse, where he spent the day haunted by the devastated look on Victoria's face. In the evening he gave her more juice and a light meal on a plastic plate. She told him that she wasn't hungry but once she had the food in her hand she ate ravenously. She had barely finished the meal when she keeled over, fast asleep. The narcotic he had added certainly worked fast.

Raising the anchor, he headed south, more because of

his own restlessness than anything. He needed to occupy himself otherwise he would go mad with anxiety. The next two days followed the same pattern. By the third day he knew she was completely clean of the cocaine. Now he needed to get her mind to start healing. She needed to *want* to get better. It had to come from within her.

30

SHE COMPLAINED INCESSANTLY about her head, her stomach, not being able to sleep, sleeping too much. He ignored her. She wept and screamed. Each bout of crying made him feel more anguished. Whatever happened, Richard knew that he had to be strong for both of them.

Victoria stopped complaining. She asked for fresh clothes and took her first shower in days. She washed and braided her hair. She was still as thin as a skeleton but the whites of her eyes were clearer than they had been in weeks.

Eight days after they had left Miami she called out to him. 'Richard, please let me out now. I'll behave. I promise. I think I'm cured. I really do.'

Standing outside the door he agonised about what to do. Then, with a sigh, he knew he had no choice. She had to want to make it herself. He unlocked the door and stood back.

Shyly, like a doe fearful of her own shadow, she came out. She crossed the salon and sat in an easy chair. The look she gave him was one of sheer defiance. 'I hate you. As soon as I'm off this boat I'm going to call my dealer. You don't get it, Richard. You may want me to live but I can't wait to shuffle off this mortal coil. So I've chosen a nice, slow suicide.'

With those words he knew that he had lost. 'I'm so sorry, Victoria. I'll…' it came out as a croak and he cleared his throat. 'I'll take you back to Miami.'

He went up to the wheelhouse and checked their

position, wiping the tears from his cheeks. There was nothing more he could do or say. He'd lost.

Hate had proven to be the seed of destruction – it always was. The cycles of violence and revenge in the Middle East proved that.

If she had never met him, Victoria's life would have been so different. She'd be completing her PhD with a life in the gentle circles of academia ahead of her. He shook his head. Hate never won. It was too corrosive. He should never have started on the road to revenge. In trying to salvage his own life he had ruined hers.

Starting the engines he reluctantly went forward and raised the anchor.

The Englishman spoke with an upper crust accent and said to the other man, 'Well?'

He shrugged. 'They have no idea where the boat is except it was headed for the Bahamas.' His name was Issa Yeslam and he had lived in America for over 20 years. He was a fundamentalist to his fingertips as well as a supporter of *Sharia* Law. He had spent months at a time in Afghanistan as well as Iraq, helping to kill non-believers. It was his duty. A sign of his commitment to the one true faith. Whenever he returned, his residency permit ensured he was waved through Customs and Immigration with the minimum of fuss.

'We'll do the same. We might get lucky. I'll check on the flights to Nassau.'

Richard glanced at the radar screen and frowned when he saw the hazy picture to the south. Grabbing binoculars he stepped outside for a better look. Huge black clouds were piling up and he could see sheets of lightning flashing across the sky. He checked the weather forecast and saw that a tropical storm was heading their way and coming fast. During the last few days he had taken no notice of the weather or the state of the sea as long as they had anchored in a sheltered spot. He did now.

The wind hit like a brick wall and *The Lady Ellen* keeled heavily to port. Down below he heard glasses smashing and anything that wasn't fixed went crashing onto the deck. Increasing speed, Richard checked their position. They were to the south of the Turks and Caicos Islands. Great Inagua was 15 miles north. Around the other side of the island he saw that there was a crescent-shaped bay. It was an ideal place to ride out the storm. Knowing his boat's capabilities he was unperturbed as he set the autopilot and began laying a course, estimating their time of arrival.

Victoria appeared from below, standing on the steps, her face fearful. 'What's going on?'

Summoning up a smile, he replied. 'Just a storm. There's nothing to be worried about. It'll delay us a few hours. But I'll get you back to Miami.' He bit his lip. He hadn't intended the last words to sound so bitter.

Coming the rest of the way into the wheelhouse Victoria sat down on the bench seat. She tried to brace herself while the boat pitched and rolled in an uncomfortable corkscrew motion.

'You'd better sit in the captain's chair. It'll be safer,' he said, adjusting the boat's heading.

She did as he'd suggested. After a few minutes, she spoke. 'Richard, I didn't mean it. I don't hate you. It's just . . . It's just whenever I'm with you I think of Val. I see her face and I can't help blaming you. She's in front of me all the time. I see her when I fall asleep and I see her when I wake up. Cocaine is the only thing that stops me from going insane.'

Looking at her drawn face, pity welled up inside him. 'I understand. I felt something like it when Ellen and the children died.'

The boat swooped and raised her bows through the waves like the thoroughbred she was. They lapsed into silence, somehow a more companionable silence than before.

The Lady Ellen chugged north. The island was 5 miles away on the port bow and the wind was howling up the starboard quarter. The sea ran before it and they bobbed along, uncomfortable but in no danger.

Then the engine shuddered and automatically shut down. *The Lady Ellen* turned beam onto the wind and began rolling heavily. Fear rose like bile in Richard's throat.

Disengaging the gears, he pressed the starter button and fired the engine. It started smoothly. He throttled right back and put her into ahead. He heard the dull clank vibrate through the soles of his feet and the safety-clutch disengage. Something had wrapped itself so tightly around the propeller it couldn't turn. Instead of stripping the gearbox the safety-clutch had kicked in and disconnected the shaft.

Putting the shaft in reverse he increased the revs slowly. The propeller guard began to cut through whatever was jammed down there. The speed of the shaft increased and for a second Richard thought they were in the clear. Then he heard another disheartening clank as the shaft stopped again.

With a curse, Richard staggered to the stern and looked over. His heart sank. It was the middle of the afternoon and an early darkness was settling in because of the storm but even so he could see the microfilament net stretching for hundreds of yards astern of them. Fishing with such a net was illegal. It trapped hundreds of tons of fish at a time.

The wild motion of the boat was dampened down and he realised that it was due to the net. All they needed to do was ride out the storm and when it had passed he could go over the side and cut them free. By the time he returned to the wheelhouse to explain the problem to Victoria he was soaked to the skin from the rain.

'It's far too dangerous to go into the water now. That stuff is lethal. Divers get caught in it and drown. It's as strong as steel, as thin as wool and floats around you, enveloping you like gossamer.' He shuddered. 'I hate the stuff.'

Checking their position, he turned to Victoria, 'How about something to drink? Some orange juice or something?'

'I'll get it.' She slid tentatively off the chair. The boat lurched and she fell against him. For a second they were staring into each other's eyes. The anguish and regret he saw there made him take a step back. He smoothed some stray wisps of hair from her face and kissed her cheek.

When she returned, he was busy checking their position for the third time. His heart was hammering when he ran their projected course on the chart. Grabbing the Pilot he thumbed through its pages until he found what he wanted. The Great Inagua's southern shore was a sheer cliff over a hundred feet high and they were heading straight for it. He checked their speed. They would hit it in half an hour.

'Victoria, we've a problem. I need to get the screw free or else we've had it.'

'What do you mean? Richard, you're frightening me. You said we'd be all right.'

'The storm is setting us down onto the cliffs of that island you can see over there.' He pointed. 'I'll send out a Mayday using the automatic beacon but in the meantime I'd better get ready to go over the side.' He pressed the alarm button on the side of the radio. The Mayday was being transmitted on VHF, UHV and HF broadcasts. Ships and boats in an area covering hundreds of miles knew that *The Lady Ellen* was in trouble. Most importantly, her location was also known. The question was, would someone come to their rescue? Richard didn't think so, not in that part of the world.

He went outside and up forward. Throwing open the

hatch he climbed below to find the gear he needed. Quickly he selected what he wanted and threw it up on the deck. Carrying it aft he wondered if there were any last minute instructions he could give Victoria. He had checked the chart and seen that the sea ran deep all the way to the cliff face. There it shallowed suddenly, the seabed rising sharply, forming the island. He went forward and knocked the pins out of the windlasses. The anchors clattered out and hung down in the water. The seabed was still over two hundred feet further down.

Back in the wheelhouse, he checked the radar one last time before saying loudly, 'I'm going over the stern. You have to do a few things. All right?'

She nodded. The wind was howling across the deck and through the rigging. The swell was long and heavy and the boat rose and fell like a metronome easily capable of riding out the storm – if it hadn't been for the island.

Pulling on a neoprene jacket, Richard slipped the diving bottles over his shoulders and tightened the straps. He wrapped a weight-belt around his waist and a knife on his right leg. He put another on his left leg and a third in the sheath on the weight belt. If he dropped one he didn't want to waste time coming back on board for another.

'You hold me with this line, all right?' He yelled above the howling of the wind and she nodded. 'I've tied the end off on that stanchion so I can't go more than a few yards away.' Looking over the port bow he could clearly see the island through the rain. The sea was smashing into the base of the cliffs, a thunderous upsurge of water rising high into the air. There was very little time left.

Opening the stern gate, Richard walked backwards down the ladder. As soon as his feet were in the water he could feel the net swirling around them. He shuddered. It was cloying and deadly. He went further down until his head was under the surface. *The Lady Ellen* was moving graciously with the swell, rising and falling maybe sixteen or seventeen feet. Bouncing with her, he began to hack at the microfilament, working steadily and quickly. He could feel the movement of the boat, the violence of the sea increasing – they were getting dangerously close to the cliffs. He sawed faster, desperation lending strength to his arms. The knife slipped and he cut his left index finger to the bone. The red blood swirled around him but he ignored it, adrenaline keeping the pain at bay.

Cutting again and again he saw huge swathes of the net drifting away. As more netting was freed there was less weight holding the stern of the boat down so the more she tossed and hit the water. One wave lifted her right out of the sea and she came down with a resounding smash across Richard's arm. He dropped the knife. The mesh was floating all around him and he was disorientated for a few seconds. He got his wits back and snatched the knife from the sheath on his right leg. Grabbing handfuls of the stuff he sawed off some more. He reached the propeller and felt around it. The net was wrapped tight, a solid mass of nylon, fused by the heat of the turning screw. By now most of the net was floating astern, clear of the boat. But it was the microfilament around the shaft and the screw that he had to get rid of. He was near to panic as he sawed back and forth as quickly as he could. Blue rope floated in front of him and he realised that he had cut his lifeline. Too bad! He didn't have time to tie it back on. He hacked some more and tore away the last bit of the nylon net. At that moment one of the anchors snagged the seabed and *The Lady Ellen* swept around to face the sea and the wind. Richard lost his grip and knocked his head on the hull as he rose to the surface. It was a stunning blow and he was semi-conscious for a few seconds. He had enough presence of mind to drop his weight belt.

Floating to the surface he saw the cliffs towering above him. The distance stayed steady for a few moments and then started to decrease as the anchor broke free again.

Spitting out the mouthpiece he summoned up all his strength and yelled, 'Victoria! Victoria! Throw the life belt.' He ditched the diving set and swam after the boat, doing the fastest crawl of his life.

She looked at him in shock. He was already five yards away and they were drifting apart fast as the wind drove the boat onwards. Panicked, she pulled in the lifeline and looked stupidly at the cut end. Lifting the life belt off the salon roof she threw it. She was so weak the belt landed less than halfway to Richard.

He was closing the gap but he was tiring fast. Victoria pulled the life belt back on board and this time, summoning up all her strength, she threw it as hard as she could. It landed on the other side of Richard and he managed to grab it, wrapping his arm around the orange corlene line.

'Pull, Victoria! Pull!' He went hand over hand while Victoria did her bit to help. He reached the stern, hung on to the ladder for a few seconds, mustered his strength, hauled himself up and grabbed the handrail. He dragged himself onto the deck. He lay on his back gasping, Victoria knelt at his side, holding his hand. Gulping air he scrambled to his hands and knees. Victoria helped him to stand. In horror he looked at the cliffs. They were less than twenty yards away. The back surge of the waves was slowing down the inevitable as it pushed them away before the next wave flung them ever closer.

Richard staggered into the wheelhouse, Victoria holding onto him. He pushed the start button and the engine burst into life. Engaging the gears he pushed the throttle hard open and spun the wheel to starboard. The propeller bit deep and *The Lady Ellen* turned her bows away from the cliffs and headed out to safety. Engaging the autopilot he slumped into the chair. Victoria was still clinging to him, tears streaming down her face.

'Hey, it's all right,' he said. 'We're safe now.'

She buried her face in his neck. 'I thought I'd lost you.'

He held her tightly, a smile of relief plastered across his face. Maybe there was a chance for them after all. Reaching across her, Richard cancelled the Mayday signal less than an hour after it was transmitted. He went outside and made his way to the bows, where he raised the anchors.

Typically for that part of the world, the storm passed as suddenly as it had appeared. That night they anchored in the cove they had been heading for. Exhausted, Victoria slept the whole night. Richard dozed, hope and anxiety mingling with each other. Just after dawn he started the engine and raised the anchors. They headed out to sea. It was mid-morning before Victoria appeared.

'Are you okay?'

'Yes, thanks. I've made some coffee.' She handed him a mug.

'Thanks. How are you feeling?'

She shrugged. 'Not too bad.' She shuddered. 'Oh, God, Richard, I thought . . . I thought I had lost you. I knew I didn't want that to happen. I . . .'

An insistent buzz from the radar warned him that a boat was approaching. A glance at the screen showed it was heading towards them. He grabbed his binoculars and focused on what appeared to be a powerful speedboat. He studied it for a few moments, alarm bells ringing in his head. He could see there were two men on board. One was swarthy looking and Richard guessed South American or . . . or Arab? Or was he being paranoid? He looked at the other man. There was something about him, his build, his bearing. Still, Richard thought, there's plenty of sea room. There was still time to turn away. Except the course made no sense. If they were heading for the island to drop anchor then they should have veered away by now to go around one side or the other.

The boat was coming nearer by the second. Looking

through the binoculars once more he tried to see if he recognised the men. It was no use. The faces were still indistinct. The radar showed the boat was now less than half a mile away. He altered course to port by forty-five degrees which would take the vessels clear of each other. Immediately the other boat turned to starboard. Now the alarm bells were ringing loud and clear. He began sounding the horn, a series of five short blasts, warning the other boat that it was taking insufficient action to avert a collision.

The man at the wheel could now be seen clearly without the binoculars. Richard had no idea who he was. He looked again at the other man and took a sharp breath. It couldn't be! Simms? Was it Simms? Christ! What in hell was he doing here?

'What's wrong, Richard?'

'We've got trouble. There are two men in that boat headed straight towards us and I can tell you that one of them is not a friend of mine. In fact I would say the reverse.'

The boat was now only a cable or two away. 'Richard, he has a gun! Who the hell is he?'

'The military attaché in the Netherlands who tried to kill me.'

Shoving the throttles to full ahead *The Lady Ellen* began to pick up speed. From less than fifty yards a shot rang out and smashed the starboard window, just missing Richard.

Using a loudhailer Simms called loudly, 'Stop your engines. I'm coming aboard.'

'What do you want?' Richard called back.

In reply another shot was fired, this time into the hull.

'He means to kill us.' Victoria's voice was surprisingly calm.

'We'll get only one chance.' His heart was racing, his mouth dry. There was still a heavy swell from the east and he turned the boat broadside to it. *The Lady Ellen* started to roll, making it difficult to stand without holding onto something. The other boat would roll even more when it came alongside.

'Go around the wheelhouse, take off your clothes and when I call for you to take a line, step out naked.'

'What?' Victoria's eyes were on stalks.

'It may distract them long enough for me to drop the diving weight onto the fuel tanks in the stern of their boat.' The diving weight was a lead crucifix weighing about 20kilos. It was used to lower to the sea bed to check depth and to give divers a reference point. By attaching a line a diver could ensure that he or she didn't drift too far from the dive boat. This was particularly important when diving in water far murkier than the Caribbean. The English Channel was a good example.

'What good will that do?'

'You'll see.' Reaching up to the small, glassed cupboard next to the door Richard flicked open the catch and extracted a flare. It was used to attract the attention of a passing ship, search and rescue helicopter or lifeboat.

'Go on,' he urged her, 'go forward.' Shoving the flare into his waistband behind his back he stepped outside onto the deck. 'Throw a line,' Richard called to Simms.

The man was glowering steadily at Richard, satisfaction written all over his face. Simms placed the gun down on the stern bench seat, stepped forward and picked up the bow rope. He looked over his shoulder and said something to Yeslam who was at the wheel.

Richard went aft and stood next to the cradle that held the heavy weight.

'How did you know where to find us?' Richard yelled. He wasn't interested in the answer. He just wanted to distract Simms in anyway he could.

'We heard your Mayday.'

'Victoria! Take the rope,' Richard called, pointing forward. The two men looked towards the bows.

She stepped around the front of the wheelhouse as

naked as a jaybird. The driver and Simms gawked at her in surprise. Victoria stood still and shook her shoulders.

They didn't see Richard's sudden movement. He lifted the crucifix above his head and smashed it down into the boat with all his strength. It ripped out the fuel lines and fractured one of the petrol tanks.

With an oath, Simms spun round and leapt for his gun, tripping over the centre seat. Richard had the flare in his hands and realised that even if he hit the petrol he would be too late to stop Simms shooting him.

The flare was the latest type, a slim tube about 20cms long with a firing mechanism at its base. Simms was raising the pistol, his finger curling around the trigger, when Richard fired. There was loud whoosh and the flare hit Simms full in the face from a distance of less than 4m. Falling backwards with a loud cry of pain, he knocked Yeslam off his feet. Simms' finger tightened around the trigger. It was on fully automatic. The bullets missed Victoria by inches before stitching a pattern along the side of *The Lady Ellen*, shattering the windows in the wheelhouse and moving inexorably towards Richard. With nowhere to hide Richard dived over the side, swimming under the hull and towards the sports cruiser. He was going to go down fighting if it was the last thing he did.

Just then, the burning flare, lying in the well of the boat, was hit by the leaking petrol. It went up with a thunderous roar right above Richard's head. The sea was turned into an inferno with debris raining down around and over *The Lady Ellen*.

Although he was short of breath, Richard changed direction and swam underwater to the stern of the *Lady E.* Climbing the diving ladder he saw burning petrol seeping across on the deck, threatening to take hold. Throwing open a locker, he grabbed a bucket and line used for swabbing the decks and threw the bucket over the side. He hauled it back on board and sluiced the deck.

He did it time and again, washing the petrol over the side, extinguishing the fire. Then he stopped. The petrol was away, the fire put out. Floating around them were bits of white plastic and other items. There was no other sign of the boat or her passengers.

Richard felt relief coursing through him when he saw Victoria was still standing in the bows, staring at the sea.

'Are you okay?' he asked gently, taking her in his arms, hugging her closely. He sounded a lot calmer than he felt.

'Yes, I think so.' She clung to him. 'I was certain you were dead. I saw the boat explode. When I looked, you were no longer there and I thought that somehow the explosion had got you as well. Are you all right?'

He smiled. 'No problems.'

Victoria gripped him tighter. 'I don't want to leave,' she said. 'I want to be with you and work it out. But I'll need your help.' She spoke in a soft voice, nervous about his reaction after so much bitterness and acrimony.

She needn't have worried. Richard smiled and said, 'I'll always be here for you.' He looked down at the sea. A body was floating away from them. He thought it might be Simms but it was badly burnt and hard to tell. He couldn't see the other one.

'These last few months have been a living nightmare. It . . . It's been like Dante's Inferno. Round and round. Misery upon misery. Hell on earth.'

'I know what you mean,' said Richard. His memories intruded and he thought back to when it had all started. If it hadn't been for a storm half a lifetime ago he wouldn't have missed the flight. He'd be dead, along with his family. Now it was ending after another storm and yet more death. He hoped it was finished. No more revenge by either side. Life had to move on, for everyone.

Epilogue

SIR EDWARD PENNINGTON-PRENTICE forced himself to smile. It was, after all, his farewell party. As Deputy Director-General of MI6 he had been fêted around various departments of the Civil Service and Ministry of Defence all week. This was the last one. Thank God.

He took a flute of champagne from a tray and helped himself to a canapé. There were about fifty people from MI6 in the room. It was the main conference and briefing room and could hold three hundred individuals comfortably. More than half those invited had cried off for one reason or another. Much he cared. He would be out of there in half an hour and in twenty-four hours he'd be abroad. He'd leave behind the Frump, his wife of twenty-eight years and be in Jamaica at the new villa on Sunday. Angela was waiting there for him. She was almost half his age but with five million pounds in the bank she didn't seem to mind the disparity. This was the amount paid by Harwazi for the information about Al-Ghoul's movements and provided a substantial part of his nest egg. It had been damned unfortunate that a few plods had been killed as well. He dismissed the thought. Retirement was going to be very enjoyable. After all, he was only fifty-seven and still in his prime. When he had been told that he wouldn't be getting the top job he had decided to go early. There was a lot he could still do outside of MI6.

'Ah, Edward, there you are.' His boss, Sir Reginald Bart-Smythe greeted him. Neither man liked each other but manners were always important. They did, after all, maketh the man.

'Reggie. Thank you for coming.'

'I wouldn't have missed it for the world.' The underlying message was clear. Bart-Smythe couldn't wait to see the back of him. The lack of sincerity in both their voices was only obvious to individuals who occupied the same rarefied strata as themselves. 'What are your plans for your retirement?'

'Oh, this and that.'

'I see. A word of caution. I suggest you don't rush off and write your memoirs. After the last fiasco we're taking a much dimmer view of such activity. The Cilla Boddington biography, while not exactly damaging, was highly embarrassing. Some things are better left unsaid, eh?'

Privately Pennington-Prentice had nothing but admiration for the ex-Director of MI5, whose biography had caused such a stir in diplomatic circles. 'Have no fears, Reggie, I have no intention of publishing any of your little secrets.'

'Good. I am glad.' His warning given, he made a grimace. 'Well, goodbye. I'm needed elsewhere.' Making no effort to shake hands the Director-General left the room. The warning had been extremely distasteful but necessary under the circumstances. Pennington-Prentice was leaving with a good deal of bitterness. The truth was, he had risen to the height of his incompetence and it was a blessing that he was leaving. Ah, well. The weekend beckoned.

The ex-DDG finished his champagne and decided that he'd had enough. He slipped out the side door and vanished into the evening. It was warm and muggy. He smiled. He'd have to get used to that. Still, the villa had air-conditioning so it wouldn't be a problem. He had told the Frump that he was retiring the following week and that he had to go to Spain for one last conference. She hadn't cared. As long as she had her bridge, he could do as he damn well liked. They hadn't been husband and wife in the true sense for so many years he had forgotten what she looked like without any clothes.

That night, he stayed at a hotel near Heathrow and dreamt

about the future. He was early for the British Airways flight the following morning but he couldn't help it. He was as excited as a teenager on his first date. Pennington-Prentice smiled to himself at the ridiculous notion. He was a mature man about to enjoy the fruits of his life's labours.

And he was starting as he meant to go on, he thought, settling down to a glass of champagne in the first class section of the plane. Yes, life was going to be very good from now on.

When the plane landed at Kingston he took his time disembarking. Now that he was there, he savoured the anticipation. He collected his suitcase and went outside for a taxi. The tall dark-haired man who had followed him all the way from London also flagged a cab.

At the villa he found a note from Angela telling him that her mother had been taken ill unexpectedly and she had flown home to Texas for a few days. She promised that she would be back on Tuesday. Disappointed though he was, he was determined not to let her absence spoil the first few days of his retirement.

In the morning, he went down to the marina and checked over his new boat, all thirty-five feet of super-charged opulence. She boasted two en-suite double cabins and every luxury that could be crammed into the relatively small space.

He intended to spend the following day at sea. Having completed an in-shore skipper's course a few months earlier he knew enough to be safe. He even went to the trouble of informing the harbour authorities of his intentions – just like he had been taught to do. They didn't seem in the least bit interested. He spent the night on board. The fresh sea air and the large brandies he'd imbibed made him sleep more soundly than he had done in years. So soundly, that he didn't hear the diver under the hull.

The following morning he sat in the boat's cockpit. He had to admit he was nervous. He had never taken a boat to sea on his own before. He had always been supervised. Today it was different. He finished his coffee, sighed and started the engines. He let them warm through, again, just like he'd been told to do. After a few minutes he let go the ropes. It was now or never. He would go as far as Portland Point and back. He edged carefully past the other boats and pontoons and finally reached the marina entrance. Outside, he moved the throttles up a few notches and the boat responded instantly. He really was having fun. He added more speed and yet more until he was flying along at over 45 knots. He laughed out loud. This was the life. He was still laughing when the bomb ripped the boat apart and blew him and her to smithereens.

Hunter spent an extra few days in Jamaica tidying up the loose ends. Pennington-Prentice's girlfriend returned to the island in a foul temper. She had flown home to discover that there was nothing wrong with her mother. At the villa she was met by a policeman who told her the bad news. She flew straight back home again.

The marine accident investigator reported that the combination of gas cooking appliances and petrol-driven engine on board the boat proved, as it did so often in these tragic circumstances, to be a lethal combination. The Jamaican Coroner brought in a verdict of accidental death.

The British government repatriated the money paid to Pennington-Prentice by Colonel Harwazi. A service was held in the ex-DDG's memory. Most of the people who attended were hypocrites, including the Frump, who could now enjoy a happy retirement with a handsome pension from the Civil Service. She never learnt about the villa in Jamaica.

The British Establishment had taken care of their traitor in the age-old way.

A Million Tears

by Paul Henke

1890. Murder and intrigue have forced the Griffiths family to flee their native Wales. They leave behind a village devastated by a mine disaster and the oppression of the Victorian ruling classes.

Their subsequent adventures represent the American Dream. With bravado born of necessity, Evan Griffiths builds a business empire – retail, transport, banking, real estate – in the frontier town of St. Louis. With an inherent sense of justice, and the support of his beloved Meg, he forges a political career. But on his right hip, Evan carries a gun. No one will ever hurt his family again.

In Wales, David yearned to travel, dreamed of discoveries. Shipwrecked on a coral island in the South Seas, he discovers himself.

His brother, Sion, dreams of flying, craves freedom and adventure. But will his dream – and Sion himself – die in the lawless hinterlands of the Wild West?

Through meticulous research, author Paul Henke expertly braids together fact and fiction, recreating the Frontier of America. With consummate ease, he conveys a vivid sense of life at the turn of the century, weaving the thread of history – and the lessons it can teach us – through his narrative.

The vitality of Henke's fiction is mirrored in the energy of his vibrant characters. On his vast canvas he captures their triumphs and their tragedies. In 'A Million Tears' he unveils the portrait of the remarkable Griffiths Family. A gem to be treasured.

ISBN 1-902483-08-1

The Tears of War and Peace

by Paul Henke

It is 1911 and David Griffiths is in Wales, bored and lonely. He travels to London at the behest of their family friend, John Buchanan, to start a new business in banking. There he gets caught up in the suffragette movement and falls in love with Emily. Against the backdrop of women's fight for votes and the looming First World War, the Griffiths build a vast, sprawling company encompassing banking, aircraft manufacturing, farming and whisky distilling.

The enmity of a German family follows them tragically throughout this period, leading to murder and revenge. At the end of the war, thanks to a change in the Constitution, Evan is invited to run for President of the United States. The family rally round for the most important battle of Evan's life.

With the Brown-shirts running rampage across Germany, David and Sion are soon involved in a battle for survival.

Sir David Griffiths is a colossus of a figure, striding across the world and through the century, a man of integrity and bravery, passion and dedication. Determined to win, nothing comes before the family.

The story is as compelling as ever. Historical fact woven into the fictional characters makes a breathtaking tale of adventure you will not want to put down.

ISBN 978-1-902483-10-8

Silent Tears

by Paul Henke

Silent Tears is full of passion and adventure. You will be captivated as three generations of the Griffiths family struggle to meet the challenges of their time.

From the depths of the depression and the rise of fascism to the abdication of Edward VIII and the Spanish Civil War, Henke's meticulous research brings the period and vibrant characters to life.

David, powerful and dynamic, at the centre of political intrigue, his love for the family is put to the ultimate test . . . Meg, his mother, stalwart and determined, guides the family with humour and devotion . . . and Susan, beautiful and tempestuous, fighting for justice. No sacrifice is too great for those she loves.

Packed with excitement, Silent Tears is a masterpiece. A novel that vibrates with sheer narrative power and relentlessly builds the emotional pressure until it explodes in a firestorm of passion and high-octane adventure. A spellbinding epic.

ISBN 978-1-902483-11-5

Tears Until Dawn

by Paul Henke

Never before have the events of the Second World War been captured so vividly. Paul Henke transports his readers straight to this turbulent period of history. From Dunkirk and the Battle of Britain, through to the final invasion, you feel you are actually there, breathing alongside his remarkable characters. This is a tale of betrayal; betrayal of Prisoners of War as they struggle to survive – and betrayal of a nation by its King.

This compelling story of a family at war is told through the eyes of Sir David Griffiths. At the height of his political power he will do whatever it takes to protect those he loves. But will it be enough?

His daughter Susan, the beautiful and tempestuous pilot, is tested to the limits of her endurance. Cousin Alex's skill in the air is legend – but can he conquer his demons on the ground? And young Richard, defying his family yet desperately needing their help if he is to survive the horrors that await him.

Tears Until Dawn is a rare blend of truth and fiction – a story you will not want to end. Henke dazzles the reader with passion and adventure in this novel of epic proportions.

ISBN 1-902483-07-3

Débâcle

by Paul Henke

A Nick Hunter Adventure

Following a summit meeting in Paris an alliance of interested countries form an elite fighting force to combat terrorism throughout the world. Based in Britain and under the command of a British General, the team is made up of Western, Russian and other non-aligned countries' special forces.

Without warning the terrorists strike. A group of bankers, politicians and industrialists are taken prisoner off the coast of Scotland and the new, untried force is sent to search for them.

The Scene of Action Commander is Nick Hunter, Lieutenant Commander, Royal Navy, an underwater mine and bomb clearance expert with experience in clandestine operations.

The enemy is one of the world's most ruthless and wanted terrorists – Aziz Habib! Hunter leads the team against Habib, backed up by two computer experts: Sarah from GCHQ and Isobel, hired by the General to run the IT for the new force.

While stock markets take a pounding and exchange rates go mad, the state sponsoring the terrorism is making a fortune. It has to stop. At all costs.

This is non-stop adventure from beginning to end. A riveting story told by a master story teller. You are guaranteed not to want to put it down!

Débâcle mixes fact with fiction which will cause you to wonder, how true is this story? Did it really happen?

ISBN 1-902483-01-4

Mayhem

by Paul Henke

A Nick Hunter Adventure

Israel faces imminent destruction, nuclear Armageddon. A series of kidnaps, bombings and senseless murders have left her isolated from her allies and threatened by enemies of old. Unknown to all but a few, the situation has been orchestrated by multi-millionaire Zionist, Samuel Dayan. His vision of a Greater Israel will be carved from the charred ruins of the Middle East.

But Dayan is up against the international anti-terrorist organisation, TIFAT, and our hero Nick Hunter. To the age-old struggle of Good against Evil, author Paul Henke adds state-of-the-art communications technology and computerised warfare. In a desperate race against time, Hunter and his team of hand-picked specialists deploy satellite intelligence and high-tech weaponry to track Dayan to his lair.

The plot twists and turns in a series of setbacks, betrayals and mind-blowing developments. Myriad minor characters deserve story-lines of their own.

Relentlessly building the tension, Henke strips his hero Hunter of all resources but those within himself – knowledge born of experience and the inability to give up. Hunter simply must not fail.

ISBN 1-902483-02-2

Chaos

by Paul Henke

A Nick Hunter Adventure

Ambitious Alleysia Raduyev has inherited the family business – the largest crime cartel in Georgia. Operating on the classic theory of supply and demand, she caters for her customers every desire – narcotics, arms, prostitution, forced labour. Her payroll has extended to include lawmakers and law enforcers. No one is safe from her tyranny and oppression.

Power base secured, Alleysia moves on to her next objective – the formation of a super crime cartel, whose actions will result in global chaos. As a deterrent to those who would oppose her, she chooses the ultimate weapon – three nuclear warheads.

Desperate to prevent a new, anarchic world order, the West declares World war III against the cartels and their terror organisations. As violence escalates, the now battle-hardened troops of TIFAT are pitched against their toughest adversary yet.

Spearheading the battle is Lt. Cdr. Nick Hunter, the fearless explosives and diving specialist seconded to The International Force Against Terrorism.

The latest TIFAT novel is a clarion call to the Western world as it comes to grips with the realities of modern terrorism.

ISBN 1-902483-04-9

Havoc

by Paul Henke

Europe is a seething cauldron of hatred. Islamophobia and xenophobia sweep the continent as incessant terrorist atrocities terrify the population. Legal and illegal immigrants are blamed for attacking the white, Christian establishment. Whipped up by the press, non-whites and non-Christians are being hounded and persecuted in retaliation for the deaths caused by the terrorists. A backlash begins.

But all is not as it seems. The immigrants are as much victims as the whites. Who is masterminding the race war? Is this an Islamic plot against the west? Or something even more sinister?

Once again this master storyteller has highlighted the fears and prejudices of a world on the edge. As always, Henke's meticulous research creates a background that is rock-solid and thought provoking. The conclusions drawn by his imagination are disturbing in the extreme.

As hero Nick Hunter battles against this latest threat to democracy, Henke fearlessly brings forbidden issues to the fore in an action packed story that enthrals the reader from beginning to end.

ISBN 1-902483-06-5

Phoenix Rising

by Paul Henke

Stephen Yorke works for Phoenix, a shadowy organisation specialising in deniable, black operations. When they are attacked and virtually wiped out Yorke turns from being the hunter to the hunted! With his stepson taken hostage, Yorke needs all of his ruthless determination to fight back.

Who is he fighting and who can he trust? Pursued across the country, he unravels a web of horror that leads him to the highest echelons of government. He discovers an unlikely ally in Catherine, an investigative journalist who has stumbled into his nightmare. But is she all she appears?

To avert disaster Yorke has to track down the most dangerous enemy he has ever faced – an enemy whose power and influence appears limitless.

The action is non-stop. Excitement and tension drives the book at a cracking, page turning pace.

ISBN 978-1-902483-09-2

A Million Tears

'The summer's best holiday read . . .'
Scottish and Universal Newspapers

'An unquenchable thirst for daring and creativity . . .'
The Sunday Times

'As a literary publicist we receive over 50 books a week to evaluate – we knew instantly that *A Million Tears* was a classic.'
Tony Cowell, *PressGroup UK*

'Henke has written a gripping story . . .'
Corgi Books

'I smelt the coal dust in Wales and felt the dust in my eyes as I fought alongside Evan.'
Dr Peter Claydon

'Henke tells interesting and exciting stories. He doesn't use bad language and writes good English. A joy to read.'
The Sun

The Tears of War and Peace

Débâcle

Mayhem

'A non-stop action adventure set in Scotland and the Middle East.'

The Edinburgh Evening News

'A fast moving tale of terror and destruction set amidst the charred ruins of the Middle East. An international force exists to fight terrorism. Terrific realism.'

The Stirling Observer

'The hero, Nick Hunter, embarks on a non-stop roller-coaster adventure from the Scottish Highlands to the Middle East. Henke is being hailed as the next Wilbur Smith.'

The Aberdeen Press and Journal

'Mayhem is a classic airport thriller. It's a veritable page turner and a cracking read.'

The Milngavie & Bearsden Herald

'A cracking good yarn. Non-stop action from beginning to end.'

Central FM radio

'Fiction becomes fact in Paul Henke's action thrillers. A superb read.'

The Northern Echo

About Paul Henke

Paul spent nine years in the Royal Navy and qualified as a bomb and mine disposal expert, specialising in diving and handling explosives. As a Lieutenant, he survived a machine gun attack by IRA gun runners in Ireland in 1976. Using plastic explosives he was responsible for blowing-up a number of Second World War mines found off the coast of Britain. He was promoted to Lieutenant Commander in the Royal Naval Reserve where he had command of various minesweepers and minehunters.

In 1979 he spent fifteen months in Nigeria where he was in charge of a saturation diving system prior to moving to the American Midwest.

He has travelled extensively, researching material for his work and is now a full time writer. He lives with his family near Loch Lomond in Scotland.

Author's Note

Thank you for reading my novel. I hope you enjoyed it. At the beginning of the book you will find my web site *and* my e-mail. I mean it sincerely when I invite you to write and tell me what you think of my books. I have had plenty of replies which, as an author doing one of the loneliest jobs in the world, I have appreciated very much.

Thanks again, and all the very best,

Paul Henke